Praise for
Raven's Ladder

"Jeffrey Overstreet's imagination is peopled with mysteries and wonders, and his craft continues to mature. Reading *Raven's Ladder* is like staring at a richly imagined world through a kaleidoscope: complex, intriguing, and habit-forming."

> —KATHY TYERS, author of *Shivering World* and the
> Firebird series

"A darkly complex world, populated by a rich and diverse cast of characters, in which glimpses of haunting beauty shine through. Sometimes perplexing but always thought provoking, *Raven's Ladder* is the work of a fertile and strikingly creative imagination."

> —R. J. ANDERSON, author of *Faery Rebels: Spell Hunter*

"With *Raven's Ladder*, Overstreet does what the best fantasy writers do: he opens a door into a new world—a beautiful, dangerous world and one that stayed with me long after I closed the book."

> —ANDREW PETERSON, singer, songwriter, and author of
> *North! Or Be Eaten* and *On the Edge of the Dark Sea of Darkness*

"In *Raven's Ladder*, Jeffrey Overstreet continues what he began with his first two novels, *Auralia's Colors* and *Cyndere's Midnight*, crafting a world rich in detail, purpose, and wonder. Each page reveals new threads of a complex, interwoven story that excites and entertains while provoking deeper thought. It has been a long time since I've read a series as captivating, meaningful, inspiring, and beautiful as this one."

"*Raven's Ladder* is a fantasy gem. The story is imaginative and truthful, the characters authentic and complex. Jeffrey Overstreet has given us a gift—a fully realized world teeming with life and wonder. It is a fully human tale, with a penetrating glory throughout. Here is a heaping portion of truth, beauty, and goodness."

—S. D. SMITH, author of the Fledge Chronicles serial

"In *Raven's Ladder*, Jeffrey Overstreet weaves a brilliant tale of intricate layers, inviting his audience into a story of deeper meaning. Not mere fiction that ends with the shutting of the book, it sneakily tiptoes into your thoughts, challenging you to ponder a little more."

—ESTHER MARIA SWATY, *Seattle City Guide Examiner*

RAVEN'S LADDER

ALSO BY JEFFREY OVERSTREET

Fiction:
Auralia's Colors
Cyndere's Midnight

Nonfiction:
Through a Screen Darkly:
Looking Closer at Beauty, Truth, and Evil at the Movies

RAVEN'S LADDER

A NOVEL

JEFFREY OVERSTREET

WATERBROOK
PRESS

RAVEN'S LADDER
PUBLISHED BY WATERBROOK PRESS
12265 Oracle Boulevard, Suite 200
Colorado Springs, Colorado 80921

The characters and events in this book are fictional, and any resemblance to actual persons or events is coincidental.

ISBN 978-1-4000-7467-9
ISBN 978-0-307-45852-0 (electronic)

Published in association with the literary agency of Alive Communications Inc., 7680 Goddard Street, Suite 200, Colorado Springs, CO 80920, www.alivecommunications.com.

Published in the United States by WaterBrook Multnomah, an imprint of the Crown Publishing Group, a division of Random House Inc., New York.

WATERBROOK and its deer colophon are registered trademarks of Random House Inc.

Library of Congress Cataloging-in-Publication Data
Overstreet, Jeffrey.
    Raven's ladder : a novel / Jeffrey Overstreet. — 1st ed.
        p. cm. — (The Auralia thread : the gold strand)
    ISBN 978-1-4000-7467-9 — ISBN 978-0-307-45852-0 (electronic)
    I. Title.
    PS3615.V474R38 2010
    813'.6—dc22

                            2009038004

Printed in the United States of America
2010—First Edition

10 9 8 7 6 5 4 3 2 1

For Anne,

who encouraged me as I climbed in search of this story,
offered meticulous, insightful criticism,
and fed me with her poetry.

CONTENTS

CAN AURALIA'S COLORS SAVE HOUSE ABASCAR?

In a dungeon beneath House Abascar, Prince Cal-raven befriended Auralia. She was only sixteen, but already condemned. Cal-raven's father, the king, had imprisoned her for breaking Abascar law and revealing colors only royalty were allowed to display.

But Cal-raven saw that Auralia was a visionary, a prophet. Her cloak glimmered with colors no one had ever seen—colors that spoke of undiscovered wonders in the world.

He was even more intrigued by her claim that the Keeper had sent her. The Keeper. A creature who brings children comfort in their dreams. A shadow who looms in the nightmares of adults who feel threatened by any power greater than their own.

So the prince gave Auralia his Ring of Trust, a pledge of protection against harm. And a few days later House Abascar came crashing down, erasing Auralia—and the ring—from the Expanse.

Their home in ruins, their king buried in the rubble, the Abascar survivors followed Cal-raven into the wilderness, taking refuge in a stone labyrinth behind the Cliffs of Barnashum.

Now their king, Cal-raven has helped his people survive hardship and a siege by bloodthirsty beastmen. But he has never stopped believing that the Keeper is watching. And he has never stopped believing that there is a better home for his people, a place where Auralia's colors shine. So he follows the Keeper's tracks in search of New Abascar.

But the road is fraught with dangers. Beastmen. A traitor with murder on his mind. A deadly menace breaking through the ground. Wicked Seers from House Bel Amica eager to seduce and enslave his people.

There are also signs of hope. Cyndere, daughter of House Bel Amica's queen, is conspiring with Abascar's courageous ale boy and with Jordam— the one beastman whose heart has been healed by Auralia's colors—to rescue slaves from the beastmen and bring hope to the Expanse...

House
Bel Amica

Mawrnas

Tilianpurth

Ruins of
House Cent-Regus

THE EXPANSE
DURING THE DAYS OF
ABASCAR'S EXODUS

Remembering, the Treasure rose in a dustcloud from the cushions. "Mustn't be late," she whispered.

A lantern's frenzied flame—the only light her captors allowed—made of her a wild shadow on walls of clay and roots. She cupped a handful of ash-dry crumbs from the bedside bowl. Then she cowled her head in a dark shawl and fitted her feet into timeworn slippers—soldier's boots she'd snatched from a passing pillage cart and trimmed to fit.

Touching the dingy rag-weave curtain she had hung on the windowless wall, she said, "I'll come back."

As if in answer, colors flickered about the curtain's edges.

The iron-barred door of her cell may once have been a garden gate before the curse poisoned the people of House Cent Regus. Locked for years, it had been her only window. But she learned to ignore the distorted shadows lurking beyond the bars—beastmen come to ogle their chieftain's favorite trophy.

One day Skell Wra had ordered the lock undone, for where could she go? Better to let his Treasure run loose. A ghost. A boast. A reminder of the fallen house his servants had pillaged.

But he could not have guessed that a spark still burned in the Treasure's spirit or that it had been fanned into flame by the glory of her own secret treasure. She would surprise her captors someday.

In her years of incarceration, she had lost the rhythm of sunrise and sunset. But a vivid revelation had rekindled memories long buried in ash. In the light of a shining relic stolen from House Abascar's collapse, she remembered the ancient songs that gave order to each day. And thus she fumbled her way back into habits that once filled those measured spaces. She established the simplest ceremonies—sweeping her cell, scrubbing her feet, cleaning stone fragments for makeshift dishes.

In recovering such common disciplines, she found strength and something more—the desire to investigate all that occurred beyond her misery's border.

During one aimless meander, she had stopped at a startling sound. Harmony.

Up a rugged stair to a low-ceilinged cave, she had moved like a moth to a flicker of light. A host of slaves, hands joined, arms bruised from long days of tunneling for the chieftain, sang House Abascar's Evening Verse. Its melody unfurled like a watchtower's flag. The exhausted prisoners seemed to draw strength from that rhythmic ritual, prodding at the darkness until it bled hope.

Her own particular hope intensified as she crept to the gathering's edge night after night. If these laborers had survived House Abascar's fall, perhaps others were searching for them on the ground that she called a ceiling. Her husband, the king. Or her son.

On this night as the Treasure crept along corridors and braved cold mockery from the parades of fang and claw that passed, her only stars for navigation were torchflares at each corner; the only moon an occasional shaft of light from the world above falling through this syrupy fog.

The vapor, pungent as boiled weeds, emanated from roots that the slaves called feelers. As the captives swung pickaxes and opened tunnels, the feelers filled them, spreading beneath the Expanse, setting a snare-net for the world. She had witnessed those tendrils drawing down prey they had caught above ground—a bird, a deer, even a man or a woman. Like a host of prowling ghosts, the feelers' cold mist crawled over her as she stumbled, shuddering, between the vein-lined walls.

When she arrived at the foot of the long stair, she heard new voices in the melodies that descended like glimmers of sunlight through a dark ocean. New slaves.

"Marcus?" she wondered aloud. "My love?" Speaking his name made the possibility seem real. "Raven? My son?"

The Treasure ascended the steps and slipped into the bowl-shaped room beyond but stayed outside the captives' candlelight.

When the music was over, the prisoners passed around a dish—a supper of scraps that might once have been seeds, nuts, weeds, insects—and began to whisper urgently, knowing they'd soon be bullied into silence. Stories rose in voices hushed and hoarse. Tales of a house busy with industry. Memories of childhood sweethearts, an elaborate prank on a duty guard, an incident with an ambassador's trousers in the midst of the king's court session, the death of a child to a winter plague. Tales of passions pursued, of dreams given shape, of creative inventions that flourished for a time.

Though these sadder stories worried the queen of Abascar like clouds of biting mosquitoes, she stayed.

"Enough." A woman's plea interrupted the man whose bitter tale of Abascar's last, vivid hours was only worsening the slaves' sorrow. "We know this tale too well. Let's hear from some new voice. You, boy...do you have the strength to tell us a story, to help us remember who we are?"

The question struck a solemn stillness.

As the boy stepped forward, the Treasure felt a pin pierce her heart. He was bent under a burden that no one so young should carry. He cast aside his outer cloak, took up the candle, and introduced himself as an ale boy. A day in his Abascar life had been a route through the whole wide house, up from the Underkeep breweries and into King Cal-marcus's palace. He took the tower stairs to the royal chambers, walked to the watchtowers on the inner and outer walls. He strolled the streets to the Housefolk, the officers' quarters, the gardens and farms, the stables and mills, and beyond to the fields, the orchards, and the huts where the Gatherers labored to earn the favor of the king. The Treasure followed the thread of his words back through passages she had made herself forget.

His small voice grew fierce and eager, for he was now describing a girl, an artist, a friend, and one who dared defy the laws that the Treasure herself had made.

Auralia, he called her.

"But the king's condemnation was a mistake," he went on. "For when they threw Auralia into the dungeon, the heart of House Abascar broke. The Underkeep collapsed—*krash!*—deep into the earth." As he spoke these words, he extended his arm and touched the candle to the edge of his sleeve. "And fire," he said, "rose up to consume what remained."

The slaves came to their feet in dismay. Some lunged forward, raising shackled hands. Too late. Flames cloaked the storyteller.

The Treasure fell backward, her arms across her face. So many of her dreams ended in just such catastrophes.

But when she opened her eyes, the boy still stood in their midst, arms raised, blazing. The people retreated as his shrill voice rose to a shout. "Don't fear. The Keeper was there, watching over, refusing to let Auralia burn."

His voice went on emboldened, his demeanor untroubled by the fire. Serpents of smoke slithered from his garments. His eyes shone. The slaves' urgent concern turned to bewilderment, then terror.

The boy began to spin, faster and faster—a small whirlwind flinging flecks of light. His hand shot out to grasp the edge of a heavy tarp, the kind the prisoners used to drag up sharp stones from their masters' mines. He cast it over himself. The cave's bright center dimmed to a faint ring of fire on the floor until the tarp stifled even that, and the light went out altogether.

The Treasure leaned forward. The cave grew quiet for long, worried moments.

Then the boy rose and cast away the tarp. Outlined in sparks, he walked in a circle. "Northchildren took Auralia from the ashes. They cloaked her in strange new skin. They gave her to the Keeper, and it carried her away. But before she left, she told me to seek the Keeper's tracks in the world. I've done so. And they led me straight to you. So listen to me."

Oh, how they obeyed him.

"I can't explain what brought our house down. Maybe the king dug too deep. Maybe it was a fire. Some have said there was something more."

"I blame that wretched queen," growled an old woman.

"But there's something else I can't explain," said the boy. "How'd anybody get outta there alive? How'd I find the Keeper's tracks in the smoke and trouble, to reach and help so many?"

"What of King Cal-marcus?" Nella Bye asked.

The boy met her gaze. His answering whisper ran through the Treasure like a sharpened spear. "He's gone, my lady."

"He...didn't survive?"

"I don't know. But he's gone." All glimmering and golden, the boy touched Nella Bye's shoulder. "I can't explain it. But I've seen Northchildren. They're not monsters. They're helpers. They give relief to the dying. Wherever the king is now, he's not beyond their reach." He looked up at the survivors. "We're not either. Auralia was right all along. The Keeper will come for us, if Cal-raven doesn't first."

A laugh burst from the Treasure. As the slaves glanced in her direction, Nella Bye asked, "Cal-raven is alive?"

"He's Abascar's new king. In the Blackstone Caves, behind Barnashum's cliffs. He's making a plan to start again. To build New Abascar. Somewhere else."

The Treasure covered her mouth. It was a joke. Cal-raven was just a boy. He could not lead a berrypicking party, much less direct a great house.

"Does he know we're here?" someone asked.

The boy's eyes turned upward as if his gaze could penetrate the stone above them. "I think I'm supposed to prepare you for his coming."

"You?" another scoffed.

"The Keeper's tracks led me here."

The Treasure observed the hushed, haunted gallery of faces illuminated by the boy's spark-lit skin. No longer sullen as livestock waiting for slaughter, they looked awake, alive. She knew this awakening. She had felt it when that colorful weave—Auralia's colors, if the boy's story was true—had flared up in her cell. She had seen it quiet the bloodlust of beastmen.

The Treasure stepped from the corner's concealment. "I think I can help," she heard herself say.

Faces turned, afraid. She knew what they saw—a creature the sun had forgotten, her own reflection sinewy, fierce, and white as bone.

"You're that wretch the chieftain keeps to mock us." The voice belonged to a toothless old man. "You brought this on us."

"And I'm the one who knows a way out of here." In her voice she heard a familiar fury. "What is more, I know someone who will fight for us."

The old man went silent, mouthing at the darkness like a fish.

"Walk with me, child," she said to the storyteller. "I suspect there is more to your story. I want to hear it all."

For the first time the boy seemed frightened.

"Don't trust her." Nella Bye stood, her hair spilling down around her ankles.

But the boy drew his cloak back around his shoulders and moved forward as against a hard wind.

The Treasure led him out and down the stair. She could see in the ale boy's smoky countenance that she amazed him—a woman free to wander the Cent Regus Core. But as this creature of courage and soot began to retell his story, his voice gained strength and fervor.

The ale boy told her of Auralia and how she flung gifts upon the Gatherers as generously as a cherry tree showers its petals. He told her of the Proclamation that had forbidden all colors and how Auralia's revelation had thrown the kingdom into turmoil. She leaned forward. Her memory sketched faint impressions, as if the boy were painting in the rain.

She paused when a skulk of white rat-beasts—all five taller than she—rounded the corner like the groping fingers of a pale hand. One in the front pushed a wheelbarrow full of pickaxes and spades. She stepped between the boy and the rats, sweeping her outermost skirt behind her so that it settled over him.

The rat-beasts approached her, pink noses twitching and oozing. Their white fur was tinted orange in the torchlight, filthy as if it had been used to sweep cobwebs. Their red eyes examined her. "Treasure," they whispered in reverence. One fell forward onto his hands and sniffed about the edge of her cloak. "Four...four feet?"

The ale boy leapt out. Anything the Treasure was ready to say was washed away by surprise.

The boy had become a little beastman. His face was painted with soil, and a mop of long, matted hair hung down over his eyes. His mouth was full of shiny fangs, and his hands were mittened in black gloves that thrust arrowhead claws into the air.

The rats blinked red eyes in disbelief.

And then he thrust his hands at them, which burst at once into gloves of flame. Painting fiery lines in the air, he leapt at them, fangs parting, and roared a horrible noise. A cloud of fur tufts filled the space where the rat-beasts had been.

The Treasure hastened on. Her little monster walked backward behind her, shaking his hands to put out their fire. He spat out the cluster of Cent Regus teeth he had glued together, and with smoking fingers he brushed away the wig of beastman hair. "That was very effective," he concluded. "I should make a bunch of these."

"Remarkable boy," she mused. "Pockets full of surprises." She shook her head. "I've some surprises for you as well, so listen close. I'll remember it as a kindness."

"If listening is all you need from me," he replied.

"This queen of Abascar once knew the very colors you describe. A merchant's young daughter she was, living with her family near Fraughtenwood. And then, on a red moon's night, a light came."

She lifted her hand, drawing in the air. "Sudden and strong, a light on the wall. Just after midnight. It flitted about and set the rat-catcher to pouncing. The girl thought she was dreaming. She rose and tried to touch it. The light appealed to her like nothing she had seen in her travels, like nothing her father and mother had ever offered or taken in trade. She laughed, and the sensation was like discovering she could play an unfamiliar instrument. She had never laughed like that before."

This made the boy laugh, and the sound gladdened her heart. Nothing thrilled her quite like her son's chirping flights of laughter.

"As abruptly as it had appeared, the bird of light was gone out the window. She felt a powerful desperation. She seized her bird net and ran into the night to catch it. But her father ran after her. He punished her."

She stopped and leaned against the wall. "The light didn't come again. She can still see it when she closes her eyes. She began to seek those colors in wildflowers, water, sunsets. She fashioned cages, collected bottles and vials, seeking anything that might capture the light if she found it."

The Treasure paused, eying a crossroads ahead. "When Cal-marcus ker Har-baron made her queen, he promised her anything she desired. She hoped to gain the power to capture those colors again. To keep them for herself. But nothing satisfied. So she abandoned Abascar and continued her search, until she was captured."

The boy took her hand, and his was hot in her cold grasp. She saw in his attentive gaze the wild confidence of one who somehow knows more than he should. His face, so strange, wore not a whisker or a hair. He was a scorched thing, a sooty sapling after a forest fire. He did not even cringe at the tiny specks embering upon his eyelids.

"Raven," she said, her voice breaking. "Look at you, all made of stars. I thought I'd never see you again."

"I'm not Cal-raven, my lady."

She closed her eyes. "Be patient with me. My mind is in pieces."

He followed her rag-skirt as it swished down crooked stairs. She led him to a simple cell and through its open gate to a ragged curtain.

"You're stepping into my story now, ale boy. I found them. Or rather, they found me. They've nested in my chamber, too much to dream of holding for myself."

The ale boy stopped, eyes widening. Colors flickered about the curtain's edge. She smiled and drew it back.

He flinched. But the colors shone without any hint of deception, and he stepped into their influence.

The Treasure held out her hand, unfolding her fingers to reveal a crimson thread. "There is so much more," she said. "Shall I show you?"

"No," he whispered. "I remember." He strode forward, gathered it into his embrace, laid his head upon it as if it were a pillow, and said, "Oh, Auralia. They're alive."

The Treasure knelt. "Tell me, little Raven. Tell me more about Auralia. Where did she find these colors? Because I want to live where they come from."

He turned to answer, but the words stopped short, for they were no longer alone.

An enormous beastman was kneeling in the open gateway, eyes bright with Auralia's colors.

"Don't be afraid," said the Treasure to the boy. "This one...he's not like the others."

"I know," said the boy, and he went forward to take the visitor's hand.

"O-raya's boy," murmured the beastman, patting the boy on the head. "You have grown."

CAL-RAVEN IN FOUR
KINDS OF TROUBLE

Auralia reached out to Cal-raven. As he approached, the flame of the candle he carried flapped like a flag in a hard wind.

Her smile was mysterious, just as he remembered it. That detail had proved most difficult. Other aspects had come easier as his hands sculpted the stone. Her humble stature. The tiny knob of her chin. Her feet—ten small toes emerging like a row of beads beneath a leafy skirt.

Cal-raven was not a tall man, and yet Auralia, slight for sixteen, had stood only to his shoulder. He could see her open hands pressing through the span of fabric that she offered to any visitor.

Almost a year had passed since he'd found her in the Abascar dungeon, wrapped in a magnificent cloak. Their fleeting conversation was burned in his memory more vividly than yesterday. Unflinching, Auralia had voiced her faith in phantoms dreamed and legends whispered—like the Keeper, that benevolent creature who haunted dreams, a silent guardian, a listener.

Cal-raven had sculpted, erased, and then reshaped Auralia's lips, her eyebrows with their question pinched between them, her whole face filled with trembling hope that others would receive and understand her vision. She had been more than human. Or better, she had been more fully human than anyone around her.

The king's hunting hound, his golden tail wagging, sniffed at the statue's ankles. "Hagah." The dog slumped down to the floor and sighed, resigned to wait.

That fabric the statue held—Cal-raven had not even tried to give it the textures and colors of Auralia's cloak. How could he? Its threads had glimmered with colors no eyes in Abascar had ever seen.

"Tell the Keeper," he whispered, "that I don't know where to go from here." He ran his fingertips along the span that spilled like a waterfall from her upturned hands. "When I was a child, I'd have called out myself. It was easier then to believe."

Auralia's expression did not change; it would not unless he changed it. Her polished eyes would not return his gaze for, in the tradition of House Abascar portraiture, they lacked detail. While each statue in the cavern was distinct—the beloved and the burdensome, the wise and the foolish, the soldiers and the miscreants—they shared that same indecipherable gaze, an affirmation of something altogether unnamable, inimitable. The mystery of the heart.

Embarrassed at his habit of addressing this likeness, he knuckle-knocked Auralia's forehead. "Last visit. Watch over these worn-out people for me, will you?"

Something shifted in the cavern behind him. Hagah lifted his head and followed his master's gaze through the long rows of statues.

"Wynn?" Cal-raven waited.

Hagah's huge black nose emerged from flabby rolls of fur and sniffed. Then the dog set his chin back down on the ground.

"You'll catch our pesky shadow in a dream, won't you?" Cal-raven said, but he gave another look back.

Why am I so agitated tonight? he wondered.

Because some of them are turning against you, replied his father's ghostly voice. *It's been almost a year. You've mentioned New Abascar, but you still haven't shown them a plan.*

The statues that crowded the Hall of the Lost listened. These extravagant stone monuments gave shape to Cal-raven's promise that he would never let his people forget the lessons they'd learned and that they would build a new house to honor those lost in Abascar's cataclysm.

But the name *grudgers,* once given to those who had rebelled against their previous king's oppressive ways, now applied to people distrustful of Cal-raven. Grudgers objected to his embrace of the foolish along with the wise; his equal concern for the weak and the strong; his insistence that every person, no matter how "useful," be fed and shown the care of their healer. Moreover, grudgers grumbled about the way Cal-raven gambled their futures on possibilities revealed to him in dreams.

Tonight Cal-raven had taken the firewalk. Lesyl's turn had come, but he had offered to patrol the passages for her. He wanted to hear her sing the Evening Verse one last time before his departure the next sundown.

"I've written a piece that can only be played by two," Lesyl had said when the firewalk brought him to the chamber of Auralia's gallery. Sitting against the wall decorated by an array of colorful weavings, she tuned the twelve-stringed tharpe, a formidable, sonorous instrument. She seemed relaxed, even happy, and oblivious that this was a farewell.

"Here." She picked up a wooden spiral. "You remember how to play the hewson-pipe, don't you? Oh, come now, don't tell me you lack the time. You need the practice." When he did not approach, she persisted. "Scared?"

"No," he laughed. *Yes*, he thought.

He had torn himself away from that conversation to continue the firewalk for fear of losing his fragile restraint. *Not now. Not yet.*

So while she sang, he paced that routine progress, ensuring that torches would not spark any mishaps, that candles burned within the spheres prescribed, that everything was in its right place.

He had led these survivors through a hostile winter and a dispiriting spring. Just as they had begun to define a possible departure, a visit from the mage sent him scrambling in another direction. Tomorrow he would slip away and venture north to pursue the vision his teacher had given him.

The day will come, Cal-raven, when you'll have no choice but to leave Scharr ben Fray's imagination behind and live in the real world. His father's fury buzzed in his ear like a skeeter-fly. *If you don't, the ground will crumble beneath you.*

Facing his father's likeness, Cal-raven felt his throat tighten. "Whose inventions plunged into the earth?"

Listen to me, boy! You're too old for toys. Who will lead the people when I'm gone? Someone whose head is full of children's stories?

"Show me someone better prepared for the task," he said. "I do not enjoy the burdens you've left me." He took the shield from where it was draped over the shoulder of the king's likeness.

The statue's lips were parted, and a strange feeling of discomfort crept up Cal-raven's spine. He did not know what scared him more—the thought of the stone speaking or the thought that his dreams might prove false.

Hagah's inquisitive nose bumped the edge of Cal-marcus's shield, and he woofed.

"You're not waiting for him anymore, are you?"

A rough tongue exploded from the hound's expansive smile, and his tail thumped against the floor.

"You've given up on them both." Cal-raven's gaze strayed to the statue of his mother. The runaway.

It was a good likeness, or so he'd been told. Jaralaine's appearance seemed an echo lost in time's clamor. But troubled scowls from older folk told him that they recognized this imperious beauty. He did remember occasional tenderness and sighs of insatiable loneliness before her disappearance. He also remembered a fury against any suggestion of a will greater than her own.

He found himself suspended between the gravity of these statues and the forested world beyond, which called to him like a feast to a starving man.

"We're all ready to be runaways now, Mother. If we don't leave soon, the bonds that bind us will break."

Hagah sniffed the base of the queen's statue.

"No!" Cal-raven shouted.

Disappointed, the dog lumbered off through the rows to settle on the lanky figure of a hunter known by his nickname—Arrowhead.

Go ahead, Cal-raven thought. *Arrowhead was a grudger. He threatened my father's life. Wouldn't hurt him to take some abuse for a change.*

Hagah would have merrily complied, but the sound of something slithering sent him bounding back to Cal-raven's boots, fangs shining beneath his retracting lip. Cal-raven blew out and dropped the candle, held his father's shield close, and knelt to withdraw the throwing knife at his ankle.

There was only silence. Cal-raven tiptoed through the statues, Hagah stalking low before him.

The dog led him to the western wall, where a corridor ran along the inside of the cliff. Hagah put his snout down to a crack in the floor, noisily drawing in air. His tail stopped wagging.

"What have you found, boy?"

Hagah stiffened. Then he began to back away from the fissure, a low, rolling growl changing into a worried squeal.

"Something nasty?" Scars like burns from rivulets of hot oil marked the floor all about the break. "Let's go. This place is giving me jitters tonight."

A puff of wind touched his ear and then—*thung!* He turned to see an arrow embedded in the wall beside his head.

He sprang forward, leaping over the dog, and ran through the corridor. Down the stairs. Through tiers of tunnels.

In the distance Lesyl sang the Evening Verse. But his pursuer—pursuers, he could hear their footsteps now—did not falter.

Hagah turned around snarling. "No!" Cal-raven knew the dog was no match for an arrow. "Run, boy!" He pointed, and the dog bolted ahead just as he had been trained.

Cal-raven did not follow. He faced the rugged wall, placing his hands against the rock. His fingertips sought hidden inconsistencies, and finding those points, he applied pressure and heat in a way he could never explain.

The stone awakened, rippling in a sudden wind.

Cal-raven's body clenched like a fist, forcing energy out through his hands. Then he pressed himself through the wavering curtain.

A midsummer evening's breeze cooled his burning face as the sand sealed itself behind him.

The grudgers are out of patience. He brushed grit from his garments. It would not take long for his hunters to find their own exit. *They were watching. Waiting for me to be alone.*

"Keeper, protect me," he murmured. Crouching, he moved away from the cliffs into narrow paths through thorn-barbed thickets that blanketed the plains.

Several turns into that maze, he sat down to catch his breath. *I must get back inside where it's crowded.*

He thought about standing up and calling for the guards on the tiers above. But they would not see him here in the brake. And what else might come in answer?

A strange wind moved through the shallow sea of thorns. Bramblebugs *skrritch-skrritched* across the plains. Something wriggled under his foot. He set his father's shield aside, tugged off his boot, and shook loose a rockspider.

He looked up through the brambled frame. A shooting star scratched a line across the night's black dome. As if excited by the mysterious sign, far-away wood dogs shrieked in song.

When he jerked his sleeve free of a bramble and stood, his rustling stirred up a cloud of twilight-suckers. These insects were always a help to hunters, for they uttered tiny shrieks of delight as they descended on fresh dung or carrion.

Sure enough, as the pest cloud dissipated, he saw two copper coins. He knew that reflective stare from a hundred hunts. A lurkdasher. A year ago the sight of this swift, bushy-tailed creature would not have surprised Cal-raven. Lurkdashers were common burrowers in beds of brush. But Abascar's best hunters had been catching little more than weakened scavengers, rodents lean for lack of prey. Across the Expanse the land had gone quiet, as if emptied by some mass migration.

If Cal-raven had been out for any other purpose, he'd have thrown his knife so fast the dasher would have fallen midsprint. But he stayed still. Something wasn't right.

The lurkdasher vanished. Cal-raven stood in the quiet, just another secret in this complicated night.

He could sense a presence, fierce and intent.

He turned his head slightly and drew in a deep breath. Only a stone's throw to his right an enormous animal, many legged, lurked in the thick web of boughs. He held that breath and waited, eyes slowly translating the contours of darkness and deeper darkness all around him.

Like a mighty hand, the creature clutched the ground, tensing knuckled legs. The bushes around it shivered as the lurkdasher stole away, and like a spider the creature raised two of its front legs from the brambles, bracing the other five against the ground. It was as big as a fangbear. Cal-raven felt a faint tremor. Then he heard a hiss, and the creature shifted its weight slightly, turning those raised limbs toward him.

Considering the sword at his side, he flexed his hand.

A crush of branches sounded to his left. His heart fluttered, a trapped bird, frantic. He turned and saw the second creature—the very same kind—with its feet planted as if it might pounce. In terrified confusion he saw the wind disturb a canvas that the creature drew behind it, a dark black sheet covering the thorns.

He did not know these monstrosities. They looked like they could outrun a viscorcat. And the forest was a long, long run ahead of him through a narrow, winding passage that he could not see clearly. But the cliffs—he might just make it back to the wall. The solid stone wall.

Ever so slowly he planted his hand on the hilt of his sword. He stepped backward, placing his foot down soundlessly.

The creatures stood as still as sculpted metal.

He took another step, drawing his sword half out of its scabbard. *No,* he thought. *The starlight. They'll see the reflection.*

At his third step the creature on the right planted its two raised feet down on the ground, digging in as if it might spring.

He heard movement behind him and felt a blast of air like a bellows. His feeble hopes went out. But something deeper than his mind, stronger than his will, unleashed a cry. He called out, as he had so many times in nightmares, for the Keeper.

The creatures leapt from the brambles and seized him. His sword never escaped the scabbard.

He had a moment to think of Lesyl, interrupted in her song, looking up to receive unexpected news, the hewson-pipe coiled beside her.

Hot limbs wrapped around him, and his feet left the ground. The creatures were shelled, bone-tough, their bellies cushioned with bundles of hair. He struggled, limbs flailing. He was falling skyward, upside down. The pressure did not increase. Nothing pierced or stung or bit. The ground, faintly chalked in moonlight, spread like the sky over his head, and beyond his feet the heavens glittered like Deep Lake at midnight. The creatures held him suspended, their vast canvases snapping in the wind as if they were wings.

And then he saw that they were wings, spread out from a towering creature.

His captors were not animals at all but hands. He hung unharmed in the clawed clutches of a monster and was carried up toward its massive equine head.

Its eyes, glassy spheres full of stars, were fixed upon the northern horizon. Flames lined its nostrils. Its mane wavered as if it were creating, not surrendering to, the night wind. And the scales on its golden neck caught more than moonlight.

A helpless toy in its hands, he watched its attention turn to him, and his fear turned to confusion.

He recognized this creature. This shape had been fixed in his mind since he first drew breath. It had moved at the edges of his dreams. In nightmares it had come when he cried out for help, and sometimes when he could not call at all. During the long days of learning, he had pillaged his father's history scrolls and hunting journals for evidence.

Nothing had prepared him for this. The creature drew in a cavernful of air, the shield-plates of its chest separating to reveal a soft lacework beneath. It held that breath. He knew it was reading him, reading the night, the skies. Then the curtains of its eyelids came down.

Are you kind? he thought. *Dreams. . .speak true. Let the Keeper be kind.*

The creature was stranger than anything he had sculpted when imagining its shape and dimensions. He felt embarrassed by his simplistic appeals, his feeble prayers. He was a mouse in the talons of a brascle, and as the creature reared up on the pillars of its hind legs, wing upon wing upon wing unfolding from its sides like sails on a great ship, he waited for judgment.

A sound like deep recognition ran tremulous through its form. Cal-raven thought it spoke his name—not the name given by his mother, but the name given by the powers that had crafted him—and every thread of his being burned with attention. As the eyes opened again, the stars within were moving.

It exhaled a scattering of sparks, but gently. The sound was like the Mystery Sea, roaring as it received the river flowing out through the Rushtide Inlet.

The air about the creature shuddered. A wave of noise beyond the range of Cal-raven's hearing stunned him, conveying a word as clearly as if the creature had spoken. He would not, in the aftermath, know how to translate such a word. But it provoked in him an immediate resolve, a reverent promise.

He would follow. What else could one do when commanded by the Keeper?

Smoke and spice clouded the air and dizzied him. He was passed from clawed hands at the edges of the creature's wings to one of its enormous, rough-fleshed feet, which held him like a woman's hand cradling a bird. The creature set him down within a footprint on the path, and a wind whirled fiercely about him. Squinting up through the storm, he saw that the creature had taken flight.

In the space of a sigh, it was gone, a succession of lights darkening across the sky, northward over the Cragavar forest. Cal-raven lay helpless and numb like a discarded doll in the Keeper's footprint.

Breath burst back into his lungs. He heaved, folding and fighting, a bird shaking away the shards of a shell.

It came when I called.

Never more invigorated, never more single-minded in purpose, he smiled back toward the cliffs. He had been changed.

In that moment everything changed for House Abascar as well.

It began with a jolt, not a tremor.

Tabor Jan had been yawning as he reclined atop a boulder and counted the brightening stars. Sleep, out of reach for many nights, had seemed almost possible.

But then the ground beneath him bucked like a furious steed. He scrambled to the path, unsheathing his sword as if he might smite the earth in reprimand. From deep within Barnashum came a sound like hundreds of drums. The shaking intensified. The refuge exhaled clouds of dust through shielded entryways.

"Not part of the plan," he muttered.

Rubble spilled down the cliffs in the quiet that followed, dust sighing into the thickets below.

"Cal-raven," he said. Another name came to mind. *Brevolo.*

Then came a distant cacophony of voices. Rivers of people were rushing out onto the open ledges.

Even as he scanned the scene for the woman he loved, Tabor Jan pushed his way through the crowds, shouting to soldiers that their first priority was to find Cal-raven.

Hagah bounded suddenly into Tabor Jan's path. The soldier seized the dog's flabby neck. "Hagah—Cal-raven!"

Thrilled by the command, the dog turned as if jerked by a chain and almost threw himself off the cliffs. It was all the captain could do to keep up with him.

He found himself running toward the sound of triumphant yelps beyond the base of the cliffs. Dog had found master. The king was alive.

Kneeling among the brambles, Cal-raven embraced Hagah, blinking as if he'd been knocked silly by a falling stone.

"Are you hurt?" Tabor Jan scanned the shadowed ground.

"Didn't you see it?" Cal-raven pointed north toward the Cragavar.

"See it? I felt it. I think they may have felt it in Bel Amica. We may have cave-ins. I'm taking you back."

"No, not the quake," said Cal-raven, exhilarated. "Didn't you see it?"

Tabor Jan braced himself. "See...what?" Then the exuberance of Cal-raven's expression triggered a spasm of alarm. "No! Don't say it!"

"But Tabor Jan, I saw—"

"Swallow that story, my lord!" He would have preferred a beastman sighting. "Don't speak of it to the people. Especially not tonight."

"Not tonight! What could bring them more comfort than to hear—"

"If the grudgers hear you respond to this quake with some wild description of a phantom on our doorstep—"

"Grudgers attacked me tonight."

"Did you see their faces?"

"No, but I became acquainted with their arrows." He laughed. "I also became quite familiar with the Keeper. Nose-to-nose, in fact."

Tabor Jan scowled. "I haven't slept for so long I'm having nightmares while I'm awake."

"It pointed me north, Tabor Jan! We've got to ride—"

"We'll ride tomorrow, Cal-raven. Just as you planned." He urged Cal-raven back toward the cliffs, and they clambered over piles of rubble newly shaken from the heights. A tumult of voices filled the sky.

Hurrying down a steep ridge, an enormous guard came stumbling to meet them.

"Bowlder, how many are hurt?"

"Cave-in!" he wheezed. "Must...dig out...three people."

"I assume you've called for Say-ressa. Without her healing hands we..." Tabor Jan stopped, stricken as he read Bowlder's expression.

He turned to Cal-raven, but the king was strangely preoccupied with the moon above the northern horizon.

TO SAVE THE KING

Wynn had made up his mind a few hours before the quake. He would take one of Abascar's horses and follow King Cal-raven on his secret search for House Abascar's next home.

You wouldn't assign stable sweeping to a tracker or a hunter. I've got to show the king I can ride among his best.

Pacing in front of the stalls, he considered the vawns and horses that hadn't been chosen. Their stalls were closed, their large, clawed feet visible below wooden doors.

The stew of smells was stifling—bramblegrass and ivy, fresh scrap-apples for bribing the animals, vawn dung and horse manure. He sneezed.

The sneeze was answered by a sharp slam of a horse's hoof against wood.

He recognized the scarred black mare by the color of her ears above the stall gate. Small but sturdy, she had a broken lip and a hide that appeared to have been raked by fangbear claws.

She wasn't the horse for stealth. But that seething, that eagerness—Wynn knew he'd found his volunteer.

Ten nights earlier—Wynn had counted them—the king had come to examine the steeds and to check the condition of his leg shields and woodscloak. He had dismissed this mare with an affectionate comfort. "Someday. But you're not ready yet."

Wynn had propped the shovel against the feeding trough and tiptoed after the king as he left. Turning a corner, he found the corridor empty and the stone wall rippling back into a solid barrier again.

He's planning to leave.

Wynn had scrambled back to the stable, climbed inside an empty feed bag, hopped to the edge of the narrow dung chute, and slid down, straight out through the cliff wall into the night. Gagging on the stench, he clambered out of the filthy sack into the cloud of rejoicing dungflies.

Behind an abandoned harvest wagon with a bad wheel, he spied a riderless vawn steaming, panting, and digging the ground with clawed hind feet.

The king stood with a boulder raised in the air. He reminded Wynn of a bittlebug he'd once watched carry a hunk of biscuit. Cal-raven bent his knees, then shoved the boulder skyward.

The stone rose, then descended to alight on the fingertip of a man Wynn hadn't noticed—a short, broad-shouldered fellow. The stranger pushed back the hood of his green cowl, laughing. The boulder spun on his fingertip. As it did, it took different shapes—a dragon with its wings spread, a raging three-horned limbaw, a woman of exaggerated shapeliness.

Then the man had pointed at the sky, and the stone reshaped itself as a spinning top that ascended into the air and moved toward Cal-raven in a slow, smooth glide. The king laughed, waiting for it to come within reach, then jumped and smashed it into a shower of sand.

The stranger was Scharr ben Fray. Wynn had no doubt.

He'd heard his father, Joss, and his mother, Juney, talk about this stone-mastering mage. The story of his exile from Abascar was legend: Queen Jaralaine had banished him for teaching Cal-raven stories of the Keeper as if they were truth.

Wynn held still, breathing dung reek and spitting out flies. A few words caught his ear: *Go north. Ladder of Ravens. Mawrnash.* Mawrnash, a place his parents had carefully avoided on the merchant routes near the Cragavar forest's northwestern edge.

Scharr ben Fray embraced Cal-raven as a father embraces his son, then climbed into the saddle and leaned over to offer one last exhortation. *Eleven days,* Wynn heard. Then the mage was borne away in swift, silent strides, the vawn's tail lifted high to keep from stirring up dust or noise.

Cal-raven had walked to the wall, put his hands against it, and paused.

"Wynn," he had said, "have you heard? The guards have seen viscorcats prowling around here. They're hungry, for there's nothing to hunt. Promise you won't breathe a word of what you've heard. Or I'll leave you for the cats."

"My lord," Wynn choked.

Back inside, night after night, he had endured the burden of brooms, shovels, and filth, gnawing on his resentment, counting down the days until Cal-raven's departure. Abascar's people were generous. But they were not Wynn's people. The merchants' life had taught him to live unencumbered by commitments. And he scolded his little sister, Cortie, when she shadowed a kindhearted woman called Merya and began to call her Mum.

He wanted to shout at them, just as his father had berated him between strikes of the lash. *Think you know better than me? I've crossed the Expanse. I've lived in the wild.*

Bang! The horse kicked at the stall gate, jolting Wynn from his thoughts.

"We'll follow the king, you and me," Wynn whispered toward the animal's ears, "but we'll make it look so easy, he'll end up following us."

He was familiar with this feeling—the fits of fright and zeal before a secretive escape.

Once, along the merchant roads, he had drawn in a deep breath of night and tiptoed a vawn through curtains of rain, closer and closer to freedom. When the storm muffled the bullfrog of his father's snore, he kicked the vawn to a gallop.

But concern for Cortie had caught him on the Throanscall's banks, a hook at the end of a far-cast line. She was beautiful and fragile. His mother had protected her as if she were a rare greenbird's egg, hoping the family would earn enough treasure to buy themselves into Bel Amica, where the girl could grow up in peace. To Pop she was just another pair of hands. Wynn had pictured her waking without him, rising with double the chores. He turned the vawn around and ventured back through the storm, spitting. Sure enough, his father stood waiting, that belt of twisted horsetail hair so much heavier and harsher for the rain.

Tonight that memory gave him pause. But if he could win a respectable position among Abascar's people, he might collect enough prizes to buy himself and Cortie a place in House Bel Amica.

The mare's breath puffed through the slats.

"Don't be scared," said Wynn. "We don't need any of them. Tomorrow we'll run."

And then, the ground shook.

For half a moment, a ghost loomed in Wynn's imagination—his father, rising alive with the belt in his hand.

Wynn ran from the stable up to the cave where children slept. Finding it empty, he staggered, steadying himself with the broom he still held fast, like a boatman with an oar but no boat, while the ground rolled in waves. He needed to see Cortie's face, know she was alive.

Emerging from the dust-choked throat of the Blackstone Caves, he plunged into the murmuring crowd. Boys and girls leaned into one another like anxious lambs on the ledge. Parents called for children. Guards shouted directions. Shattering blackstone shrieked deep within.

As the crowd quieted, gossip spread like foam tossed over rapids. *A chamber's collapsed. Some have been buried.*

"What is it with House Abascar?" Wynn muttered, straining to hear names. "What is it with all the collapses?"

He dropped the broom when he saw his sister. He caught her up just as the news took a terrible turn. Say-ressa, the healer, was among those buried inside when a wall became a cavalcade of rocks.

"Why?" Cortie whispered, wide-eyed. "She's the one who makes things better."

"Don't worry," he told her, worrying. "I'll take care of you."

Cortie put her head on his shoulder. He thought she was crying, but then her tiny hand patted his back. "Don't be scared, big brother," she whispered.

That's when he realized he was the one who was shaking. "This is stupid," he said. "Come on, Cortie. I'm finding you a safer place to sleep."

They tiptoed down into the dark, all the way to the armory's piles of shields and plated armor. Cortie crawled into one of those hollow, burnished suits and hid like a cat.

"Stay here tonight," Wynn said. "Sleep here from now on. I don't want to come back and find you've been crushed."

"Come back? Where are you going?"

"Tomorrow night Cal-raven's gonna..." He heard voices, soldiers approaching from the stable cave below.

He seized a heavy metal shirt made for a massive defender—probably Bowlder—and crouched down within it. He watched reflections from the soldiers' torches flicker in golden ripples all around. Peering out through the right-arm window, he counted six silhouettes. They carried quivers. And they were angry.

In those urgent whispers, he learned about the ambush, the king's escape, the quake's interruption of their pursuit, and their intent to try again before they were found out. Soon.

When the voices diminished, Wynn dared to stick his head out through the suit's open shoulder. The soldiers had set down their quivers and left a torch in a torchstand. Leaning into one another like hunting dogs, they were halfway up the corridor toward the crowds.

"Conspiracy." The word was delicious on his tongue. "Cortie, it's a conspiracy." He trembled with a sense of purpose, his head rising through the open collar. "This is it. I'll show Cal-raven I'm useful. And he'll never assign me to stable duty again."

In the shine of the armor where Cortie lay hidden, he saw himself—a small head and feeble arms emerging from this massive metal shirt. He jerked his arms inside and ducked down, troubled by the reminder of the distance between him and a full-grown soldier. Then he crawled out, a snail abandoning a shell. "I'm going after them, Cortie. I gotta find out who they are."

She blinked her eyes sleepily. "Pop says you should stay in the wagon," she yawned.

Dust floating on the air crackled as the torch's flicking tongue caught and consumed it.

There goes Wynn, thought Luci to her sisters. And then her smile boasted, *I told you I'd find him.*

Luci's identical sister Madi raised her chin in defiance. *Foolish orphan. He's just spying on the big folks again, jealous of anyone important. Let's leave him alone.*

The triplets rarely spoke aloud to one another. Thoughts passed between them clearly, but they often confused which one was thinking, and their feelings rarely matched. This frequently left them looking pained as they wrestled in mental entanglement.

Luci thrust out her lower lip. She would take a liking to any boy she pleased, and her sisters would have no say in the matter. *You're the one who wants to grow up and marry Cal-raven,* she snapped in a wordless retort. Brushing off her weed-woven trousers, she stepped out from behind the stone slab that had fallen across the corridor just outside the armory. Following Wynn, she heard the quiet clatter of her sisters' stonecrafted jewelry close behind.

Madi, Luci, and Margi were as different in opinions as they were alike in appearance and gifts. Born stonemasters, they took regular lessons from Abascar's only master of that art—the king. Cal-raven had shown them how fingertips could read a rock. Like the gift of firebearing, healing, or wild-speaking, stonemastery was evidence of direct descent from Tammos Raak, the man who first crossed over the Forbidding Wall into the Expanse, followed by the parade of children he had freed from captivity.

While they were proud of their stonemastery, they kept their telepathy secret. Double blessings such as theirs were rare indeed. Those so greatly gifted were often assumed to be schemers and crooks.

When the triplets' parents had joined the assembly in the quake's aftermath to wait for Cal-raven's instructions, Luci had turned to her favorite distraction—the rascal merchant boy who had, much to his own dismay, charmed her.

But what had begun as distraction turned troubling the farther Luci led her sisters in pursuit. Wynn seemed afraid, his concentration so fierce that he had not noticed his followers.

They emerged from the tunnel to walk along a high tier under the night. Wynn was well ahead of them, shadowing the soldiers as closely as he dared. They followed him up a weedy slope.

Summer constellations glistened—the Golden Heron, the Healerfish, the Wildflower, and the Changeling. And there, low on the northern horizon, the Kite People, six clusters of stars like men and women in flight, trailing strands of dust that bound them to a single blue star with a wavering aura. The sisters paused together, and not for the first time. Starlight always enchanted them, as if it were a strange music composed only for them.

Luci led them through the bowl where they had helped Cal-raven sculpt a towering Keeper and along narrow ledges, tempting gusty winds to cast them over the cliffs.

Coming around a bend, they saw the soldiers slip into a crevasse in the cliff face. Wynn climbed along the vines just above the entrance and hung there like a bat, upside down.

The girls, seeing him stop, clustered together on the path. He saw them, hissed, and waved them off.

Luci ventured on, bare feet padding along the path. "You're gonna get in trouble," she whispered.

Wynn held out a hand to quiet her, listening intently.

Wind moaned through the Red Teeth, the field of stone spears far below the precipice. Margi, who seemed drawn to danger, grew distracted and crawled to the edge to look down. Luci could feel her thinking of things they could sculpt with those jagged lances.

Wynn's head snapped back as if he'd been struck by what he heard in that crevasse. He let himself down soundlessly and approached the sisters.

"Run, Luci," whispered Madi. "He's angry."

No, thought Luci. *He wants our help.*

"You'll get us into trouble," Madi growled, coming up to Luci's shoulder.

Wynn wagged a finger in their faces as if they were obstinate children. "If you want Cal-raven to live another day, you need to help me. Right now."

Luci could see the moon like red jewels in the boy's wide eyes, but those eyes were on Madi. She stepped closer and rested her wrist's beaded bracelet on his shoulder to win his attention. "We promise to help," she said just as Madi said the same thing. They turned and scowled at each other.

Wynn spelled out instructions. All memories of the quake fell away. This conversation made them feel hot and cold at the same time. A different kind of quake had begun, and when the shaking stopped, the world would be changed. They would be changed. Here in the open, under a rising red moon, the sisters' doubts dissolved. In a sudden decision, as final and immovable as the stone, they sealed the crevasse and trapped the soldiers inside.

3

RIDDLES IN THE DARK

Krawg found the king kneeling in the entry cave, stroking Say-ressa's bloodied cheek. Lying beside two others nearly crushed in the cave collapse, Abascar's beloved healer rasped through a dust-choked throat while her apprentices guessed what they could about unseen injuries.

"Would this be of any comfort?" Krawg, his knees popping, approached the king, offering a purple scarf.

Cal-raven took it with cautious hands. "Auralia made this." He nodded to acknowledge Krawg's generous sacrifice. "Thank you."

"Has healing properties, it does," Krawg muttered. "It's Warney's."

He felt the heat of displeasure in the crowd behind him. Some would protest that a scarf with healing powers was just the sort of superstition the Gatherers were prone to believe. Among Housefolk, suspicions lingered that the Gatherers, former criminals, had all gone rather strange in the head during their hard labor outside the protection of Abascar's walls. But the king had given the Gatherers a chance to prove themselves responsible.

Krawg and Warney, famous thieves, had become resourceful and productive; through the winter they helped House Abascar gather a harvest from this barren region. Krawg approached the king with some confidence, for Cal-raven respected their experience, and he was not one to doubt claims about the power of Auralia's colors.

"You look like a Bel Amican," Cal-raven told Say-ressa after binding the scarf around her head. "As lovely now as you were when you caught Ark-robin's eye."

Krawg withdrew, wrapped in joy for having provided help. He knew the subtle ministry of Auralia's colors, knew the scarf would cool the healer's fevers. He had a scarf just like it, after all. But his was yellow, and he would never part with it.

Somewhere Warney was sweeping the shaken caves. Stalactites had shattered, cobwebs had come down, and walls had broken to puzzle pieces. Krawg moved instead to help others deep within to sift debris from the shallow reservoir of water that sustained them.

"Didja hear?" That tattling was Hildy the Sad One, a gossipy old Gatherer drifting by on a raft, her sifting net neglected at her side. "Five defenders have gone missin'. Five. Didja hear?"

Saying most things twice, as always, she kept on, speculating about who the five might be and the grisly ways they might have died. Krawg rowed away. He'd heard enough trouble already today.

At the darkening of the next long day of recovery, what had been a fuss of guesses over the missing defenders' fate settled into a burdensome quiet punctuated by fitful coughing from the quakedust.

Krawg crawled into his blankets, assuring himself that the distant thunder came from the sky and not from the ground beneath. Beside him, Warney's bed lay empty, but Krawg was too wrung out to worry, sore from the toil of hauling debris.

Soon after the last thought left his head, footsteps awakened him.

Lurching awkwardly between the sprawl of slumbering laborers, Warney's scarecrow silhouette advanced. In the faint candlelight, Krawg watched him kneel and pat the floor to find his folded mat of reeds.

"Spit it out, Warney. Somethin's got you running scared. Are the beastmen back?"

"Hope not." The mat crackled as Warney smoothed it. "I'm just losin' my mind."

"That's been certain for years. But what's the story?"

"It's the season, Krawg. Bad things happen when a red moon's up. Sayressa's half-crushed. Some say the quake's a sign we don't belong here. And there's something else." Warney shivered, wrapping himself in bug-eaten blankets. "Don't make me say."

"How can I sleep if your bones keep rattling? What do you think you saw with the eye you haven't lost?"

"Saw? It's what I *heard* that bothers me." Warney burrowed deeper into his cocoon. "Help me forget. Tell me an Auralia story."

"I've told you—no bedtime stories about our little girl." Krawg pressed his head into the yellow scarf he had rolled for a pillow. "I have bad dreams about what happened to her."

"Gimme riddles then."

Krawg picked at his fingertip calluses. "Fine, I'll fold you a riddle if you promise to tell me what's tied you in knots."

"If our cave don't collapse, I'll tell."

Krawg sat up and cleared his throat. "Who am I?" He stared into the darkness of the cave's high ceiling.

Fish nibble my toes,
my head's in a cloud,
got so many riches,
I'm boastful and proud.

Warney's silence might have been deep thought. Impatient, Krawg embellished his trick.

One crown sinks,
then the next one dies.
My eyes, they're blinded
by moonlit skies.

Warney noisily gnawed at his lips. "Fish nibble my toes," he repeated. "Is it a ship?"

"You're close. Bring her in to port."

"House Bel Amica!" Warney gasped. "Built on a rock in the Rushtide Inlet. Clouds around its head."

"And the two crowns?"

"King Helpryn, dead in a shipwreck. His heir, Partayn, slain by beast-men. But what's that line…'blinded by moonlit skies'?"

"Moon worshipers, Warney. Those fish-brained Bel Amicans spend too much time out on their boats, I tell you."

"Maybe *we* should pray to the moon." Anger flared on the edges of Warney's words. "Ask it to help us outta this mess. Gimme another riddle, Krawg."

"Tell me what scared you."

"In the morning."

Another breeze wafted through the cave, the earthy perfume of a warm rain stirring up another wave of sneezes.

The beastmen come a-hunting,
but I'm always underground.
And on a map of the Expanse,
I just cannot be found.
When the floor fell out from under me,
I fled to a safe haven.
Oh, what will become of me?
Go ask King—

"Cal-raven," Warney almost shouted. "House Abascar."

"Until we get to some new home and become New Abascar, that's the whole of it."

"What'll we be when we get there, Krawg? Will they need us anymore?"

"Someone's coming!"

A torch bobbed in the dark as a soldier found his way through the maze of sleepers.

"He's looking for you," said Krawg.

"I had nothing to do with it," blurted Warney. "But I heard the screams. Screams, Krawg. Coming from a solid stone wall."

"I've come for you, Krawg," said the torchbearer.

"Tabor Jan?" Krawg recognized that broad jaw line, the obvious displeasure. His fingers clenched his pillow as if he might wring comfort from it. "I gave up thievin' many years ago. Ask anybody! They'll tell you—"

"King's called for you. Bring your stormcloak."

Krawg lurched from the blankets. Warney's whimpers returned. "Where—"

"Think I know?" he snapped. "Don't expect me anytime soon. And, Warney, don't let anyone take my bed."

The stone underfoot gasped at the rain's beating, and the streams that washed over the clawed feet of six groaning vawns were heavy with sludge from the quake.

Did you come to Barnashum because I called for you?

Cal-raven closed his eyes and tried to remember the creature. Its scales had rustled like leaves of ivy layered on a stone wall. Its wings had struck at the air like great sheets shaken free of dust. He had called; it had appeared. He had asked for guidance. If he could befriend it, summon it for help...

Lightning shattered night's dark glass. The flash revealed two figures advancing from the cliffs—Tabor Jan with his hand fastened on Krawg's shoulder.

The one riderless vawn in this half circle of six sneezed a spluttering hello to the shadows that approached. The animal seemed eager for a rider so they could all charge north to the shelter of the forest.

Tabor Jan shouted back toward the descending path. "Wynn! I won't say it again."

Again? Pugnacious, that merchants' orphan. In the next faint flicker, Cal-raven glimpsed the boy standing still on the path.

Wynn's fierce voice cut through the rain. "I gotta talk to the king!"

Tabor Jan's tone made it clear that his forbearance was at an end. "You've got your own tasks. Go back to the stables. This work's for men, not boys. Soldiers' business."

No, Cal-raven thought. *This isn't even soldiers' business. This is in that uncertain region between revelation and madness.*

The next storm blast rang out like a threat.

"Fine!" the boy barked. "I won't tell where to find the missing soldiers." With that, he turned and ran back up into Barnashum's heavy shadows.

Cal-raven scowled down to Tabor Jan.

"I'll look into it, but I suspect it's just another lie, my lord. Merchant trickery. He's used to getting what he wants."

Uneasy, Cal-raven surveyed the companions he had chosen.

He could read Shanyn's face. She was wondering why he didn't just trim the boy from Abascar's story. Shanyn never liked unnecessary fuss, especially before a ride. He liked her bold, blunt counsel, and he depended on the strength of her sword arm in matters both military and practical. For a bonfire, she'd shear all the branches from a cloudgrasper in the space of a song. Nobody knew if she had sharp spurs or a gift for wildspeaking, but steeds responded to her with speed no other could inspire.

Bowlder shifted in his saddle, staring at Shanyn. Women were his only fear, and one so confident and strong set his broad, pulpy face to twitching. Cal-raven had chosen Bowlder for his muscles more than his mind, in case they stumbled into trouble.

They would also need accurate arrows, so Cal-raven had called on Jeshawk as well.

Without explanation, Cal-raven had also summoned Snyde, his father's ambassador of Abascar's arts for thirty years before the collapse. But Snyde was no trained traveler; he bundled the reins tightly in his hands as if he might fall even before the vawns set out.

Tabor Jan waited beside the last vawn, hesitating to help Krawg into the saddle. "Are you sure about this, master?"

"Remember when we first arrived, Captain? I trusted you to ride out and investigate the smell of smoke. You were gone a long while. But, true to your word—"

"True to my word, I returned with good tidings," Tabor Jan interrupted. "Your trust in me was well placed. That's why you should take *me*, my lord."

"My trust *is* well placed, Captain. That's why I need you to stay. The quake unsettled us all. The people need a leader they trust."

"What is so important," snapped Snyde, "that we ride out in this tempest while the people are troubled?"

"We ride to find chillseed," said Cal-raven. It was all he would tell the company for now. He didn't want them frightened by his true destination. "Say-ressa's fever is fierce, and chillseed is the surest help we know." He turned to Krawg. "Gatherers learned how to find it in the wild, didn't they?"

"Blindfold me, my lord, and I'll still find it for you!" the old man exclaimed.

"Captain." Cal-raven watched Tabor Jan reluctantly help the old man into the saddle. "Keep a close watch on the Cragavar. Keep our stonecrafting sisters close so they can—"

"We'll be watchful, my lord."

Cal-raven urged him to keep the people busy storing up food and fashioning wagons and wagon wheels in case they needed to set out from Barnashum soon. Then he turned abruptly to Krawg. "Why do you keep staring back at the caves? Have you forgotten something?"

Krawg bowed his head. "I reckon, my lord, that I can find chillseed faster if I have help." His hands opened and closed as if they were swallowing the rain. "He's light as a bundle of bird bones. He could sit behind me on this animal. Surely..."

"He?" Cal-raven smiled. He had expected this. He nodded to Tabor Jan, who hunched his shoulders against the rain, mumbled something, and trudged back into the caves.

Storm light splashed across the northern darkness, as seven riders on six vawns departed across the flooding plains. The distant Cragavar forest seemed frayed and worn in patches, a dark and ragged blanket.

Tabor Jan waited out in the open longer than was safe. He listened to the low wind and surveyed the star-glint on the thorns of rain-wet husker-brambles. Just as this weather would beat the summer's loose husks from that sea of tangled boughs, so Abascar's new troubles would purge the remnant's weaker aspects. Only the most resilient would endure to the next season.

He knew he would survive. But what of his friendship with the man who knew him best?

His shadow leapt out ahead of him as a torchbearer came up from behind. "There you are." It was Brevolo's voice. She took his wrist and drew it around her hooded stormcloak, leaning into him. They stood watching the wind and rain. "So he didn't take you with him. Look at it another way. Now you're in charge."

"I've never been a superstitious man," he murmured. "Never glimpsed a ghost. Never heard voices. I think those who claim visions of Northchildren are a little too fond of madweed. I've inherited no magical gift, at least none that I've noticed."

"There are still tricks you haven't tried," she laughed, relentless in flirtation.

"I tried to talk to an animal once—a rabbit. The thing ran away up a dry streambed, drawing about a dozen other long-ears into flight. Like it had warned the rest that there was a madman on the loose."

"Let Cal-raven be Cal-raven," she said. "You have your own path. And frankly, I'm uncomfortable following anybody who bases decisions on dreams. You should counsel him more forcefully. Abascar would do better with a practical leader like you."

As a child, Tabor Jan had chopped wood, raised boulder walls, and hunted. His renown had increased because of the bundles of firewood he could carry on his shoulders and because of his willingness to carry them wherever the king's men commanded. That strength had gained him armor, a horse, and responsibility. His rise after that came from a near-perfect record for hitting his mark with the first arrow shot, even from the back of a charging vawn.

Like anyone else, Tabor Jan had dreamed of the shadow that lurked in the forest. But he had been troubled by his father's scorn for the idea, just as he was troubled by Cal-raven's certainty that it existed and could be trusted like some infallible guide.

The myths that Scharr ben Fray had poured into every question Cal-raven raised seemed as unlikely as the fables about how the long-ear got his ears and why the vawn must suck for grubs.

"It doesn't matter," he said. "Cal-raven's brought us this far." He looked up at Barnashum, envisioned Cal-raven standing in many places at once, exhausted from sealing one tunnel after another, from toppling giant stone columns down upon the beastmen attackers.

"Remind me one more time about how he saved us from the siege, and I'll knock out your teeth." Brevolo dug an elbow in just below his ribs. "His stonemastery's a gift. We're all grateful for it. But it's still a mad gamble to follow him."

He said he saw the Keeper. Right here.

A prickling crept up the captain's spine, a sense that he would never see his friend riding back toward Barnashum.

"He still hasn't told me how he knew the beastmen were coming or how he knew exactly when they would charge. I wish he would. He carries burdens he needn't bear alone."

"Come inside." Brevolo took his hand and pulled him toward the tunnel. "Tomorrow will be a busy day. We've overstayed our welcome here. Don't you think Abascar should get ready to leave before Barnashum gives us another warning?"

He shivered and cursed, trudging after her. This would not be the night he had wanted it to be. A wedding would certainly raise the people's spirits. But this was not a good time to ask Brevolo to join him in burning tattoos on the backs of their hands. It was an old fireside rumor that promises made in stormy weather would never last in sunlight.

Very well, maybe I am a bit superstitious.

It was lonely out here. And Brevolo was as beautiful when she took off her armor as she was frightening when she put it on. When he sparred with her in swordplay, he came away with scars, just as he did when she kissed him. He would postpone his plan awhile longer. But only as long as he could stand it.

"If there is a Keeper," he said as they stepped into the corridor, "I hope it brings the king back safe. I'm tired of surviving. I want to start living."

She kissed him. They watched the storm worsen. Beneath the sky's flickering canopy, the thrashing trees of the Cragavar danced—dark, wild, out of control.

4

THE SECOND SIEGE
OF BARNASHUM

T he touch of tiny fingertips on her forearm, light and cool as snow-flakes, woke Say-ressa to orange candleglow. Three pairs of tearful eyes gleamed down at her where she lay in the healing cave. She was accustomed to seeing worry and grief here, but not for her.

"Luci, Madi, Margi," she whispered through the cobwebs of her illness.

"Can't you make yourself better?" Margi mumbled.

"Healers need strength," she sighed. "It will take time for mine to return. But don't be afraid. The king's gone to find chillseed. I'll be back on my feet soon."

The triplets were clad in their handmade animal costumes—a cat, a rabbit, and an owl. They exchanged worried glances, then bowed so that their long yellow hair veiled some unspoken shame.

Behind them, a familiar silhouette towered in the doorway.

"Is that you, my love?" she asked.

Her husband, Ark-robin, was not as he had appeared so many times in her dreams, draped in a mantle of dust and rubble from House Abascar's collapse. This time he was a silhouette illuminated through a shroud. Diamonds fell from his eyes.

"Release me," she said to him, "or give me something to do. I'm useless here. A burden."

She felt that touch on her arm again. Lifting her head from the pillows, she gasped as if rising to the surface of a dark lake.

The glowing figure in the door faded.

She had been mistaken. These girls had not come to comfort her.

"I'm listening."

"We're scared," said Madi, her cloth rabbit ears flopping beside her face.

"Tell the guards what scares you. They'll put your minds at ease."

"We're scared to tell the guards," said Luci, eyes wide in the large painted circles of an owl's watchful face.

The feline, Margi, only nodded, fingering the curling stone claws of her costume.

"I have to stay in bed," Say-ressa whispered, "until my fever is gone." Even as she said it, she knew the fever had worsened. Chillseed might not be enough now. "I must get well, for there are others in worse condition than I am. They need my help."

"We know," said Madi. "That's why we're here. Their voices are..." She raised the tip of one rabbit ear. "They've stopped calling for help."

"Calling for help?" Say-ressa winced as a groan rose from the darkness at the edge of the cave. She extended her hand toward the sound. The others lay in stiff bandages while bones began their slow reunion.

Luci drew wild pictures in the air. "We didn't mean to do it, but Wynn said we'd save the king. I didn't want to—"

"I didn't want to either," Madi asserted, tears blurring the painted whiskers around her nose.

Margi glared at them. "It wasn't wrong. We saved the king."

Say-ressa sensed something else between their words, like a charge in the air during a lightning storm. *They're thoughtspeakers. I can feel it. Doubly gifted.* "What," she asked, "did Wynn tell you to do?"

"Wynn's like my sisters," sighed Madi. "Always sneakin' around. He's the one who found them."

"He did what was necessary," muttered Luci. "He showed us the cave where they were hiding, and we sealed it."

"How many hours ago?"

The girls looked at one another.

"Last night." Madi flinched as she said it.

"Get me crutches." Say-ressa turned to prop herself up on an elbow. "You'll have to take me there."

"We're scared," whispered Luci.

"I'm not." Margi folded her furry sleeves before her like a shield. "They deserved it."

"Say-ressa!" Tabor Jan entered the room in a bluster, crouched, and laid a hand on the healer's shoulder. "My lady, you're to remain still." He turned to the girls and growled in suspicion. "Why aren't you having supper with the others?"

Say-ressa grasped the captain's arm. The girls shrank together like baby mice in a burrow.

To any other eyes it was an ordinary patch of wall, textured by heat and storm, cooling in the dusk.

But to Tabor Jan, who had patrolled the ledges of Barnashum's cliffs, it was a terrible confirmation. A cave's mouth had vanished.

He unsheathed his sword and stepped back but not too far back. The precipice was near, and the dizzying space below made his stomach turn. He hated heights.

"Open the cave," he said to the triplets.

Placing hands one beside the other across the center of the stone face, the girls set the stone to rippling, then running.

A breeze gusted out through the widening crevasse, cold and foul. Tabor Jan felt his muscles pull taut as the bowstrings of the defenders on either side.

No one emerged.

Tabor Jan stepped forward.

A voice, then—like evening dove song.

Tabor Jan peered into the dark, then strode through. His archers came behind him.

Blinking into the wedge of dusklight as if it were bright sun, a grey-haired soldier lay against the cave's far wall, heaving for breath in a pool of blood gone cold. His right arm was a bloodied stump, ending where the elbow should be. He smacked his lips dryly together. And then that voice again. "Coming through the floor," he cooed. "It's got me. It won't let go."

"Dokkens, where are the others?" Tabor Jan's feet were sticky, for bloody lines crisscrossed the floor like ribbons from an opened package.

"My arm first. Then the rest of them."

Black lines led to a corner of the cave and a break, the source of the chill. That burrow was far too small to have provided an escape. But the floor before it was littered with spots of gore and fragments of bone. Tabor Jan sank to his knees.

"The rest of them," sighed the dying man. "Left me alone. For hours and hours."

Hearing a faint cry, Tabor Jan turned in time to see the triplets flee from the entrance. He grabbed an archer's wrist. "Go after them. Don't let them say a word to anyone."

The archer stood paralyzed by the horror of the spectacle. It took a shout to send him staggering away.

Tabor Jan took hold of the grudger's remaining hand and winced at his desperate grip. "What happened?"

"Came through the floor," Dokkens groaned, eyes wide and staring at the ceiling.

"What came through?"

"Branches. Or roots. So fast we couldn't..." The man gestured toward the crack. "The smell. Do you remember?"

Tabor Jan's nostrils flared, and a long-sealed door in the back of his memory opened. "The abyss beneath the Underkeep." He looked at the crack again. He could not bring himself to ask any more questions. "The rumors are true. But the rumors spoke only of some terror in the Cragavar. Has it come so far?"

"The quake," Dokkens whispered. "If this thing caused the quake, it's coming through. Could be anywhere."

Tabor Jan stood up. "The quake." Pieces were fitting together in his mind to reveal an unexpected trouble.

In the distance someone sounded a horn, sonorous and urgent. An alarm. Tabor Jan looked to the second archer, who nodded and flew from the cave as if he'd been waiting for an excuse.

Tabor Jan was alone with Dokkens. There was no one here to guard the cave. But he was captain of the guard, and this horn was a summons he could not refuse.

He shouted in surprise as a hand grasped his shoulder.

"You'd better answer that summons," said Scharr ben Fray.

"What are you doing here?" Tabor Jan looked past the mage. "Is Calraven with you?"

"He's far from here. It's for the best. I'm here to help." Scharr ben Fray moved forward, put his hands to the wall, and melted shut that bloodied break. Then he turned and put his hand on Dokkens' forehead. "Go, Captain. Get the people out, and arm them with torches. I'll do what I can for this one."

Another urgent horn blast spun Tabor Jan around and drew him out so that quickly he was running along the ledge, afraid of so much more than the open space alongside him.

He followed the shouts to the armory, where Brevolo readied an arrow and her sister Bryndei held a torch. Before them great tendrils like roots were thrashing, powerful as the tails of oceandragons. Limbs bashed at piles of armor, denting shields, crushing breastplates, bending and snapping spears. The break in the ground from which they lashed cracked and expanded under the pressure of their advance. From within that pile of empty, battered armor came a shrill scream.

"Who's there?" he cried.

"Cortie!" said Brevolo in a voice unlike any he'd heard. "We've been trying to get to her. Tabor Jan, what in the name of Har-baron's host are we fighting?"

Bryndei lunged and waved her torch, and the tendrils jerked back like spider legs.

The ground rumbled. New lines spread like veins through the stone.

Brevolo fired arrows into one of the writhing roots. But another slithered across it, snapping the shafts as casually as one might brush off biting flies. Only fire sent the branches recoiling.

The ground's become Abascar's enemy again. We've got to get out in the open.

As three soldiers ran up to him, Tabor Jan shouted, "More torches! Fast!"

He heard a gasp, and he turned just in time to see Bryndei caught by the ankle. She dropped her torch. One of the tendrils snatched a shield and smashed it down on the flame to crush out the light.

In darkness the clamor intensified. Tabor Jan called for Brevolo. Brevolo called for her sister. Bryndei screamed.

The shield came free of the torch, and in its failing glimmer he saw Cortie, unconscious, limp as a rag doll, suspended in the coils of a root. Bryndei was nowhere to be seen. And then the light went out again.

5

A Second Exodus

Like shards of stained glass, scraps of Auralia's weaving glimmered, reflecting light that had no discernible source.

Beside a blue river of reedcloth, Lesyl knelt, considering the collection —useful crafts like scarves and stockings alongside mysterious patches that blazed just for color. "Leave whatever can be spared," Tabor Jan had said. She folded the reedcloth, gathering the colors until the whole span was bundled like a bedroll. *Cal-raven would never spare these.* She tried to bind the roll with leather straps, but her hands trembled, and the knots collapsed.

Softly she hummed a memory—a summer's evening on Deep Lake's glassy surface with her father's hands on the oars and her mother's lips to a claywhistle. She could barely hear her own melody, for the tunnel roared with the tumult of change. But she sang anyway. The song slowed her breathing and stilled her frantic heartbeat until she could bind the straps fast.

"Have you seen Wynn this morning?" It was one of the triplets, dressed as an owl. "We can't find him anywhere."

Lesyl folded the girl's cold fingers into her own. "No one's found him yet, Madi. I'm sorry."

"I'm Luci," sighed the girl. "Madi's asking other folks. A horse went missing, you know."

"Yes. We think he fled after the king's departure."

"He didn't mean to hurt anybody."

"Luci." Lesyl took the girl by the shoulders. "Wynn meant well. So did you. We all make mistakes with good intentions."

"What if the king's dragged him off to punish him?"

She laughed bitterly. "The king has more important things to do."

"Did he tell you that?"

"No." She heard the resentment in her own voice. "He told me nothing. But he'll do what he thinks is best."

"Then what about Wynn? What if those things that killed the grudgers—"

"No," Lesyl answered forcefully. "We've lost seven to that monster. No one else."

"Madi thinks he ran way." Luci folded her arms like a disgruntled schoolteacher. "We hate boys."

Lesyl gathered the girl into her arms. The bones behind Luci's shoulders were so small, like the bones of a bird before its wings find feathers.

"Wynn shouldn't have run away," said the girl. "What good is he to the rest of us if he heads out into the wild without telling us where he's going?"

Lesyl realized she was squeezing the air right out of the girl and released her. "Here. I've wrapped my string-weave in cloth. Take it. But, Luci, it's my most precious instrument. Not a scratch or a broken string. Do you understand? Go to your sisters. Stay close to the grownups. And don't step on any cracks."

As Luci ran off, Lesyl stood and strapped a heavy pack over her shoulders—a bundle of musical instruments. Then she tucked the roll of reedcloth beneath her arm and lifted a bag of Auralia's sculptures, garments, and inventions.

Cal-raven would thank her. "Her colors will gleam like jewels in a crown, from the gates of New Abascar right up to the palace," he had said, lying beside her. For one fleeting night they had watched Auralia's colors cast dancing light across the ceiling. He had touched her left hand with his right. At first she thought it was accidental. But then his fingertips traced her knuckles, drew a circle on the back of her hand and another on her wrist, his touch as gentle as a first kiss. *He's tracing a marriage tattoo*, she had realized. *He's pondering the question.*

Stifling the memory, she departed the chamber, troubled by new cracks that had spread on the walls behind the gallery. She wanted to remember what they had made of this place, not how it had gone wrong. She would carry the details close and weave them into music for a day when the people were ready to lift these heavy memories again.

Shouts racked the corridor. Defenders repeated Tabor Jan's commands. Wear boots, not shoes, if you have them. Bring flasks of water from Barnashum's reservoir. Keep families together. List the names of those who shared your caves, and give every name to the counters who wait on the tiers. Get outside the caves as quickly as possible, for we'll descend to Barnashum's threshold at the sounding of the Midmorning Verse.

Parents hauled children along by the collars of their jerkins. Old men and women hobbled, bracing themselves on crutches, walls, or each other. Lesyl watched one shove away a swordsman who offered to help with her overloaded wheelbarrow. "I'm not some Gatherer weakling!"

Gatherers wore nervous smiles. Danger, sudden death, flight, the wilderness—this was the life they'd once known. But for Housefolk, what semblance of security they'd constructed here in Barnashum now lay in pieces. Creases crossed every brow.

Tabor Jan approached like a charging bull—shoulders hunched, teeth bared through his ragged beard.

Lesyl grabbed his arm as he passed. "This isn't the departure he envisioned," she said.

"No. We had plans. So many nights. So many maps."

"Where has he gone?" The question leapt past her better judgment. "Why didn't he tell me he..." She pressed her eyes shut, but it was too late to hide her emotion.

She felt his hand on her shoulder, an awkward press of comfort. "He doesn't like to worry you."

"He doesn't *trust* me."

Tabor Jan pulled at his beard. "He trusts you. He trusts us both. But I did hear him say that soon he would need to shut out other voices and listen for something deeper."

"That sounds like him."

"I'd probably lose my temper if I heard what Scharr ben Fray has stirred into Cal-raven's soup. But who am I to question our king's decisions? His plot to defend us from the Cent Regus attack was like fighting fangbears with fishing nets. And yet it worked."

Somewhere up the corridor there was a clamor of clattering metal, followed by outbursts of anger and blame.

"I should go." Tabor Jan leaned forward as if pulled by an invisible tether. But Lesyl still had hold of his sleeve. "Stuff your questions, songbird!" he grunted. "We've lost too many already to that blasted creature. And I don't think last night's struggle convinced it to leave. We'll talk about Cal-raven later." He jerked his arm away and marched up the corridor.

His steps slowed, and he paused. "Forgive me," he called back over his shoulder. "It's...it's a terrible day. I'm so tired I can hardly tell left from right." His eyes met hers. "The king will return. Then..."

"Then." She nodded.

As she took up her burdens again and moved on toward the open air, they seemed heavier than before.

A plan. Oh, for a plan.

Like an ache after a recent wound, shame burned at the edges of Tabor Jan's concentration. He had not intended to hurt Lesyl.

He stepped into every cave along the corridor, calling out for stragglers.

He had not seen Brevolo this morning. She had disappeared after the ordeal in the armor cave the night before, refusing comfort. It was her way in everything—self-reliance. She would never seek from him, nor he from her, the kind of sad, consoling whispers Cal-raven shared with Lesyl.

He could not fathom why those two would complicate their troubles by staying up all night in search of words to describe them. Brevolo was complete and content, even if she snarled about everyone else. He hungered for the rough sparring of their conversation.

The corridor ahead sloped into steps that ascended into darkness. He ran the full stair. Each chamber he passed was silent and empty until he reached the top. Hushed voices haunted the last cave.

Inside, a small, silver glowstone illuminated the features of a stout old woman hovering over her frail, bedridden husband and dabbing at the tears dripping off her nose. "Vyrna," he said, but then swallowed his reprimand.

Vyrna had come to be known for her quiet compliance and service among Abascar's elderly. These days she rarely left her crippled husband's side, passing the hours by braiding intricate patterns into her long silver hair.

"They said to leave Jak where he lies," she rasped in a voice that had been frail since the dust and ash of Abascar's fall. "They said he'd slow everyone down."

"Jak will slow everyone down, and many will thank him for it." As Tabor Jan raised the old man from the stone bed, he was surprised to find him as weightless as a child. "The world's changing out there, and our maps can tell us only so much. We need our elders."

"I'm no use," Jak protested in a squawk like an angry gander. "I'm a heavy load."

As the foul air blasted through the gaps in Jak's remaining teeth, Tabor Jan turned his head and choked. "We're a body," he answered, grabbing hold of a speech he had heard Cal-raven give many times. "Don't let muscle tell bone its work is done."

"Bone?" That brought on a cackle and wheeze. "Zat what I am?"

"He means you're tough, Jakky," said Vyrna like a schoolteacher to a child.

"Brittle 'n' rotten. That's what he means." Digging his fingers into Tabor Jan's arm, the old man whispered, "Just put the pillow over worthless Jak's face. It would take you no trouble at all."

Tabor Jan heard a faint crumbling of stone somewhere in the dark. There was no time for discussion. He began carrying Jak to the stairway. "Anyone who'd pass you by has got no gratitude. You're Abascar's experience, a memory as deep as a well."

"Well's gone dry, Captain," Jak sneered. "Can't even remember breakfast."

"Seeds," muttered Vyrna, hobbling alongside. "Seeds and knuckle-nuts."

"If we left you behind"—Tabor Jan felt his grumbling cargo grow heavier as he thudded down the crooked stair—"our strength might carry us a fair distance, and fast. But how would we be any better than beastmen? If we measure everyone's worth by brains or brawn, well, why not leave all the children behind?"

Jak scoffed something unintelligible.

"What begins in love," said Vyrna, "should end in love as well."

"What's that?" Jak barked.

"Somethin' my mum used to say. Babies to oldies. Loved in the womb, loved still until the tomb."

"Take a look at your dear Vyrna, Jak." Tabor Jan leaned against the wall of the stairway, catching his breath. He swung Jak's head around so the man could stare into his wife's mole-spotted face. "She's a treasure. Would you insult her generosity and tell her she's not worth seeing every morning?"

Jak muttered something about intolerable noises that Vyrna made in her sleep.

Vyrna lowered her already failing voice and said, " 'Twas that scurrilous boy, Vorcin's son. He's the one who told me to leave Jak in his bed."

"Dignet?" Tabor Jan winced, wishing he hadn't heard. Now he'd have to live with the knowledge, and he knew that someday he would find young Dignet and act on it.

At the base of the stairs, he sat down, exhausted, with Jak lying across him like an old hound.

Vyrna finger-combed her husband's circle of sparse hair. "It's all right, Jak. We'll take you out into the sun. It'll do you good."

Merya's husband, Corvah, lumbered past, a hulk of a man, cradling his infant. It was still a startling sight—Corvah, whom so many had determined to be dead on account of daily drinking, now up and purposeful and carrying his pink and mewling son.

"You see?" Tabor Jan turned Jak's head, as if it were a doll's on a pivot, so the old man could witness Corvah's passage. "You see? New Abascar's strength is in its heart as much as its head and its arms. We'll show the world what can be made from broken pieces."

As Meddles the Weaver came into view shoving a cart full of folded blankets, Tabor Jan thrust out his leg to block his path. "Ballyworms, Cap'n!" the Gatherer shouted. "I coulda smashed your shin to splinters!"

Tabor Jan brought Jak to the cart, set him down there, and leaned in close to Meddles's ear, which stuck out from the Gatherer's wild explosion of hair like a mushroom. "Push carefully. He's fragile. And when you have time, find the old fool some freshweed to chew. If his breath gets any worse, the leaves of the Cragavar will curl up and fall."

Adryen and Stasi, Abascar's cooks since Yawny's passing, approached. "What about food?" asked Stasi. "You know how the king loves bramblebug honey."

"And I've made bundles of bean sticks," said Adryen.

"Some we'll have to find on the way. The Gatherers'll help. Shame to leave those cavefish drying on the racks, though. Bring what you can carry. And remember—anything you lift now will feel ten times heavier by the time..."

His voice failed, for there was Brevolo, drawing a sledge through the corridor's dust. Lying on its wooden bed, pale in the cocoon of a thistleleaf quilt, Say-ressa might have been a statue of white chalk. "Our healer's not fit to sleep in the open, Captain." The swordswoman's face was expressionless. "She's fallen so far that we could lose her to something as slight as a flyspider bite or a scratch from a venom thorn."

Brevolo had not called him captain in a long time. It was a retreat. "We'll sift the Gatherers' wisdom to see what other help we might find in the wild until Cal-raven brings the chillseed."

"It's not just the sickness, Captain. It's the loss of her husband and daughter. Say-ressa's been dreaming of Abascar's fall."

"Try singing to her of the Keeper." Scharr ben Fray had appeared so quietly, Tabor Jan wondered if the mage had walked right through the wall. "She might find comfort."

Brevolo's eyes blazed, and Tabor Jan could read her thoughts. *So it's true. This is the one who made Cal-raven mad.* But she kept her mouth shut, too bruised to muster the strength for an argument, and she dragged Say-ressa's sled away without giving Tabor Jan so much as a glance.

"What a burden Brevolo must carry," the mage quietly mused. "Having lost her sister, she'll be afraid to let anyone else be close to her for a while. I'm sure you remember that feeling."

Tabor Jan did not reply, but he was stunned by Scharr ben Fray's knowledge of his older brother's death. It had happened so long ago. Lejor Jan had been prone to illness all through his childhood, and then a winter plague proved too fierce and took him. *How dare you trouble me now with such a memory!*

But then he saw Scharr ben Fray raise his hand to address an invisible audience. "I'll raise an image of Bryndei in stone on the wall of New Abascar, with her torch lifted high as it was when she was taken from us. For she was one of Abascar's bravest."

"What are they?" whispered Tabor Jan. "What monsters are driving us from our home?"

"The Blackstone Caves have never been your home, Captain. Barnashum belongs to the wild. We're meant for a far better home than this."

"Where do we belong, then?"

Scharr ben Fray fixed him with fierce attention, dark eyes gleaming beneath the cowl. "That, Captain, is the secret your king is chasing."

"Is there an answer?"

"We know, somehow, that we are out of place. I've made it my life's work to understand why that is so. And I'm close, Captain. Closer than ever to the answer."

6

DRAWN BY VISION, DRIVEN BY FEAR

Exhausted by its tantrums, the storm that had pursued Cal-raven's company for a night, a day, and another night finally subsided. The sun came up smug and bold, casting golden rays. The continent of cloud broke apart, its remnants melting away like dollops of butter across a hot pan.

In the boughs of a full-grown cloudgrasper, a giant in this patch of the Cragavar forest, the king lay in his hammock. His mind was inclined to see in metaphors, for he was fresh from dreams, spectacles inspired by the campfire story Krawg had shared the night before.

Krawg was fond of stories about magicians and enchantments. His art improved with every telling. In this particular story, a stranger paid a gang of pickpocket brothers to rob a magician who ruled the Expanse. After the robbery's success, the robbers fought one another, arguing over some foolishness such as the true and proper name of the one who had hired them. They forgot that they were brothers, calling each other "bushpig" and "snake in the weeds." In the commotion the treasure they had stolen was smashed, and they raised jagged shards to attack one another. Lanterns fell sideways in the melee that ensued, and their hideaway caught fire.

Walls burned away, revealing the magician, torch in hand. As the brothers called out for his help, he smiled, and his face changed. Lo, the man they had robbed was the man who had hired them, tricking them into exposing their wicked nature. Their crimes were undeniable now, and they would pay a terrible price. Laughing, the magician turned and walked away while the fiery house collapsed upon the thieves.

The story had clearly shaken its teller, past crimes paining his conscience.

But in Cal-raven's dream, the scroll had unfurled to reveal a different ending. The Keeper had burned the house down on the thieves and then, with a sweeping thrust of its mighty wing, scattered the story's characters and sent them off in flares like shooting stars.

Cal-raven felt the dream slip away. But one element remained as clear as these sideways rays of daytime. *It's not just a dream anymore. The Keeper is real.*

The hammock swayed slightly among leafy fans. Birdsong spread. He pushed off the rainskin and hung it from a tree branch to dry in the sun.

I know the truth at last. And it's just what I always claimed. I call for the Keeper's help, and it hears me. I must have won its favor somehow, searching for its tracks or sculpting its likeness.

Birdsong was not the only music rising from the Cragavar. The breeze spilled rainwater from the leafy boughs, from one broad green hand down to be caught by another, surrounding Cal-raven with a pitter-patter symphony. Far below, he heard the happy concert of humming vawns. Mouthless, the reptiles sang in short, dissonant hoots and snorts with no discernible pattern or rhythm. Between the notes they noisily sucked mud through their nostrils, chewed the worms and grubs with the teeth that lined their throats, then sneezed out the leftover soil.

As if joining in with the vawns, Snyde was singing an old Abascar folk tune, "Up the River Throanscall."

Cal-raven closed his eyes and fought against thoughts of the coming confrontation, the ugly business he must carry out along the way to Mawrnash. Breathing deeply, he tried to remember childhood lessons in how to be still.

We have far to go. I cannot afford any delays.

His worries were as aggressive as weeds. He could not forget his last sight of Say-ressa in bandages, her fists clenched as she battled against death's ruthless agents.

A strange gravity from the east tugged at his attention. Were he to give in to those beckoning phantoms, he would be drawn back across familiar ground to the desolation of his father's house. He lifted a shield against that temptation. No hope could be found in those ruins.

He turned westward, drawn by another sort of gravity. Bel Amica. The beastman who had warned him, saving Abascar's remnant from a siege, had said that only Cyndere, the heiress of House Bel Amica, could be trusted to help House Abascar. Cyndere would welcome them with shelter, sustenance, and a future. It would take only a few days' ride to enter an opulent house.

Memories of his last visit to those foggy, busy avenues taunted him. All that his people needed, all that he could not give them, could be found within Bel Amica. He'd come close to the queen, mapped much of her palace labyrinth, and learned just how intoxicating that house by the sea could be. He had wandered in mirror-lined marketplaces, watched triumphal ships return from faraway islands, seen the fishing nets burgeoning. If his half-starved, exhausted people ever tasted those riches, all that had survived Abascar's collapse would be ruined. He mouthed one of Scharr ben Fray's lessons: "The greatest threat to what is best is something persuasively good."

There was only one direction open to him now—the path into vision, the way to New Abascar.

An arrow slammed into the underside of a thick bough nearby. Dangling from its shaft was a sling, and glittering seeds were spilling down into the campsite.

Cal-raven laughed. "Chillseed!"

"The Gatherers found it, my lord!" came Jes-hawk's happy cry. "And in less than two days! Let's go home!"

The company was jubilant with relief, and the king proclaimed Krawg and Warney as "Abascar's Masters of Herbs."

But the joy dissolved as Cal-raven handed the sling of chillseed to Shanyn and announced that now they could begin the second stage of their mission.

Shanyn flinched. "You can't mean it. You brought me because it's dangerous out here. I beg you—"

"And I've begged myself to find a better solution. I covet your company. But the mind must rule the heart in these matters, and you can get back to Say-ressa faster than any of us."

"Must I go alone?"

"Send Gatherers," mumbled Bowlder.

"Starvation and illness are as dangerous as beastmen and bandits," Cal-raven growled. "Krawg and Warney can find food and healing herbs. Further, they look like ordinary travelers. Where we're going, we mustn't attract attention. Shanyn looks like nothing less than a king's defender." He shrugged. "Really, must you be so impressive?"

He did not get the laugh he wanted.

"I can be ugly if I have to be." Shanyn exchanged a furtive, troubled glance with Jes-hawk, a fleeting connection that told Cal-raven more than he had guessed about them.

"Shanyn will take the chillseed," he said with finality. "We'll go on, following signs Scharr ben Fray left for me. He says they'll lead to an answer for Abascar. If Red Moon Season passes before we get there, the vision will fade."

"Vision?" Snyde groaned.

"If my teacher is right," said the king, "then we'll return with a story more exciting than anything shared at this campfire. It may be that the people of Abascar will rise up and march out from Barnashum with new hope and a new purpose." His speech inspired a worrying silence. Cal-raven cleared his throat. "Shanyn, I am grateful. Ride fast for Barnashum, and I suspect you'll arrive before midnight."

❧

The bristling plains were restless. Seedpods crackled. Springnippers sprang. And the golden waves of brush seemed to undulate, a trick of the light as a gauzy haze muddied the sun's glow.

Quarreling and distressed, the people made their way down Barnashum's cliffs and out into the maze. Archers and soldiers formed a protective perimeter around them as they entered the dark sea of thorn-barbed branches through which a host of beastmen had charged only a few months past. Who could say what prowled there now?

Flies moved in clouds across the paths. A flock of peskies appeared, darting through the tapestry of boughs and twittering giddily as if the exodus were the most exciting thing they'd seen all summer. But when a brascle crossed the sky, the peskies vanished, and the people of Abascar wished that they, too, could take cover. *When brascles soar, beastmen prowl*—so went the children's verse.

Tabor Jan scanned the parade for the mage, eager to learn what he could about this new threat growing in the ground. But Scharr ben Fray had not appeared since their encounter in the corridor.

The sun had only begun to descend when Tabor Jan moved to the front of the line and entered the Cragavar. As he did, he heard the archers behind him hiss a warning.

A vawn skulked beneath the trees. The creature was not trying to hide; her head wagged low, her long reptilian tail swishing the ground behind her. She shifted from one heavy hind foot to the other, her pathetic little forelegs stuck in their perpetual crumb-begging pose. She seemed anxious and uncertain.

Scharr ben Fray emerged from the crowd. He uttered a call that sounded like a vawn's own shrill salute. The creature raised its head high, trumpeted a three-toned reply, and knocked saplings aside as it tromped eagerly through the underbrush.

"Rumpa!" The mage slapped the vawn's shoulder with affection. "This is Rumpa," he said to Tabor Jan. "She's the ale boy's vawn. But it seems she lost him somewhere."

"The ale boy?"

"You call him Rescue."

"Here's Scharr ben Fray," whispered a boy excitedly to the captain. "Will you ask him to tell us a story tonight?"

"I suspect he'll have too much on his mind to bother." Tabor Jan watched as Scharr ben Fray rode Rumpa on a winding progress between clusters of shoddy shieldfern tents. Sure enough, the old man was as immune to the awkward applause of his admirers as he was to the glares of those who distrusted him. His gaze seemed enthralled with scenes invisible to others. He leashed his vawn to a hanger-tree, then entered the glow of their smokeless, crumblewood bonfires without so much as a nod to anyone.

Despite his gratitude for the help of Cal-raven's teacher, Tabor Jan became uneasy in his presence. That head held a library of history and experience. But when the mage revealed any lines from those mysterious scrolls, he spoke with calculated restraint.

As the mage approached their makeshift bench, the boy sprang up. "He wants to talk with you!" It was almost a squeak, as if he did not understand that the old man was flesh and blood, could see and hear him.

Scharr ben Fray barely acknowledged the youth as he sat down, folding his legs beneath him and staring into—no, through—the flames. Tabor Jan refused to flatter the mage with questions. Instead, he lifted his shieldfern plate, folded it, and poured what remained of his supper into his mouth, then cast the leaf aside.

Scharr ben Fray answered as if he had been asked. "You'll have chillseed soon. The rider will be here even before I've bid you farewell."

Tabor Jan folded his arms, noisily chewing the seeds, berries, and roasted scratchwings. He would not ask how this secretive meddler came by such information about approaching riders. In the hour before the company had stopped for that first laborious endeavor of setting up camp in the trees, Scharr ben Fray had vanished. *Just when his wisdom might have been most useful,* Tabor Jan thought, *he's off on secret business. And even now he seems uninterested in what's going on around him. He's solving puzzles only he can see.*

"Ravens," said Scharr ben Fray, rocking back and forth slowly. "Gossipmongers, they are. And spies. Eager to impress me in hopes I'll reward them. Interpreting their noise is a chore. But they give a good report. Calraven's almost to Mawrnash. All according to plan."

Mawrnash? The captain choked on a seed. *Whose plan was that?*

"Yes," continued the mage. "I'm southbound for House Jenta, the garden that grew me. The brotherhood may be some help to us."

"The brotherhood? Would you ask them for parchment for us to throw at the beastmen?" Standing, Tabor Jan seized a small, stripped sapling he had dragged to the fire and cast it onto the orange glow. "Those sulking scrollreaders have never shown Abascar kindness before." He spat out a tough shred of scratchwing. "And I thought you'd left that world behind long ago."

"Maps, journals—to reach Abascar's destination, we'll need reliable guidance. My older brother knows more than he lets on. Best to know the obstacles in our path before we face them. Don't you agree?"

As the sapling crackled and blackened in the flames, it writhed in jerking spasms. It reminded Tabor Jan of the time he'd killed a bonestalker in just this fashion. He hadn't seen one of those headless nighttime predators in years, but then, a bonestalker was hard to see at all. With limbs and body as narrow as sticks, the eyeless, bloodsucking insect wore its bones on the outside—coal black and unbreakable. Its knife-claws skewered prey, and a whiplike tongue drew blood as through a straw. He'd seen a bonestalker climb a man's leg and kill him, and he swore from that point on that he'd seen the most frightening killer in the Expanse. Now he knew otherwise.

"The dangers we face out here consume my attention." He brushed crumbs from his beard. "I cannot bother to worry about unknown obstacles just yet. I want you to tell me how we're going to fight the menace that drove us from our caves."

Scharr ben Fray lowered his voice. "Do you think I came just to say good-bye?" Then he stood and walked to the edge of the fire. He leaned in close, then thrust his hand into the fire, seized the writhing sapling, and cast it to the ground.

"What are you doing?" the captain exclaimed.

"Hush!" Scharr ben Fray knelt over the black, burning branch, his head cocked as if listening. Then he leapt to his feet and cast the wood back onto the fire, where it exploded in sparks. He fixed Tabor Jan with a summoning gaze. "Follow me."

They moved out through the perimeter of the watchful archers until they came to a crowded grove of coil trees. Scharr ben Fray cast an anxious gaze back toward the camp, eyes filling with firelight as if his skull were a lantern.

"That was quite a performance," Tabor Jan scoffed. "Don't you think the people are jumpy enough?"

"I've been across the Expanse since winter," said the mage. "I've questioned birds, lurkdashers, even fangbears. Few animals remain in the territories we've traveled, Tabor Jan. Those that do are quick and good at hiding. They speak of a predator rising from the ground. I've learned that the Cent Regus know a great deal, for they grumble about something that they call feelers. Birds call them Deathweeds."

"Deathweeds."

"I gather they come from the Core of the Cent Regus lair. The arms of some underground creature that spreads like a weed. The curse has cast its net. And now, at last, it's drawing in its catch. It seizes any living thing, save for those already corrupt with the Cent Regus curse. And they seem linked to a single mind—a single appetite. For the living."

"We know they're afraid of fire." Tabor Jan stared into the distant red flare.

"So far, our only weapon. If I could find myself a firewalker, I'd make him our chief agent in resisting such a monster. I had my eye on one, but he got away."

"Why did you pull that small tree from the fire?"

The mage scratched his grizzled chin. "It smelled funny. And there was a sound...a strange sound."

"These Deathweeds... I recognize the stench. I smelled it more than once deep beneath Abascar in the Underkeep."

Scharr ben Fray nodded. "I am not surprised. I have long suspected that what shook House Abascar to its foundations was more than an earthquake, more than a fire. I believe that the menace either rose up to break the ground apart or else the fire came first and awakened it, setting those powerful limbs to thrashing. Either way, I think the Deathweeds helped bring Abascar down."

Tabor Jan had the sickening sensation of being trapped, as if he could feel those wretched roots troubling the ground beneath him. "Are we any safer out here?"

"I'm not sure," sighed the mage, looking up into the darkling boughs. "If Deathweeds can burrow through ground, they might corrupt the trees."

"If they can break through Abascar's foundation and shatter the stone of Barnashum..."

"Barnashum's stone is soft. Abascar must go north. The mountains of the Fearblind North are made of tougher stuff. They might keep out the curse. Difficult to know. The sooner the remnant of Abascar crosses the Expanse to find a new foundation, the better."

"You want us to go beyond Fraughtenwood? To the Forbidding Wall?"

Tabor Jan laughed, incredulous. "Such a journey seems too foolish to risk on a guess."

"Cal-raven will return with something better than a guess." There was that smug, knowing smile that Tabor Jan resented. "His most difficult challenge is this—to get the people past an easier and more alluring possibility. Abascar's prejudice against the Bel Amicans is failing fast."

"Cal-raven has no desire to go to Bel Amica. The Seers have—"

"You know your old friend better than that. Cal-raven hates the Seers, sure. But his desire to walk through those halls and marketplaces again is almost unbearable. He wants it so badly he scares himself. That's why he's desperate to find something, anything else. He knows that the distractions of Queen Thesera's house could be Abascar's undoing."

A commotion drew their attention to the north end of the camp. The guards' shouts were hostile at first but quickly turned to excitement.

Tabor Jan could not help but cry out in the dark. "Shanyn!"

"It's begun," sighed Scharr ben Fray. "I wish you good ground, safe campsites, and the best of the Cragavar's summer bounty. Yours is the greatest exodus since Tammos Raak led the children of the curse over the Forbidding Wall into the world we know today. I will leave you to tend to the healer."

Tabor Jan welcomed the swordswoman into the firelight even as he heard Rumpa's stride fade. He let others explain the exodus to Shanyn as they carried the bundle to the beds where Say-ressa and the other wounded lay in fevered sleep.

Tabor Jan placed a hand on the healer's burning forehead while Shanyn folded the chillseed pods in a cloth, pounded them to powder with a stone, then cast the powder into a bowl of hot water and stirred up a cloud of steam. Tabor Jan held Say-ressa's head while Shanyn spooned the tea into the sleeping woman's mouth. And they waited, a crowd of golden faces shining in the dark all around them.

Not far away gentle notes of music drifted along like sparks from the fire, and Lesyl's voice rose in a quiet, hopeful song. "Help is coming. But the night is dark and long. Help is coming. Until then, kindle me a song."

7

CAMPFIRE IN THE CRAGAVAR

O n the third day of their journey, four vawns followed Jes-hawk as he rode in a sulking slump.

Cal-raven smiled sadly, understanding the archer's disappointment all too well. Now both of them had hearts divided.

The company slowed only to skirt the edge of a vast, overgrown berry patch, the vines interwoven into an impenetrable wall. They picked berry-rolls—thick, juicy husks that curled into scrolls as they grew; when unrolled, they exposed rich beds of crimson berries, shiny as fish eggs. Soon Warney's grin was as red as the stains down his tunic.

I'm not the only one who has missed the forest, Cal-raven thought.

During their run through sparse stands of haircloak trees, a long-ear was startled from its dig in the lee of a fallen tree. The stag-sized rabbit bolted, and Jes-hawk was off in hot pursuit. It was an hour before the exhausted archer returned, more discouraged than before, and the way he chewed a gob of root-gum, he might as well have been cursing.

Dusk began climbing the grass and the tree trunks. Cal-raven had anticipated a swifter voyage. Even now the red moon would be peering over the Forbidding Wall, glowering down on the Expanse like the eye of the overlord from whom Tammos Raak had fled. He could sense the company's weariness, and Say-ressa would tell him that he was not a good judge of his own need for a pause. At his order Jes-hawk drew them aside into a canopied chamber of violet trees.

A light rain returned; sharp hissing notes sang from the fire. Breezes teased the flames, and Cal-raven knew that these winds moved on the momentum gained while rushing across Deep Lake.

Snyde looked as if he'd been belly-kicked by a vawn. He had not spoken more than a few suspicious questions on their journey.

"The ride seems to have bruised you," Cal-raven laughed. "Shall I ask the Gatherers to weave you a pillowed saddle?"

Snyde froze in that hunched position, as if caught in some treachery. Then as he straightened, his scowl melted upward into a smile broad and toothy. "You misunderstand the nature of my discomfort. I'm unworthy to travel in such…prestigious company. You should have brought a rider who would have been more able to defend you in a fight."

"Are you expecting a fight, Ambassador?"

Snyde began digging dirt from beneath his nails with the corner of a folded leaf. "I only hope my king will return to Barnashum unscratched."

"Oh, I think I'm as vulnerable to scratches in Barnashum as I am out here."

"What are you insinuating?" Snyde snapped.

"Insinuating? Why, Ambassador, I was only referring to the quake that buried our healer. You haven't forgotten the quake, have you?"

Snyde's face was hot and red as the moon. He sank slowly back down to the grass. "Why did you bring me here? I'm old. These lungs do not contend well with breezes so heavy with blossoms. I'm an ambassador of the arts. I should be indoors revising the verses of the royal—"

"There will be new choruses sung in New Abascar," Cal-raven said. "The people will compose them."

The ambassador looked as if he'd been struck in the forehead with a frypan. "Composed by…Housefolk? By Gatherers? In House Abascar the king and his ambassadors provide the people with their songs. If the songs do not follow the patterns and themes established by our ancestors, we won't have music. We'll have a nursery's squall."

"I'm not interested in dogs who howl on command, Snyde. Our house is full of dreamers who have heard new melodies, new verses. New Abascar will be a kingdom that manifests all the colors its people have to offer, united by that golden strand that's been sewn through king, cook, chemist, and carver."

"What"—Snyde blinked—"strand?"

"The Keeper who haunts our dreams. I've begun composing lines for a chorus that describes its dimensions, the number of its wings, the way its hands can snatch a person up as easily as an owl grasps a mouse."

"Such particularity," Jes-hawk observed, still gnawing on the root-gum. "Dreams of the Keeper give us many different pictures. Aren't you asking for trouble by requiring people to favor your definition?"

"Ah, but that's just it. Most have only dreams. What if I told you the Keeper's been observed?"

"When did you see it, my lord?" Jes-hawk asked. Not "Have you seen it?" or "Did you catch a glimpse?" but a direct challenge. Lowering his voice as if he were speaking with a friend in private, he added, "You've never made such a claim before."

All eyes were fixed on the king.

Cal-raven smiled, the secret roiling within, steam in a kettle. Then he slapped Krawg's shoulder to disrupt the challenge. "Krawg, another story! What'll it be?"

"Nobody paints pictures of Tammos Raak's escape better than Krawg," suggested Warney.

Cal-raven clapped his hands. "Incredible. The very tale I had in mind." And it was, for the culmination of the story occurred in the very place they quested for, even though none of them yet knew their aim.

"Which version shall it be?" Krawg asked. "The death of Tammos Raak? The blessing of the ladder? The rescue by sky chariot?"

And so it was Krawg who told another tale.

⁂

Krawg's storytelling had first impressed Warney in the early days of their thievery. Krawg had filled long hours with tales to calm the nerves of his anxious co-conspirator while they lay in wait for a door unguarded, a wagon unobserved, a treasure momentarily forgotten.

Warney had learned so much from Krawg in those days. He had learned from the master burglar's powers of observation—the same piercing gaze that made Krawg a master thief had spotted the infant Auralia in the river-bank reeds.

Krawg was also good at losing himself. His thievery had trained him in concealment, a skill enhanced by his resemblance to a tangle of gnarled, knobby branches. He could wriggle his twig-thin frame into any nook or cranny and wait, with patience and fierce attention, until the golden moment when he could emerge and snatch what did not belong to him. Running with the long, loping stride of a fieldbounder, he'd take some predetermined avenue of escape—a trapdoor, a ladder, a hideout with myriad corridors, or a dark barn with loose floorboards that could be quickly lifted to expose another hideaway and replaced over his head.

That urgent need for a hiding place was what had brought the two out-casts together. Krawg had been running to avoid arrest. Warney had run to escape his sisters. Seven sisters, in fact. All grown, they had never left home or the parents who babied them, and they shared their mother's loathing for Warney.

What was it exactly that had made his mother treat him as a curse? Warney shuddered to think of the accusations. To comfort himself, he affirmed that it was crazy for a parent to hold a grudge for some damage done in childbirth.

"I labored to flush him out into the open," his mother had shrieked at his sisters. "But he was a burglar from the hour he was born, for he held on to my insides with some ferocious grip, refusing to let go, though I watered and bled. The baby catcher had to pry Warney's wicked little fingers free. That's why he's got such long fingers today. On the way out he'd stolen some-thing else. Something precious I'll never get back."

What had he stolen from his mother? In his darkest moods he deter-mined he'd taken her heart. For how else could he explain her merciless nature? Whatever the case, his sisters branded him "the Bandit." As he grew, any object's disappearance was blamed squarely on him. His sisters took to stealing anything that belonged to him—his pillow, his leaf-roll, his shoe straps, his dinner.

He'd schooled himself in stealth so he could recapture his belongings from his thieving sisters. He'd mapped out a network of hideouts in case he had to make an escape like that famous Midnight Swindler—the uncaptured crook called Krawg.

Warney knew Krawg by reputation. And, in fact, by admiration. For how could he not be impressed by a thief who always escaped without hurting anybody, without any evidence to point to him? Krawg had become a secret hero, a pilferer who perplexed the smartest guards.

Once, Warney dashed into a decrepit stable, gripping his favorite feathered hat, which he had just repossessed from his sisters. Stumbling through old piles of dung, he dove to the floor and, lifting an overturned food trough, concealed himself, fitting it over him as neatly as a coffin.

He panted into quiet, endured the stench that saturated his temporary cell, and drifted into a fantasy in which he was the Midnight Swindler himself.

He could never have guessed that the floorboards beneath him were loose or that Krawg himself lay beneath them, hiding from a dispatch of furious guards. And even if he had, how could he have suspected how mightily Krawg was striving to stifle a sneeze?

Whether it was the force of the eventual sneeze, or Krawg's powerful lurch from a lie-down to a sit-up, or Warney's spasm of astonishment—it didn't matter in the end. Warney rose from the floor like a boulder from a catapult. And the boat in which he sailed brained the ornery goat that a merchant had just bullied into a stall.

Krawg and Warney had run together, cursing at each other even as they took turns leading the escape. They learned in their hurry that the merchant was a guest from Bel Amica, and they would never forget his rage. He gave chase like a wild pig, fast as a fitter, thinner man. And it was not until they clambered over a fence into a children's schoolyard and hid themselves behind archery targets that they were still again. Thus began one of the longest tests of their endurance.

Crouching at the end of the yard, holding the targets before them like shields, they whispered angry accusations at each other. But as the steam of tempers dissipated, Warney's admiration kindled Krawg's sense of pride. Soon Krawg regaled his fellow escapist with an array of stories about his wild exploits.

So their ritual began, and Warney came to think of stories as whispered and exciting prologues to some daring disappearance with a prize.

In those early days, Krawg's stories were exaggerated and—Warney came to believe—stolen. Their twists and surprises were as hot as a panpatty snatched from the fire, and Warney learned that his hero, now his friend, was as skilled in plundering histories and biographies as he was in robbing laundry from the line.

But in time Warney's doubts conjured questions, and those questions both aggravated Krawg and provoked him to narrate in more elaborate detail. Pleased to find an attentive companion whose curiosity seasoned his stories, and so delighted to train an apprentice in thievery, the Midnight Swindler had welcomed the Bandit as a partner. But there was never any doubt which thief was in command.

Together they had weathered a hundred crimes, and while they harassed each other unceasingly, they also had formed an unbreakable bond. It endured through their disputes, as when Krawg stole Warney's occasional sweetheart. (That story always ended when the girl absconded with both of the thieves' broken hearts.) It endured when they were captured and beaten and when Warney lost his eye in an epic escape. It endured when they were exiled from the safety of Abascar's walls and were made to labor in the harvest until they were old.

One night Warney had wondered, "Krawg, what would drive a wedge between us since not a woman or a wound has ever come close?"

Krawg had given it some thought. "Satisfaction," he sighed. "Riches would keep us from conspiring, either to snitch what's not ours—but we don't go that way no more—or to claim what's ours rightfully. We'd get lazy and fat, and where's the fun in that?"

Warney, stunned with the insight, had slowly wagged his head. "Gotta 'gree with ya there."

Tonight as Krawg applied his talent to a story of ancient adventure, he lavished detail upon each scene, detail that often had nothing to do with the story but so enriched it with food for the senses and kindling for the imagination that Warney remained enthralled.

Sometimes those meanders would bring the story's biggest surprises. And like some lucky wanderer who runs away, gets lost, regrets his foolish wanderlust, and stumbles inexplicably upon his own home, Krawg would reach the end of the tale and tie all fraying strands back together.

No story was told more often, in versions more varying, than this—a tale of rebellion, escape, ambition, and tragedy. Tammos Raak, hero to kings and thieves, had stolen children from a formidable cursemaster and led them over the Forbidding Wall. He had delivered them triumphantly into the Expanse and established a house called Inius Throan. Together, they lived in an ongoing celebration of freedom.

And this is where the storyteller came to a fork in the road. Threadweavers in each house blamed the breaking on founders of other houses. They painted starkly contrasting pictures of failure and betrayal. But each tale concluded with Tammos Raak fleeing to save his life from rebels, wolves, or—in Krawg's version—monsters. The hero had climbed up the tallest of the world's starcrown trees and vanished in a cataclysm of fire that left a cavity called Mawrnash.

Krawg's story, like other versions, was lit by the wrathful eye of the rising red moon. But the detail he imagined led Warney and his companions down a new trail. Warney forgot himself until Krawg fell into a silence, lost in the sadness his own words had opened up.

"Who knew," said Cal-raven, "that a Gatherer could tell a tale we've heard a hundred times and make it something new? Your role in New Abascar is already established."

Even Bowlder, who hated Gatherers, nodded.

This praise, and the color that covered Krawg's smiling face, filled Warney with unexpected dismay. He had not imagined that Krawg might ever step into some new purpose. And if he did, what then would become of Warney?

8

KING OF BIRDS AND MERCY

K aww!" rasped Warney.

The raven glowered, guardlike. Its talons squeezed a path-barring branch as if to wring out its sap.

"Brains as brickish as old bread." Warney lunged and thrust out his hands. "Kaww!"

The raven stared at Warney's eye as if it were a grape.

Krawg pushed past, his netcaster propped against his shoulder like a spear. He marched right at the bird, and when it finally flew, the branch it had weighed down sprang up, disrupting a cloud of long-legged willowflies that swarmed about Krawg's head. With foul announcements, he swung at the bugs with the caster.

Warney hurried along until the river's roar forced him to shout. "Awfully far from camp. And the sun's already high up. How do we know the king won't ride off 'n' strand us?"

"Cal-raven'll never abandon his own. Let's catch breakfast where it can still be got. Nuthin' left in the woods. Critters are as gone as the starcrown trees of Mawrnash."

Warney made after his friend, gnawing on questions that Krawg's campfire tale about Tammos Raak and the starcrown trees had inspired. "Why'd they call 'em starcrowns?"

"The way they caught stars in their branches."

"And Mawrnash, where they grew... How'd it get a name like that?"

"Why, for the Mawrn, of course." Krawg climbed over a fallen tree and staggered down a steep riverbank, his feet punching up gobs of mud with each step. "You hear me comin', fish? Comin' to getcha!"

"Mawrn, Mawrn. That does me no good if'n I don't know what a Mawrn is, Krawg."

Krawg stalked across the pebbled banks and toed the edge of the narrow watercourse that rippled through the ravine. "The Mawrn's a creature that's made of dust. Scattered across the ground—every speck a watchful eye and a whispering tongue. You can't go near it without it knowin' you're there."

"And what's it do when it knows you're there?"

"Nothin' probably. But it drives the best men crackers, I tell you." Krawg raised the netcaster and fired. The dart sailed in a high arc, the stream of silvery webbing unspooling behind it. When the barb stung the far shore, the net laced the surface of the golden water until weights sank it to the bottom.

Krawg took the caster and plunged its sharp point into the soft ground to anchor the line's silvery span. "Once you've walked through the Mawrn, the Mawrn goes with you. Your shoes, your hair, your lungs. And then, the Mawrn owns you. Reads your thoughts, every grain a gossip. Nothing's hidden from the Mawrn."

"Jellypots," Warney scoffed. "You mock me for believin' in Northchildren and then start shovelin' vawn nuggets like that? Mawrnash. Makes the Keeper sound as common as a dinner roll."

"I never said the Mawrn is *real*," said Krawg. "It's just a campfire story, made up to explain a big hole in the ground."

Glancing back, Warney witnessed the bird hopping along through the branches as if striking the notes of an ominous song. "That blasted raven's following us."

"The king?" Krawg turned, surprised.

"No, not *Cal*-raven. What am I? His mother? I've never called the king by anything but his formal name." Warney snatched up a seedcone and threw it at the bird. The raven leaned to dodge but continued to stare at Warney as if it recognized him. "A shame, really, to name a child Raven just because he took his first steps chasin' some blasted bird."

"Cal, rava?" asked one of the ravens.

Warney stood quite still.

Then, one by one, more ravens began to appear as if summoned by the first.

Nervous, Warney strode along the shore upstream, the bird in unhurried pursuit. Arriving at a fallen tree that formed half a bridge across the water, he climbed onto its span and cast a pocketful of dried beetles into the stream. They glittered like jewels and pattered the water. The fishermen waited for fish to follow the bait into the net.

The ravens were all around Warney now, closer, perched on every twig and branch of the fallen tree. They began to caw, as if working up courage to push him into the stream. "Now, which one of you summoned Cal-raven from his cradle?" Warney grumbled. "Kawww. Kawww!"

Another raven spoke. "Cal, rava?"

"Krawg, one of these ravens is askin' for the king!"

Krawg waved his arms and rasped, "Shush! You'll scare the fish!"

Warney pointed at the guilty bird.

"What berries you been eatin', Warney?"

"Cal, rava?" asked the raven.

Warney lost his footing and hit the water with such a splash that the ravens scattered. Krawg dove in to grab him by his sodden hood.

"Ballyworms, Krawg!" Warney choked, thrashing. "It called for him!"

"You've just scared off the king's breakfast. We gotta move upriver." Krawg dragged him to the shore.

"I gotta tell the king." Warney clambered back up the muddy riverbank and dashed into the trees.

As he ran, he heard the ravens' frantic pursuit, glanced back over his shoulder, and nearly collided with an approaching horse and rider.

Tumbling off the path, he recognized the man and shouted, "Master Cal-raven!"

Jes-hawk came running not far behind the rider. "Warney, let the king go. Come and see!"

Warney followed the archer back to the campsite, then further south into the woods to a flat patch of ground punctured by thousands of tiny beetle burrows. Bowlder and Snyde were circling a depression in the brittle earth. Warney reached out to grip a young tree like a walking stick to save himself from falling.

"Seven," Jes-hawk agreed, scanning the trees. "Seven toes on this foot. And whatever it was, it came through sometime this morning."

Warney's eye bulged, and his grin was a fright. "Didja find a baby lying inside?"

"Cal-raven heard something, woke up, and rushed out of the tent," said Jes-hawk. "Then came an incredible noise. We followed him here."

"Did he hear the birds?" Warney asked. "Ravens everywhere! Calling his name!"

"Told you they were off eating mushrooms," muttered Bowlder.

Snyde laughed quietly, kicking at the footprint so that its soft edge collapsed. "And you wonder why I'm concerned about the king. He leaves us behind to chase a monster. Oh, a very bright future awaits us."

Jes-hawk cursed. "Saddle up. We don't want to lose him."

Just then Krawg stepped out of the trees with a net full of wrigglers. He glanced about. "Did I just let pinchers nip my ankles for nothin'?"

"You said the king wouldn't leave us," Warney blurted. "Well, he has."

※

Following the massive footprints, surrounded by ravens calling his name, Cal-raven crossed the river and rode northward. He rode for hours, confident his company would keep up as he moved along the western edge of Deep Lake.

"Listen for the path." He repeated Scharr ben Fray's words to himself. "Listen."

The ravens' cries seemed to coax him north and west, through the Cragavar.

"I was there, Cal-raven," the mage had said as they tossed stones to each other on the threshold of Barnashum. "I stood in your father's courtyard when Auralia revealed the colors of her craft. The greatest mystery I've ever seen. That girl had knowledge that even the wisest of my Jentan brethren lack. Since that revelation, I've been crisscrossing the Expanse, looking for the right answers. You've seen the colors too. We both want to know where they come from. Well, I've seen something new. And if you are to go forward without doubt, you must see it too."

"See what, exactly?"

"That's just it. You need to see it for yourself, my boy. If you don't, fear will get the better of you."

He rehearsed his teacher's instructions again. *Mawrnash. While the red moon is high, find Tammos Raak's tower. Climb to the crown.* The instructions confounded him. *The great starcrown trees burned to ash. How can I climb a tree that has fallen?*

He ascended a rise and arrived in a wide space between trees. There he examined yet another footprint, a seven-toed signature. He waited.

His companions ascended behind him, regarding him with worry. Their vawns slowed, panting, and snuffled at the ground. He flung out his arms, triumphant at his discovery. "Scharr ben Fray promised me that the path would be clearly marked. Birds that call my name—that's what he intended. But this? The Keeper's tracks? Even he would be surprised. This is what I'm meant to do."

"You mean to lead us even farther from Barnashum?" Snyde snapped. "I appeal to your memory. You once rode away from House Abascar, and the ground collapsed beneath it. Five nights ago you ventured outside Barnashum's refuge, and a quake shook the Blackstone Caves. Now here you are, several days' ride from the people who call you king. And you propose to keep on riding? Basing your decisions on vague and muddy impressions?"

Cal-raven went very still. "Jes-hawk, relieve Snyde of his reins. He'll be heading home to help the people who concern him so fiercely."

"Wait!" Snyde sputtered. "I cannot go back alone!"

Jes-hawk, smiling, brought his vawn alongside Snyde's. The old man clung to his reins in desperation as Jes-hawk reached across to tug at them. Their vawns grumbled. A well-placed boot toppled Snyde from his vawn, and when he rose, he was costumed in mud.

"You'll have time on the walk back to think about the benefits of loyalty and the disadvantages of treachery."

"Treachery?"

"Shall we do this now?" Cal-raven spurred his mount forward so that his boot was close to Snyde's face. "Tabor Jan and I knew someone in Barnashum was plotting against me. On the night of the quake, grudgers attacked me in the Hall of the Lost. I counted six. After the quake, five soldiers went missing. I think they fled, but their leader stayed behind to watch for another opportunity."

Snyde tried to wipe the mud from his face with his sleeve but succeeded only in smearing it.

"Where did your five little helpers go, Snyde?"

"You're insane." Snyde bit off the words.

"Stonemastery is a marvelous gift. You can open windows in solid walls and hear your own people conspiring to kill you. We planned to bring all six of you out to the woods and deal with you. But you came after me sooner than I'd expected."

Snyde looked searchingly to the others. "What's he talking about?" They regarded him with scorn. "What an abhorrent, presumptuous—"

"Where did the other five go? Are we going to see them somewhere along the way?"

"We all know your willingness to believe incredible things. But this"— Snyde waved his arms—"this is incredible." He seemed to be stretching, loosening up, as if preparing to make a grab for the knife strapped to Cal-raven's ankle.

Jes-hawk notched an arrow into the groove of his caster.

"How did you know I was outside Barnashum when the quake struck?" Cal-raven asked.

"What are you talking about?"

"You just told me that on the night of the quake I ventured outside. No one knew that. . .except my pursuers and the captain."

Warney had wasted no time. He now sat astride Snyde's vawn, backing it slowly away.

"You surround yourself with crooks and disregard those who protected your father from false counsel." Snyde clenched his teeth but kept on. "Your people disrespect you, and you tolerate it. You attend to dreams and follow signs left by a dangerous man your father had the good sense to banish. And a disloyal witch enchants you with music unfit for a king—songs about trouble, doubt, even pity for beastmen. Where are the songs that exalted House Abascar and taught our children who to despise?"

"Lesyl sings the truth. That's the foundation of New Abascar. And you speak of crooks? You swore allegiance to my father when he appointed you ambassador. By those vows you are bound to serve his successor. But you've mocked me. You've planned my assassination. And you complain of crooks? That you climbed to such favor proves how flawed my father's house had become. What shall we do about you?"

Cal-raven reached out swiftly, clasped the line of tarnished medals on Snyde's tunic as if they were a fistful of coins, and stripped them from his jacket.

Snyde cried out in shock. Then he lunged, seizing the knife.

Jes-hawk's arrow found its mark, its feathered end protruding from the attacker's ankle. Snyde stumbled backward. The knife fell. He tumbled down the slope and, clutching at his ankle, came to rest among the roots of a gnarled coil tree.

"Snyde ker Bayrast," shouted Jes-hawk, "I denounce you as guilty of conspiracy to kill the king." He notched another arrow to the caster. "No trial is necessary. We all witnessed that you took the king's weapon and threatened his life."

"My father's law," said Cal-raven quickly, "demands execution. But this isn't House Abascar. I'll leave your sentence to a higher authority, the master of this territory."

Snyde's reddening face resembled nothing more than an infant's in a petulant outcry. "What authority?"

"May the Keeper show you patience that you might learn from your mistakes, as I hope to learn from mine. Go home. Of course, you don't believe in the Keeper, do you?"

As Cal-raven turned his vawn about and rode on without another word, starlings crossed the sky, drawing night like a sheet behind them.

"You're a disgrace!" came the ambassador's roar behind them.

"Shall I silence him?" Jes-hawk raised his caster.

"No. We'll see how far his divided mind will take him."

9

WHITE DUST

Straying from the sight of the stag hunters, young Cal-raven, only eleven years old, prodded his horse off the trail.

A sharp chill had daggered him from the shadows of that dusty, overgrown rise to his right. It was summer. What was this sudden river of winter flowing over the hill? Moving through violet trees, he found a sort of stair—an old mudslide's hard, rippled clay—to carry him up and over the ridge.

As he reached the top, his father joined him. Bracing for reprimand, he was surprised. "You are your father's son," King Cal-marcus boasted. "Such curiosity. But you must avoid this place, both for its history and its deathly air, even though it calls out to descendants of Tammos Raak."

"Something's wrong, Father." Cal-raven shivered. "It's winter here."

"It's the dust. Ice that doesn't melt."

They stared across a vast white crater, a bowl full of wasteland.

"They call it the Mawrn. No one really knows what it is. It can't be found anywhere else in the Expanse. Look there, at the way the crater's edge stands jagged against the sky. My grandfather called it Two Giants. Trace that side and this, and you'll see the outline of two people lying down."

"Yes. Their foreheads meet." Cal-raven pointed across the crater. "And where we're standing, their toes touch. But why is this here? How'd it happen?"

"Did Scharr ben Fray never tell you the story of Tammos Raak's escape?"

"Many times. Tammos Raak's children rebelled in the house of Inius Throan. They all wanted his crown. He fled, and when they caught up to him, he climbed the tallest starcrown tree. Then something happened."

"Yes, but what? Some say they burned the trees to catch Tammos Raak. And this crater's full of toppled starcrown trees. But this—the Mawrn..." His father rubbed his thumb across his forefinger. "It isn't really ash, is it?" Reaching to tousle his boy's hair, he laughed. "Maybe you'll solve this mystery someday, Raven. Still, promise me you'll never let the question draw you down into that pit."

Surveying the dusk-dim ground, Cal-raven was again troubled by the violence of the scene. The trees appeared to have been shattered and half buried by some tremendous plow. Boughs, trunks, and roots—all painted with bone white dust—seemed paralyzed in anguish.

"What is it?" Jes-hawk rode up and, gazing over the white cavity, whistled a long falling note through the window of his smile's missing tooth.

Cal-raven unsheathed a farglass. Gazing through its lenses, he sifted the view for one great tree still standing. But there were no straight lines here. What appeared to be dragons made of dust crawled, wrestled, and leapt about the ground below.

Turning the scope, he considered the crater's western wall. A cloud branched upward against the blue of evening like an ink-black coil tree. A constellation of lanterns and torches was awakening along that stretch—buildings connected by paths that spilled down to a complex of platforms deep in the crater.

In the dim light he saw high-reaching beams turning on pivots. From the beams, ropes carried miners and supplies down into dark pits as if to bait underground monsters. One of these cranes reeled in a pallet crowded with buckets, which were loaded onto wagons that crawled like beetles to an illuminated structure, its windows aglow. A chimney spewed smoke, drawing a line against the bleached landscape.

"A mine?" Jes-hawk shook his head. "What do they dig beneath cold ash?"

Cal-raven pointed to a cluster of cabins, dark boxes on the bluff of the crater's western edge. "That's a Bel Amican way station." He slipped out of the saddle, knelt, and let the silvery sand run through his fingers. "We've seen this powder. And recently. Do you remember that Bel Amican Seer who said he would help us?"

"Do I remember the liar who led beastmen to attack us? Master, when I·practice, I imagine he's my target."

"We recovered a box of this dust from a thief, and we returned it to that Seer. He treated it as precious. Mawrn. The Seers carry Mawrn. I think...I think they're mining the dust itself."

Jes-hawk's gaze seemed fixed on the distant way station.

"You smell the hot meals. I know. But we didn't come here for stew or soft pillows. We have people waiting for us." Cal-raven flinched, bowing and casting his sleeve across his face as a breeze blasted them with the stinging white grit. His vawn groaned, agitated by the cold and frustrated that she could snuffle no grubs from this chalky ground.

"You're going down there, aren't you?"

"Yes, but I have no business with Bel Amicans. I'm looking for something else. A particular tree, if you really want to know. Or what's left of it."

"How do you expect to find it without interruption? They've seen us by now, surely."

"Go back to the company." Cal-raven eyed a feathered silhouette that waited patiently inside the edge of the crater, almost within reach, clinging sideways to a root that protruded from the gradual slope of the wall. "The ravens will show me the way."

"I can't let you—"

"When the Bel Amican welcome party arrives, introduce the company as travelers who have abandoned Abascar to seek a better fortune."

"They won't believe us. The best way to draw attention away from you is to go to that way station like reasonable travelers."

"Kramm!" Cal-raven aimed a kick at the archer's leg.

But Jes-hawk caught the king's buckled boot of muskgrazer skin and pulled it right off his foot. He held it up as if threatening to cast it into the crater. "You know I'd rather go down into that cauldron of ash with you than sit among strangers with a glass of ale and wonder what's become of you. Tell me you know that."

"Bloody vawn crolca, Jes-hawk. I know it! You'll have that hot meal. But you must be the blandest of visitors. Tell boring lies. Laugh at their jokes. Stare into your bowl. Offend no one. Accept no challenges. If the Bel Amicans will rent you a room, pay for two nights, just in case. Plant an arrow in your window frame so I can find you when I come back."

"When do we come looking for you?" Jes-hawk handed back the boot.

"You don't."

Eager to make progress while faint blue light still lingered on the western horizon, Cal-raven descended into the lifeless jungle. Binding a scarf across his nose and mouth, he followed the birds through unmoving swells of earth, vines, branches, and roots.

"Great Keeper," he spoke through the cloth. "You came to me last time I ventured out alone. Come again. Show me where to go." Nothing happened. Nothing moved, save for boughs that twitched without any wind and ravens darting through the dusty tangles.

Soon after the sky's last notes of purple had dissolved into black, a blue glow caught his eye. He crouched down, peering through a dark web of boughs. The light was quiet, delicate.

He worked his way cautiously through the maze until he found a passage straight to a patch of ground shrouded in blue mist. Seizing the farglass, he fingered the notched edges of various lenses, pulling some from their slots along its wooden span, fitting others into place. When he found a combination that magnified the clearing, a memory surprised him.

I've seen this blue before, in the cloak that Auralia wore.

Coiling out into the night air on fragile green stems, delicate blue flowers emerged from between the bulky stones of what appeared to be an ancient well. Steam spilled from the ring of stones, infused with light from the flowers. It beckoned to him like an oasis in the eastern Heatlands.

Suddenly a shadow stepped into the picture. Surprised, Cal-raven reached out to catch himself against the wall of branches. His hand closed tight around a bough, and a thick, sturdy thorn ran right through his palm and out the other side.

His cry caught in his throat, and tears sprang into his eyes. Pain lanced his arm. He jerked his hand free and pressed its wound with his other palm. He rocked back and forth, then fumbled in the pocket of his jacket for a traveler's bandage roll. When his left hand was wrapped, he raised the scope again with his right.

Enveloped in steam, the figure lifted a wooden cover, which brought from the well a new flood of cloud that filled the clearing.

It was a man, bearded and broad shouldered. He was clad in layers of rags, twigs, feathers, and fur, a costume made of all that had been shed on the Cragavar's forest floor. He was lifting a bucket from the well.

Surely, Cal-raven thought, *there can't be water in this pit of ash.* But when the man placed the cover back over the well, Cal-raven saw a spill wash a dark line down the side of the bucket.

The stranger strode away slowly, bracing huge hands on both sides of the bucket to keep from spilling another drop. But for a prodigious nose, his face was hidden in a thick, filthy mane. His ponderous progress was almost comical, his steps uneven, as if his body were a burdensome suit. As he turned and disappeared up another path, Cal-raven glimpsed an unnatural bulge at the back of his neck that caused his robe to swell between the shoulders.

Cal-raven hurried to the clearing, his hand ablaze. Kneeling, he picked a few of the blue flowers. *I'll have to ask Krawg and Warney about these.* They surrendered without resistance, and he wrapped them in another span of clean bandage.

The mist's rising scent was sweet, promising water as pure as a mountain spring. He leaned over the well and inhaled deeply and thought he heard water flowing steadily below. His whole body tensed, demanding a drink. He had to fight the urge to climb down into the well's mouth to submerge himself. "Bring back the bucket, Ragman," he murmured.

And so he pursued the stranger, following the footprints until they ended at a solid wall of intertwining boughs. But as he paused, the branches untangled and opened for him. Ravens, gathering along the top of the hedge, clucked and muttered approvingly.

I'm getting close, Teacher.

The hunchback was not far ahead, ascending to a small dome encrusted with the same moon-pale grains that dusted the landscape. He climbed a stairway up the side, past glowing windows, the wooden steps groaning beneath his considerable weight. Someone opened a door for him.

Put the bucket down. Cal-raven almost spoke the wish aloud.

But the man ducked to push through the door, his effort casting a spray of dust and debris out onto the doorstep. The door swung almost closed, leaving a narrow line of golden lanternlight.

Cal-raven heard quiet, happy laughter, like musical gusts from the old wheeze-box Obsidia Dram used to play in the breweries.

The birds were behind Cal-raven now. And they were noisy. "Cal, rava. Cal, rava."

This isn't the way.

His tongue stuck to the roof of his mouth. His throat felt coated with dust.

"Give me a moment." He gripped the stair's rail and moved up to the door.

But as he leaned to peer into this strange abode, the whole flock flew at him, greatly distressed. As he turned to hiss at them, the door burst open. His bandaged hand was seized in a cold, hard grip. He was pulled, stumbling, inside. The door slammed behind him.

He found himself face to face with a woman wrapped in a winding white shroud.

She seemed all bone and blue skin, withered and wretched. Wisps of long black curls fell down around her skull of a face. The lids of her eyes drew all the way back into her head so that her blazing, bloodshot gaze was impossible to meet. While one hand was fastened around his forearm, mean as a mousetrap, the other caged a bird's broken, wing-splayed body.

She madly cackled through a thin-lipped grin, "We hope-hope-hoped you'd come."

She shoved him down onto a rickety bench. "Help yourself to the wah...to the water," the withered woman wheezed. The bucket steamed on the round table in a ring of three misshapen clay goblets.

As if new to walking, the woman staggered and collapsed onto another bench, then spidered her open hand across the tabletop to pick a few stray crumbs from an unwashed plate. She kept the other hand closed around the bird's crushed body. "It's what you've come for, isn't it? Folks get thir-thir-thirsty out there. Out there in the Mawrn."

"I'm in the wrong place," he stammered. "I'm lost."

"Haven't we heard the same-same-same story from every strange-strange-stranger who visits us here?" She lifted her empty hand high over her head and let it fall back with a sharp *crack!* "Welcome to Panner Xa's prison. What'll we call you?"

Now it was Cal-raven's turn to stammer. "P-prison?"

Under a ceiling of redbrown reeds tightly aligned, the walls curved to the floor, rugged with the crater's crumbling pearl. Everything within that circumference—counters, basins, benches, tables, chairs—seemed crooked and badly made, broken in some small but distracting way. Skeletal wooden devices, each equipped with gleaming metal teeth, and pans holding portions of dust spoke of their work breaking down the crater's crystal shards for mysterious purposes.

Moving among the tables, barrels, and chairs, the ragged giant carried plates and bowls in a teetering stack to something resembling a kitchen. He set them down, and the stack fell over, fragments of clay clattering and scattering. When he came back to the table, he stopped.

The woman had released the bird from her hand's bony cage, and now Cal-raven could see it clearly. It was a common shrillow, lying on its back with sparsely feathered wings cast open, eyes closed, tiny yellow feet jutting into the air.

"Found it while I cleared webs from the tower's tun-tun-tunnel," she whispered to the hunchback. Her gestures seemed to direct his attention to a large, barred, black gate against the north wall.

The old man surrounded the bird with his heavy hands as if to warm it. Then he reached into the thick thatch of his coppery hair and drew out two long pins, which he gripped together as tightly as a dagger for a fight. He puffed a weary sigh. Scooping the bird up, he carried it across the room and tiptoed clumsily up a short stair and through an open door to a balcony.

"Old Soro fixes everything," the woman muttered as Cal-raven watched for the giant to return. "The water. It's what every-every-everyone needs. What else is worth a sideways spit in this graveyard? Hey!" As if slapped awake from a dream, she seized a goblet and plunged it into the bucket, then presented it to Cal-raven. "Drink up, young man. This-this-this is our only bit of joy today."

When he didn't obey, she planted it hard on the table before him and a splash spattered out. She poked at the drops and sucked her fingertips noisily. "Old Soro, he put out this cup for you. Drink it. The Seer returns. We'll have to hide the bucket."

Panner Xa. A Bel Amican Seer.

His obvious dismay set the woman laughing darkly. "Overseer of the Mawrnash Mine. Panner Xa." She filled her own goblet and drained it in a rapid sequence of gulps that rocked her whole fragile frame. "That's better," she sighed, and her voice was softer.

The hunchback tiptoed back into the chamber, murmuring like Hagah when gnawing on bones. He marched to the table, filled the third goblet, and returned to the balcony.

"Be quick," the woman hissed, "and you might get out of here without a beating. Not long until moonrise."

"You called this a prison," Cal-raven remarked. "How can I leave?"

"Oh, Panner's not yet got her hooks in you. Stay clear of her potions. Stick to the well water. And then it's up, up, up Tammos Raak's tower for you!"

He stood, knocking the bench down behind him. "How do you know?"

"I was right?" she gasped. "Old Soro! He's come for the tower! Oh, you've come to the right place, young man. The Seer won't let anyone near it. Forbidden to anybody except her monstrous ilk. Can't say why. Don't know why. Who are you, anyway? You speak like you're from Abascar."

"Abascar is gone." Cal-raven set the bench right, sat down again cautiously, ready to run if necessary. "My purpose is my own. Why are you so eager to help me?"

"Because I'm getting stronger," she said, lowering her voice. "The Seer doesn't know it yet. But Old Soro's helping me."

Cal-raven lifted the goblet and sniffed the water. He was so terribly thirsty. "The two of you are slaves?"

"Captives. Let me see your injury." Before he could devise a polite refusal, she stood, grabbed his arm with her cold fingers, and thrust his hand into the bucket.

"Oh."

The water was warm at first, soaking through the bandage and stinging his wound. But then something like heat and cold spread from his hand into his arm. His thirst faded even though he hadn't tasted a drop. He choked.

"Captives," she said. "Me, ten years now. 'Twas the Seers' potions did it."

Dark tears were filling his eyes, as if his body were drawing water from the bucket and flushing some corruption from his head. He wiped them on his sleeve, a dark smear. The colors of the room brightened. "Is this a potion?"

"No," she exclaimed, and he followed her bitter gaze toward uneven shelves on the wall. They were lined with jars of murky sludge. He realized he could smell the concoctions across the room.

"Panner Xa won my loyalty with those. I wanted to be beautiful. And, oh, they did the trick. I enjoyed some fame for a while. My sister wouldn't walk with me through the market anymore. Jealous, you see. So I tried to quit the potions, and the headaches almost killed me. Then I ran out of money. I begged the Seers to give me more. But I couldn't pay. So Panner Xa brought me here. Potions, if I'd help." She pointed at the jars as if blaming criminals. "Years. They've taken years from me."

He pulled his hand from the bucket. Colors brightened steadily all around him. He noticed bright ribbons on a workshop table—gold, red, and green—and something that looked like an enormous purple kite. "I'm sorry," he said. "I really must leave."

"Yes," she hissed. "Yes, you must. The Mawrn has told her you're here. She'll be angry." She closed her eyes, and through her frail eyelids, she still seemed to be staring. "There will be beatings tonight."

He flexed his hand. The pain was gone, drawn out like the thorn itself. He looked at the bucket. He looked at the woman. The drink had quieted her quaking. Her voice, still shrill and birdlike, was no longer broken into stammers. He looked at the cup she had filled for him.

"There." She pointed to the northern wall, to the dark, barred gate. "That's what you want."

"How do I know this isn't a trap?"

She swiped her hand across the table. Dust billowed into the air. "Mawrnash is a trap. The dust is all over you. When it gets its tiny claws into your skin, your lungs, your mind, all the Seer has to do is close her eyes. It's their power, man of Abascar. She sees you clearly."

He had heard such rumors before. This time they did not make him laugh.

"That is why I never escape," she sighed.

He reached for her this time. When he took hold of her arm—such a fragile bone within that sleeve—he felt heat and something more. The humming pulse of resilient life. "What is your name?"

"Call me Gretyl."

"I'll help you, Gretyl," he said. "I hate the Seers as much as you do."

"No," she laughed, looking toward the balcony door. "You won't. But Old Soro's here with me. Panner Xa thinks he's just another servant. But he's going to rescue me. He told me so. He went out one day and came back with water. Strange water from deep beneath Mawrnash. It helps. Soon I'll be strong enough."

"What is he?"

"Soro? He's a kite-maker. Wandered in here, just like you, one night while Panner Xa was gone. Said he came down from a mountain workshop to look for his family. Said they'd been taken from him. There's more, but he doesn't like to talk about it."

Cal-raven picked up one of the stray shrillow feathers from the tabletop. It was hot as a candlewick, and he dropped it. *The water. What has it done to me?*

"I asked him to take me back with him," Gretyl sighed. "Told him I could help him make his kites. He won't do it. Says it's against the rules, whatever that means." She shook her head. "He'll have new scars tonight."

"I've got to get you both out of here." He dusted off his sleeves and shoulders. "But first I must do what I came to do."

Gretyl took up a crooked walking stick, awkward as a newborn fawn on her spindly legs. "Let me show you something."

On the balcony, under a night sky newly brushed with crimson, Cal-raven watched Old Soro raise his cupped hands as if in prayer to the rising red moon. His head was bowed, hair falling over his face, and he breathed deeply and heavily through his nose, just as Cal-raven's father had when deeply asleep in his chair before the fire.

"Now," said Gretyl, seeming unconcerned at how the platform groaned beneath their weight, "we are standing at the top of Tammos Raak's tower. The very starcrown tree he climbed."

Cal-raven laughed, for they were not far from the ground. He searched the dark, straining to discern the reddening contours of the landscape. "I don't think you understand. I'm supposed to *climb* a starcrown tree. All the way to the crown."

"And this is where you start. Look. The Seer has built her house into the top of Tammos Raak's tree." Gretyl gestured to the dark ridge from which this white dome, this crystal shell, emerged like a skull at the end of a spine. The ridge ran off into the dark, then rose up the curving incline of the crater all the way to the rim. "That's it. What's left of Tammos Raak's famous starcrown tree," said Gretyl, "lying where it fell." She pointed up to the crater's northern edge. "There, the tree's very roots, right on the bowl's brim. When the trouble came and the forest was destroyed, the tallest starcrown was the last to fall. It fell inward, across the rest of the ruined forest."

This great ridge of earth. This line of broken pieces. It was a toppled, shattered column—a tree that once stood as broad as fifty marrowwood trees bound together and as tall as seventy stacked root to crown.

This, if he was to believe Gretyl's claim, was the tower Tammos Raak had climbed in final desperation, the tree that had then come down, along with all its proud species, when a mysterious flash seared the sky and scorched the earth.

The more he stared, the more he could see the truth of it.

"This, where we stand, was once the treetop that touched the sky. And there..." High above them at the rim, an array of roots splayed out like the headdress of some wild forest king.

"The crown," Cal-raven gasped. "It's not the treetop but the roots."

It would be like climbing a mountain—to cross from this moon-silver hut to the high ground where the base of the tree was half torn from the soil.

Gretyl's grin was almost vicious with delight. "You won't have much time. Panner Xa's coming home soon."

As if to encourage him, ravens appeared, threading through the sky. They settled on various branches along the incline of the fallen tree and called to him.

The Ladder of Ravens. What an intolerable trickster you are, Scharr ben Fray.

He raised his farglass as if he might discover some clear path through the obstacles. "If I'd known, I would have taken a vawn around the crater and climbed up from the other side."

"There's a better way," she whispered, looking at Old Soro.

At that the old man drew his raised hands down, pressed them against his breast, and then shoved them out, spreading his fingers and flinging the shrillow's crumpled form into the darkness. The ravens were silent, surprised. Then a fluttering cry like a laugh fell from above. Diving from the sky, the shrillow appeared, darting in wild figures about their heads.

"I thought it was dead," Cal-raven laughed.

"I told you," Gretyl whispered. "He's good at making things fly." She stopped, cocked her head, then snapped her fingers. "The Seer's on her way. Come back inside. Soro, will you open the gate?" Shrugging, she leaned in to Cal-raven's ear. "He's like this. Doesn't help unless you ask him."

Old Soro dropped the dark gate's heavy crossbeams to the floor. Then he gripped the gate's edge with his massive hands and grunted as he pulled.

Cal-raven marveled at those hands, those arms, and their strange, fibrous flesh. Old Soro seemed crafted from the stuff of the forest, as if his whole body were a costume.

With a gasp, the gate came open, snarling along the filthy floor. Cal-raven recoiled from the stench of rotten wood.

"In you go," Gretyl urged.

Old Soro half turned—the closest he had come to facing Cal-raven. Within the frame of a ragged, braided mane and a bushy, braided beard, a dark face returned his gaze. Or was it a mask? That bold and noble nose, those cracked and wounded lips—they might have been a woodcarving, adorned with eyes of black glass, inscrutable.

"Go, Raven," said the weary giant in a voice like boulders breaking.

The name caught Cal-raven by surprise. "Who are you?" he growled back. He had not identified himself. Even if he had, he would have introduced himself with his full and proper name. Old Soro had addressed him as an intimate friend or family member, speaking only the half of his name that his mother had given him. In Abascar such a privilege had to be granted, or it was a sign of disrespect. "Are you ignorant of Abascar custom, kite-maker?"

Old Soro laughed wearily—that musical wheeze-box sound again—and shook his head.

Gretyl cleared her throat. "Please, now, please-please-please. Your time's running out."

Cal-raven, watching the hunchback carefully, spoke to Gretyl. "You've been generous. But I'll climb the tower just the way my teacher instructed me. My teacher's always right."

"The Mawrn," Gretyl squeaked.

All around the chamber dust was lifting from surfaces—swirling over jar lids, whirling into tempests across the floor. "The Mawrn, it knows. She's coming. Go, King of Abascar! Which-which-whichever way you desire, go now!"

Cal-raven rejected the open gate. He leapt back up the stairs to the balcony instead. Stepping out into the crater's cold air, he felt the strain of an invisible cord newly strung. "I've made you a promise, Gretyl," he said. "In the meantime call for the Keeper. It'll watch over you."

Gretyl seemed not to hear him, shrinking into her shroud.

Old Soro, meanwhile, sighed, pushing the dark gate closed.

10

THE REVELHOUSE

I n everything, Jes-hawk was an archer.

Rigorous in discipline, precise in thought and aim, he drew his attention taut. Given a target, he refused to miss. And in the moment before he fired, there was a tension, almost as if he expected the target to fire back.

While his companions hurried toward the revelhouse glow like prisoners toward an escape, he stared at its front door and planned how they would pass through it.

As the company approached, they were dutifully welcomed. One young woman promised she'd stable the vawns, then paused and cupped her hand in automatic expectation. Jes-hawk dropped small chips of blackstone from Barnashum into her palm, and she was surprised, clearly calculating what she might get for such material in trade.

Krawg and Warney stumbled toward the revelhouse as if already drunk. Jes-hawk shouted after them to wait, but they blithely waved him off.

"Gonna be like shooting at a target in a windstorm," he muttered, chewing a gob of root-gum.

At the door the sleepy guard yawned, "You'll answer for your friends, or I'll have 'em thrown out. State your names, purposes, and places of—"

"Abascar survivors," Jes-hawk declared. "Before the collapse we apprenticed for merchants. Now we've struck out on our own, a company ready to clasp hands, bond in blood, make and stake our claim."

"It's a hard life," sighed the guard. "But then, life was especially hard in Abascar. Least, that's what they always say in Bel Amica." He eyed Jes-hawk as if measuring his temper. When the archer didn't respond, the flicker of alertness faded. "Welcome to the Mawrnash Mine. It's a place for hard work, not trouble. It's almost moonrise, so you're just in time for the casting."

Jes-hawk nodded.

"And since you've never heard of that—casting's when the hostess puts out coins. All the chips are fish-side up. At the whistle each miner turns a coin. Those who have the mark of highest value become the first wave of workers into the mine on the next shift."

"Fair system," Jes-hawk grunted. "Leave it to luck."

"Luck? Leave it to the moon-spirits." Condescension dripped from the guard's every line. "They can see which of us wants to find a fortune, and they reward unclouded desire."

"You've learned your religion well."

"And you had better too." The man's humor had soured. "Our Seer doesn't take too kindly to those who mock our faith."

"I mean no disrespect, but will my company find welcome here?"

"The main room's for the miners. But there are a few quieter rooms along the side for merchants and travelers. We see all kinds. Many stay to try their hands at mining. The Seer pays well. Our doors are open to you. Not because we trust you, mind. Our Seer—she sees everything that happens here." His grin showed what teeth he had left. "You'd do well to tell your company that."

The revelhouse shook with noise. When Jes-hawk stepped inside, he found that the raucous laughter and the rumbling of boots on a wooden floor came from drunkards in the throes of disorderly dance, driven by cacophonous percussion.

There was no shape or harmony to their dance. In storytelling and other forms of art, each Bel Amican worked alone to draw attention to his own particular style. They danced and sang *at*—not *with*—one another, each person a whirlwind of his own invention.

Moving through the tumultuous crowd, Jes-hawk felt as if he had been immersed in ale, for the tint and tang of beer saturated the air. Colors were muted, everything brushed with gold. Light spilled from torches, candles, and the two roaring fireplaces set into columns in the center of the space. That light reflected and refracted from mirrors hung throughout the room.

Krawg and Warney were lost in the crowd, so Jes-hawk moved straight for the bar and stood next to a miner who was pondering seven empty, sticky glasses. The Mawrn clung to the miner's bald head and eyelashes, clotted in the corners of his eyes, and powdered his mustache and beard like a spill of flour swept up in a baker's broom. Propping himself up on the bar, he wheezed an incomprehensible greeting and clasped Jes-hawk's hand, not like a friend, but like a wrestler.

"Runekere. Mine overseer." An eighth glass appeared before him, full to the brim. "Look like you never mined a day in your life."

"Merchant. And archer. For hire."

"Abascar. Can tell it by your talk. Need fast currency? Panner Xa thinks she sees everything, but I see miners stuffing their pockets and sealing dust between the layers of their cloaks. Could use a sharp-eyed shooter to catch 'em in the act."

An ale boy interrupted them and asked what Jes-hawk wanted—wine, ale (brown or sunny), or a glass of something called Six Hard Slaps.

"Shame about your house," Runekere went on as if addressing a grand hall. "You Abascars, you shoulda turned to the moon-spirits. Our Seers came to see your drunkard king, you know. Tried to persuade him to accept our Bel Amican faith."

Jes-hawk accepted a clay mug of dark brew. "I remember. Long time ago."

Runekere clapped him on the back with such force that half of the drink washed out of the mug and across the dripping bar. "I know exactly how you feel. A man without a house. I may never see my wife and daughter again." Every statement was somehow a cough and a shout at the same time.

"Why not?"

"They're in Bel Amica, safe and sound. We've good position on the rock there. Views of the Mystery Sea. But I work here now. And I wouldn't trade it for anything."

"You like it here?"

"Oh, my family, they enjoy what I send 'em. For me, it's all about the thrill of the getting, you see?" The man rubbed his thumb across his finger-tips. "Show me something that feels better than getting."

Jes-hawk turned his attention back to his drink. How long had it been since someone had poured him a mug of beer? "You should go home awhile," he suggested. "Take some time to enjoy the rewards."

"What do you have?" Runekere seemed prepared to laugh at any answer.

Jes-hawk shrugged and lifted his mug. "Nothing anymore."

"You'll need equipment. To get equipment, you'll need currency. To get currency, you've got to prove your worth."

Jes-hawk swallowed a smooth rush of the beer. "My worth to whom?" he asked.

"The Seers."

The beer was blended with something that reminded him of lamp oil. "I thought a queen ruled Bel Amica."

Feigning severe conviction, Runekere said, "Queen Thesera rules Bel Amica, and I'm her loyal subject." Then his face changed to a wry grin. "Ah, but who rules the queen?"

"So, as long as we impress the Seers—"

"They'll buy your service, but it's a bargain for what they give you." Runekere grabbed a passing ale boy, slipped his hand beneath a shoulder strap that held up the boy's trousers, and snapped it hard against his chest. An array of tiny glass vials pinned to that strap came alive with swirling clouds and splashing liquids inside them. "Potions and enchantments," said Runekere, running his thumbnail down that row of vials as if plucking the strings of a harp—*pung, pung, pung, pung, pung!*

The boy glared, then turned to Jes-hawk. "You wanna buy a sniff or a sip? Whatcha need? Cure for a sore head? Sleep for the night? Or a little something to make a lady sure you like 'er?"

Jes-hawk thought of poor Tabor Jan, sleepless back in Barnashum. But he held up his hands and declined.

A drunkard pushed in to the bar, separating Jes-hawk from the mine's overseer. The brute wore little more than a leather loincloth, showing off his miner's musculature. Every knuckle of the fist that he pounded on the bar bore a rune tattoo to spell out an obscenity. "Another!" he roared at the hostess.

When the hostess came to answer him, Jes-hawk was impressed to find that she could stare the inebriate in the eye. "You know the rule," she barked through gemstone teeth, her voice as rough as any man in the bar. "If I give you another and the Seer hears about it, she'll chop off that hand before you can put down the glass."

The brute brought his fist down again as if trying to destroy the bar. The woman did not flinch. "Go sit down and wait for the casting."

Sulking, the brute threw himself into a corner.

"Idiot," said a man to Jes-hawk's right. Draped in a ceremonial robe, slumped against the bar, he was small, his nose sharp and his chin receding, his eyes like bruises above even darker bruises. His expression appeared to be permanent, forever groaning "See what I mean?"

"Cesylle," he said and did not extend a hand. "Seer's apprentice."

"Indeed." Jes-hawk introduced himself, practicing his summary, and took another swig of the strange beer. But as he did, his attention was caught by a barmaid, a thin and worried woman with a garment cut low in the front, high in the back, with crescent cuts on her hips.

"Like her?" sneered Cesylle. "Make a play, Abascar man. You'll be lucky to get even an insult from that one."

Jes-hawk glanced back to see miners gathered in rapt attention around tables made of broad slices from tree trunks larger than any he'd seen. Ale boys and barmaids scurried about, placing coins on the edges of the tables.

As the barmaid walked by again, Jes-hawk saw her face. He grabbed the edge of the bar to steady himself. "What's your name?" Surely it was the drink doing this. Surely his eyes were deceiving him.

She did not look at him, not even when Cesylle said, "Visitor's asking your name, woman."

"How much is he willing to pay for it?" she snapped, bending to draw a clean tray from a stack under the counter.

"Hey," Cesylle laughed, "give him a chance. This penniless straggler might be the best—"

"Ask her if she'd like to see a hawk," said Jes-hawk. He thought of his father, Jes-wick, and his mother, Say-julan. "A hawk, or a wick, or a julan flower."

The woman spun around in amazement.

"Turn!" Runekere, the overseer, shouted the command. At once, the miners turned their coins, stamping them down on the tables.

"Call!" Runekere shouted. "Full moons?" Several miners, burly men and formidable women, raised their coins high in the air. "You have first dig of the night. Be ready when the horn sounds. Any half moons?" Another chorus and coins raised high.

"Lynna." Jes-hawk's eyes were locked upon his sister's. He nearly jumped over the bar to embrace her.

But Lynna moved quickly around the bar, and standing behind him, she leaned in. "You," she whispered. "Don't. Know. Me."

He answered loudly, with a garish grin, "Why, thank you. I find you rather attractive as well. Tell me, how does a barmaid stay safe around so many amorous men?"

"Test my temper," she snapped back. "You'll find out."

"There's a lot I'd like to find out," he laughed. "Let's find a quiet table."

With a glance to Cesylle, she said, "I'll give you one chance to make your case."

Cesylle's eyes bulged. "You," he muttered to Jes-hawk, "are my new hero." He made a gesture as if he wished to erase them from his sight. "But you'll never have Bel Amica's most beautiful. Emeriene, sisterly to the heiress. She's all mine." He emptied his glass and spoke to the bar. "She's waiting for me back home. And here I am. Here I am." Something like regret entered his voice. "Moon-spirits. They'll wring you out."

Jes-hawk's sister took his arm and pulled him through the assembly. Jealous gazes followed them.

Too many half-moon coins had appeared on the table. Too many miners would assemble for the night's second shift. When accusations of cheating began, someone threw a mug into another miner's forehead, inspiring a barrage of beer glasses.

But Jes-hawk clasped his sister's hand beneath the tabletop, unnoticed in the corner.

"Lynna." It felt good just to say her name. "I kept watching for you at Barnashum."

"I'm sure you have your reasons for hiding in a cave, but I'd rather have a life."

"This?"

"I want to be a Seer's apprentice."

He tightened his grip on her hand and nodded back toward Cesylle. "It certainly hasn't done him any favors."

"We suffered enough in Abascar. I deserve better."

"And this is better?"

"You know how many fought for this job? My moon-spirit saw my determination. He—"

"Your what?" Jes-hawk laughed but quickly wished he hadn't, for it struck her like a slap. "Forgive me. It's just...you've changed. Why work here and not in Bel Amica?"

"This is where fortunes are won. I made my reputation fast."

"Can't imagine how." He withdrew his hands.

"Make your words count, Brother. We may not be ignored for long."

"Come with me. Cal-raven's leading us out of Barnashum soon. We'll build a new home."

"When?"

"Soon. It'll be better than Bel Amica."

"Have you ever seen Bel Amica, Hawk? I'll eat from the sea and have my pick of a hundred eager suitors. My moon-spirit tells me I'll be famous." She looked past him, her eyes gold with reflected light. "They could use you on the fishing boats. Put your bowstring to work firing hooks into a grey giant, a seawyrm, or even an oceandragon."

"I get seasick just thinking about it." Jes-hawk drank the mug dry. "Always preferred the sun to the moon anyway."

"The moon is subtle. It draws the eye, sets us dreaming, sends wish dust down on everyone. We breathe it in, we dream great dreams, and we learn what we were meant to become. In Bel Amica a beggar one day is a hero the next."

Jes-hawk ran his hands across the tabletop. "Wish dust? Is that what they're mining?"

She smiled. "I heard a story. Moon-spirits fought over power. In the struggle a box full of their power broke and fell into the forest. Others say the spirits wanted to test the people of the Expanse to see whose desire ran the strongest, so they buried a lode of wish dust here. They'll bless the one who gathers most."

He reached for her again, but she withdrew.

"For the first time, Hawk, I have everything I need."

Staring into his empty mug, he felt the cords of his mind slackening. "The old Abascar's gone. Cal-raven pays attention to his people. You can have the full attention of a king."

"Ever heard of Captain Ryllion?" Lynna poked his knees playfully with her toes. "He's gonna be king someday. He always gets what he wants. And I've seen him watching me." She started bouncing the way she'd bounced while watching their father frost a cake.

"I think you've been sipping too much of what you serve."

She reached to squeeze his hand. "Still want to protect me, huh? I guess that's a brother's job." She leaned forward and suddenly seemed concerned. "You said Abascar's coming out of Barnashum soon?"

"Soon."

She looked down into her hands. "I'll think it over."

Something struck him across the face. "Oh!" he gasped. Then again, and he fell sideways to the floor. "Oh!" Once more, as if someone were smacking him with a platter. He cried out again, and the world seemed to spin.

When he opened his eyes, he saw his sister's face—or rather several images of his sister's face—fading in and out of focus. She was laughing. "Somebody served you Six Hard Slaps."

The hostess's voice rose. "We have time for a game before the horn. And it's my revelhouse, so it's my choice. Storytelling it is!"

With a mix of groans and applause, the crowd drew back from the table in the center, and a few men made their way into the open space, bowing to the hostess.

Jes-hawk ignored the proceedings, too grateful to see his sister's face to be distracted.

So when he finally noticed that Krawg had entered the contest, it was too late to interfere. He felt a sudden dismay, as if he had fired an arrow that sailed clear of the target to strike the judge of the contest instead.

Any child in the Expanse could have narrated the first tale of the evening's contest.

A rebel, Tammos Raak, rises up against an oppressor. He rescues his children from slavery. He conspires with birds and dragons. He flees, blazing a trail of fire over mountains no one has ever crossed, escaping southward into the Expanse. With newfound power beyond anything the tyrant has known, this rescuer raises up a fortress from the very stone of its foundations. From its fourteen towers, archers can defend it against any siege.

Justice and freedom. That's what gave the conclusion such a punch. As Tammos Raak's children inherited varying measures of his gifts—stonemastery, healing, wildspeaking, thoughtspeaking, firewalking—the revelhouse roared with approval.

Through Warney's vision, already blurry from drink, the place seemed a riot. Crowds loved this story, willfully forgetting the tragic chapters that followed. Warney had always loved it too. Somewhere in his heart he was like the enslaved children, his plague of sisters was the curse, and Krawg was Tammos Raak, leading him to a new life and freedom at last.

Warney tried to catch Krawg's gaze. But Krawg seemed lost in thought, tracing lines on the wooden tabletop.

The next miner told a story of a blind Bel Amican child who was beaten and robbed and left in an alley for dead. Descending from the sky, a magnificent moon-spirit found him there. The boy's devotion to that guardian spirit led him to give his last coin in a dying gesture. The moon-spirit took the token and blessed the boy with sight, with healing, and with justice.

Warney felt he might just lose his drink. The mirrors seemed to be swinging on their hooks. He had never been to sea before, but the revelhouse seemed a Bel Amican ship carrying him out on the waves.

The hostess called for Krawg.

11

THE SIX TRICKSTERS

"O nce in a night-skied world," Krawg began, "six boastin 'n' thievin' tricksters flew between stars. They rode astride dragons of fire 'n' bluster, creatures they'd made from pieces of the pillage they'd snatched from a hundred worlds."

Warney snapped the handle from his mug.

Staring into golden space as if through a window open only for him, Krawg continued. "Thieves of riches, stealers of spells, their saddlebags were stuffed full of power 'n' oddments. Cloaked all thickly with stuff from their hideouts... Oh, did I tell you 'bout the tricksters' hideouts? They draped themselves in dustclouds, way out beyond the stars."

The drinkers were blinking up into the ceiling and scratching themselves.

"They wanted to dazzle each other, those tricksters. With flash and with startlements, all kinds of shocking. So when they faced each other in open space, all 'round some great floating table as vast as the Mystery Sea, they cast the tools of their sorcery across its jeweled surface. They were fit to show, you see, that they could make great things with materials common and plain. Their contests always aimed to prove which spellcaster was best and bedazzledest.

"All six had met on many occasions, out where none of them night-sky dangers could snap at them nor any hunters track them down.

"One by one they'd send up flares—storms of fire 'n' lightning. Smoke from their displays trailed out in rivers 'cross the sky. Ships they'd raise would sail in the clouds, and sometimes they caught a current of wind that would carry them gleaming in great streaks of light that scorched the space between stars."

Among the listeners, rumors rumbled. "I've seen such things. Great streaks of light from one end of the night to the other."

"But the dragons," someone shouted. "How'd they make dragons?"

"The tricksters' secrets would be unbrainable for you or me," Krawg whispered. "But they'd show off those dragons—oh yes they would. They'd set them after each other in fiery chases and violent clashings. For them dragons were flown like kites on their masters' strings, swift to jerk and leap at whispers 'n' cues."

Krawg's mouth sagged open as he stared into the ceiling's dark rafters, great arcs of rib bone from a seabull. "Still, among those six battleful illusionists, no two could agree on who was the greatest. They'd each count the others down—five to one. But they'd never admit no lesserness. Not for a hummingbird's wingbeat.

"On this pertickler meeting, a seventh contender appeared. Not a one among them would admit surprise, for none dared seem lesser of mind or experience. The stranger, he didn't seem to think his presence was anything unusual either. Seemed right at home in their company.

"He was not much like them. His clothes were snatches and left-aways. Smelled like a forest, he did. Smiled all younglike in a keen way of mischief. Hands? They were knobby and raw from some hard labor or perhaps a disease. He spread out his tools as each of them had done." Krawg moved his hands over the tabletop. "Took dust from the ground, unprecious stones, and some twigs. Took a flask of water, poured it into a clay bowl. Them other thieves, their smiles went crooked. How could so much nothing help the boy play against them?

"And so they went about their contests, lighting up the dark with blazes and lashing each other with curses. A fight broke out over a firework, for one claimed another'd stolen his colors. A second row rose over a certain song of thunder. But they never did each other no harm, for they feared to group the others against them. They focused on showing themselves superior in craft, each aspiring to be the master of all they saw. And while they agreed that the newcomer couldn't best them, each one worried, for he seemed so calm 'n' ready.

"That stranger didn't say much, but he seemed to enjoy the contenders' shows. One sent stars a-dancing, and he applauded the idea. One gripped the edge of a cloud-sewn canopy, and in a flourish like a servant shaking out the sheets, he whisked it away to reveal an army all decked out for battle, and the stranger laughed in surprise.

"But when it came the stranger's turn, he smiled 'n' nodded 'n' opened his hands. In them lay a boy and a girl, all dressed up in colors like unfinished dolls."

Krawg hesitated. He seemed startled at his own announcement. Then, cautiously, he continued. "The tricksters guffawed, for each of them had fashioned puppets that could sweep their floors and sew up their shoes. And they scoffed, for these children were smaller than small, poorer than poor, simpler than simple."

Krawg paused for a long time. His hands were trembling. He stared down at the table. Revelers fired anxious glances about the room as if watching a sudden incursion of grasshoppers. Krawg trudged ahead.

"But then this newcoming trickster, he plucked two golden hairs from behind his ear. He took them and threaded needles fashioned from bone. Then he thrust those points right through the hearts of the boy and girl, stitching them round about until they pulsed. He drew those needles right up through their throats and on through the cords of their voices, then ran them through their minds in mysterious tangles."

Some of the listeners pressed their hands to their hearts, others to their throats.

"The raggedy boy, he yelped at that piercing sting. And he leapt up so fast he startled his maker. The stranger laughed and hugged the boy, and they danced, each thumpin' a drum. It weren't a dance meant for show. It was just a burst of happy and hooray. And them tricksters that watched, they forgot about the contest. For a few forgetful moments, they were accidentally happy as well.

"And then the maker turned to that raggedy girl he'd made, and the boy got nervous and picked at his stitching. The girl sat up and sang out a song that set her maker to laughing. The tricksters' smiles, they faded fast, for they were baffled 'n' vexed. How could inventions surprise their own maker? How could a doll know gratitude or make up a tune?

"This troubled them as the raggedy boy struck sparksticks that flared into light, as he painted his hands many colors and then painted the maker's as well. The raggedy girl, she touched the tricksters' faces and spoke a poem. The words she crafted meant many things at once. The tricksters felt she had pulled out their stuffing into the light, and it was muddy with sadness and shame. This scared them, for how could anybody's puppet know such stuff?

"The girl's maker touched her shoulder lightly. 'For your kindness,' he said, 'I'll show you a secret.'"

Krawg suddenly clapped his hands together and laughed.

Warney gasped, struck with a wild notion he had never dared suppose. Old Krawg was making all this up. This wasn't some old story he'd refashioned his own strange way. No, old Krawg was weaving a tapestry all on his own.

A tang of sweet smoke tainted the air, but Warney gave it no heed as Krawg continued.

"Much to the girl's surprise, wings unfolded from her shoulders. She took to flitting about, swimming around the stars quick as a fish in the sea. Her maker smiled like an old grandpa at play with his children. He needed no more fancy stuff. The game, you see, was done as a bun left too long in the oven."

The hostess, interrupting Krawg's story with a sharp curse, scuffled her way back to the kitchen. "Nectarbread," somebody muttered.

Krawg would not be distracted. "But the raggedy boy," he lamented, "well, he'd picked at his stitches too long, and his insides were coming out. 'Why can't I fly too?' he asked. 'Oh, I've got something else special for you,' said the maker. But that was no good for the boy. 'Make me fly!' he cried, and the maker, he breathed a deep one. Then he snapped out a stitch in the boy's sewn back. Wings sprang out, and skyward he flew. The boy and the girl, they laughed and they danced. But the boy laughed too loudly, and as he swooped low, the tricksters, they noticed a wrinkle, right there between the boy's brows.

" 'That's all for today,' said the maker. But it was clear he'd shown only a spark of his magic. This threw them all mad into fits. All the six tricksters' cold and cruel inventions did only what they were told. Creatures flown like kites. Machines with wheels that turned. Spells that did as they were designed and never surprised. But who could invent such a creature, with a mind and heart of her own? And all the girl's ways with words and mystery! What of their devising could imagine such surprises, could say one thing and mean another?

" 'How is it,' they asked, 'that you fashion such life? What treasure have you dug up?' "

Krawg leaned forward as if he'd stopped at the edge of a precipice. When he exhaled, it was the sound of a well gone dry.

But then his eyes widened. And he rubbed his hands together as if contemplating a perilous dive.

"The stranger, he smiled without fear. With a fatherly affection, he said, 'Don't you have a notion by now? I've come to call you home with me. Give up your boasting. Don't waste more days on thieving. Come back...' " Krawg choked, looking down into his empty hands. " 'Come back home, my friends, and you'll have all you need. I've missed you there. I've drawn golden threads of will through hearts like these before. Yours were the first that I threaded.' "

All around the storyteller, rasping shouts of surprise burst out, filthy cries of alarm, like bushpigs growling all through a swamp. Krawg cast Warney a look of nervous glee, an expression Warney hadn't seen since the heyday of their thievery. Krawg's reckless gamble was working.

The old man continued with heightening zeal. "And so them tricksters threw tantrums and quakes. They roared like lions with tails caught in traps. They barked like dogs who catch sight of the gorrel. They declared themselves their own inventions and refused to follow this dollmaker anywhere.

" 'I'm taking my children back home,' said the stranger with a sigh. 'And I plan to make a thousand more. The parties we'll have. The feasts we'll devour. The colors we'll give to the world.' "

At that, Warney's mind lit up, and he smiled, for he knew the source of his friend's inspiration.

Meanwhile, the hostess quietly took new drink orders, glad to have her customers so enraptured. More were pressing in through the door, straining to hear the story and whispering questions to catch what they'd missed.

"One of the six tricksters came forward then, arms folded 'cross his chest, like so. 'What if I don't believe that you made us?' he scoffed. 'What if these scrap 'n' stitch children are just illusions? Are two other tricksters in contract with you, hiding in those woven costumes?'

" 'I've said all you need to hear,' said the stranger.

" 'If those wretched toys have untamed minds, they'll leave you,' sneered the tallest trickster, the one with the curl to his lip. 'If you're smart, you'll crush those sparks. You should control your inventions like we do.'

"Before he could laugh, that trickster fell back, his very own fireworks exploding in their boxes. The dragons he'd stitched came undone. And while he moaned over the mess, the stranger took his children and disappeared. Victorious."

Warney surveyed the revelhouse, gazing into the mirrors to study the listeners' rapt attention.

"So that's it then!" roared the miner who was waiting for his turn at the contest. He stood up and pounded his mug on the table a little too sharply, and it shattered. The hostess cried out and disqualified the man, which brought the last contestant to his feet.

"You think you've heard a tale?" he squeaked, failing to muster the confidence he wanted. "I've got a tale of King Helpryn and how he fought an oceandragon and saved our glorious house from—"

"The stranger here isn't finished!" came a voice. It was the revelhouse guard who had come in from outside and forgotten his duty. "Look! He's serving up more!"

Krawg stood. And as the hush fell, a voice not his own rose up in his throat, bitter and twisted. It reminded Warney of the Krawg he had known in the days before they found Auralia together—an angrier Krawg, a jealous and spiteful Gatherer.

"The tricksters," said Krawg, "they pursued the powerful stranger, all jealous with rage. When they found him after years of chase, they were threadbare 'n' crazy. And when they saw the whole new world he'd made, all wild with color and life and a whole mess o' children, they wept and they cursed. 'What can we do to match such invention?'

"So they made themselves a moon of dust from all their failed attempts throughout the starry vastness. And they crouched down behind it, peering 'n' plotting how they might assail the stranger's wondrous world. Behind the moon they molded imitations, all frail 'n' forgettable, which only made them madder. So they besieged the dollmaker's inventions and took hold like sucker-worms, throttling every beauty, choking out the pulse of life. They flooded fields he planted. They fouled oceans he spread.

"But they could never quite capture his children, for he protected them, and they followed him, ever refusing to stray.

"In time the stranger grew angry at the tricksters. 'I'll raise a fence,' he told them, 'one you cannot trespass. We'll play there out of your sight so we do not offend you anymore.'

"'Oh,'" said that snarling voice of a Krawg long gone. "'We will steal your children away,' the tricksters ranted. 'We'll fool them into unstitching themselves. They'll curse you. There'll be no more play, only war. Those wills you've invented—they'll abandon your arrogant hands. We'll overpower them and prove that we are too strong to be mere inventions of yours.'"

Krawg now seemed somber. He massaged his hands as if they ached. Warney knew, somehow, just what he was thinking. All those hard lessons of life as a thief were burning in his memory, scorching the path of his story.

"The maker sighed and said, 'The more you unstitch what I've made, the more you'll fray and fumble and fail. But there is a golden thread that runs through everything. Should you ever lure my new family into forgetfulness, that golden thread within them will burn with secrets of the weave they were meant for. If even one of my prodigal children traces that thread and follows it through all your snares and illusions, he'll find his way home. When he does, I'll give him the power to bring everyone else back with him. Slaves and crooks, kings and queens and heirs to thrones, thieves and killers, youngsters and old folks. He'll bring 'em back by way of the innermost strand, a thread that can't be broken. And so I'll draw all threads back into my weave.'"

In the quiet that followed, somebody murmured, "Bet that didn't make those tricksters too happy."

"No," said Krawg. "This only stoked their wrath. 'If you're wrong, we get to keep those that leave you,' said the tallest. 'And you may not do more to bring them back across your fence.'"

The story seemed to have taken control, and Krawg could not stop himself.

"So the maker took his children behind a great curtain. And the tricksters set about their wicked arts in full view of that shelter."

A commotion erupted in the revelhouse doorway. Crowds pressed inside to make room for another. But Krawg seemed not to notice, and so the story went into its final chapter.

"Just when the tricksters were weakening, worn-out in their attempt to lure out the children, one young boy—that first raggedy boy that the stranger had sewn—he spun himself out to the edges of things, curious about the tricksters' displays. He stumbled in his steps for a moment, the wrinkle gone deep in his brow, and gazed at the world beyond the dollmaker's fence.

"He was troubled to see what the tricksters were doing out there in the moonlight. It bothered him how nothing they did made any music, only trouble 'n' noise. But the more he looked, the more he got dazzled by the power in their show. He wondered what it would feel like to step out into that silvery light and smash something with a hammer of his own. Surely he could try it and nobody would know.

"Caught there on the boundary, the boy was questioned by his smiling maker. He made an excuse and said the moonlight had drawn him there. 'But the moon,' the maker told him, 'it does not truly shine. It only casts back light that it has stolen from the sun.'

"The raggedy boy was ashamed of his error and even more upset by his lie. How could he have thought of breaking away? But he knew that others had witnessed his distraction, had sensed his rebellious desire. When he returned to his place in the play, word spread that he was forgiven. And he resented that mark in his history. He thought less of himself and feared that his master thought less of him for failing. He did not want to bear that pang of shame alone. So he called for a game of Seek and Go Hiding. And while his master covered his eyes and counted to fourteen, the boy lured all the younger children to the boundary. And the maker, letting them go, wept behind the hands that covered his face for the counting.

"Seeing their advantage, the tricksters thundered like storms. They burned gardens into deserts. They swept lakes into the sky and brought the water down in storms to flood. They lunged at the children and—"

A sound like a snake's hiss pierced the quiet all around Krawg. And then a voice slashed through the revelhouse.

"That one."

The blade of that voice severed the taut lines of attention connecting every listener to Krawg's story so that each one slumped like an unstrung puppet.

Krawg stood with his hands raised as if trying to catch some mysterious falling light. Then he fell against the table, breathless, sweat streaming down his brow.

The figure who had shouted was hunched in the doorway, for she was too tall to stand upright in the frame. Cloaked in what looked like a red tent, she clasped one grey hand to her beard. That chalky flesh was somehow immune to the tint of golden light.

At first the revelers thought the knifelike nail of the pointing finger was aimed at the trembling storyteller. "How many?" Her words cut their ears. She stalked forward in unsteady strides that suggested she walked in her own personal earthquake.

But she passed Krawg and loomed over a man sitting at a table against the wall. The man, snoring spittle onto the table, had both hands thrust out before him, clutching half-empty mugs among a dozen other empties.

The hostess slowly stood up, clearing her throat. "I told him, Good Seer. I told him if he drank another, he'd suffer the punishment. He knows the rules."

Panner Xa slowly searched the crowd until her wide eyes, two shining moons, fixed upon a bald and shirtless brute in a black cloth mask. "The rules!" she shrieked.

The brute stood up as if he'd been shouted an order, unsheathed a gleaming blade, marched straight to the table, and in one clean strike severed the drinker's left hand. As the guilty drunkard lurched to his feet in surprise, the brute snatched up the hand left on the table. Warney had time to notice the bright runes tattooed on the knuckles before the hand was cast, dripping, across the room and out an open window.

The Seer's eyes followed that hand, and her crooked lips smacked dryly together.

The drunkard blinked at the blood pump of his newly opened wrist as puddles of beer reddened and spilled off the table's edges. He coughed three unintelligible announcements, then fell straight into the arms of the brute, who dragged him outside, snatching a torch from its stand on the way through the door. A searing howl, a sizzling sound, and then sobs. The brute returned and planted the torch back in its stand as if this were just part of his routine.

The Seer, seething, scoured the room with her gaze. "That story," she quietly laughed. Then she lurched across the room as if one leg were longer than the other. Her elaborate headdress, a mane of red seaweed tendrils, whispered and rushed as she moved to the storytellers' table. Her large, pale hand shot forward like the muzzle of a slayhound to clasp Krawg's throat. "Who taught you?"

"Taught?" he rasped, flailing. "Me?"

Warney stood up. He could not help it. Something within drew him forward to his friend's defense. But when the Seer cast him a wild glance, those strange, bold eyes swiveled loosely in their sockets to pin him to his place.

"Never again," she instructed him. "Never again."

Krawg's feet dangled just above the ground, his face purpling. Spittle foamed at the edges of his mouth.

The Seer dropped him and lurched toward the hostess. "Arrived?" she demanded.

"Tonight, Good Seer."

"How many?"

"Four. Deserters from the hiding Abascars. Trying to be merchants."

"Four." She turned and looked at Jes-hawk in the far corner. "Steeds?" she barked.

"Five," came a voice from somewhere in the crowd.

"Five." She stamped her foot, and a sound like a swarm of bees filled the room.

Warney shrank against the wall as the revelhouse air filled with dust. It rose from the tabletops, the floor, and the bar. The Mawrn wafted from nostrils and mouths. It skittered out from under tables. Revelers twitched and itched as it crawled from their sleeves. The Seer turned to the window, seeming to direct the dust in streams and ribbons into the night like a legion of ghosts on a hunt.

And Warney knew their prey.

"Red moon," mused the Seer. "Red moon." She moved to the window and stared out at the crater as if she could read every grain of dust in this darkness. Again the hiss: "Tressssspasser." She sniffed the air deeply, and then she left the revelhouse, noisy and crooked as a wagon with a broken wheel.

A harsh grip clasped Warney's arm, and he shouted.

It was Jes-hawk, leaning in close to his ear. "Take Krawg to the bunkhouse."

They moved to the table where Krawg lay shriveled as if years had flowed from his veins. Jes-hawk knelt, muttering, "Blast of a story, old man. I'll never forget it." Then he slipped an arrow from a sheath inside his boot and gave it to Warney. "Plant this in the window of your room, as the king instructed. I'm going out there to look for him."

12

WHAT CAL-RAVEN SAW
THROUGH THE GLASS

As Ruffleskreigh the cleverjay watched the man-fool climb, she thought about redfish.

Silver-scaled. Juicy-eyed. With tails that trail like ribbons in the current. Feasts of pink meat that taste best when wriggling. But a redfish swims deeply, far from a cleverjay's claws. Haughty hunters like flashdivers snatch them as easily as jays pluck berries from briars. Cleverjays hate them for that.

But if Ruffleskreigh could fulfill the task assigned her, her master would reward her with a redfish feast.

Wait for the ravens to bring you a man called Cal-raven. Lead him up to the roots of the tree. Help him solve the puzzle just the way I have shown you.

The mage had bargained with the ravens as well, but they were simple minded and settled for a promise of wrigglers. For that, the greedy flock had flown in all directions, shouting "Cal-raven" to every traveler they saw, hoping to win some tasty prizes for themselves. She had laughed at the sight. She had known to push for a richer prize. And the mage always made good on his promises.

She coasted across the crater, feathers sifting the breeze, and alighted on a bough just ahead of the man-fool. He was surprised to see her, with her tall, glowing crestfeathers—so much more impressive than the ravens who were now almost invisible around him.

Light glistened on the climber's neck and shoulders, and his breath was labored. Weaklings, these wingless creatures. Ground-bound and easily discouraged. And this one was more foolish than most, ascending to a worthless perch that offered nothing tasty, nothing shiny. He still had far to climb.

She laughed. The man shouted harshly at her.

Beneath the starcrown's layers of moss, something scuttled noisily, and the man turned in a fright. *Only a dustrat,* she thought. *But he fears the beastmen. And should.*

Hopping easily from branch to branch, Ruffleskreigh coughed the man's name again. "Hurry," she hissed, proud of her eloquence. "I want my prize."

She liked her master, liked the way he spoke to her. The old mage knew more words than any of her cleverjay kin—words written in the cage of her ribs since she first cracked the wall of her eggshell, words written between the rapid beats of her *fum-fum-fumming* heart.

When the climber was halfway to the top, the bird stretched her wings and moved ahead. She could not leave. Not until he reached the enormous nest among the tree's splayed roots. Not until he found the pieces of the puzzle and assembled them just as the mage had.

She strained to curl her tongue just so and croaked his name: "Cal-raven." Then, "Higher. Higher."

He scowled at her, and she laughed in disdain, for he was already failing, already rejecting her counsel and heading off in the wrong direction. She would have to fly at him and drive him back to the path the mage had marked.

At that moment she noticed that Cal-raven was not the only man climbing this fallen tree. Startled, she shot straight up into the starlight and hovered there, clucking curses at whoever dared to delay her redfish feast.

⳥

Crafting the cleverjay's likeness from the potato-sized stone in his hand, Cal-raven narrowed his eyes, trying to sustain his faith in this garrulous guide.

At intervals in the bird's incessant chatter, it brought its tail feathers forward, making a horn around its body, and called Cal-raven's name in the voice of Scharr ben Fray—an uncanny impression. Then it snapped those feathers back, bobbed its yellow-capped head, and tapped its prickly feet. It seemed to think it knew other words as well. He caught something that sounded like "fish," "tasty," and "prize." The ravens were quiet, probably intimidated by the brash newcomer.

Shaping the bird's trumpet, his fingers remembered the contours all too well. A cleverjay had been one of the first figures he'd crafted as a child. Maybe he'd take it back to Barnashum and give it to Wynn—a peace offering to keep the boy from growing a grudge.

The bird lifted and flew back over his head, calling him to retrace his steps.

Uncertain, he followed, and he winced when he found that he had left the tree's trunk and wandered off along a broad bough. As the effect of Soro's well water diminished and the vivid details of night faded back into darkness, hunger and exhaustion took hold. "I hope you've left me something to eat there, teacher. Otherwise, I'm going to roast your bird."

The bird drew him along, climbing the tree's rugged backbone, past its outspread arms, moving back through time from its youngest heights to its ancient roots, which were spread like the tendrils of some threatening sea creature on the crater's rim. With each step he felt more likely to fall back down to the dustbowl floor, to the fallen starcrown's ash-buried head, into the clutches of Panner Xa.

He slumped against a near-vertical column, a bough as big as a Cragavar marrowwood tree, branching up from the starcrown's center. He clung to its mossy skirt and glanced back over his shoulder. *I won't make it to the top by moonrise. I'll have to camp in the tree. And wait for tomorrow.*

A rustle from a branch above cast a faint skiff of dust across his head. He looked up to curse the bird.

Lantern light revealed two large, leathery feet on the lowest branch of that treelike bough. The man holding the lantern seemed a part of the tree.

Old Soro's glittering eyes regarded Cal-raven. "Trust me." The instruction came in a cavernous whisper through that thick weave of beard. "Your own understanding will not get you to the top in time. Give me your sword. I'll show you a straight, clear path."

Cal-raven laughed. "My sword? I need my sword. Especially if the Seer's coming after me."

"You're afraid. I heard you call for the Keeper."

His hand was on the sword hilt, but he could not decide whether to draw it in defense or cooperation. "The Keeper's kept me safe this far. It won't fail me now. So I don't need your help."

"A claim like that requires a lot of faith."

"I don't need faith. I've seen the answer."

How did he get ahead of me? He's not even out of breath.

"You seem to have everything figured out." Soro seemed burdened beyond the weight of that hunch on his back.

Cal-raven tightened his grip around the hilt.

Soro snapped off the crooked branch he'd been holding to keep his balance. Then he reached the hooked end of the branch toward Cal-raven and sent a water flask sliding down its span to swing by its strap at the end. "Drink."

Need overpowered suspicion. Cal-raven took the flask and drank deep.

The fierce, cold purity of the well water shook him. At once the stars burned brighter. The water carried the smell of stone passages deep beneath the earth. His ears were battered by the sound of his heartbeat. As he drew the flask away from his face, the scent of the Cragavar north of the crater filled his nostrils, borne by the wind coursing southward.

Even before he hung the flask back on the hook, he asked, "How did you get here ahead of me? I'm exhausted, but you aren't even out of breath—"

"I know it's unlikely, but perhaps I know a few things about climbing Tammos Raak's tower—things that even the king of Abascar might find useful." In a hissing spill of ash, Soro jumped down to land hard on the tree's trunk beside Cal-raven, the branch in his hand like a walking stick. He drew in a deep wheeze and sneezed.

Cal-raven waved the cloud of Mawrn away from his face.

"Let me show you something." Soro smiled, and Cal-raven could see stitches across the dark wood of that masklike face. "Ready?" He raised his makeshift staff as if he would strike.

Cal-raven drew his sword.

"Consider this a second chance." Soro brought the branch down and plunged its sharp, broken end through the soft bark between them.

Cal-raven heard a sharp crack. The solid foundation of the ancient tree shuddered. Breaks branched out like veins, splitting and fragmenting the pet-rified surface. He cried out. Soro leaned on the branch, widening the gap in the bark. The ground collapsed beneath Cal-raven.

In a rain of debris, he fell through the rotten marrow and landed against a wall of dry, spongy wood in the starcrown's core. He began to slide, along with a river of rubble, down an open burrow within the tree, and he clawed at the honeycomb surface. As he grappled, his foot found a ledge—a bar of wood nailed into the wall. A step.

If there's one, there must be. . .yes, another.

He laughed, shaking his head.

When the rush quieted, he looked up through the break Soro had opened. The stars were wild with light. There was no sign of the hunchback.

He looked ahead through the tree's dark hollow. Although the way was narrow, the air foul, and the walls chattering with insect life, his path through the core of the tree was now straight and unimpeded. Through translucent curtains of cobwebs, he beheld a warm crimson glow, a sphere of light far away.

"Perhaps the darker path was the better one," he muttered.

His hand found the farglass still bound to his belt. Then he cursed, for the sword sheath was empty. The blade was lost, buried somewhere below in the dark heart of the starcrown.

He began to climb. And the more he strove, the more strength he found. With every grasping lunge upward, his hands pushed through crumbs of rot-ten wood and rotbeetles to find another hold. Along some stretches he found dangling ropes of ivy—ivy!—heavy with clusters of bittergrapes. There was life to be found in the dark's hanging garden.

His thirst quenched, he thrilled with life, sure that he would find the top before the moonrise.

When at last Cal-raven leapt up into the open maw of the starcrown's fallen roots, he fell forward onto a bed of wind-stripped grass. Wind from the north roiled in this cave, beneath the flare of unearthed roots. He thought of a story he had invented as a child—a tale of being swallowed by a dragon but fighting on within its belly and refusing to give up.

I've climbed up through its throat. I'm sitting in its open mouth.

He rested on all fours, sucked in chestfuls of cold night air, and enjoyed the exhilaration of the well water's enchantment.

I've made it to the top, Scharr ben Fray, by a passage kept secret even from you. For once, I know something you don't.

He gazed out through the hanging tendrils of ancient roots and took in the view of the world below and beyond—the forested spread of the North Cragavar. Beyond that he saw the darkness of Fraughtenwood and then the rising land that became the mountains of the Forbidding Wall. Wind whipped back his thin braids and blasted dust from his face until his skin burned.

Between Cal-raven and the opening, a table waited like an altar for a sacrifice. Chalky, uncrushed boulders of the Mawrn rested on its round surface, holding down a heavy cloth that rippled like a skirt. Perching on the table's edge, the cleverjay regarded him with one eye, then the other.

He crept past the table and glanced down over the lip of the cave's mouth. It was a long drop to the ground where this tree had been planted. But some of the starcrown's roots still stretched downward, robust as pillars, anchored in the slope of the crater's outside edge.

It hasn't given in. Somehow this fallen tree's still drawing life from this ground. Like Abascar. He looked toward the rising moon. Already a bold red gem rested between two of the Forbidding Wall's fangs. *I'll raise a new kingdom yet.*

The cleverjay tapped at the tablecloth.

He sat down and unsheathed the farglass.

The cleverjay screeched, impatient. She flew at the Mawrn rocks as if they threatened her until they lay vanquished, crumbling into powder on the cave floor.

The table. That's what Scharr ben Fray wanted me to see.

The bird paused, dusted her beak, eyed him intently, then carefully pronounced a new word: "Window." She scratched at the black tablecloth like an aggravated bull before a charge.

Cal-raven stood, drew the tablecloth away, and cast it aside. It flew, full of wind like a ship's sail, and spread itself flat against the cave's back wall.

The bird alighted on the tabletop—a large round pane of glass. "Window."

Cal-raven leaned over to look through it but saw only the stone column that supported it. "Window?" He took hold of the edge and rattled it. "It's... loose." Lifting the heavy pane away from the pillar that supported it, he held it up, and looked through it.

The glass presented a warped, distorted image of the back of the cave. The view made him dizzy. He set it down on its edge and looked at the bird, who now pecked about the exposed surface of the stone column.

A groove, wide as Cal-raven's thumb, cut straight across the column's flat surface.

"Ah." He lifted the tabletop and set it upright, neatly snapping the edge into the column's groove.

"Ha-ha!" cackled the cleverjay, hovering in place.

"Window," Cal-raven pronounced, brushing off his hands. Then he took a few steps back and said, "Oh. Oh, yes."

The glass magnified his view of the northern mountains so that they seemed to rise right in front of him.

Standing on its high curve, the cleverjay clucked proudly. "Look," she said.

Cal-raven studied the distorted picture, eyes tracing jagged mountain peaks that towered like an array of charred chimneys draped in a swirling blanket of cloud. Soon moonlight would spill over that blanket, revealing the details of those severe mountainsides.

"So the Seers watch the North. Why? What do they see? Is that why Tammos Raak fled to this place when he was in trouble? Maybe he could see something. Oh, listen to me," he snorted, "talking about these stories as if they were true."

The blurred silhouette of the Forbidding Wall seemed so close he felt he could touch its sharp peaks. And as he watched, a bright line burned across the cloudy tide beyond the mountains. It thickened and, as if spilling over a dam, poured between the towering peaks and painted the spaces between the mountains in crimson, then rushed down toward Fraughtenwood. What had seemed an impenetrable wall now revealed passages winding through rank after rank of heightening mountains.

"Where are you?" His whisper puffed white dust swirling into the air, fragments that, when magnified by the glass, looked like tiny moons— colorless, pockmarked, and cold.

He leaned closer. Through the blur of the magnified specks, he looked to the threshold of the Forbidding Wall. A strange symmetry drew his attention: a row of vertical lines like bright spears of an advancing legion, their tips pinpoints of light in a row, close together, almost imperceptible. Their perfect arrangement was consistent and, thus, unnatural. It was something made by men.

"By Har-baron's severed arm."

He began to count, and in his excitement he forgot to breathe. *Thirteen. Thirteen.*

"One more," he whispered, stepping from side to side, trying to find a patch of the glass that would show him a clearer view. "Show me one more."

He could see, even from here, that this line of bright towers disappeared behind a rocky ridge. "There must be another." He straightened and looked at the dome of the half-risen moon. "There must be fourteen. Inius Throan. Fourteen bells in fourteen towers."

His hand brushed the farglass in its sheath. *What might I see if I could look even closer?*

He set the farglass down on top of the stone pillar, its open end flat against the glass pane. Then he leaned down and looked through the viewpiece.

I told you the legends were true, Scharr ben Fray would smugly say. *Think of it. Gardens, just waiting to be reawakened. Walls, impenetrable. A throne. I can already see you there.*

He drew out all of the farglass's lens discs. Then he began to restore and remove each lens, one at a time, to test the combinations. Each variation sharpened certain aspects of the view, enhancing the texture of the rough mountainsides, magnifying the light, or blurring those slopes to reveal flocks of birds or clouds of dust carried along on the winds that rushed down from the north.

He leaned away from the scope, left it resting against the great glass disc, and let his eyes take in the spreading crimson flood.

His teacher's lessons rose from the past, loose pieces of a puzzle finally fitting into place. *Dangers haunt Fraughtenwood, and beyond the threshold of the Wall, it's worse. But the stories of Inius Throan, that first house of the escape, tell us of wonders. The city became deserted only when Tammos Raak's children turned against one another. They descended into the Expanse to stake their claim, to follow their hearts and shape kingdoms that would fit their desires. They wanted more than he could give them.*

"But now. Inius Throan lies open. Empty. Waiting. Father, you should see it. Like a king's crown waiting to be claimed."

"In-ee-us," chirped the bird. "In-ee-us." Then, apparently satisfied, the cleverjay disappeared into the night, uttering a farewell that sounded like scorn. One grey feather remained on the air, drifting slowly into Cal-raven's hand. He absent-mindedly threaded it into one of the braids that ran back over his ear.

Somewhere behind him in the starcrown's throat, a dull thud reverberated. He glanced over his shoulder. *The Seer. She's coming after me at last. And it seems I have to figure out my escape on my own.* His hand sought the hilt of his sword. It was gone. He turned to face the burrow that had led him here.

As he did, the air in the cave suddenly changed. A glow shimmered in the air, swirling slowly.

"Auralia." Cal-raven fell to his knees.

It was as if the threads of Auralia's magnificent cloak had unraveled to float in the air. Colors he had seen only once before, shining in the Abascar dungeon, clouded in the open space and danced against the canvas of the dark tablecloth at the back of the cave.

His gaze traced those strands, finding that they wound together, streaming from the eyepiece of the farglass. A ray of moonlight, shining across the clouds above the Forbidding Wall, had struck the window and passed through the scope's lenses, breaking apart and expanding into the cave, a web of luminous filaments.

Cal-raven exhaled the breath he'd been holding, exhilarated. *Scharr ben Fray did not anticipate this.* He scrambled back to the scope. *Where do they come from?*

The moonlight had set fire to the surface of the thick country of cloud.

Something within that blazing miasma caught the light. High above the mysterious towers and the mountain peaks, it lit up like a splinter of the sun, firing a fierce beacon straight to this—the place where the tower of Tammos Raak once stood.

That beam, passing through the pillar's glass pane, suddenly proved too intense for the lenses of Cal-raven's scope.

They shattered.

Cal-raven felt a fragment of light shoot straight as an arrow into his vision. The burn cut deep into his head. He staggered away from the farglass, grasping at his left eye.

A voice cut through the cooling air, a hiss in the starcrown's ancient throat. "Tressssspasssser."

Cal-raven grabbed the broken farglass, then stumbled, half blind, to the edge of the starcrown's root-lined cave. He blinked down at the long, wind-blasted slope of the crater's outer edge. Through the fire in his head, he could not see what waited for him.

A hand, deathly grey, thrust up from the burrow and groped for a hold on the ground.

Cal-raven jumped.

13

A Traitor's Bargain

J iggerspit, I'm cold. And I don't want to stay here."

At Krawg's complaint, Warney paused outside the revelhouse and draped his own cloak around his friend's hunched frame.

"I smell rain comin'. Let's get inside." They limped along like brothers joined at the shoulder, their journey to the bunkhouse slowed by a herd of wild grubswine that crowded the avenue.

The bunkhouse host, a thin man with skin dark as a Jentan's, blinked at them with runny eyes.

He's heard of us, Warney thought. *Already we're "those troublemakers from Abascar."*

He reached for excuses that had once helped the Midnight Swindler and the One-Eyed Bandit escape from Abascar guards. But Krawg produced a small leather pouch and handed it to the host.

Opening it, the host nodded. They moved inside.

"Ballyworms, Krawg!" Warney whispered. "What'd you give him?"

Krawg managed a feeble smile. "When that blasted Seer picked me up, my hand found her pockets. Packed with Bel Amican moon coins."

A familiar sensation of smug triumph warmed Warney like a swig of apple brandy. He hadn't known Krawg to steal so much as a crumb in Barnashum. He could not remember the last thing they'd nabbed that hadn't belonged to them—except Auralia.

He hauled Krawg across a mud-caked rug into a fireless fireside room. As they pushed through a crowd of miners, Warney and Krawg learned a great deal about Krawg's performance.

Apparently Krawg had spoiled his chance by using language of the lowest sort. They ranted that "Abascar poor folk" were famously "muck mouthed." A young woman squirming in an old man's lap spat the word "Gatherers" like the husk of juice-weed. "I counted exactly seventeen utterances of *kramm* and six, maybe seven, of *crolca*. Should purge such talk from Bel Amican camps."

"Offended, are they?" Krawg muttered. "And yet listen to them—all sneers 'n' scoffing 'n' judgment."

Worst, Krawg's story had spoken of sorcery and spells inconsistent with the moon-spirit religion. "That tale might send folk off to behave like tricksters, practicing dark arts and conjuring. String him up and flay him, I say."

Only Warney could understand Krawg's rasp, for the story had worn out his voice. "Haven't they ever played make-believe?" Krawg coughed, spat. "Did they forget the hows and whys of makin' stuff up?"

Trudging like weary rock goats up the steep staircase, they were buffeted by the insults. That ranting Abascar vagrant had broken every rule in the house, they said. He'd talked for too long. The story went places they hadn't expected. Hadn't he learned the formulas? Hadn't he learned that people prefer happy endings? What kind of story stopped with a question?

"Jiggerspit, I'm cold," Krawg growled again. "And I don't want to stay here."

"Still," muttered a creaky miner who had stopped at the top of the stairs, "there was something there in the dirt of that story." He watched Krawg and Warney ascend as if they were only a phantom of memory. "Some meaning under it. Or perhaps creeping along behind."

"Well, out with it then!" said a younger version of the old man as he placed his foot on his elder's hindquarters, grabbed his shoulders, and straightened him with a tug and a *crack!* "If you can't spit out what your story's about, where's the sense in it? Shouldn't punish listeners by making them..." He paused and thought for a moment. "By making them think!"

"In finer speech it might've made a finer tale." The old man gave Krawg another curious glance.

"Nah," said the younger. "You heard the room when he finished. Quiet as the grave. Not a whistle, not a stomp. So really, how good could it be?"

Warney urged Krawg farther down the hall to another stairway.

"Cold," Krawg whispered. "Don't want to stay."

"Gotta 'gree with you there."

As they walked, Krawg grew smaller and heavier for hearing the complaints. At the end of a crooked hallway, Warney opened a narrow door and found a three-bunk room crowded with broken pickaxe handles, coils of rope, and piles of discarded grey Mawrn sacks with broken seams. Flies drifted drunkenly over a mop bucket's sludgewater.

Krawg crumbled to the floor. "Cold." Warney winced at the shallowness of his breath, the sound of a punishing fever. He dragged Krawg to the bunk. "You need," he groaned, "Auralia's yellow scarf. It cools your brow every time."

Krawg was already snoring, lips spluttering together like the cinch of a balloon as the air gusts out.

Warney checked Krawg's pockets. "You had it with you in the revelhouse. I'm goin' back."

And so he went out and tiptoed down the corridor, hoping nobody would recognize him as Krawg's companion.

Down in the gathering room, among those few stragglers who had not lumbered off to bed, talk about Krawg's story had changed. Their voices were stern with disapproval, but they went on repeating its unfamiliar twists and surprises as if they were riddles to be solved.

Back in the quieted revelhouse, Warney found the yellow scarf lying in a puddle under the table where he had listened to the tale of six tricksters. "Wish you were here, Auralia," he murmured, "to help me bring Krawg back to rightness. Hope your weaving does the trick."

Three newcomers blocked the exit. Warney hesitated. Two of them looked excited, laughing, money in their hands. The other, stout and confident, beamed as if he'd just won the better end of a bargain. He put his hands on their shoulders in some ceremonial parting, then looked toward Warney.

It was Snyde.

Warney turned and strode toward the kitchen, pretending he belonged there. He passed through a bustle of barhelp too busy to notice him, and then he was out a back door and into the night's red glow.

A solitary rain cloud sent a shower slanting against the back of the revelhouse. Warney shuddered as miners and grubswine passed him, and he bowed his head to stare at the mud.

All thoughts of Snyde fell away when he saw what one of the grubswine was sniffing. A severed appendage lay with fingertips pressed to the ground as if it might scuttle away.

The drunkard's hand. Warney kicked the heavy, dull-minded grubswine away.

The hand's flesh was dull and grey, and its ragged wrist did not look as if it had been severed by a sharp blade. Warney looked closer. Black stitches lined the edge, threads that had been broken, as if this was a glove modeled to pass for flesh. *Like some old man's mitten nibbled by mice.*

Even stranger, it had long and curling nails, more like the Seer's than the drunkard's. Most perplexing of all, the knuckles bore no runes like those Warney had clearly seen indoors.

Warney hurried along, trying not to look at the ground for fear it might be littered with carnage. But the image of the hand stayed with him so vividly that he forgot all about what else he had seen in the revelhouse. For a while.

❧

Vawns complained as they dragged a wagon out of the crater to level ground, and the miners' complaints were even darker as they coughed out the gritty corruption they had breathed in the Mawrnash mine.

They were too tired to notice when Cal-raven, like some loose bundle of quarry, tumbled out the back and crawled into a huddle of abandoned, unhitched wagons that leaned like cattle stooping to graze. One cart was still rigged to three handsome horses, whose ears pricked forward through the rain as they stared up the avenue in expectation. Cal-raven leaned against a wheel and rested while bruises from his adventure pulsed and punished him.

He pulled off his boots, knocked out loose debris, and massaged his ankles with his thumbs. Shutting his eyes, he studied the aura that flickered in his left eye. That red burn had faded to pale orange, congealing into an angular shape.

The sound of clanking dishes and a lively melody from a copperflute drew his attention toward the revelhouse just beyond the stables. And now he could smell it—bread, fresh and hot, seasoned, soaking up drizzled honey, dripping as lumps of butter softened into golden syrup. He smelled molten cheese in a tangy tomato stew. He smelled spiced yellowroot and baked fish. He imagined himself slipping inside and washing the ash from his throat with a flagon of fizzy ale. It was almost worth the risk.

The aromas summoned up Bel Amican evenings—scenes from streets he had not walked in several years. He had proved to his skeptical father that he was smart enough to explore the house on the edge of the Mystery Sea. In disguise, he had learned their resources, their intentions, their limitations. He had formed alliances. And oh, he had eaten well; friendships opened doors to lavish feasts where even the mockery of his father and House Abascar could not spoil his enjoyment. His last escape had been costly: a blind boatman smuggled him out through one of the waterways beneath the great city's stone foundation. He had suffered not so much from the risks involved but from the ache of leaving pleasures behind.

A guttural snort made him jump. A grubswine had shoved its snout into the boot he had removed and, after some delighted snuffling, was now trying to free its head. "Wait!" Cal-raven growled, but the pig was gone at a full run, blind with the boot on its head.

Cal-raven got on all fours. *How can I go after it if I can't see? This must be what Warney's world is like.* He began to crawl, sneaking between the wagons until he reached the edge of the avenue. Across the rain-sludge lane, the stables waited. *Our vawns are in there. Can a vawn catch a grubswine? Or should I go boot stealing?*

A figure stepped out a back door and lit a pipe. Cal-raven squinted at the man's boots. They seemed familiar. He strained to get a better look.

Snyde.

Snyde. Alive. Calm and confident.

Cal-raven froze. *I should've kept him beside me.*

Snyde looked up and smiled toward the cluster of wagons. Cal-raven realized that, in spite of the shadows, the old traitor knew he was there. He cursed the starcrown tree for swallowing his sword and reached to his ankle for his knife. Then he came slowly to his feet.

The bowl of Snyde's pipe glowed so that his toothy grin glittered in crimson.

"I hope you've come to confess," said the king. "I hope this means we can trust you to—"

Cal-raven woke to pressure on his wrists and a violent, shattering pain as if his bones had been sharpened to razors. He was lashed behind a galloping vawn.

He fought to clear his head, which struck stone after stone. Roots battered his ribs. He tried to wrest his hands free, but they were bound fast. He opened his eyes, and past that burning scar he saw only shadows and deeper shadows.

Another vawn strode along beside.

"He's waking!"

"Just in time to feel the fall." The voice shifted as one of the riders turned to address him. "You should thank us. We were paid to kill you, and we said we'd dispose of the body. But we'll be paid again if we leave you in a pit for the slavers."

Slavers. If I survive, I'll be in for a world of trouble, most likely far from here.

He struggled to get his feet under him. His hands clutched feebly at stones. His mind went out like a candle.

When he woke again, hard hands were rolling his body like a log across wet, rocky ground. His captors had placed a bag over his head and pulled its drawstring tight. Then the rolling stopped. He heard birds and saw, through the cloth, a morning glow. He heard a sound of branches and brush being cleared.

"Don't go dyin' on us. Traders won't pay if you do."

A sharp boot tip hooked his belly and gave him another violent turn.

"Over you go!"

He felt the ground fall away. He plunged down a narrow shaft. A jolt to his bound wrists nearly pulled his shoulders from their sockets, and he dangled like bait, upright in space. Somehow the binding between his wrists had caught on a protruding stone.

The light above him went out as a lid was placed over the hole.

It was not exactly sleep that he knew then. Just cold, and aches that pulsed like embers.

At times he became aware of sounds far below, like branches scraping against one another in the wind. But there was no wind. He heard the uneven patter of seepage from the rain dripping down to spatter on stone at the bottom of the chasm.

Daylight illuminated the fabric across his face. He heard voices. Women's voices, urgent and secretive. Something cold and metal struck his left hand, then his right. He realized that someone was fishing for him with a hook on a rope. He felt the hook scrape his wrist, then catch the wire that bound him. He felt a sharp tug. He was rising, his body thudding against the wall again and again.

"Keeper," he gasped, "where are you?"

Then he swam in a cloud of bright blue light, feeling and thinking nothing.

In his dream he faced a hard north wind on a rocky promontory.

He was out of breath, exhausted. He wore a new riding uniform, not unlike his father's—garments fit for a king. His left hand held a ring binding three heavy keys, each painted with mysterious hues of Auralia's colors. His right hand gripped a heavy sword.

He looked down at its gleaming blade. It was a sword of the finest craftsmanship—newly forged. In its shine he was startled by his own reflection. He was older. His hair was long and unbraided, his scarred visage stormy with indecision, his eyes dark with despair.

Sounds of pursuit troubled the path behind him, and he looked to the Forbidding Wall as if searching for some sign of help. The mountains were close, and a winged shadow blurred through that looming wave of cloud above them. He called to the Keeper, but the shadow did not respond. He called again. The figure's flight ended abruptly, the full sails of its wings collapsing. It fell from that billowing canopy, its body writhing as if in anguish. It crashed hard onto a rocky mountainside and was still.

Cal-raven cried out. Something stepped onto the stone behind him. He cast the keys over the cliff and watched them fall. Then he turned...

He woke, trembling, and heard the heavy drum of hoofbeats. He fought to keep from sinking back into the miasma of painful dreams.

A small hand touched his shoulder. "It's all right," said a voice. A boy's voice. He recognized it but could not think of the name. His concentration shattered once again.

Morning's birdsong was distant, the chorus keeping to the forest and avoiding the crater. Sunlight scorched the slatted shutters with bright gold lines. The bunkhouse roof dripped leftover rain to the grey sludge outside.

"Saddles, Krawg." Warney began to unwind the yellow scarf he had wrapped around his friend's feverish head.

"I'm warm." Krawg turned over and pulled the dusty, moth-chewed blanket over his head. "I'm warm, and I don't ever want to leave. Go away."

"Feet on the floor," Warney hissed in his ear. "Jes-hawk's hot as a poker. Company's saddling."

Krawg snorted. "Barnashum's no home. It's a warren for long-ears. And all those beds are hard."

Warney folded his arms across his chest. "So you're gonna stay then? All by yourself? How'll you pay for it?"

"I'll swear lasting allegiance. I'll scrub their crolca pans if I have to."

"Something's happened, Krawg. We gotta ride."

"Come back later."

Warney opened the shutters; light struck Krawg's face. "Gorrel pooey!" he spat. Warney dragged the blanket away and pulled Krawg up to sitting. "Ballyworms. My legs have lost their memory."

With Krawg leaning on his shoulder, Warney staggered down the long, loud stair and into the dawn-lit avenue. "The light hurts," said Krawg.

"It's the drink," Warney sighed. "It's like a brick to the head." And then he groaned, dropping his pack onto the avenue. "These bags're heavier than they were last night." Panting, he lifted it again and proceeded to tell Krawg about all that he'd heard the night before while the miners meditated on the remarkable narrative. "For the love of Yawny's stew, Krawg! D'ya reckon they'll sing our song in Bel Amica? I s'pose we'll never know."

"We'll know, all right. I'm gonna dine on that fish soup again if I have to pick the lock of Bel Amica's back door. The bread, dipped in thick red oil. And burrow cheese, Warney. Muskgrazer cheese. Yellowbrick cheese. Whipped cheese. And that caraberry ale, like honey to a fangbear."

"We're goin' back to Barnashum. Cal-raven must've got what he came for. That means he's got a plan at"—Warney slowed to a stop in the road—"last."

As Jes-hawk led vawns from the stables, Warney noticed that his own was missing and that an unfamiliar young woman sat astride the king's steed, smiling as if she'd won some sort of contest.

"Either I'm sicker than the boy who ate snails," said Krawg, "or that's not Cal-raven riding Cal-raven's vawn."

Jes-hawk held his arrowcaster ready in hand, and he surveyed the avenues like a hunted man.

"Where's the king?" Warney murmured.

"A vawn's gone missing." Jes-hawk lifted up a single boot. "I found this on a dungheap."

Warney's jaw dropped. "Where's the rest of him?"

14

SISTERS ASTRAY

Wild dogs in a frenzy of claws and teeth kept Tabor Jan from stepping out from behind the rock above the grassy gully. The scene troubled him. Dogs only fought like this if they had run out of prey.

With low expectations he had left the camp in search of something to hunt. The dogs were more wildlife than he'd seen in these six days, yet he wished they would disappear. He'd heard enough barking, seen enough biting on this laborious journey already. He was losing his grip on the patience and resolve that Abascar needed to see in him.

One of the dogs charged off in desperation, the others hungry in pursuit; they disappeared north and west.

He descended into the gully and followed it along a dry creek bed until it rose into ground where trees made room for jutting stone teeth. *If I kept going this direction, someday I'd reach Bel Amica.*

It was only a matter of time before the travelers decided that Bel Amica was their best option. Famished and hot-tempered, they were already fighting over blankets and shoes. They complained about the sick they carried, the sledges they dragged, and the wheelbarrows they pushed. Some grumbled about the route Tabor Jan had chosen, for the lowlands offered streams and pools; others agreed that this higher ground would help them see trouble coming from a distance. Everyone cursed the buzzers and stingerflies.

Darkening the gloom, the three injured in the cave collapse had worsened along the journey. Tabor Jan knew better than anyone how much they needed Say-ressa's calming influence, her healing arts, her quiet counsel. But she remained asleep. He had given up taking a turn at her bedside. It only increased his feelings of helplessness.

Instead, he took to patrolling the edges of the parade, watching for the king.

Golden banners of sunlight unfurled from the tops of tall evergreens. He pulled a leaf from his pocket and unfolded it, opening his meager midday meal. The dried fish was in short supply, so he contented himself with a handful of crisp grainseeds, nuts, and berries.

The quiet was troubled by a cascade of bark from a high pricklecone tree, and there was Brevolo climbing down.

Unnoticed, he admired her for a moment, for she seemed to have absorbed some of the sunlight. She reached the ground and stood sadly in a drifting shower—dust that sparkled, seedpods slowly whirling.

Her tawny tunic had frayed over her knees from scrabbling against tree trunks. Her arms were tattooed in the manner of Abascar swordbearers, with barbed and winding lines cascading to her wrists. Her hands were crisscrossed with scars from the labor of clearing paths. She had not unbraided the narrow lines of her black hair since they had moved out of Barnashum, and every day those tresses seemed more alive with bits of colored leaves, as if she had always dreamed of sleeping in the wild. Her boots, golden laced, patched, and patched again with spans of leathery rock-goat hide, left shallow prints in the dewy summer earth.

Every day of their march, he walked with her for a while, though she would not speak. During the days she patrolled a stretch alongside the parade's western side, and occasionally she climbed a tree to look for signals. It occurred to him that she might just disappear; she had very little binding her to their company now that Bryndei was dead. In the evenings he sat nearby, hoping she would sense his respect for her solitude and yet find comfort in his companionship.

Brevolo drew a span of cloth from her belt and unwrapped a shrillow's egg. She held it into the light to illuminate its sheen of black and yellow stripes.

"Better not let anyone see that," he said.

She placed the striped, warm egg in his hands. "You're carrying a king's concerns. You should eat a king's meal. Anyone can see you're discouraged."

"Me? Brev, I'm not the one who lost—"

"And don't waste more time on me. This world's grown dangerous for hearts that care too much. You'll break. And then where will we be? Two ruined people. In a ruined house." Her eyes, a crystalline blue, would not meet his. The lines around them had deepened since the departure. "If Calraven's right, if there is something that watches us, then why..."

He wanted to put his arms around her, give her a safe place to crumble. Instead, he held the egg as she walked away through the golden rays.

Warney awoke and found his head on Krawg's shoulder. Alarmed, he sat up.

Riders. I heard riders in the night.

Krawg made a sound like a boiling pot of stew and kept on sleeping. His face was wet with sweat, and Warney breathed a sigh of relief. "Fever's broken. Chillseed worked. You'll be back to perfect soon."

They rested against a bank of moss that might have been a fallen tree. The blackened remains of last night's smokeless fire crackled and coughed. Bowlder had roasted gorrels on both nights since they left Mawrnash, and they had all become miserable on this diet of unchewable and tasteless meat.

Day seven since Barnashum, he thought. *We're halfway home. Well, the caves aren't home exactly, but they're the next best thing. It's quiet as a dead man's drum. Where is everybody?* He sat up.

Bowlder crouched at the foot of one of the vawns, trying to raise it so he could pluck out a thorn that had set the steed to grumbling. Refusing to budge, the animal stared, dull eyed and drowsy, at the soldier.

"Where's Jes-hawk?" Warney asked.

The brooding soldier gestured to the vawns, of which there were only three.

"Did ya hear them riders last night?"

Bowlder nodded. He was tickling the vawn's toes with a feather now, hoping to get a reaction.

"Is that what Jes-hawk's gone to check out?"

The soldier shrugged.

"Seven days in unfamiliar lands, and the only signs of beastmen we've seen are a few filthy arrows. No prey, no beastmen, I s'pose."

Bowlder, digging his fingers into the soil beneath the vawn's foot, stood up and strained, growling and cursing. At last the vawn bent its leg at the knee, exposing the bottom of its scaly foot. Warney dashed to Bowlder's side, squatted down, and scowled. "A whole stickery branch is stuck deep here." He nimbly pinched the strand between its thorns and jerked it free. As he did, the vawn kicked and sent Bowlder staggering backward, a wind gusting through his nose. When he fell, his head hit the earth with a thump. Warney tossed the thorn branch aside and ran to kneel by the unconscious, mountainous man.

The vawn lifted its foot and snuffled at the open wound, whimpering.

"Things just keep gettin' worse," Warney fussed. "The king's disappeared. Krawg's sick. Bowlder's hurt. And now I'm the only one awake in this camp. What'll go wrong next, I wonder?"

The vawn sighed, feeling some relief. Then, before Warney could cry out, it set its foot back down squarely on that very same bramble. Its eyes bulged, it flung its head back, and it shrieked and stamped in a fury.

That was the moment Jes-hawk came dashing through the trees to the camp. "They're in the forest!" he shouted.

"Who?" Warney backed toward Krawg. "Beastmen?"

"No! I think it might be the..." Jes-hawk stopped, stunned at the sight of Bowlder's sprawled body. "Is he still asleep?"

"Rather," said Warney.

"And where's Lynna?"

Warney blinked. "I thought she was with you."

Jes-hawk turned as white as the ash of the firepit. "I told her to watch the camp. Riders passed right by us last night." He ran to the animals, which grumbled nervously. "Where's the king's vawn?"

"Gone," groaned Bowlder, sitting up slowly and clutching his chest. "Gone. With Lynna. And all her belongings. Gone before I woke up."

Jes-hawk stared about as if he would run in every direction at once. "How? Were we raided?"

"You know we weren't." Bowlder tried to get to his feet, thought better of it, and lay down again.

"Why would she leave?" Jes-hawk hustled about the clearing, studying the leaves and grasses. "For two days we've been talking about Barnashum and Cal-raven, and she's been full of questions." He dashed a few steps into the trees, listening, his eyes scanning the ground. "She was so excited about seeing everybody again."

Bowlder shrugged. "She's a Bel Amican now. Of course she went back."

Jes-hawk looked likely to attack the soldier in a fury, but Krawg surprised him by speaking while his eyes were still closed. "Will you track her?"

"I learned to track by playing Seek and Go Hiding with Lynna when we were children." Jes-hawk began to untie his vawn. "I learned to track, but Lynna learned to hide. If she's decided to go back, I doubt we'll catch up with her." All of a sudden he unsheathed his sword and swung it hard against a tree, slicing halfway through the trunk.

Warney crouched down and helped Krawg sit up. "Glad to see you're up again. If you'd gone and died on me, I'd have given you a beating you'd never forget."

Bowlder bound back his long black hair into a tail, strapped his sword belt back on, and draped his woodscloak around him. "So...who were the riders?"

Jes-hawk slumped to the ground. "I didn't see anything of the riders but their wide, trampled path. I did see something else—a great company in the woods about a day's ride between us and Barnashum." He shook his head. "I hardly believe it myself, but it appears our return journey's been cut in half."

"How?" asked Warney.

Bowlder scratched his head.

"Something's happened. And it can't be good. Abascar's coming to us. On foot."

What did the Keeper look like in your dream?

It was Madi's question, and her two sisters thought it over as they lay silently, the crowns of their heads almost touching, their toes pointing toward the brightening sky, their legs swaying like cloudgrasper trees.

It was the seventh morning of the march. The travelers were rising from their blankets and grumbling about the hard work of finding anything more than fruit for breakfast.

In my dream, answered Luci, *the Keeper had a neck like a tree, with bark for skin and moss for hair. Its body was so big that if it stood over you, it would protect you from a storm.*

That's not what I saw, said Margi. *I saw something come out of the sea. Like a dragon, it pulled itself onto the shore. Its wings had scales. Its head was like a horse's head, just like what Cal-raven sculpted.*

I'm hungry, Madi mused.

Which of us is right, do you think? asked Margi. She held up her hands, weaving her fingers together in contortions, trying to make the outline of the creature she had seen. *The Keeper can't be all those things.*

Oh yes it can, Luci thought. *It can change. Who's to say what powers it has?*

I'm not just hungry, thought Madi. *I'm thirsty.*

Isn't it strange? Luci was wondering. *We all dreamed of it at the same time. That hasn't happened since we were kids.*

We are kids, thought Madi.

"Maybe it was here!" Luci got to her feet, leaf fragments clinging to her arms so they seemed like feathers to complete her owl costume. "Maybe it's playing a game of Seek and Go Hiding. Let's go look for it."

"She just wants to go looking for Wynn," muttered Margi. "She keeps hoping he'll catch up with us. But he won't. It's been days." But she got up anyway and followed her sister, her fluffy cat tail hanging from her belt and dragging along the ground. Madi stopped to put on her rabbit-ear hat, then hopped along behind.

They scampered through the grumbling crowd, singing out the Gatherers' names as the ragged harvesters carried nets and baskets into the brush.

They tried to ignore Brevolo when they saw her, for her sadness frightened them.

And then they were out across the damp ground of the woods.

Madi noted that there were plums and pears and hard-shell applenuts all over the ground. "Fruit's falling early," she said, plucking a plum from the ground. "Ugh. It's fine on one side, rotten on the other."

"Leave the fruit," said Margi, and her painted whiskers twitched as she wrinkled her nose. *If the Keeper's hiding, we'll have to look for clues.*

They followed a path that wound through an old, disordered orchard. The ground sloped downward sharply, and soon they found that the gully was thick with knee-deep grass, with the burdened fruit trees leaning out over them on both sides. They stopped and looked about.

What a very fine place to play, thought Luci. *The light in the trees. And I think there must be a stream up ahead.*

Something isn't right, thought Margi.

A large stone tumbled down the slope toward them, and Madi had to jump out of its path. It crashed against the opposite slope, then rolled back to settle in the creek bed. They looked at the stone. They looked back up the hill.

Maybe it's the Keeper, thought Luci. Margi squealed in excitement.

My ankle hurts. Madi grimaced as she sat down in the grass and pulled down her stocking. *I think I twisted it.*

"Maybe we're not following the Keeper," said Luci. "Maybe it's following us!"

"Let's draw it out into the open then," whispered Margi.

Madi felt a strange sensation, like terror and delight all at once. She got up to follow her sisters on a run up the creek bed, trying to ignore the flare of pain in her foot. The path led them around a bend, guiding them into a darker place where the gully narrowed and the boughs above them reached to interweave with those of the opposite bank, as if the trees were bracing against each other to keep from falling.

"Can't go any farther! Gotta stop!" Madi hopped on one foot, the fabric of her rabbit ears flouncing against her cheeks.

"Shh. Look."

In the dark, dense trees up ahead, a figure like a torn strip of the sunlight beckoned to them, then moved as if carried on a silent wind into the shadows.

Did you...

...see that?

Silence cloaked their fearful contemplation. And then they all spoke the word together.

"Northchild."

Where'd it go? Luci took a few steps forward.

What's that there? Margi pointed up the shadowbound slope ahead, far above where they'd seen the shimmering phantom. *A lamp's been lit in a window. Is that a Northchild cabin?*

They huddled closer together, bumping knees and elbows, Madi and Margi holding Luci's leaf-feathered sleeves to keep her from running uphill to investigate. The window's warm light wavered like the glow through the curtains of an inn on a winter night.

We should run, thought Margi. *I've heard that Northchildren tear people up, eat their insides, and then drag the bodies over the Forbidding Wall.*

Why would anybody build a fire indoors on a hot summer day? asked Madi.

Margi's answer was assured. *To roast the people they've captured.*

They're roasting Wynn, thought Luci. She broke free and began hurrying up the slope, quiet as an owl taking flight.

Margi padded after her on all fours, her feline tail swinging behind her.

Madi hissed in outrage, then slumped down to the ground. *I'm not going. Sheepskulls, both of you. I'm the oldest. I know best.* She unbound one of her sturdy toughweed slippers and flexed her foot, pressing all around the knobs of her ankles to see if anything felt wrong.

Voices, came Luci's clear and anxious thought. *Voices in the house. They're telling stories, I think.*

What's that language? asked Margi, suspicious. *It's not Common.*

It's beautiful, thought Luci. *Look. There's no fire. It's the Northchildren. They glow.*

Madi could no longer see her sisters. They had gone around behind the shack. Taking a stone the size of a bread loaf, she softened it with stonemastery and drew out handfuls, which she released so that they hardened into smaller stones—perfect for throwing in case anything approached her. *I should aim one at Luci's head,* she muttered. *Knock her wits back to where they belong.*

Luci, if you climb that stair, they'll hear you! said Margi.

Margi, come and see! They're reading to each other from scrolls written in fiery script. And then...

Their lights have gone out! They're hiding from us! Luci, what are you doing?

Madi looked up. The magic drained from her hands. She sat still as a suspended breath.

Luminous apparitions tiptoed in a line down the slope just ahead as if they were anxious to slip away, alarmed at having been discovered. They were tall and elegant like kings and queens, features veiled by shimmering shrouds. Some of them paused to glance in her direction. Then they moved on through the narrowing gully into the deep woods' shadows.

The sound of distant water came to Madi from the dense trees ahead. When it did, an urgent thirst brought her to her feet.

What a strange cabin, came Margi's thought. *They sat together, in a circle.*

Madi limped along the path, slowly at first. But as she came to a place where the trees had descended the slopes and now embraced each other in the soft earth of the creek bed, she lost sight of the last shining phantom.

She stepped into the trees.

Madi, are you coming up?

I cannot climb, she answered back. She tried to stop thinking about the apparitions. If her sisters sensed what she had seen or what she was doing, they'd come charging down the slope, and she would never find the North-children.

She pushed through thick ferns, trying to focus. It was colder here. The sound was louder now, and she was almost certain she could smell a creek.

A circle of light appeared, a glow from within a ring of stones. *A well,* she thought.

The light began to fade.

They've gone into the well.

What's that? came Luci's eager inquiry. *You've found them? They have a well?*

If it hadn't been for small, twinkling blue flowers coiling from between the wellstones on green stems, Madi might have passed right by this place. *I'm thirsty,* she thought.

Horses? came Margi's urgent question. *Luci, do you hear horses?*

Is Tabor Jan coming after us? Are we in trouble?

They told us not to stray out of sight!

The horses are coming from the other direction.

Luci! Hide! They're not from Abascar!

Madi? Where are you, Madi?

Madi couldn't move. She could see the riders now in the dark trees up the western slope.

Luci, get in this closet! Quick!

They're on the stairs! Margi, they're coming inside!

A storm of turmoil—her sisters' panic and dismay—filled Madi's head. They'd been discovered. They'd been seized by strangers, who were dragging them from the house.

Run! came the urgent, harmonious message.

A man on horseback wandered down through the trees toward the well.

Madi leaned her head over the open mouth of the well, her rabbit ears flopping in front of her. She found a rope bound there to an iron ring. Far, far below she saw faint flickers of light, like candles in a heavy wind, and she heard water rushing as powerfully as a river.

"You there!" The shout was harsh and commanding as hoofbeats quickened through the trees.

Madi climbed onto the stones and sat with her feet dangling inside, then pushed off, grabbing hold of the rope and trying to let herself down. But the rope was damp and slippery. It began to slide through her hands. Looking up, she saw a torch over the well's mouth, and then her pursuer leaned in to reach for her. She quit fighting the rope and let herself slide farther down, trying to evade his reach.

But the rope had been severed, and its frayed end passed through her hands. She fell.

"Madilyn!" Luci cried out as the soldier carrying her mounted his horse.

I can't feel her! Margi's thoughts were shouts.

Dizzy and sick, the girls leaned forward, holding the horses' manes with their left hands, clutching at their hearts with their right. The horses, the shouts of the men in their bristling vests, and the barbed throwing spears in the riders' hands were all so alarming that the two girls had no time to make sense of it before the riders joined a large troop riding in a circle around the perimeter of the Abascar camp.

The sisters saw the people crowding in together, shouting in a defiant hubbub. Abascar's archers were down on their knees, arrows notched to bows and trained upon the moving circle.

Then a massive rider in a sweeping cape and wooden mask dragged both girls from their horses and pushed them into a run, advancing swiftly behind them.

As Luci and Margi were welcomed into the crowd, the man behind them roared, "People of Abascar, put away your fears." It was a boastful and commanding voice, sharp as a sneer. "You look as if you're being attacked. In truth, we're carrying heavy arms to defend you. We're your saviors."

Tabor Jan stepped from the crowd, sword unsheathed. "We summoned no rescuers. Leave us. This forest is not the property of any house."

"Things change," snapped the voice behind the mask. "Everyone knows that the house of King Cal-marcus fell to pieces. Surely we can't leave the forest to the beastmen. And the philosophers of Jenta? They hide in the desert. The forest is not their concern." He spread his arms as if presenting the whole world to the travelers. "House Bel Amica accepts what the Expanse has offered them. We're expanding our territories." He advanced toward Tabor Jan. "We'll show patience with ignorant trespassers. But, yes, you do need permission to pass through this—"

"House Abascar survives," said Tabor Jan. "We have not entered into any bargain with Bel Amica about changing borders. We move through open country on the orders of our king."

"Your king?" The challenger looked about. "Should I not speak with him?"

After an uncomfortable hush, Tabor Jan said, "King Cal-raven has gone on ahead."

"Oh, I'm sure he has. Until he returns—and let's pretend, for a moment, that he will—let me treat you as guests and escort you to House Bel Amica for shelter, hot meals, and soft beds."

An elated cry burst from someone in the Abascar assembly.

"Ah." He pointed to his wide-eyed audience. "Perhaps some of you have some sense after all. While you rest, Queen Thesera's advisors will offer just the guidance you need to determine Abascar's future."

"We are not interested in listening to the Seers," Tabor Jan seethed. "Nor will we take one step toward House Bel Amica unless our king directs us to do so. His party will return shortly."

"His party? Would they by any chance resemble these?" The challenger snapped his fingers.

The circle broke, allowing four more riders through. Before each one of them was seated a bound and bag-hooded figure.

"A few nights ago," said the man, "these trespassers slept in the Bel Amican way station at Mawrnash under false pretenses. They informed us that they had broken away from Abascar and had no intention of returning."

Shanyn emerged from the crowd, panic in her face, but Tabor Jan waved her back.

The man, whose stature resembled that of a powerful beastman, strode to one of the riders, reached up, and seized the bag over a prisoner's head. It came free, revealing a bruised, bloodied face.

Jes-hawk! thought Margi.

"I'm told there was a fifth member of their party," the challenger mused. "They claim he is out there on his own." He made a clicking sound with his tongue and then withdrew his mask. A wild, ragged mane, striped white and black, fell about his shoulders, framing a face patched with white bandages that concealed all but his flaring red eyes and his bearded jaw. "It's possible your king has been abducted by mercenaries or killed by the Cent Regus.

Perhaps something surprised him. Have you heard of the menace that lurks in the ground?"

Blinking through the swollen bruises, Jes-hawk looked around, amazed. Then his face contorted with rage. He looked back to the circle of riders. "Where's Lynna?" he roared, blood and spittle spewing from his lips. "Where's my sister? Let me see that wretched traitor so I can—"

The giant knocked him to the ground as easily as a bear cuffing his prey. Jes-hawk lay silent in the dirt. Shanyn started forward again, but Tabor Jan seized her and held her back.

The challenger bowed. "Forgive me. I've forgotten my manners. I am Captain Ryllion." And with the same hand that had struck down Jes-hawk, he reached out and clasped Tabor Jan's hand.

Margi could see Abascar's captain wince at the force of that grip. "Soon you and your people will forget all about the troubles of the past." Ryllion grinned, and both sisters felt a chill at the sight of those beastly yellow teeth. "And eventually you'll agree," he said, "that this was a great day for Abascar."

15

SNYDE'S FALL

And that's what happens!" Snyde barked, spinning the vawn on its heels so he could address any vengeful pursuers. "That's what happens when you try to put down Snyde ker Bayrast!"

He was riding back to Barnashum. He had considered taking his chances in Bel Amica, but the thought of starting over—unknown, without leverage or authority—changed his mind. Some of Abascar's survivors still valued the words of King Cal-marcus's aging ambassadors. He might reassemble his sympathizers there. So after stealing back his vawn from the Abascar company at Mawrnash, he had taken to the woods.

For a few days he saw nothing more interesting than trees and passing rainstorms. Nevertheless, he sensed someone—or something—following him.

He tried to cheer himself by remembering Cal-raven's startlement and the blow that had struck him down. Now, with the king out of the way, Snyde could make House Abascar listen to him again. He had followed King Cal-marcus's instructions with excruciating attention for so many years. That was how he had been taught, this son of the famous Bayrast ker Boon. He could bring back the old law and sweep the filth—all those Gatherers and insubordinates—out of his sight.

After Cal-raven's company had abandoned him in the forest, Snyde had staggered southward, fearful of Cent Regus savages. To his surprise, when an ambush came, his attackers weren't beastmen but bandits. Finding no currency, the robbers threatened to leave him there, bound, unless he told them something useful.

Whole and beautiful, the idea had bloomed. He'd told his assailants he could show them a soldier carrying treasure from a fallen house. They'd find a fancy farglass and a sword of the finest Abascar craftsmanship. He also promised them money but refused to tell them he had concealed it in his vawn's saddlebag for safekeeping.

The bandits agreed to follow him with a promise of punishment if his claim proved false. He convinced them that their target was dangerous. "Kill him first, then take what he can give you. He'll track you down if he survives." They boasted that their crimes were precise and clean.

Snyde liked that turn of phrase. Cleanliness was important to him.

"I have to get back indoors," he now told the vawn after a tailtwitcher scolded them from a nearby tree. "Away from all this disorderly nature."

As if it had heard him, a structure revealed itself through the gloaming— a hunter's hut like the kind that had once sheltered him and his father during hunts. This was not House Abascar's territory, nor did it belong to House Bel Amica, but the houses had negotiated some shared shelters in the neutral ground of unclaimed wilderness. This was one of those crude wooden boxes, long neglected.

The idea of setting foot in such a derelict structure annoyed him, but his exhaustion overpowered his distaste for dust, moss, and rot.

Snyde climbed down from the vawn and paused to brush the creature's shed scales from his trousers. He hated the hard work of steering these filthy reptiles. No matter how hard he whipped this animal, it stumbled, swayed, brushed against trees, and would not follow instructions.

Examining his hands, he found that he had dirt beneath a thumbnail, and he began to carve at it with the edge of his pocketknife. When he couldn't scrape the darkness out, he cursed and bit into it, tearing off the soiled edge. Better not to have nails at all than to be found with soiled edges.

"Never let them catch you unpolished," he said, mimicking his mother's shrill command.

Inside the hut Snyde found a table, a few dishes dusty with the remains of dead insects, and a decent clay goblet that contained the ghost of something sweet.

A quick inventory of the cupboards turned up only an abandoned tailtwitcher nest. But Snyde was never content with a quick inventory. He searched the cupboards again and tapped on their wooden frames, certain that somebody had concealed something here. It was just the way people behaved. He had learned this from a lifetime of careful observation and rigorous recordkeeping when it came to others' failings, crimes, and indiscretions.

An aggressive attention to propriety—it was what he had inherited from his father.

Whenever Bayrast ker Boon passed through a crowd, people sprang to attention and bowed. The troop commander had intimidated his soldiers into extravagant respect and precision so that they snapped into salutes as sharply as puppets on tight strings. He had improved his son in the same way.

In the privacy of his room, recovering from his father's beatings, Snyde would carve the names of everyone he knew into the wooden frame of his cot and then make a mark to represent every offense, every indiscretion. He became a resourceful spy and relished the sharp impact of justice, especially upon those who had mocked or annoyed him. He enjoyed the moment a transgressor realized that judgment was inescapable. He savored the work of ensnaring young women who had rejected him, catching them in some kind of gossip. And he learned how to draw attention to certain laws at certain times, to show he was on the respectable side of a very stark line.

Wherever Snyde went, he found that almost everyone else was wicked by comparison.

"What's your secret, filthy old house?" he muttered, kicking at the walls and floors and listening for a hollow note. He stared at the stones beneath the table. A small puffdragon was peering out between two of them.

Puffdragons were rare vermin—squirmy little lizards without arms or legs, and when their yellow tongues flicked into the air, sparks burst forth. Some travelers kept them caged for the purpose of lighting campfires or torches in the wild, but most avoided them because of the stink that lingered after each puff. If a puffdragon wriggled its slender green ribbon of a body into walls or under a house and stayed for more than a few days, the house would absorb an indelible stench—that is, if the monster didn't accidentally burn it down first.

"So," he said, "how deep is your burrow, little lizard?" He reached forward, then drew back, remembering that the brown bristles of its spiny head were not thick hairs but sharp, barbed needles. He rattled the tabletop, which turned out to be a heavy, loose disc of wood propped precariously on the crooked pile. The lizard shot out of its den with a complaint that sounded like a drunkard's fit of hiccups, punctuating its passage with putrid smoke— a line of dark and dissipating clouds—as it escaped.

Snyde knelt down and pulled one of the stones free. Reaching in, he drew out a dusty brown bottle. A cork still tightly sealed it. He held it aloft as a trophy. "This rare bottle of Abascar brew goes to Ambassador Snyde ker Bayrast."

One night Bayrast had come home furious. King Har-baron had promoted his own son, Cal-marcus, to serve as the new captain of the guard. Bayrast felt the position was owed to him.

To Snyde's sharp sense of fairness, this was unfortunate but entirely acceptable and lawful, for King Har-baron could appoint whom he liked. But his father surprised him with the ferocity of his displeasure.

In the morning he found his mother spreading cream over bruises on her face. Looking at him sternly, she had said, "Never let them catch you unpolished."

Snyde wished she had taken him with her when she vanished later that same day.

No one organized a search. People gave each other troubled, silent glances when his mother's name came up among the Housefolk.

And then one night his father came home carrying a fur merchant's hat. He hid his bright green prize under his bed mat, never saying a word about how he had acquired it. The one time Snyde asked, his father said only, "I straightened out something gone crooked."

Snyde later heard the news that someone had found a fur merchant beheaded in the forest and a woman bludgeoned to death at his side.

Snyde began to watch his father closely, newly aware that the man could, in fact, transgress. And one evening he followed as the bitter commander crept to the bedroom window of a soldier named Ark-robin, who had just married a beautiful young woman—Say-ressa.

An idea struck Snyde as clearly as a hammer strikes a bell. He lay resonating all through the night, plotting what he would do.

Ark-robin found an anonymous note on his doorstep in the morning. It exposed Bayrast's transgression. The very next night Ark-robin set a trap with the help of Prince Cal-marcus, and in the morning King Har-baron stripped Bayrast of his medals and sentenced him to hard labor outside the walls.

Snyde had come forward, admitting that he had exposed his father. He won King Har-baron's favor and was appointed as a royal informer, a surveillance officer among the people.

Bayrast lived among the Gatherers for a short time and then vanished.

Meanwhile, Snyde's resourcefulness earned him a position directing Abascar's artists. It kept him moving throughout the house so he could spy on the behavior of others without drawing much attention to himself.

During Cal-marcus's reign, Snyde had been so highly favored that Ark-robin's young daughter, Stricia, often asked him for advice on how to win Prince Cal-raven's hand in marriage. He had made Stricia something of a project, for he greatly enjoyed the way she bowed and called him master. Such a pretty girl. Such soft hands.

He put the bottle on the table. "What man with any brain could have rejected her? She should have been mine." He had never touched strong drink and had often boasted of that very thing. But he was very thirsty. Perhaps it was only juice.

He took out a knife and dug at the cork. The cork crumbled and fell into the drink. He cursed, poured some of the crumb-cluttered liquid into his hand, and sniffed its sweet perfume. "Honey." He tested it with the tip of his tongue. Indeed, it was sweet, and it tingled in his throat.

He poured it into the cleanest vessel he could find. But the bowl was cracked, and honeywine began to seep onto the table. So he gulped down all that remained in eager, noisy swallows.

"How," he roared through a burning throat, "can anyone say they enjoy such stuff?"

A few minutes later he was throwing more branches onto a fire and singing at the top of his lungs, forgetting all fears of beastmen. He was happy—excitedly so.

He danced in front of the fire, singing one of the exaltations to King

Cal-marcus. But he did not get far before he went down on his knees to weep for the loss of the king he had so dutifully adored and, even more, for the loss of his privileges.

A great wind rushed through the house. The gust swept soot out of the fireplace, spreading it across the floor, even as it carried a swirl of sparks out the window into a night that had crept up while he wasn't paying attention.

"Sorry, mother!" he exclaimed. "I'll clean it up! Go back to bed!"

As he stared out into the darkness of the moaning trees, he heard a moon-hound howl somewhere, a hungry and lonely sound. He shuddered. *The wilderness is a horror! The heavens declare chaos.*

He had a sudden vision of Cal-raven surrounding the hut with an armed host.

Look what the drink has done to me. That wretched hunter, leaving it here to tempt a thirsty traveler.

The vawn outside shrieked in sudden distress, and Snyde sprang again to the window. "No."

He took a brand from the fire and ventured out. "Thieves, I'll burn you!" he roared. "Wolves? I'll set your fur on fire!"

The vawn was untouched but afraid, raking the ground with its hind feet as if it would dig a hole and hide itself.

Snyde walked a circle around the reptile and the tree where it was anchored. Then he walked a wider circle but found nothing.

Crossing the space between the vawn and the hunter's hut, he halted abruptly and gasped. He had almost stumbled into a deep and strangely shaped cavity.

"That," he mused, "is one big footprint." He glanced about at the shadows. He pressed his forearm against his mouth to silence his voice. *I will not entertain any thoughts of mythological creatures. The world is what has been proved.*

He heard a sound like branches breaking, sensed a darkness descending.

Looking toward the hut, he watched its beams bend and break, the whole shelter collapsing under the weight of a winged colossus.

16

BROWN AND MOUSEY

The scar burned through Cal-raven's sleep. Like a hook caught tight around a bone, it dragged him up from the blur of half dreams into waking.

The air was thick with dust and honeyweed pipe smoke. Canvas-filtered sunlight inside the carriage felt warm against his skin. He'd been stripped to his leggings and boots and covered with a thistleleaf blanket. If he moved, he would learn just how badly he was broken.

Two women laughed coarsely outside the canvas. As the carriage tilted up a steep slope, he watched red bouldernuts tumble along the floorboards until they disappeared under the bench where he lay. He tried to lift his head and groaned.

"Shh."

A boy sat against the front of the canvas, knees drawn up to his chin, bound at the ankles. His wrists, too, were tied and pulled back behind his head where they were strapped to one of the struts that supported the canvas. He appeared to have been dipped in mud. "Are you actually awake?" he whispered.

"I told you," Cal-raven moaned, "not to come after me."

"I'm sorry," the boy whispered. "I came after you to warn you. Snyde's a traitor."

Cal-raven clenched his teeth, realization worsening his pain. "I know, Wynn. I knew all along."

"We're captives," the boy announced.

They were paid to kill me, he thought. *But they sold me instead. I've never been so grateful for the greed of wicked men.*

"How long have I slept?"

"Don't know. You were asleep when they picked you out of the hole. And we've been on the road two days since. Maybe three. Not sure. I can't stay awake either, not since they caught me. My horse got away." Wynn had the cleverjay figurine caught between his bare toes and was slowly turning it around and around. It must have fallen from the shreds of Cal-raven's jacket when his captors pulled it off of him.

If the birds saw what happened, maybe Scharr ben Fray will come. Or... At the thought of the Keeper, he raised his head, and the flare of pain knocked him flat.

"If you'd listened to me," Wynn muttered, "we wouldn't be here. I was gonna warn you about—"

"I knew already, Wynn. You can't just charge ahead, thinking you know better than everyone. You endanger us all."

Wynn went on as if Cal-raven had never spoken. "Grudgers. They were plotting against you in the caves. Six of 'em. But don't worry. I took care of five."

Cal-raven coughed into his hand and was alarmed to see spots of blood. "You'd better explain that."

"Found them plotting. They talked about Snyde. I sealed 'em into a cave and came to warn you."

"Sealed them in? How did you..." He stopped. "You didn't drag the girls into this, did you?"

Wynn's smile stayed, but his hands clenched into fists behind his head, and his gloves of dry mud cracked.

"I knew, Wynn. I was going to draw them out, away from the people, and reckon with them in the woods."

Wynn's face flushed red. "Well, you didn't."

"No. The earthquake came, and five of them disappeared." Cal-raven endured the pain to sit up. "What happened after you sealed them in?"

The boy frowned. "Don't know."

The wagon lurched to a stop. Cal-raven heard vawns snuffling in the brush and two women whispering. He heard branches snapping as the women walked away from the wagon; then their voices echoed into a deep space.

Another slave pit.

The voices quickly turned bitter and mean. The pit was, it seemed, empty, when they had apparently been expecting new captives to sell.

"Did you tell anyone that you'd captured the grudgers?" he continued. "Or that you were coming after me on a horse?"

Wynn shrugged.

"So, thinking you could save me from Snyde, you rode right into the slave traders' hands." He sighed. "And you probably told them you were following me."

"I didn't say your name!" he squealed a little too loudly.

Their captors' debate ended abruptly. One climbed through a flap in the canvas to land between the two prisoners, and she pinched Cal-raven's cheeks. "Ay, yummy. The pretty one's awake."

She was younger than he was and not unattractive. Above her freckled, fierce expression, a shock of short red hair jagged out about her head like a crown of autumn leaves, and her pointed chin was scarred with a scab. "You're gonna do as you're told, aren't you? Hate to have to bruise you any worse."

"I'm going to win you a fortune bigger than any you've imagined," he replied as the wagon began to move again.

She clapped her hands against his face. "That'll be sparky." She leaned in and kissed him hard on the lips. When she drew back, he glimpsed his own astonishment in Wynn's expression.

"Hmm." She licked her lips as if sampling wine. "A few lessons and you won't be bad at all." She wagged her finger at him. "Our little secret, redbraids. I gotta take what I can get when Brown's not looking."

"You're not going to sell us?"

"Eventually, sure as sap is sticky, we'll take coins for you." She pinched his nose, her hands frantic as tailtwitchers. She took a small clay pot out of her pocket and waved it in front of his throbbing nose. "Slumberseed oil. Breathe it in. You'll forget all about what hurts and sleep a few more days."

"Maybe I don't mind the pain."

"Ooooh, strong man! That's just sparky, 'cuz"—she fingered the claw marks on his face—"there's plenty more scars on the way."

"Can I try some?" asked Wynn.

"I've other potions," she went on, ignoring the boy. "They'll make you forget your heart's true favorite. Then you and I can stop wasting time and have some real fun. Time's short. We'll knock on Bel Amica's door in two days."

Cal-raven could not stifle his surprise.

"Yeah, Bel Amica. Seers'll buy you right out of our hands. I suspect you'll end up on an island somewhere." She picked at a jagged fingernail and watched her story sink in.

"And what if we don't play along?" Wynn sneered.

"They've got these sharp little tools that can carve a tongue right out." Wynn pressed his lips tight shut.

"Thesera knows about this?" Cal-raven's mind hastened to make sense of these revelations. "She consents to such slavery?"

"All she knows is that we catch trespassers and crooks so the Seers can punish them, teach them discipline, and train them up as resourceful laborers. She's happy to let the Seers take care of nasty business."

"The Seers must pay you handsomely," he said. "But I can do better."

"Redbraids is a bargainer," she groaned.

"Too bad," came the other's voice beyond the canvas. "Mousey, keep your hands off him. It's my turn for special company."

"The heiress herself invited me to Bel Amica." Cal-raven struggled to hold her narrowing gaze. "She wants to surprise the Seers."

"And what kind of surprise would you be?"

He thought fast. "The Seers keep watch over everything. It's hard to surprise them with any kind of honor. I'm a stonemaster." He nodded toward Wynn, who lifted up the tiny cleverjay sculpture with his toes. "Cyndere wants a statue for the Seers. But I have to arrive in secret, without any kind of fuss."

"What statue?"

"When you've helped me get inside, I promise I'll mention your names to Queen Thesera. But if Cyndere tells the queen that I've gone missing, there may be some investigation."

Mousey stuck her fingernail under his chin and tilted his head back. "How do I know you're a stonemaster?"

Wynn kicked the stone to Cal-raven's feet. Mousey put it in his hand. The cleverjay's harsh edges softened and melted.

Mousey backed away from him.

He lay calmly and said, "You're saving me days of travel by giving me this ride."

For a brief moment Mousey's eyes flashed in desperate hope. But then the driver's mocking laughter sounded outside. "Liar." Mousey opened the pot, and a sharp, bitter vapor washed across Cal-raven's face, clouding his thoughts.

"No!" Wynn cried. "Don't! He's not what you—"

"Wynn!" Cal-raven shouted. "Not another word, or I'll ask them to throw you out the back."

"How did you plan to get into Bel Amica?" Mousey asked.

Cal-raven took a deep breath. *Cyndere warned me not to trust anyone else.* "A token. I'm to send it to her through a Bel Amican guard."

"What token?"

"I have yet to sculpt it."

Mousey looked at Cal-raven's hands. "Melted that rock like it was cheese on a hot pan." She scratched the scab on her chin. "You hearing this, Brown? This bloody fellow's a friend of the heiress." He could see the ovens burning hot within her mind. She was beautiful and feisty, just the way his father had described his mother when he spoke of finding her—an orphaned merchant girl in the wilderness.

Mousey leaned in and stroked his hand. "You know," she whispered so Brown wouldn't hear, "if what you're saying is true, I could be a friend to you in Bel Amica. Help you get settled. I've always wanted a room of my own with a view of the sea."

"Tempting," he whispered back. And for a moment it was. "Consider this a promise." He took a shred of the softened stone and sculpted a ring around her finger.

"Sparky!" she gasped. He watched a shudder ripple from her shoulders to her fingertips. "I knew you were good news when we pulled you out of that pit."

"Mousey!" Brown was upset. "Put out that fire. He's mine."

"I'm just puttin' him back to sleep!" Giddy with conspiracy, Mousey pressed her small round nose to Cal-raven's. She smelled like a summer pear. "Believe me, if you're lying, I'm gonna ask if I can be there when they hurt you." She had freckles—countless flecks of freckles fanning out across her cheeks. He was so distracted by them that he didn't see her raise the clay pot.

You fool. Remember what happened last time you let yourself be seduced by a stranger. It was his last thought before the wave of slumberseed perfume plunged him back to sleep.

Two days and several empty slave pits later, they gave up the wagon for a rowboat. As if caught and reeled in by some far-off fisherman, the boat was drawn from the stream into the Rushtide Inlet, that great spearhead of water where five tributaries joined in a rush out to the Mystery Sea.

In the middle of that bay, a family of islands was bound by sweeping arcs of stone to one tremendous, central hive—the rock of House Bel Amica. From his seat on the floor of the boat, Cal-raven could see it all come into view.

"It's a whole 'nother world," said Wynn. "It's like we're being pulled into a dragon's jaws."

Mousey grinned so broadly that she revealed several missing teeth. "You're not the first to see it that way."

"The story of the stranded dragon." Cal-raven opened his tied hands as if presenting the story. "I heard it as a child."

While Wynn looked concerned, eying the city on the rock with suspicion, Mousey rubbed her hands together, clearly eager to tell the story. And she did.

In an age long since past, she said, an enormous oceandragon traversed the Mystery Sea. Eventually the dragon became bored with its limitations. Skydragons could fly wherever they wished, and earthdragons could swim if necessary, but oceandragons could neither fly nor walk.

One season the oceandragon decided it was tired of borders. So it ventured eastward until it encountered the edge of the great continent of the

Expanse. In frustration, the dragon refused to turn and take the necessary route around this mass of land. Instead, it tried to push the continent out of its path.

Other dragons tried to talk sense into the oceandragon's tiny mind. But the stubborn creature insisted, too proud to give up, until it eventually expired, leaving only this dent in the coastline—which came to be known as the Rushtide Inlet. Eventually the sea claimed the oceandragon's body. But its great skull remained there, rising from the waters in the cleft of the inlet as a lesson: heed your elders.

"No, no, no," said Brown, whose tight black garments, black hair, and white-painted face contradicted her name. "That's not the story's lesson. The dragon's skull is to remind us that we should never set out on a mission we cannot complete."

"When my teacher told me the tale," said Cal-raven, "he came to a different conclusion. Impatience can blind you. If you don't stop to consider all paths, you'll get stuck in the wrong one."

"Whatever the lesson," said Mousey, "the story's meant to explain the shape and place of the rock that's home to Bel Amica. In truth, it's bigger than the skulls of a thousand oceandragons put together."

Whether for Wynn's benefit or just to hear herself talk, Mousey went on to explain that Bel Amica had filled the rock's vast cavities with homes, markets, temples, and galleries. She pointed out the palace towers and immense, flag-decorated domes. She identified residences, outbuildings, and platforms anchored like barnacles all over the rugged surface. Walls spanned sections of the rock, she explained, so watchmen could monitor the harbor, the mainland, and the sea. As she spoke, a silver cargo train descended around the rock on a spiraling track.

Cal-raven grew distracted, losing himself in memories as he studied the crisscrossing avenues that ran in tangles all around that stone foundation like the wire of a Bel Amican beastman trap. The streets were lined with sculptures of eagles and oceandragons. Massive seashells served as canopies for great halls and chambers, gleaming white in the sun, and when the wind whirled around the rock, they sang in sonorous tones. Gardens and orchards in green and gold burst from jutting promontories. Flags flapped in the hard wind, streaming ribbons of colors.

This is what drove my mother to covet. And she could not have it, so she punished us all.

Clouds of birds swarmed about the scene, now swelling like a puff of smoke, now shredding and streaming like webs on the wind. They rose from shipyards along the inlet banks to engulf the bridges, besiege the tall towers and the slender spans that connected them, and then spread themselves across the broad flats of the rock to Bel Amica's marketplaces and craftyards.

"It's like twenty Abascars, isn't it?" Wynn whispered.

"And we're seeing only the shell of it."

Brown scowled while Mousey leaned out over the prow of the boat.

"My pa told me how they got rich," Wynn continued. "He said they learned to build ships, which they sailed until they found islands. And the islands are all covered with good stuff."

"That's part of the story." Cal-raven shook his head as Brown's oars brought them into the shadow of the foundation. "Incredible. Everything I might've recognized has been replaced."

"There's an old Bel Amican joke," said Brown. "If ya don't like the view here, wait a few minutes." Her eyes interrogated Cal-raven, testing him for a lie. "Your accent says Abascar, but you've got memories of this place."

"Long story."

"If we're going to find a way to get you inside, we'll have to do some fast talking. What do we call you?"

"Marcuson."

From the "mouth" of that skull-like rock, a long floating bridge ran to the mainland. This was Bel Amica's primary entrance, the path to the front gate. But other bridges sprouted out like whiskers from the base of the rock, leading to complex wooden walkways and mazes filled with boats that covered the inlet like lily pads.

Brown drew the boat through the maze toward the harbor caves in the base of the rock. The stone here was rugged, and creatures of many colors and many legs clung to it, some ogling the boats with beady eyes on the end of wavering stalks. The hulls of larger boats loomed over them.

"Ey! Ey! Bring it in!" A grey-haired guard in a green uniform gestured to them from the end of a dock's wooden span.

Brown, who looked more like Mousey's burly brother than a sister, turned the boat, her muscled arms bulging as she drew them alongside. Mousey leapt from the boat and saluted the guard. During her hasty whispers, the man squinted at Wynn and Cal-raven as if sizing up muskgrazers for slaughter.

"Ey then, ey there," he said in a voice burnt out from smoking. "She says you've a token for the heiress."

"It's for Cyndere's eyes only." Cal-raven wished he could stand without help. "She invited me and told me to alert her directly."

"How did she expect you to manage that, ey then?"

He shrugged. "Her invitation was too short for details."

"Show me this token."

Brown sighed, kneeling to unbind Cal-raven's feet and hands. "Jump in the water," she said, "and you'll feel my dagger between your shoulders."

She helped him to his feet, and he grimaced at the sharp reports from his bruised knees and his battered arms. Leaning on her shoulder like a drunkard against a friend, he said, "You'll be glad you trusted me."

As she held him up before the guard, the man assessed him with an icy squint. "Ey then, mystery visitor. I'm Henryk. You're lucky it's me you're facing. I've brought in surprise visitors for Cyndere before." He glanced out to the open water as if he half expected to see someone swimming toward him.

Mousey shifted her feet, cleared her throat.

"Anyway," said Henryk, "I've known the heiress since she was the age of this boy. So I will relay your message on my own two feet." With a guffaw he added, "If I can remember it when I get there, that is. So give me a name. Give it to me twice."

"Name's Marcuson," said Cal-raven. Then after an awkward pause, "Marcuson." He reached out his shackled hands and offered a small sculpture.

That small, detailed figurine was the best representation he could manage with his wrists bound. If Cyndere had indeed sent this beastman, she would recognize the wild mane, the sharp pointed ears, the leonine lines of the messenger's face. And if there was any doubt after that, he'd etched the Abascar rune for royalty in its base.

Henryk lifted it to the lamplight. "Ey, boyo. This reminds me of something. Why is it familiar?" He wrinkled his nose and squinted at Cal-raven. "What did you call yourself again?"

"Marcuson."

"Boiled crolca," Mousey whispered. "Your life's on the edge, and you send the queen's daughter something to remind her of the monsters that killed her husband. If Cyndere burns up, the trouble's all on you, Marcuson."

Henryk looked again at Cal-raven for a long, silent moment. Two officers approached from the harbor cave, baring bad teeth as if threatening to bite him.

"Take the boy to a holding cell," Henryk told them absently. "This one I'll lock up myself."

"He promised us we'd be rewarded," Brown barked, standing up and lifting an oar as if she might paddle them all. Meanwhile, Mousey got into the boat and lifted Wynn up to the two snarling officers, who seized him by the arms.

"I'll see to your payment when I return." Henryk turned from Brown to Cal-raven and held up his hand in caution. "Step carefully, ey, boyo? Don't want to spoil your surprise. I'll escort you to your quarters." He pushed Cal-raven forward up the stair, following the guards who were buffeting Wynn with questions.

"Don't worry!" Cal-raven heard the boy shout. "I'll get us out of this!"

Then, with jarring abruptness, Henryk steered Cal-raven through a crevasse in the wall so narrow that they had to turn sideways to slip through. "Keep moving," Henryk whispered.

Stepping through a curtain, they entered a zigzagging corridor.

"Your room is at the end."

Twenty corners later, having passed many sealed doors, Cal-raven stumbled into a small chamber with a stone bench, a barred window, and nothing more. When Henryk let go, he found he could not stand on his own, and he landed like laundry below the window.

"Wait here. As long as it takes. If you leave, I can't protect you anymore."

"Leave?"

"Don't toy with me, ey, boyo? I know what you can do." He lifted the statue and gave Cal-raven a nod of assurance. "My memory may be feeble, but I have this to remind me of my task. Just stay put and enjoy the view. I'm off to speak with the heir."

"Heir?" Cal-raven shouted, confused. "No! It's for the heiress!"

But the heavy stone gate was already sliding shut.

He would not walk through it again for days.

17

BAURIS AT THE WINDOW

This is my favorite part."

Bauris did not see the spoon that Emeriene held up to his chin. The sunbeams breaking through the convergence of midmorning storms seemed to please him; he blinked into the light like a satisfied house cat. He did not know that he had fragments of seaweed porridge clinging to his extravagant mustache.

"This is the part where she comes back."

Sisterly Emeriene drew the spoon back, stunned out of the half sleep of routine, and set it on the tray. She rose, stepped behind him, and rested her chin affectionately on his shoulder so she could share his view. "You spoke," she whispered, placing her hand on his bald pate.

Bauris wept joyously into any bright light these days. But he had not spoken a word since they brought him back to House Bel Amica. The old soldier had vanished from the Tilianpurth outpost the same day that the missing heiress had returned from her vanishment in the forest. A search had turned up nothing. Several days later a servant girl had found him crumpled at the bottom of an ancient, overgrown well in the woods and laughing. Laughing.

The old man, beloved like a favorite uncle of both Emeriene and the royal daughter she served, had treated them like amusing strangers since his ordeal. Emeriene had questioned him, provoking only a slight tremor of distress in his expression, never any kind of answer. Some of the healers decided that his fall into the forest well had knocked out his capacity for speech.

Bauris had been in Queen Thesera's service for many years and in his fractured state was treated with favor and tenderness. But he seemed to dwell somewhere else, where everything was bright and surprising. He often laughed out loud, even after they'd blown out the evening candles and left him to his dreams.

"Have you come back to us, Bauris? Do you remember?"

He nodded.

She returned to her chair beside him, lifted another spoonful. "What happened down there in the well? How did you stay alive so long?"

"It must have cost me. I...I've forgotten things."

"Your memories? You lost them in the well?"

"But she came back anyway," he whispered. He jabbed at Emeriene with his knobby elbow. Porridge dripped down his chin onto the napkin spread between the tray and his collar. "She's here."

"No, Cyndere's not here, Bauris. Archery practice this morning. And she had to go down to the shipyards. Those sailors thought they could buy the Abascars for slave labor. Fools, the lot of them."

He glanced at her directly. "This is my favorite part."

Emeriene dabbed his moustache and chin with the napkin. "The wind's dusted you again. That's what makes your eyes red, you know. There's more of the Mawrn in the air all the time." She sighed, gazing at the grit on her fingertips. "If only it really made wishes come true."

Bauris's tray rattled. A distant rumble grew louder.

"Look, Bauris. The train." The sisterly pointed down at a promontory that jutted out from Bel Amica's foundation and into the fog like the prow of a ship. The rust red arc of a train rail crossed that stony point, and the mist swirled as the engine arrived—a black swan gliding on a swift current, twin sails spread out behind like wings. A parade of wooden carts rattled along after the engine, containers piled high with newly harvested oilpods from the sea, purple and gleaming. They reminded Emeriene of the fish eggs King Helpryn had loved to slurp from a spoon or spread on cheese bread.

Bauris's eyes followed the blue line of Emeriene's sleeve to her hand and then finally turned toward the train. As it disappeared again into the fog on its circuitous, spiraling journey, he nodded like a schoolboy feigning interest in his studies, then raised his eyes to the skies again. He put his hand on the pile of parchment scraps on which he had sketched image after image of simple boats crowded with vague figures.

"The current," he insisted. "It draws them upstream."

Emeriene tapped her fingers on the edge of the tray. "Currents can't run upstream, Bauris."

He laughed with a warm fondness and tried to stand. "She's here," he announced.

"Cyndere? No, I told you. She's going down to the shipyards." She scooped up another spoonful of the porridge. "What's set you to talking?"

"Her father tried to talk her out of it." Bauris looked down. "But she wouldn't listen."

"You're dreaming, aren't you?" She rested her small hand on his scarred forearm. "I have to go down to the kitchens to prepare Cyndere's meal. But if you're going to keep talking, I should send someone who will listen."

His expression seemed to mirror her own pity. "They're not going to miss Cal-raven's big surprise. They're all going to be there."

She stood up. "Cal-raven! Didn't I tell you? Ryllion's messenger said that Cal-raven left those poor people of Abascar many days ago. Rode out on some kind of mission and never came back. Vanished. Just like his mother the queen."

Bauris pressed his lips tight together as if trying to hold on to a secret.

A knock drew her to the door. She walked unevenly, her left leg in its permanent toughweed cast, and paused before a mirror just inside the door to brush her dark hair back over her shoulders. Her hair had grown so long that she once again looked as she had before she'd married Cesylle and borne two boys. It felt good to remember life before Cesylle, before the loneliness of being forgotten.

When he returned, Cesylle wouldn't notice the length of her hair. He never noticed anything. She hadn't seen him in a long time, and he had committed their young sons to training down at the shipyards to become pilots of their own ships someday. The boys still had their baby teeth, but Cesylle had already trained them to strive for that dream and beg the moon-spirits to grant their wishes.

As she reached to answer the door, she saw that Cyndere had chalked a small bird on the lintel.

It opened, and a massive, muscular viscorcat burst into the room and padded right past her, whiskers sprung straight out from his face. "Blackpaw!" Emeriene exclaimed. "Come to see your best friend?" The cat trotted right to the window, ears sharp and high. As the soldier embraced the cat, Blackpaw's purr rumbled like the rail train passing.

"Wouldn't Deuneroi be glad to see that?" Cyndere stepped through the door and set her bow and quiver of arrows against the wall.

"My lady! I wasn't expecting you." Emeriene turned and gestured to the window. "You'll never believe it. Bauris spoke!" She took Cyndere's cape and hung it on a hook beside the mirror.

Cyndere looked down at Bauris. He did not look up.

Emeriene repeated the ramblings, and Cyndere shook her head. "Strange that he'd mention Cal-raven."

"Maybe he heard some gossip. Maybe he dreams about leading a search party."

The cat had set about bathing Bauris's face, and Emeriene remembered her duties. She took a dustbrush to the room's sparse furniture, sweeping white powder into a pan. "Are people still shouting at you?"

"They're afraid. Afraid we'll all suffer if we share some wealth with those poor survivors. But Mother is on my side. She remembers losing a husband. She wants to go to sea just to feel closer to my father. So she understands that it is my love for Deuneroi and his vision that drives me to serve House Abascar. She remembers that he died while trying to help them."

"But Ryllion... Isn't he trying to ship them off?"

"Ryllion's king of Bel Amica in his own mind. He thinks he should be able to do what he wants with Abascar's survivors. Have you heard him lately?"

"He speaks of nothing but the beastmen he's slaughtered. I heard he's showing buckets of teeth as trophies."

"I don't want to know how he managed to kill so many in such a short time. Part of me doesn't believe he could. Part of me is sick just to think it might be true. He's up to something." Cyndere leaned out the window as if to catch an eavesdropper. The fog teased her short, golden hair until she drew the curtain closed. "Thank you for dusting. We can't let the Seers hear us speaking of this."

Emeriene emptied the pan into a cloth bag and tightened the drawstring.

The door opened, and two sisterlies bustled in, carrying a tray piled with steaming hot towels. "Bauris!" Emeriene exclaimed, accepting the tray and dismissing the servants. "Murfee's on his way up to bathe you and take you for a walk."

Bauris's contented expression did not change.

"No matter how many times I tell them!" Emeriene set the tray on the table and picked up three small bowls of oil. "Don't they know you're too old-fashioned to bother with prayer lamps?" She handed the bowls to Cyndere, who drew the curtain open slightly and proceeded to cast the shells, one after the other, out the window. As Bauris laughed, delighted, they could hear the distant clatter of shells shattering on the rocks below.

"I miss the old traditions," said Cyndere, "the prayerfeathers we held as we thought of our ancestors crowded around, witnessing our lives. It felt good to ask them for their wisdom and to offer up things to them on the Memory Trees, to show them respect. I don't know if those beliefs were true. But I think they were closer. Closer than this…this obsession with wishing for our own success."

"You're not here to complain about the Seers." Emeriene slumped down in the chair beside the door.

"I need your help again, Em."

"Of course you do."

"I can't explain it all yet."

"You never do. But I'm your faithful fool. You know that. Did something happen down at the shipyard?"

"Not exactly."

"Dukas!" announced Bauris, looking intently at the viscorcat. "His name isn't Blackpaw. It's Dukas."

Cyndere looked at Emeriene. The sisterly shrugged. "No idea. Go on."

"Down at the shipyards," Cyndere continued, "I explained that nobody's hauling any Abascars off to the islands. Their future lies with the council. And this morning I got the vote that I wanted."

"You can govern the Abascars?"

"No, that's not what I want. I belong to Bel Amica, not Abascar. But the council will recommend that Mother summon volunteers. She'll choose one volunteer to serve as a principal tasker for the Abascar people."

"And the Seers can't interfere?"

"Mother promised. She all but worships the Seers, but she loves me even more. She'll appoint a principal tasker who will report to me—and only me. This tasker will place the Abascar people in apprenticeships and tasks throughout the house until a decision about their future is made."

"So now all you need is a good volunteer." Emeriene clapped her hands. "Good. That should be easy. Everyone wants a position of power, some way to climb the ladder of your mother's favor. People must be sending up prayers to their moon-spirits already. Whoever prays the hardest." She laughed.

"We need someone patient and observant. Someone who will take the time to find a good place for each survivor. Someone who knows how to organize and direct a large crowd of people with efficiency and a firm hand."

"And I can help you find that..." Emeriene stopped. Her smile faded.

Cyndere had that look again—that patient gaze, waiting for Emeriene to understand.

Emeriene stood up. She sat down. She stood up again.

"Emeriene, I want you to volunteer to be House Abascar's principal tasker."

"The what? For the...who now?" Emeriene eased herself slowly from the chair to the floor, dizzy with the surprise.

"Em, I trust no one more than you. You manage my life. You direct the staff of sisterlies. You hate the Seers as much as I do. And you have more experience fighting Ryllion than any of us. Volunteer, and the matter will be resolved swiftly and surely."

Emeriene pressed her hands against her pounding heart.

"I will not let you suffer."

"My responsibility is to care for and protect you—as it has always been."

"I'm not dismissing you."

"Don't try reading my mind. You're bad at it." Emeriene scowled, her fingers playing with the strap that bound the cast around her left thigh. "I have no ambitions. I want to serve you for the rest of my life."

Cyndere stood up. "Em, trust me. I'm not letting you go."

"But you'd have to. You change your plans every few minutes, running here and there. If I don't chase you, you'll miss your meals."

"You *will* be serving me. My mind is divided. I need to continue my endeavors to save the Cent Regus beastmen from their curse. We're closer now than ever. But I also must ensure that the people of Abascar receive fair treatment. Do this for me if doing it for them is not enough. Do it for my peace of mind."

A netterbeak landed on the other side of the curtain. Bauris held very still, staring at the bird's outline. Then he leaned forward and, with excruciating care, drew the curtain aside so he could see the bird more clearly. The netterbeak glanced back at him but held its perch defiantly. It shifted from one webbed orange foot to the other and clucked.

"I miss the sky," Bauris sighed. The bird flew, and one of its feathers drifted back in through the window and came to rest on his open palm. He looked at it, water spilling from his eyes. "I miss the sky so much."

Cyndere pulled the curtain back to open the whole window. "The view's clear now, Bauris," she said, kneeling to look into his face. "The sky is right there."

"The troublemaker." Bauris reached out and pinned the feather through the hair just above the heiress's ear. "She's come back."

"Yes, yes, I'm here, Bauris," Cyndere said. "It's such a pleasure to hear your voice. We thought that you—"

"No," he said, grasping at her sleeve. "You don't understand. She's come back. The witnesses will come in greater numbers now just to watch it happen. This is my favorite part."

Cyndere combed her tousled hair back with her fingertips, perplexed.

"The sky was closer," he said. "For a while it was very, very close."

"The sky's right there, Bauris," said Emeriene. "Right where it's always been."

Cyndere went and sat beside Emeriene. "I have a smaller favor to ask you."

"I hope I like this one better."

Cyndere touched the toughweed cast on Emeriene's leg. "I need a disguise."

Emeriene remembered the many times at Tilianpurth that she had loaned her cast and gown to Cyndere as a disguise, while she posed as Cyndere so no one would know the heiress was out meeting a secret friend in the woods. "You want to trade places again for a while. Is that it?"

"I need to dress like a sisterly so no one notices me. Just for tonight."

"If you're thinking about returning to Tilianpurth without me—"

"No. No tetherwings. No beastman waiting for me in the shadows. No, this time I must slip through my father's secret tunnels on an urgent errand. Those passages are the only way to get past the Seers unnoticed anymore."

"And if your mother comes looking for you? I can't shut the door against her."

Cyndere thought for a while. "Mother's head is full of celebration details—the parade, the voyage to the islands, all the madness ahead. Just remind her how much she likes birthday surprises."

"And are you preparing a surprise?"

Cyndere smiled. "For everyone. And for you, perhaps, most of all."

18

THE WALL THAT
TALKED BACK

Seven hundred and sixty-two stones—angular fragments of turbid green glass—puzzled the wall of Cal-raven's prison.

He had counted them. Reflecting tremulous light that shifted with the movement of buoyant clouds, they were a quieter sight than the world beyond the window.

In the years since his last visit, House Bel Amica's simple wooden boats had become larger, sleeker. Few bristled with oars. Now most were tugged by ugly seabulls, their bulbous white heads surging through the waves like boiled eggs bobbing in brine.

He might have enjoyed the spectacle, but gulls buffeted the air about his window, seeking entrance so they could poke about for food. Farther out, the birds besieged the Bel Amican ships, frantic, fighting for perches along the masts. Fat birds. He hated them. He wished for a bow and arrow.

Busying his mind with plans, he tried to ignore the birds' maddening din, the ache of his bruises and wounds, and his worries.

And there was good reason for worry. The eye of his cell opened to water in unsettling proximity, and a stiff wind would bring the waves right in; the barnacles clinging to the sill were testament to that.

Trust Cyndere, the beastman had told him. Again and again he sought to recall exactly what the beastman had told him at Barnashum. The creature could have killed him but had saved him from a deadly fall instead and had tried to convey some urgent message. *Trust Cyndere and nobody else.*

Long ago Cal-raven and Cyndere had explored rocky tide pools together while their fathers held conference along the sandy shoreline, out where the inlet opened to the Mystery Sea. Cal-raven had sworn that someday, when he was sovereign, he'd make Cyndere his Abascar queen. As they were still children and Cyndere's older brother, Partayn, had not yet been slain by beastmen, she was not likely to inherit House Bel Amica's crown. But they had been only six or seven years old, dreaming childish dreams. Cal-raven's father, amused, had patiently explained to him that such rash alliances were foolish. At the time Cal-raven had not understood the bitter regret in his father's words.

Cyndere said she would give me whatever I need. I need to be back with my people.

The walls moved, or seemed to. In his weariness he felt as if he were trapped in a wavering boat. Mist wafted in, sometimes in fine drifting clouds, sometimes in sudden cold spray. He sank down onto the bench and closed his eyes. The pulsing white burn in his vision seemed to be fading.

In his mind's eye he stood again in the crown of Tammos Raak's tower. Light through the farglass flowered into Auralia's colors. He felt himself drawn to the eyepiece. Instead of seeing the piercing light, he watched a wave rise, Seers borne upon its curling crest, lashing their seabull steeds. Light passed through the wave, and he saw all the riches of House Bel Amica sweeping forward. In a moment they would flood his cell.

He shook himself awake, gasping. Breathing deep and slow, he quieted his heartbeat. Water trickled down the black mortar between the stones to seep through the floor of porous sediment. This went on endlessly—water coming in, water draining out.

This could drive a man into madness.

Just inside the door lay a pitcher of water, a tray of fresh bread, and strips of dried meat.

Others all around had awakened to rations of their own and hissed their disgust. He joined the chorus, carving a clump of rock from the wall and hurling it against the door, where it splatted and stuck in a star-shaped clod.

To keep himself from further nightmares, he sang a Barnashum tune. He saw Merya rocking her child to sleep, saw Tabor Jan reassuring the people, saw the triplets sculpting stories. He walked among the statues in the Hall of the Lost. He imagined his own voice in harmony with Lesyl's. Despite her frequent appeals, he had never sung along with her, not loud enough to be heard. But now he raised his voice and sang as if the words might summon her. It was good to think of her and not the constant chaos.

Toward the end of the second day, he began to discern voices—other prisoners shouting through the pinprick pores of the wall's solid sponge. He pressed his ear to the rough surface and listened.

A speaker was coming to the end of a tale about hunters at sea preying upon oceandragons. "Best leave the monsters alone," he intoned. "We were not meant to know everything. And the moment we think we've mastered the mystery, it will turn on us and tear our ships open to the sea."

That night, lulled into drowsy discomfort, he heard the voices again, this time in labored prayers; prisoners were calling to their moon-spirits for deliverance.

Meanwhile, the bruises and gashes on his face, his ribs, his hands and feet pulsed their own aching laments.

In the morning he had a visitor. A pink sunclinger had crawled through the window.

Cal-raven gingerly pried its seventeen legs free, which took a very long time. Once the last leg gave up its grip on the stone, he examined its headless, star-shaped body, bejeweled with sparkles, tough and gritty as the bottom of a pan when the stew's burnt dry. He turned it over and watched countless white filaments flailing in the air beneath its grand legs as they slowly bent to find a new hold. In the center of that star was an open mouth, eager and ravenous, ready to accept whatever those limbs would carry in.

Cal-raven threw it back out to the inlet.

At once a torrent of birds cycloned from the sky to clash in competition, feathers flying. The splashing frenzy ended as quickly as it had begun. One of the gulls remained floating on the water, head bowed with the weight of its catch.

Cal-raven choked when he saw what was happening. The gull was trying to swallow the sunclinger and had worked two of those long legs into its gullet. But the other limbs had wrapped around the predator's throat, adhering and holding tight. The weight was wearing down the bird. Slowly the sunclinger throttled its attacker. Eventually the bird would either choke to death or drown, and the sunclinger would break away to its undersea abode.

Cal-raven cursed the bird. He cursed the sunclinger. He cursed the spray that had saturated his garments during the night. He felt sick from breathing the salty mist.

Turning back to the wall of glossy green stones, he ran his fingers along their rugged, broken spans. He surrounded one of the stones with ten fingertips and applied soft pressure, concentrating on contours. His wounds flared in protest. With a deep breath, he released all other thoughts. A channel of softer lode shifted slightly. His fingers sank into the mortar, encircling the hard green block, and he drew it smoothly from the wall.

He cupped it in his battered hands, molding it as if it were a brick of green clay. Without considering his intention, he began to shape the Keeper. It was the first time he had done so since seeing the creature in the waking world.

Its edges and lines were complex, and he liked the possibilities. If he pressed, he could feel a difference in the stone's density, find a line, clear away all that was unnecessary. This was where most sculptors went wrong—finding a line, they immediately pursued it. It was just as important to explore all around it, for sometimes there were stronger lines hiding deeper or fractures waiting to be discovered. Any hasty work would come out crooked and crude. Without this patient study, a sculpture would not last. But a shape consisting only of the soundest stone—that would weather storms. It would speak of something pure and true. It would unite generations.

The cell had seemed like such an ugly place, but now it was alive with opportunity. Everywhere he turned, he saw suggested lines, contrasts waiting to be broken, cracks waiting for pressure.

Hours passed. The work absorbed his attention. When he awoke from the effort, he was seated far from the window. As he lifted and turned the sculpture of the Keeper, it filled with light as if it might come to life in his hand. It did not much resemble the creature that had found him on that violent Barnashum night, but it was a good figure. He put it down and stared hard into that radiance. As he did, the white flare in his left eye suddenly returned, bright and harsh.

He set the sculpture of the Keeper in the window, then lay down, folding his arm under his head. As he gazed past its silhouette, the voices began again, murmuring beyond the wall like the waves.

The prisoners' voices wove into his dreams. He did not know how many hours had passed—perhaps a night and a day—when he seized suddenly upon one word, bold as a knot along a thread of speech. Had he heard it or dreamed it?

Auralia.

The name startled him, like the face of an old friend suddenly appearing in a crowd of strangers. He pressed his head against the porous stone as if he might push right through it.

And again, *Auralia.*

A woman's voice was raised in the fever of a story. He could catch only pieces, but he began to sense that the tale as he knew it had been very much revised. The real Auralia had not organized a revolt against his father. And the Keeper was not "Auralia's moon-spirit."

A blare of horns shattered his attention and drew him to the window. The tones flared high above him. He could picture them sounding from a hundred towers encircling the house, flags lashing at the sky like torchflame. Bel Amicans would be congregating on great platforms to see some wonder or receive some proclamation. How easy it would be to climb out the window and slip unnoticed through the masses.

Don't make me come find you, Cyndere. I'll trust, but only for so long.

He slumped to the floor.

Hunger and thirst began to get their claws in.

On the fourth morning the king awoke to find another meal waiting for him, and the sculpture was gone from the windowsill.

He drank half of the water, devoured the bread, then chewed the meat to a flavorless plug and spat it out the window. Again the birds came down.

The harbor was busy. Broad flats floated past, bearing subdued huddles of people listening to instructions from their guards.

The flats moved between fishing boats and vanished for a time behind a magnificent ship drawn by a team of seabulls. Sunclingers held to the ship's wet hull just above the water, gleaming brighter and brighter, absorbing the light. Useless creatures. But glorious.

Wooden planks creaked above him, making him aware of a walkway and of other witnesses to this spectacle. Some steps were heavy—a large man, perhaps. The others were light and quick, two children. And then the laughter confirmed it—a man with two, no three, children. He must have been carrying the third. The children were counting and naming the sunclingers—Slimey and Grasper.

When the ship had moved out to sea, the crowded flats were far away, drawn to dock at the edge of the inlet. He thought he could see people moving off of them and into a series of spacious white tents.

"Can we go see the strangers, Papa?" a child asked.

Cal-raven heard a cough from somewhere beyond the wall, somewhere close. As he turned, he felt a flaring pain from his neck down his back—a cramp from a night sprawled on a wet stone floor.

Even though he was alone, he began to feel pressed upon from all sides, as if people were looking in and listening through the walls.

He woke to darkness and a quieter sea. Loose threads of scented oil touched the air. Somewhere voices were raised in dissonant litanies.

Do they think the moon hears their prayers?

And yet how many times had he addressed the empty air? How many times had he heard his father ranting in solitude as if someone might hear?

The ale boy sought the Keeper and was led to save so many lives. I spoke to my father as if his ghost might hear. I told him I wanted direction. And the Keeper appeared.

He stood and raised his voice, calling out, "I do not ask you to give me riches. Or power. Only that you help me to lead my people, to bring them into a place we can call home."

"Who are you?"

He turned back to the wall of green stones, astonished. The voice, so near and sudden, sent his hand grabbing for the hilt of a sword long gone.

"Who's that?" he asked.

"I asked first." It was a voice like a boy's, but harsh, hushed, and urgent.

He walked toward the wall. "I am from Abascar. Brought here. Imprisoned without explanation."

"You're a trespasser."

"I was dragged into Bel Amican territory by slavers." He eyed the green stones and heard a faint rustling of heavy cloth. "I had intended a proper visit. I've been summoned by the heiress."

"Bel Amica has no heiress. Haven't you heard? Partayn has returned. He's restored to his proper place, first in line for the throne."

Cal-raven was stunned. "The house must be overjoyed. But my claim remains." He trailed his fingers along the wall. "What is your offense?"

"I won't lie," came a weary sigh in return. "I'm tormented for pursuing what I most desire. You would think that this would please the Seers, who urge us to follow our impulses. But I tell you this: if your impulses run counter to those of the Seers or their favored followers, they do not hesitate to thwart your ambitions."

He walked slowly along the wall, trying to find the point where the sound was strongest. It seemed to shift. *Keep him talking.* "I've been led to believe that the men and women of Bel Amica pursue happiness here in freedom."

"We're free to follow whatever paths we like. But does anyone see that all the paths we're offered—for work or pleasure—have been carefully mapped and baited by the Seers? They keep us busy pursuing our whims. We dash about from this to that, more selfish all the time. Paths that might lead to any good are made complicated or concealed altogether. It is hard to make people care anymore, because their attention is enslaved."

"Masses are easily fooled," Cal-raven agreed. "My... King Cal-marcus once convinced Abascar's Housefolk to give up their freedom. They agreed in order to gain his favor and to rise in power and status."

"Ah, but Cal-marcus's people resented his authority. Here, the people are more than happy to do their tempters' bidding, because the Seers give them such enthralling and flattering potions. Bel Amica's becoming a land of pleasant dreams, and we're all so happily asleep that we may never awaken to do what should be done. I'm in trouble because I believe there are better possibilities. There are healing waters out there, running deep."

"Are there?" He leaned in closer.

"And colors. Such colors."

The word gave Cal-raven a start. "You speak of colors. As I lay here, I heard a tale of Auralia through these walls."

"Yes, we've heard stories about a young woman who caused trouble at Abascar. Bel Amicans love stories about rebels."

"Auralia was not a rebel. She would not have done harm to anyone. She was a very young woman with a vision she wanted to share."

"You knew her?"

His answer stuck in his throat, for it would have been a lie. He pinched the base of his ring finger, thought of giving Auralia his Ring of Trust to protect her against his father's judgment.

"Tell me, Abascar man, why were you coming to Cyndere? Have you deserted your people?"

"Abascar's king has a plan for them, but the people are hungry and weary. He has reason to believe that Cyndere might send help. I'm here to find out."

"Send help? Cyndere is already helping them. Just today the people of Abascar—well, whatever is left of them—were given shelter and meals here, in Bel Amica's safety."

The words bewildered him, like the answer to a riddle he had missed in his sleep.

"They're in a spread of tents down at the shipyards. Didn't you see them carried in?"

"What?" Cal-raven gripped the windowsill. His heartbeat fell out of step. "Impossible," he whispered.

"They fled their caves, escaping some kind of invasion."

"Beastmen?"

"No, something else. But there are rumors everywhere. Captain Ryllion intercepted them in the forest. The queen is deciding what to do with them."

"By what authority?"

"They're under her protection. They are eating her food. Would you rather they were handed over to the Seers?"

Cal-raven turned sharply toward the voice. "I was under the impression that Queen Thesera did the Seers' bidding. I know what the Seers are made of."

"No one," said the prisoner, "knows what the Seers are made of."

Cal-raven began to press at the edges of the window, widening it.

"Cyndere," the voice cautiously continued, "has become concerned about these people. Would you trust her to look out for them?"

"Can Cyndere protect them from the Seers?"

The stranger was silent.

Cal-raven waited.

"The Seers," the voice quietly continued, "have been sinking their hooks into the queen for years. Many of us have wondered why they don't just take the throne for themselves. But they have not gone so far yet. And they seem to enjoy their...their work."

"You know a great deal about what is going on for someone locked up here."

"I told you. I know too much."

"I have to get out of here. I have to get back to my people."

"And what do you think you could do for them? They have a capable captain."

"Tabor Jan is here?" It was unthinkable. And then, before he could stop himself. "What about Lesyl? Have you heard of a musician called Lesyl?"

"I am not free to converse with the strangers," the voice said dryly. "And you'll bleed yourself to death digging at these walls. This is coarse, punishing stone."

"If you can help me speak with Cyndere, I'll free you from this prison when I leave."

"Why do you want to speak with Cyndere?"

"I told you. I came here by her invitation."

"I'll ask you one more time, Abascar man. Why do you want to meet Cyndere? Many zealous men are eager to speak with her these days. She may have lost a husband, but she's still young. And Queen Thesera is so eager for grandchildren."

Exasperated, Cal-raven pushed his fingers into the wall. "What do you mean? I just told you! I'm looking out for the best interests of my people."

"Your people?"

He bit his tongue. He had used the phrase once too often. He bared his teeth at his faint reflection in one of the stones.

"If Cyndere promised to help you, she will. But it'll be a gamble. She's cornered, you see." There was bitterness in the voice. "The Seers are puppeteers, and Ryllion's their favorite toy. He's Bel Amica's captain now, with all defenders at his command. If he gets his way, he'll direct the watchmen, too, and all patrollers on the streets. Queen Thesera's besotted, even though she's twice his age. If she could make herself younger—and the See s have made her think it's possible—she might invite him to sit on Helpryn's throne. Cyndere and her brother are struggling to preserve what little sense their mother has left."

Cal-raven sighed. "Perhaps it's folly, then, to put my hope in Thesera's daughter when the Seers have Bel Amica surrounded. But I have to take that chance."

Even the birds were quiet. Wind whistled across the widened window.

"You see things clearly now," came the hushed voice. "Wait until the Seers' potions take hold of you."

"The Seers won't seduce me. I've bested one before. One who promised aid to Abascar but instead led a swarm of beastmen to our doorstep."

The voice sharpened excitedly. "One sure way to stay locked up is to speak openly of Seers in league with beastmen. Why are you telling me?"

"Because you're locked up too. What harm can it do?" He put his hand against the wall, suddenly uneasy. "Will you keep quiet about what I've told you?"

"I've kept your secrets before."

"What do you mean?"

"You don't think you slipped away undiscovered the last time you were here, do you, Cal-raven?"

He stepped away from the wall.

"I followed you through the evening revels. My disguise was much more convincing than yours. And I know what scared you away. But don't worry, King of Abascar. I haven't told anyone. The secret's too much fun to spoil.

Still, you cannot blame me for wondering—can you really be trusted this time?"

The haze of Cal-raven's confusion suddenly cleared. The answer took a clear shape in his mind even before he could ask the question. "Who are you?"

He heard a shifting, then footsteps.

He flung himself at the wall, his hands burning into the stone.

When he broke through into the next cell, it was empty, and the door was shut. There was a lingering scent of rosefruit in the air. Small footprints marred the dust, but they led straight to a solid wall—a wall upon which was chalked the likeness of the beastman who had delivered Cyndere's message.

Heavy boots sounded in the corridor outside. He struggled back through the opening into his cell. And even though he groaned for the ache of it, he scooped up piles of misshapen stone and slapped and pressed them together, hoping to repair the wall before anyone looked inside.

19

QUEEN THESERA
TAKES COUNSEL

Full-grown, but enthusiastic as a puppy, Drunkard careened from side to side, a black blur barking at the netterbeaks and bumping into her brother Trumpet in his golden, stately stride. Holding one leash in each hand, Cyndere laughed, envying the dogs' joy. Both knew they were off to visit their mother, Willow. The old grey hound would probably be curled at the queen's feet before the fireplace.

As they crossed the narrow footbridge from the slender, unadorned stalk of the Heir's Tower toward the stout monolith ahead, Cyndere's gaze climbed the dark scar lines of her mother's crooked tower. Those marks recorded the builders' responses to Thesera's frequent requests for a taller tower. For Cyndere, the lines were the rungs of a ladder her mother was climbing in hopes of escaping this world and all the loss she'd suffered in it.

Cyndere had grown up in the Palace Tower, listening to her parents' footsteps in the chambers above her own room. Through one window she had watched the sea for oceandragons until she accepted the disappointing theory that they had left this world; through the other she'd waved at her brother, who lived in the tower set aside for the heir. Years after their father's death, when reports came that Partayn had been slain by beastmen on the road to House Jenta, Thesera had insisted that Cyndere move into the Heir's Tower to be formally acknowledged as Bel Amica's next queen.

While the burden of that future pained her, Cyndere found some relief in the distance from her mother and the Seers, especially when she married Deuneroi. And when Deuneroi, too, fell victim to the Cent Regus while seeking survivors in Abascar's ruin, the Heir's Tower became Cyndere's hideaway, a place to mourn.

When Partayn reappeared, Cyndere's life was transformed, her ambitions rekindled. Partayn joined her in the Heir's Tower, accepting only a small, simple room for himself. But the two were rarely to be found in their chambers. They worked together zealously in Myrton's greenhouse, plotting rescue for the Cent Regus prisoners and seeking a cure for the Cent Regus curse.

Cyndere gazed down through the fog to the complex of structures within the palace wall on the crown of House Bel Amica's rock. Since childhood she had loved this view of the domed greenhouse, a great tortoiseshell of gleaming panes crafted by the glassmakers. It had loomed large in her childhood, as had the man who worked within.

Emeriene's father, Myrton, the royal chemist, still labored there, seeking cures in herbs, wildflowers, seeds, and roots. There, Cyndere and Emeriene as children had played and learned how to care for all things green and growing. Later, after long days in the royal court, Cyndere and Deuneroi had spent many nights under Myrton's tutelage, studying tinctures that might become antidotes for poisons.

But now the sight of Myrton's laboratory and gardens saddened her. The greenhouse, which had once shone in the morning sun, was now in shadow. The hulking, mirrored structures of the Seers' laboratories surrounded Myrton's greenhouse as if to taunt it. The Seers, rising in power after the death of King Helpryn, had subverted Myrton's work. Taking the old chemist's secrets, they had conjured potions that acted swiftly to please the senses, numb pain, and disguise blemishes. In offering these, the Seers won the hearts of the people and of Queen Thesera as well.

Myrton's treatments, meanwhile, which worked with more subtlety and were often bitter medicine, fell into disfavor. His resources were stripped away when the Seers convinced Thesera to build up Bel Amica's militia as if it were wartime. He sank into seclusion in dark rooms, his spirits enfeebled by the loneliness of rejection.

Now the Seers, with the help of their champion, Captain Ryllion, were on a campaign to capture and train the beastmen. Ryllion would slay any Cent Regus he could not reform into obedient dogs.

This morning the sight of the greenhouse troubled her. Suddenly she was not so eager to go see her mother. She took the dogs on a walk full circle around the tower and paused to gaze out over the Rushtide Inlet.

The horizon was marked by the sails of Bel Amican ships as they moved through the inlet. When they reached the Mystery Sea, their sails leaned, buffeted by the wind. The ocean, always temperamental, permitted their passage begrudgingly.

Watching that distant drama, Cyndere felt a strong kinship with the sailors. "Deuneroi," she whispered, "I need your help today."

Released, the dogs shot through the purple curtains, claws clicking and scraping up the stone stairs, yelping their way into the queen's receiving chamber.

The strong, honeyed scent of incense told Cyndere that her mother was not alone.

Stepping into the large, round room, she kicked off her silver-scale slippers so she could feel the thick red woolen carpet underfoot. Reflections welcomed her, mirrors framed in gaudy gold, catching and casting the light that filtered in through the domed glass ceiling.

Reunited with their mother, the dogs whimpered happily and lay down beside her in front of the fireplace. Willow sniffed them fondly, her tail slapping the floor.

Cyndere moved through more curtains into her mother's bedchamber. She glanced to the vast bed, its oceanic quilts in disarray as if the queen had dreamt of a tumultuous storm.

But her mother, who could so often be found sitting up in bed and addressing uncomfortable guests, was seated at the washtable, her back to her daughter, her face down in a pan of a thick, white, fizzing paste. A towel was swept about her neck. Her bejeweled hands hung limp by her ankles. Her feet were tucked under, her toes in their purple slippers pointed backward.

"Oh," came a timid hoot. Beside the queen on the table sat her pet whiskiro. Bunny, like all whiskiros, looked like an overstuffed rabbit without any forelegs, just two bundles of toes emerging from beneath a furry belly's bulge.

"Mother, I'm here." Cyndere sat on the edge of the bed and tried not to look at the Seer who bent over her mother.

Tyriban Xa—a woman painted in brash colors and exotic tattoos as if she were trying to hide her spindly, emaciated form—moved as awkwardly as a stork, clad in almost as many white feathers. Each of the Seers had particular talents; Tyriban Xa was renowned for her capacity to transform the appearances of men and women.

A splash from a small glass vial, and that white paste darkened to green. Cyndere waited. The Seer drew the queen back in her chair so that her face emerged from the gurgling soup.

The queen laughed. "I'm busy."

"You called for me. Remember? The sun's already high in the sky. You wanted to discuss the council before its session begins."

Tyriban Xa glared at Cyndere, put her hand behind the queen's neck, and then leaned in with a small brush. Her toothy grin murmured into Thesera's ear as she began to scrub her face. "Why not postpone this council until your face is ready?"

"It won't be ready?"

"Why face the council in a mask, my perfect rose? In just a few days, you can show them your true face."

"A mask? At the most important council session of the season? No, the council must, with proper ceremony, pledge allegiance to Partayn for the coming days while I am off to the islands. Partayn will be sovereign during my absence." The queen slammed her fist on the washtable, rattling the trays, spoons, and brushes. "Make my face ready, Tyriban. Now."

"Mother, Partayn is not the only subject for the session today."

"You're troubling the queen," Tyriban Xa chirped. "Why not let her do one thing at a time?"

"Mother, are you so old and feeble that we should treat you as a weakling?" Cyndere walked to the window and opened the curtains so that light fell on the Seer, who raised her hands to block it. "I suspect the Seers are not happy about today's session."

"I am not old!" Thesera shouted.

"Old," hooted the whiskiro.

The Seer wriggled her long, curling nails like a cat clawing the air. "We make no political decisions. We only mean to…improve." She lifted a bowl of flesh-colored putty in one hand, took careful aim with the other, and flicked a dry flake of makeup from the edge of the queen's ear.

"Mother, we must appoint a tasker for Abascar's people. The Seers are rallying support for Ryllion."

The whiskiro clicked its tongue and said, "Oh."

"I think that's a grand idea!" the queen managed to exclaim as the Seer puttied her nose. "Ryllion will make them cooperate."

"That's what I'm afraid of. Abascar needs a caretaker, not a punisher."

"Are they really so frail?"

"They're exhausted. Many are sick. They came for help, desperate for grace. We stuffed them into crude tents and fed them table crumbs. Can you imagine sleeping beside the harbor's din? Soon they'll feel betrayed and begin to resent us. They'll wish they'd never come."

"House Abascar's collapse is not your mother's fault." The Seer spoke like a schoolteacher to an impertinent child. "Those people should—"

"Has my mother given you such privilege that you dare interrupt me? Paste your mouth shut with some of that glue, or I'll—"

"You'll what?"

"Noise, noise!" shouted the queen, pounding on the tray. "Tyriban, do your job and begone, or I'll summon Myrton to repair the damage you've done." She snatched the whiskiro and tucked the animal under her chin, where its worried mutter smoothed into a purr.

"Mother," said Cyndere, stepping close to lay her hand on the queen's. "Remember our plan?"

"My memory's failing now? Yes, I remember." The queen tapped her purple-slippered toes.

"As I promised, I've come with names of those who have volunteered to serve."

"Why not Ryllion?" sang the Seer.

"There's another matter, my little beachcomber." Such sudden affection in her mother's voice put Cyndere on her guard. "We must decide who will be your escort to my birthday banquet."

"Drunkard," Cyndere snapped, and the black dog trotted in, tail wagging giddily. "Drunkard will be my escort."

"Squawk, squawk," groaned the queen. "You need a man to worship you."

"I'm a widow, mother."

"Why must that make a difference?"

"So...*you're* bringing an escort, then?" Cyndere asked.

"Why not? I want the people to see that I still have certain powers."

"I won't accept Ryllion. Not as my escort nor as the Abascar tasker. Everybody knows he's looking for a shortcut to the throne."

"Why, look who has arrived!" exclaimed the Seer, clapping her hands. "You speak the good captain's name, and he appears!"

The dogs had all come in now, backs hunched, baring their teeth toward the door where Ryllion stood.

Cyndere bared her teeth as well, stepping between the soldier and the queen as he ducked into the room.

Ryllion's transformation in recent months had become impossible to disguise. His hands were enlarged, the nails gone dark on his fingertips. His jaw jutted forward, and his eyes were harsh and burning gold. His hair, once yellow as straw, was now striped with black. Beneath cloaks perfumed to cover other changes, he trembled as if always on the edge of violence.

At the soldier's name, the queen had lurched up in her chair. "You're not ready, my sweet rose," said the Seer, clasping the back of her neck. "We have to soak you again." The hand forced Thesera's head down into the vat of warm jelly, and she did not have time to take a breath. "She's going to be beautiful, Captain," the Seer sang.

"The queen is always beautiful." Ryllion flashed a grin at Cyndere.

The Seer went on smiling. "Closer to her true face all the time. She is so patient."

Cyndere stepped closer to block him from taking another step. "You're still barging into bedchambers without permission."

"The queen," said Ryllion, "does not have your inhibitions."

"You used to address me respectfully."

"I used to call you heiress." Ryllion smiled. "With Partayn back in his rightful place, how would you have me address you?"

"I'd rather you didn't."

"My moon-spirit sent me." His voice was hoarse, as if he had swallowed a torch. "Told me I might be of service to the queen."

"You came because you saw me visiting my mother, and you do not like to be kept in the dark."

Thesera suddenly planted her hands against the edge of the vat and pushed. The Seer let go, and Thesera's head flung back. Green jelly dripped and wriggled down beneath her collar while a wash of it splashed across the floor. "Mirrors," she panted. "Don't let the captain see me like this. I'm not finished."

As she reached up to her face, the Seer grabbed her hands. "Don't touch. It's still in a delicate state."

"It itches. I hate this part."

"A few moments, then the bath. You'll look young again, my queen. If only your daughter would observe what we can do to erase what time and grief have wrought."

"Is Ryllion still here?" the queen's voice came, trembling.

"Shall I command him to leave?" asked Cyndere eagerly.

Ryllion stepped past Cyndere as if she were a piece of furniture. "I've a report for you to carry to the council." The dogs surrounded and stopped him. When Cyndere moved to stand with the defensive hounds, she shuddered to see how much the soldier's eyes had become like an angry dog's. "The Seers," he said, "have finished their examination of the Cent Regus carcasses from my recent sweep. A ship now carries the dead out to sea to be tossed overboard, where nothing of their corruption can taint our ground."

"I'm pleased you've cleaned up the mess," the queen said, "but why must you report such ugly details?"

"He's looking at you," said Cyndere, "but he's talking to me. He knows my objection to this slaughter. And he knows that the Cent Regus are not a threat. It's one of the ways he gets even."

"Some of the materials that are saving your mother from time's abuses are made from elements that were wasted on those monsters," snarled Ryllion.

"And why not?" intoned Tyriban. "Consider this very paste, which was taken from—"

"Noise! Begone! All of you! Tyriban, clean me up. It's time for the council."

"Patience, my queen." The Seer cast a withering glare at Cyndere. "I will not speak again." She ripped the skin of makeup off Thesera's face. Cyndere cringed at the sight of the transparent visage hanging between the Seer's hands as it slowly sagged, the mouth turning down into a grotesque frown, eye cavities drooping. As Tyriban shook it out like a handkerchief, Cyndere turned away and slumped to a couch.

Somewhere out in the harbor, a distant voice rose in a melancholy sailor's song—something about a white horse galloping on the sea. Cyndere never heard that melody sung without her mother pointing out that it was Helpryn's favorite song.

"Your father loved that song," sighed the queen.

Clearing his throat, Ryllion knelt. "My lady, I am ready to humbly accept responsibility as a principal tasker for Abascar."

"You do nothing humbly," said Cyndere.

Another voice had taken up a harmony line in the song of the faraway sailor. But this voice came from the base of the stair, quickly approaching.

Ryllion winced and licked his large teeth. But the dogs, distracted from their defense of the queen, began to wag their tails again.

Queen Thesera spun around in her chair. "Partayn!" she shouted, arms open wide. With her hair pulled back tight, her face—green and dripping—seemed drawn into a smile as manic as those of the Seers. "My son!"

Partayn stepped into the room, brushing the curtain back over his shoulder as if it were a cape. Ryllion ducked as if afraid of the man, and he was gone from the room in an instant.

"Thank you," Cyndere sighed. "You're the only one who can make Ryllion feel he might not be in control. It's the best way to get him to leave."

It was back—that black, wooly beard that Partayn had been wearing on the day he returned, as if from the grave, to House Bel Amica. His mother, so shocked at the news of his arrival that she could not stand for a full day, had demanded that the beard be shorn even before he arrived in her chamber, even before she embraced him, weeping so loudly and long that she could be heard from the base of her tower.

There had been no report of his survival, no warning of his impending return, only Wilus Caroon, that cantankerous Tilianpurth guard, arriving unexpectedly. Captain Ryllion had hastened out on horseback across the long floating bridge to Bel Amica's front gate, where he loudly chastised the old soldier for abandoning his post.

But Caroon had sworn that his appearance was an act of obedience.

To whose authority? Ryllion had demanded.

Caroon gestured to the one-man carriage harnessed to his horse, then asked for Cyndere and the queen to come down and meet him. Ryllion denied that request. Caroon then asked to be given an audience with the royal court, which Ryllion also refused.

Partayn then stepped from the carriage. He informed the speechless captain that, for his insolence and rudeness, he would not be invited to the homecoming celebration unless he consented to get down on all fours and serve as a footrest.

Ryllion demanded all manner of proof. So the gratuitously bearded survivor climbed atop the carriage and turned his face toward the queen's tower. He began to sing.

As Partayn unfurled his voice, his lineage was unmistakable—he was one of the blessed, one of the descendants of Tammos Raak. His was a voice that charmed harmonic tones from panes of glass throughout the house. Flames became fierce at the sound of his song. Dogs stopped barking and sat at attention. Cats purred. Some swore that bottled ale improved. The train drivers threw the brakes to silence their wagons so all could hear that distant music.

Cyndere had been strolling through fog along the inlet's sandy shore. Drunkard and Trumpet had been bounding and barking at the surf, while Shakey and Willow strained at their leashes, dreaming of being so young again.

It was Willow who had turned, woofing a question into the air. Then Shakey had joined her in wild excitement, ears pricked toward the house. Cyndere surrendered, letting them lead.

And then she heard his voice.

Her laughter turned to breathlessness. She dropped the leashes and ran.

When she reached the floating bridge, she saw a man standing on a carriage, surrounded by a mob. She saw the singer's hands raised to the sky, saw that long, wild beard. Then the song suddenly halted a few notes from its conclusion. His eyes met hers. And in the midst of that preposterous beard, she saw her brother's crooked smile.

Partayn said what he always said when he saw his sister approach. It was an affectionate exaggeration of what their father always said when they, as toddlers, had come into a room. Helpryn had folded his hands over his impressive corpulence and boomed a long, smiling "Yes."

"Yes," Cyndere whispered to her brother in return. Then she ran to him and wept into that scratchy beard. The crowd had surrounded them both, embracing their embrace.

Reports rushed like bees from the gateway to the top of Bel Amica's rock. The story spread along the Rushtide Inlet, down into the harbors and shipyards, and eventually out to the island-bound ships, where many asked permission to come home and hear his voice again.

Later by the fireside, while their mother sat across the room, staring in a saucer-eyed shock that looked likely to be permanent, Partayn had told them—and only them—the story of his escape and his unlikely rescuer.

Cyndere had thought herself wrung out of tears, but they came coursing again. When she could muster her voice, she found the courage at last to tell her mother of Jordam the beastman and how she had come to befriend him.

"Please," she begged, "please may we welcome him? May we honor and acknowledge his courage?"

At Thesera's blunt refusal, Partayn had taken the goblet—a gift to welcome him home—and thrown it into the fireplace. "If Bel Amica has no gratitude for my rescuer," he said softly, "then I will leave this house as quickly as I've returned. And Cyndere will go with me. We will fulfill Deuneroi's vision on our own, somewhere else if need be. For if my father's house no longer leads in courage, I want no part of it."

So, with the sharp knife of fear, Thesera carved herself a tiny room in that troubled, confused, ailing mind. In that room she could resist the Seers on this one small matter for the sake of her children. And when the Seers challenged her, she roared as if she might become a beastman just to hold her ground.

She agreed that her children could offer Jordam gifts in thanks. But she begged them not to throw the house into turmoil by presenting a beastman to the people. Further, she convinced them that Ryllion and the Seers would find a way to harm him, and they should keep their meetings secret. If they would do this, she would protect their endeavors to keep Deuneroi's vision alive.

Cyndere had seen the beastman again. She had thanked him. And Jordam had promised that Partayn was only the first of his rescues.

In the queen's chamber, with his beard grown back, Partayn suffered his mother's embrace, then suffered further as she begged him to bring back that youthful, beautiful face.

"That face no longer exists," he sighed. "You saw the scars."

"The Seers could erase those scars," she whined.

"I'll wear what life has written on my face." He pulled a scrap of parchment and a piece of seachalk from his pocket. "The honesty...of scars..." he murmured, scratching that down.

"You'd write a song for everything, wouldn't you?" Cyndere laughed affectionately. "You would speak in song if you could."

Mimicking the Seer, he raised his hands and crooned, "Why not?"

How she loved that sparkle in his eye.

"Mother thinks Ryllion should govern the survivors. I disagree. I—"

Partayn interrupted, the sparkle flaring into a blaze. "I also disagree!" He turned to the queen. "Listen to me."

"Here we go again," sighed the queen. "Things you learned in captivity. Can you speak of nothing else? Gloom, gloom, gloom."

"I learned among the prisoners there—prisoners from Abascar, from the merchant roads, even from our own house—that in order to help others, you must know them. You must take the time to imagine how the world looks to people without homes or how it looks to one who carries the burden of the Cent Regus curse. Otherwise, they won't trust you. Nor will you learn anything from them. And think of all we can learn from Cyndere's beastman."

"Cyndere's beastman," sneered the Seer. "Some animals should never be pets."

"Get out!" Partayn snapped.

The Seer did not move.

"Let me speak to my children," said the queen with a note of surrender. "Alone, Tyriban."

The Seer bowed to Thesera in an extravagant show of deference, then departed in a flurry of feathers. As she passed, white dust clouded behind her and settled on the mantel and on the floor.

Cyndere quickly snatched a broom from beside the fireplace and began to sweep up the dust. Partayn joined her, taking a cloth from the washtable, folding the fine white grains into its fabric, then tossing the bundle outside the chamber.

"If we want to avoid making enemies of those survivors," said the heir, "we need to work with someone who knows them well."

"You'd appoint someone from Abascar? How could you trust such a one?"

"Their captain, Tabor Jan, is a good man. He has the people's respect. He led them out of Barnashum." Partayn glanced at his sister. "And he won't let Ryllion push him around."

"I will not give someone from another house a position of privilege in ours."

"I agree," said Cyndere. "And I have a better idea. We appoint someone we know and allow that person to appoint an advisor from among Abascar, who will be given limited privileges and remain under close watch."

"Now we come to it," Thesera snapped. "Speak the name you've clenched between your teeth all morning."

A bell rang at the curtain.

Her cast thumping with every second step, Sisterly Emeriene limped into the chamber. "Forgive me for my lateness, my lady," she said to Cyndere.

"But the courtroom had to be swept and the places at the tables all prepared." Blushing, she bowed to Partayn, then stepped forward to kneel before the queen. "I am at your service, as always," she said. As she did, a strand of long black hair fell loose from her headdress.

Queen Thesera and the whiskiro stared down in the very same blank-eyed astonishment. "Oh," they said.

20

A Precarious Beginning

When the girl handed Warney the bowl of supper, he scowled as if she'd just sneezed into it. "What is it this time?"

"Wild rice and jewelfish with sea beans, all wrapped up in surfgreen." She squirmed on tiptoe. "You pick 'em up and eat 'em whole."

A spasm seized Warney. He put the bowl down and examined the crowd in the dull green light of the sun-warmed tent. Many were wrapped in blankets and shivering from the contagious chill. Warney's years in the wild had toughened him against such affliction. But he shuddered anyway at the thought of chewing something that had recently wriggled along the ocean floor.

"Have anything...simpler? Gorrel stew or bread with honey?"

The girl thrust out her chin. "Eat, or don't." She reached for the bowl. He gave it to her.

Ryllion and his troop had herded the Abascar travelers for days through the forest, then out across hills dense with fields where the wind cast up purple dustclouds, through orchards and vegetable patches, and at last over ridges that lay like the backbones of dragons. Then Warney had seen a discomforting spectacle.

The earth ended. To the west there was nothing but water, water stretching out of sight—violent water that seemed intent on devouring the coastline. To the north he saw the Rushtide Inlet cutting a deep wedge from the land, welcoming the waters of several converging flows. "So that's how rivers die," he moaned.

The sight of House Bel Amica was even more distressing. That great island of stone engulfed in cloud seemed larger than five House Abascars.

When Krawg, transfixed by the sight for a long time, turned to face him, his expression was almost as startling as the landscape. "Isn't that better than great?" Krawg cackled like a crow. His mouth—a cave of yellow stalagmites—closed, the smile replaced by concern, and he put his cold, hard hand on Warney's shoulder. "Too much to see for a one-eye?"

"Send me back to Barnashum," Warney had whispered.

The survivors were then driven onto broad floating platforms to suffer an unsteady passage through the inlet. Warney had marched what felt like an endless trek—up a rickety stair, across a damp wooden deck, through a border of long, whispering grass, through a gate in a fence made of fish bones, to the array of white tents, their walls and ceilings sewn from the broad leaves of an undersea tree.

Through the night Warney had tossed and turned, terrified of the waves' constant murmur, the sound of the end of the world. While the blankets provided by blue-robed "sisterlies" were as soft as any he'd known, he regarded their puffy, perfumed fabric with suspicion. He'd slept better among rags on Barnashum's hard floor.

He and Krawg shared a tent with the oldest survivors and the children. "Those less capable of serving the spirits," a soldier had muttered as if Warney could not hear him.

Krawg was gone, having cleaned his bowl within moments of its delivery. Warney hated it when Krawg went off suddenly on his own.

He slipped to the tent flap and peered outside. The evening's azure gleam cast golden sparks over the inlet. A low wind moaned through wildgrass beyond the fish-bone fence. Krawg was down there—a dark blue cape, his arms lashing about in the air. He had kept himself from frustration by narrating story after story to the survivors. Now he had a new audience—a crowd of Bel Amican youngsters, their hair windblown into tangles, listening in awe.

"I thought it was just a season, your storytelling fit," Warney muttered, stepping out. The monitors were all busy delivering bowls of soup, so he wouldn't be missed for a while.

When he reached the fence, he saw that its upper edge was a line of razor teeth.

Krawg was making up some nonsense about the last stand of Captain Ark-robin during House Abascar's collapse. But Warney was quickly drawn in by the dramatic conclusion. He became so enthralled he hardly noticed the clouds of yellow sea froth that the wind carried up from the inlet surf or how that lacy foam shattered when it hit the fence and alighted on and around him like lodes of sparkling jewels.

The children beyond the fish-bone fence clapped at the tale's conclusion and asked for another.

"Aren't you supposed to be working?" Krawg asked.

"We're s'posed to wait for the *Red Oceandragon*," said the eldest boy, with the fishing pole and the stitches on his cheek. "When it gets here, we gotta clean it."

"Ocean...dragon?" Warney whispered.

"It's a boat, you old sheepskull," Krawg muttered. "Okay, another tale then. Have you ever heard of a girl called Auralia?"

The children looked at one another as if Krawg had introduced a foul smell. "Don't tell that story," said a girl, crossing her arms.

Krawg put his face through the open jaw of some sharp-fanged fish. "Why not?"

"Auralia stories are for naughty kids to try to scare them into behavin'."

Krawg laughed. "That's not the Auralia story I was gonna tell. I knew the girl myself."

"The *Red Oceandragon!*" shouted a scrawny, shirtless, mud-smudged boy. The children rose and leapt down the muddy slope to the sand, where they ran to the dock as a slow ship approached, sails painted full of light.

"You keep wandering off," Warney growled.

"I'm not your hound," Krawg snorted.

"We've been partners since you started teachin' me how to burgle. And now you're done with me?"

"I came back for you when Cal-raven called me to—"

"You keep starting things without me. You venture into some crazy storytelling contest and almost get us killed."

"They weren't gonna hurt—"

"And now you keep makin' off to rattle 'n' spin big crowds with broke-brain stories about tricksters and stuff, and where do I fit? What happens to me?"

"I know what I'm for," Krawg barked. "At last. I been thievin' and berry pickin' for well about fifty-three years. And I plan to live quite a mess more. Some got their healin'. Yawny had his stewpot. Auralia had her colors. But me? I may not know what's happenin' in the world, but I can think of what *might* happen. And to me, that's a stitch more interesting. Don't even plot it out ahead of time. I just picture the people, and off they go a-talkin'. It's like reachin' up and snatchin' stray threads from the air that'll weave a perfect jacket. Now I know how Auralia felt."

Warney was silent while Krawg caught his breath. Then he sighed, "Well, why don't you just kick me in the teeth for sayin' anything at all."

They sat in a long silence as the golden sky faded to a muddy yellow over the sea.

To the north, rail tracks of the delivery trains, market platforms, ancient statues of eagles—all these intricate details of Bel Amica—vanished in shadows. Lights emerged in constellations as if the rock was a glowbug hive.

Over all this, the copper moon shone, brightest of all evening lights.

Krawg sighed. "Warney, have you ever seen anything so..."

"Frightening?" To Warney, the people disembarking from the ship looked like beetles marching out of a nest for some kind of itchy business. The line passed along the strand, slowing when one of them pointed up the slope toward the tents. Warney felt as if they were looking at him, those dark shapes that had come from the sea. Then the line broke, and two sailors approached. "I'm goin' back in before these buzzin' waternippers decide to drink my blood." Warney stood as if to depart.

"Please yourself. I'm stayin'," said Krawg.

"You two!" came voices from the approaching men. "Are you from Abascar?"

The sailors clambered over the embankment, approached, and knelt at the fence. Both were lean and muscled from lives of hard labor. The one with the sharp eyes and thin beard held a wrench. The other, his grey shock of hair blown back as if he spent all his time at the top of the ship's mast, carried a coil of rope over his shoulder.

"We're from Abascar too!" said the bearded one.

"We didn't know until recent days that so many of us were left alive!" exclaimed the other. "How did you all survive out there?"

The first man, Wilsun, his hands hardened by years of driving Abascar's mine-hammers, had found work and quick success as a repairman on the ships. The other, Willup, once a brewer of Abascar ales, now managed shipments of Bel Amican ales and wines to the islands.

"Have you been out on a boat yet?" Willup seemed made of enthusiasm. "Once you've sailed, you'll never stay landbound."

"Really?" Krawg sighed.

"It's a fine life," agreed Wilsun, "so long as you don't get caught up in that moon-spirit nonsense. My lovely Clayre's here too. She works on the rock." He gestured to House Bel Amica. "Teaches children about the history of Abascar and the kings and queens of its past. She's strong as a bottle of hajka."

"We're on our way to find out about the council," said Willup. "We're hoping the queen's assigning hunters to patrol the inlet."

"Hunters?" Krawg's hands opened and closed like birds snapping at bugs.

"We lost a boat last week." Wilsun's face turned grim. "Here in the harbor. Something attacked from the water. Third time since the season's first red moon. Boat was smashed open. Something left a nasty black stain on the wreckage."

Warney dug his nails into Krawg's shoulder.

"Council's also going to decide what to do with you!" exclaimed Willup. "And who's going to be in charge."

"I want to work with you!" Krawg exclaimed. "Give me a task on the ships!"

Wilsun glanced skeptically at Willup, who seemed ecstatic about the idea. "I'll recommend you!" he rejoiced.

"What can you do?" Wilsun asked.

"I'm..." Krawg glanced at Warney. "A storyteller. Well, and I've had a lifetime of work as a harvester."

"You might learn to harvest fish, then," Wilsun mused. "It's not like Abascar; no one's standing over you shouting the rules. You'll have to prove yourself. You'll sink or you'll rise."

"Hey, what's the word on the healer?" Willup asked.

"Healer?" Krawg glanced back at the tents. "Say-ressa?"

"Is it really Say-ressa? She came with you all? She taught my wife, Marey, everything she knows back when we were just Abascar Housefolk! We heard she was sick."

"Haven't seen her since we arrived," said Warney sadly. "They wrapped her in a blanket and carried her off."

Wilsun elbowed Willup. "Time to go. Sunup's gonna be here all too soon." He turned apologetically to Krawg. "If we're not at the dock by first light, others will talk their way into our place. We have to be the best at what we do, or we get kicked down the ladder and have to climb again."

"And here," said Willup, "fastest has a lot to do with best. Sleep tight."

Krawg and Warney were alone again at the fence.

"What's gonna become of us, Krawg?"

Krawg shrugged. "We'll have to fend for ourselves here."

"It's like we're gonna be Gatherers all over again, isn't it?" Warney snatched at the grass as if he'd tear it out and cast it away, but the roots held tight.

"It's nothing like being Gatherers," said Krawg. "As Gatherers, we lived in the woods with beastmen behind every tree and vermin all over everything. Here, this is how people are supposed to live. With water and sky. It's restful."

"Restful? Gotta disagree. The water never rests. And just look at them birds. Scary."

"They like it here." Krawg stood up, towering over Warney with a scowl. "Can't blame 'em. The forest is better than Barnashum. But this is better than the forest. I like these stones. And the sound—it's washin' away all the thoughts I don't need. Never been here before, but somehow I've come home."

Warney stared out at the horizon's faint halo. "I keep hearin' that things'll get better. But we get where we're going and find it's time to start climbin' all over again. Everywhere is steep."

Krawg seemed hypnotized by the activity around the *Red Oceandragon.* "I can learn to get up early again. Learn to pick fish from the sea like berries from trees. Learn the stories that sailors like to hear."

"And what about me? What'm I for?"

"You'll answer that in Bel Amica."

"I just want the sort of busy that feels like play. You remember, don't you? Like we did when we were less than several years old. String and pebbles and wimple-ball and Stamp the Tootle. Play, Krawg. Like Auralia did all day."

"What do you want to do?"

"What do I *want* to do? Ballyworms, Krawg, I don't even know what I *can* do. Every place I go, I hear my sisters screamin', 'You're not even fit to pick apples.'" A horizon cloud infused with purple light from the vanished sun drew his eye. "I got nothin' on the inside."

Krawg did not reply.

Warney shuffled back to the tent.

From one of the benches along the side of the long rowboat, Tabor Jan eyed the rower. "For a fellow who defends a house by the sea, you sure seem afraid of the water."

Bel Amica's Captain Ryllion kept his gaze fixed on the dark waves. Across his knees lay an unsheathed trailknife, a massive broad-bladed tool typically used to blaze paths through thick brush. The fact that it was Ryllion rowing them—alone—was clearly meant to intimidate and aggravate Abascar's people.

Leaning over the sides, the ten companions Tabor Jan had selected to accompany him to the rock seemed entranced by the water around them and Bel Amica's glittering mountain above.

Tabor Jan hated the water's unsteadiness almost as much as he hated heights. He wanted level ground, a clear direction. His discomfort took the shape of aggression. And since the rower of this boat was the man he'd most like to throttle, he had to fight to remain seated.

Ryllion was younger than he'd expected but enormous, with features that seemed oddly distorted. And those hands... Was he wearing gloves that exaggerated their size?

"I'd recommend that you quiet down." Ryllion steered them alongside the base of Bel Amica's rock, past one docking cave after another. "Or you'll be the first I throw overboard if it comes for us."

"If what comes for us?"

Ryllion glanced at the others. "Your leader here, he's nervous. Is this what Abascar folk are made of?"

"He's the only one on this boat I'll be calling captain," snapped Jeshawk. "He's the king's protector."

At that, Ryllion laughed, and a glimpse of his teeth—fangs, to be sure—shocked Tabor Jan. "The king's protector? Where were you when your king disappeared?"

"Do you see our people bickering or fighting?" Tabor Jan asked quietly. "No. We are waiting. Waiting in good faith for Cal-raven to return from his mission."

"If he ever commands you again, I'll eat my boot." Ryllion looked past Tabor Jan. "What about you—the swordswoman with the lovely blue eyes? Are you as confident of Cal-raven's wisdom?"

Tabor Jan glanced back in alarm. Brevolo did not lift her gaze, but her clenched jaw made it clear that she was wrestling with possible answers.

"I smell disappointment." Ryllion smiled as if he had just discovered a valuable secret. "We'll have words later, swordswoman, when you can confess without offending your kinsmen. I may have some use for you."

With a swift stroke of the oars and a frightful force, Ryllion turned the boat so suddenly that the passengers were thrown against the side. "I'm amused by your fighting spirit," he said as the darkness of the harbor cave engulfed them. "But you'd better watch your words around my master."

"Your master?"

A bright green glowstone on the end of a staff illuminated the giant waiting for them on a ledge inside the cave. The ghastly, skull-like face staring out from beneath the fanlike headdress grinned fiercely down at Tabor Jan. It was Pretor Xa, the Seer who had led the beastman siege on Barnashum. Tabor Jan looked down, hoping his own appearance had changed enough that the Seer would not recognize him from their recent encounter.

"Welcome, proud House Abasssscar," seethed the Seer. "Welcome. I hope you've enjoyed your boat ride. Consider that a little introduction to House Bel Amica's new kingdom—the sea."

Tabor Jan and his companions came awkwardly to their feet. Ryllion sheathed the trailknife and sprang like a viscorcat from the boat to the platform. The boat rocked wildly behind him, throwing them back to their seats.

"I won't waste your time," said the Seer, pointing to a stairway that led up into the rock. "Your new principal is waiting."

"New principal?" Ryllion turned to the Seer. "But wait. I'm the new principal."

"The queen's made up her mind." The Seer's smile never faded, but it was clear that something had not gone the way he had planned. When he spoke again, Pretor Xa's words were sharp-edged. "Queen Thesera has chosen Sisterly Emeriene to govern the Abascar people."

Something like a yelp burst through Ryllion's teeth. "But you promised—"

"The Abascars will show her nothing but respect," said the Seer. That white head swiveled, and those wild eyes caught Tabor Jan in an accusatory glare. "Isn't that right, Tabor Jan?"

Tabor Jan refused to acknowledge the question. Instead, he watched Ryllion's massive jaw chew on the Seer's bitter news.

"Emeriene will attend to your people, but listen to me, Captain." The Seer's arm shot out, and he grabbed Tabor Jan by the beard. "Should anyone fall ill..." The Seer tightened his grip, twisting the beard until Tabor Jan winced. "Should anyone be injured... Should anyone need counsel..." That grip tightened further until Tabor Jan's head tilted and he gasped. "You would be wise to consult me before anyone else. Without my attention things can go from bad to worse."

He could feel Jes-hawk and Brevolo tensing to defend him, but he waved them back. "A gracious offer," he wheezed. "But you have already taken those who needed attention. And the silence about their condition has not given me reason to believe—"

Pretor Xa released him and clapped his hands, and a door opened somewhere up the stairway. Another soldier in a uniform like Ryllion's appeared, leading a figure in a white gown.

"Tabor Jan?" came the voice, shaky with disbelief.

"Say-ressa?" Tabor Jan felt as if his feet were nailed to the dock boards. Brevolo ran up the stairs and caught Say-ressa in an embrace. The willowy healer, who had seemed so pale, so fragile when strangers had carried her away a day earlier, was strong and full of color, laughing with the radiant joy that inspired healing in so many others.

Tabor Jan held back, his gaze shifting from the bright circle of Say-ressa's face on Brevolo's shoulder to the Seer, whose satisfied attention was still set on him like an opponent who has gained an advantage.

"Thank you," said Brevolo to the Seer. "Thank you. May we take her back to our people? There are many who need her attention."

"Of course. But she will tell you about what we, too, can offer the sick." Pretor Xa loomed over Tabor Jan so closely that the captain could see the dark space behind those eyeballs as they bobbed loosely in their sockets. "You can depend on me," he said. "Don't forget that." It sounded like a threat.

Tabor Jan would have replied with something regrettable, but the Seer gestured to the stairs. "Your new tasker waits. I advised the queen that your people deserved to be overseen by Bel Amica's best." He clucked his tongue behind that ferocious grin. "But Thesera's choice shows that she views this assignment as more custodial in nature. Like sweeping. Or throwing out the scraps."

Stone eagles with gemstone eyes and severe, regal expressions perched on pairs of pedestals along the narrow stairway that Tabor Jan ascended with his companions. Some were depicted in flight, tilting with outspread wings, great fish caught in their talons. The captain recognized these as the emblem of the house. In recent hunts with Cal-raven, they had come across outposts in which eagles had been joined or replaced by a howling wolf with crescent-moon eyes. This passage was older and one favored by royalty.

At the top of the stairs, they strode up a corridor and stepped through heavy curtains into a long and stately hall. Open to a view of the starry evening sky, the hall revealed they were on a low outcropping of Bel Amica's stone, with the rest of that tremendous house looming—a dark mountain—above them. Green and needled trees stood like watchmen on the heights, bent from years of storms. Gulls canvassed the rock, crying and wheeling. Even as Tabor Jan felt a thrill of delight at the view, he suspected that it was intended to make the observer feel vulnerable and small.

He brought his attention back to the hall. Dark wood panels lined the walls, housing a portrait gallery. Lavish purple curtains hung on either side of each, as if the pictures were windows into the past. In those frames, Bel Amica's rulers stared out with fierce authority—the line from Queen Thesera all the way back sixty generations to someone's perception of Tammos Raak himself, a muscular figure with skin dark as marrowwood and eyes like beacons.

On one side of the room, a fireplace was alive with quiet light from a pile of driftwood. On the other, a long table was laid with plates of small saltcrust rolls, open shells with gleaming meatpods, cheese, and bundles of bright purple surfberries.

"Please, help yourself," came a voice from the far end of the hall.

Brevolo came up beside him and whispered, "Have they appointed a child as our overseer?"

"Hush," he whispered. "Let's wait and see."

A small figure strode unevenly across a carpet of fangbear furs that had been stitched together so that the predators' faces snarled ferociously in all directions. She wore a dark blue gown and head scarf, and she walked with a limp. Her dark eyes were stern, and she folded her hands before her as she bowed.

As she drew near, he dropped to one knee.

"Oh, that isn't necessary. Thank you, but I'm not royalty. I'm here to serve you. Please, eat." She did not speak with a high, formal manner. Tabor Jan thought she sounded practical and even a little eager to please. Like a common hostess.

When the company did not make a move toward the table, the woman walked to stand at the corner. "I assure you, there's nothing to fear. This is a safe place, and we chose it to honor you. Not even the Bel Amican council assembles here. It's one of our oldest chambers, a place where kings and queens have welcomed special guests for generations. Alas, the queen is busy, but her daughter will join us soon."

Brevolo walked to the table, and she gasped when she saw savorsweet syrup for the bread. "Thank you," she said. Then she said it again several times as her gaze swept across plates of sliced meat, small cups of fish eggs, and bunches of seagrapes.

"My name is Emeriene."

"I am Tabor Jan ker Tanner. And this is Brevolo kai Galarand."

"In House Abascar I suppose I would have been Emeriene kai Myrton. My father is Myrton, the royal chemist." The woman seemed genuinely pleased to greet them. "I've always appreciated that tradition of yours in Abascar, giving honor to a father or mother in your name. Bel Amica has no such tradition. Once people reach a certain age, they can change their name if they wish. Tabor Jan—what does it mean?"

"I was born Jan—named by my mother for a man from old stories. An invisible watcher. Apparently I was nearly silent as an infant. Then my father began to notice that everything I did, I did as if to a drumbeat. He was a firm believer in order. So he named me for a drum. They argued, but both names stuck."

"You are King Cal-raven's man-at-arms. And captain of the Abascar defenders."

"I am."

"Your people have survived some horrible ordeals."

"We still suffer," said Brevolo, and Tabor Jan restrained himself from silencing her. He did not want to hurry into complaints.

Emeriene shook her head. "I'm sorry. Some of us have wished to offer you more help. Others have made it...difficult."

She turned then and addressed the whole company. "I speak for Queen Thesera, her son, Partayn, and her daughter, Cyndere, when I say this: You are welcome to House Bel Amica. Forgive us for our slowness in giving you the attention you deserve. We mean to help you forget your troubles, find rest and healing, and begin again."

Brevolo looked up sharply, and Tabor Jan could sense her objection to the idea of forgetting what she had lost. But he touched her arm and then touched his lips to suggest patience.

"Enjoy the food. Enjoy the fire. Each of you will have an opportunity to express concerns, and we will respond as best we can."

"We?" asked Jes-hawk.

"One of your own will be a representative who will report to me and advise me. Now, I would speak with Tabor Jan awhile. So, please, be at peace."

She led Tabor Jan to the far end of the hall where a three-paneled tapestry depicted a king—most likely Helpryn—standing on the arc of a bridge and blessing a boat that passed beneath. The tapestry was upright, its panels folded to enclose a smaller portion of the hall with three cushioned chairs behind it.

Tabor Jan hesitated, then followed Emeriene out of sight of the company.

She sat in a high-backed chair that had bold wooden feet carved like eagle talons. She gestured for Tabor Jan to take the identical chair opposite her. Another fangbear fur lay between them—and this one had a head with jaws open, facing him. The floor beneath was made of flagstones smoothed as if by centuries of water and flecked with winding lines of bright crystals.

"I hope your people will enjoy relief from scrabbling for food and shelter in the wild," she said. "We'll give you work that's more agreeable than the stuff of mere survival. At least for a while. That is the queen's firm decision. The question of your future is still in play, of course."

Turning, he found that he could see through the tapestry that separated him from his company. He could watch them whisper to each other as they devoured the delicacies at the table.

"You may be pleased to know that we found a boy belonging to Abascar. Wynn, he calls himself. We've put him to work on the docks under strict supervision."

Tabor Jan shook his head. "Not really one of ours, but we took him in, and his sister, Cortie, after beastmen killed their parents. He must have run off on his own."

She laughed. "You took him in even though you were struggling to survive? Is Abascar really that generous?"

"We have a gracious king," Tabor Jan said. "Cal-raven is the best man I know." He took a deep breath, then posed his first test to his questioner. "He'll be coming for us soon."

"Yes," said Emeriene. "So I understand. Cal-raven. Explain that name to me, will you?"

The sisterly was certainly taking her time. He eased further into the chair to appear comfortable. "Cal-raven took his first steps toward an open window, and his mother found a raven feather there. It's another tradition— take a name from the place where a child first walks. And then, the royal family can bestow a forename from among the first children of Tammos Raak. Ark, Har, Say, Cal—there are many children mentioned in the old stories. Royalty can give these names to anyone as an honor, as a badge of privilege, in gratitude. Only family may address them without their forename."

"I met Say-ressa," said Emeriene. "So she was Ressa before she impressed the king."

Tabor Jan would have told the story, but he was interrupted when a great rattling noise, like a parade of wagons down a rocky path, broke the silence, and he joined his companions in looking up.

A vast ceiling emerged from a sheath in the face of the rugged stone. The sound, he later learned, came from dozens of wheels hidden along its edges, which ran along tooth-lined tracks atop the chamber walls. The view of the rock above, its platforms and windows, its torches and flags, was replaced by an intricate network of glass panels that glimmered darkly with filtered light.

Emeriene shrugged. "Sometimes we must assemble here in the rain. And at night we must protect this chamber from the bats." Lowering her voice, she said, "It will be better for us if it's closed. Less chance of anyone else listening in."

"We're being watched?"

"Perhaps."

The ceiling came to a jolting stop, and the Abascar representatives stood with chins raised, mouths open, gawking. It seemed so simple, so practical— and yet Abascar had never seen such a thing.

The panels were richly hued. Describing them later to the other House-folk, they would fumble for words, speaking more of emotions than metaphors. For what was it like, looking into that abstract collage of fragments and colors? Nothing like a night sky. Nothing like reflections on water. A field carpeted in bright autumn leaves? Perhaps, but these colors were so much brighter.

Tabor Jan returned his gaze to Emeriene and found her examining his company carefully.

"Jan, the invisible watchman," she murmured.

"My lady, I am duty bound to command our people so they're ready when the king returns."

"You're so sure that he'll return. Is it not true that Cal-raven was born of a queen who abandoned her people?"

"Cal-raven has applied himself to the survival and restoration of House Abascar from the moment he became king. He is fixed upon one thing—raising that house again."

Emeriene regarded him quietly for a long time. "Did you know that Cyndere extended an invitation to your king many moons ago? Before spring was fully awake? It's true. She offered him refuge, resources, anything he might like. He never responded. In fact, he drove off her messenger. With a sword."

Now it was Tabor Jan's turn to press his lips shut. Cal-raven had shared Cyndere's invitation with him. It had included the warning *Trust no one in Bel Amica but Cyndere.* But the king still had not divulged how he had received this message.

Emeriene continued. "There are those here who would exploit Abascar's need and make slaves of you. Your king has enemies, it seems. More than you might realize."

"I'm acquainted with some of those...enemies."

"The same villains who would ruin Cal-raven have arrows ready for Cyndere and Partayn as well. This effectively unites us. If your king does come to Bel Amica, he will need to be carefully guarded by those loyal to him, just as Cyndere and Partayn now have guards everywhere they go. I would assign you to patrol atop the walls that line and divide Bel Amica's avenues and yards. What better way for you to freely move about the city and oversee your people?"

"Very well. But, Sisterly Emeriene, when Cal-raven arrives, it will be to gather us and go."

"I think that the heir and his sister will support Cal-raven's plan. But we will have to work quietly together. Or the Seers, who have ways of making things difficult, will interfere."

Tabor Jan began to relax.

"I would ask a favor of you in return. Bel Amica is changing. You would think that devotion to the moon-spirits would unite its believers. But followers listen to their own desires, believing them sacred. They justify whatever they do, saying their behavior was commanded by a guiding spirit. This sets neighbor against neighbor, sister against brother, husband against wife. We flourish, for those believers strive mightily, and some fulfill desires for grand and honorable things. But the fact remains—they compete against one another. We are free here in House Bel Amica to pursue what is best. But in the name of that freedom, there are those who embrace and justify what is worst, undermining what remains of the queen's hold on order. This evil spreads quickly and quietly, for no one has the right to call it what it is. Greed."

"My lady, what does this have to do with us, with my being a watchman?"

"I would ask you to be eyes for Cyndere and Partayn as well as for your people. Study the Seers' activity, especially those closest to the queen. You know who I mean. And if you breathe a word of this, I'll ship you off to the islands faster than you can skin a... What's easy to skin?"

He smiled. "Shockwyrms, perhaps?"

"Faster than you can skin a shockwyrm."

"I will not speak of it." He was surprised to find he meant it. She was persuasive. And powerfully attractive. No wonder she had such influence in this house.

"Keep a close eye on Captain Ryllion," she whispered.

A more welcome command he could not have imagined.

"He's up to something. As the Seers' favorite apprentice, he's become a puppet, even as he flatters himself for the privilege."

"You feel strongly about this."

"It's happening to Cesylle, my husband," she said with sudden force and bitterness.

So there, he thought, *is a thing worth knowing.*

"You're the least likely person we'd set to spy on our own chief defender. We have no reason to trust you."

"So it would seem."

"But I've chosen an advisor who already knows your people well. An advisor who has always spoken highly of you."

"You said you would choose an advisor from among our people."

"Partayn has a company of agents, the royal brotherhood, who serve him discreetly, just as the sisterlies serve Cyndere. My advisor is a new officer in Partayn's brotherhood. He'll be the one to find tasks for your people."

In the corner a curtain parted, and a woman with short yellow hair and a gown of green scales appeared. She wore a tiny emerald in the left side of her nose and silver slippers. Realizing that his surprise had brought him, slack-jawed, to his feet, he bowed. He had no doubt this was Cyndere herself.

"Are we ready?" the woman said to Emeriene softly.

"Only if you are still certain."

"I am."

As questions shouted in Tabor Jan's head, Emeriene turned and cast him a worried smile. "We will speak again soon. For now, I leave you in the care of the queen's daughter." With that, the sisterly set aside the tapestry screen and departed.

Cyndere stood beside Emeriene's chair. "Please, be seated, Captain."

Startled to be addressed by his title, he obeyed. "It is an honor and a privilege."

"I've come to introduce you to a friend. I want you to trust him and not to pester him with complaints or questions."

She reached down and threw back the fangbear rug. Then she slipped her fingers beneath a hidden seam around one of the flagstones. "My mother's ancestors were very fond of secret passages," she said. "We didn't want Ryllion or the Seers to trouble or threaten Emeriene's new advisor before he met with you. So we took rather drastic measures."

She lifted the flagstone. Cold air breezed up through the open space.

A man in a robe belted with gold ascended from the concealed stairway. He moved cautiously, as if confused. He wore armbands similar to those worn by the men who had escorted Partayn on his visit to the survivors. But despite the uniform, he had a bruised and haunted look about him, as if trying to shake off a bad dream.

"Where am I?" he asked.

"You are in good company," said Cyndere. "Thank you for accepting my invitation, at last, King of Abascar."

The man, realizing a presence behind him, turned to face the Abascar company.

Behind him, Tabor Jan was the first to drop to his knees. "My lord," he gasped. "My king."

21

ABASCAR SCATTERED

The ocean-vine apple sparkled like a green moon in the sunlight as Tabor Jan held it aloft. "Have you tried one of these?"

Cal-raven could see countless shining juice beads sealed within its translucent rind.

"They just came in on a boat from, oh, I forget which island. They're the best."

"The best what?" asked Cal-raven. At his side Hagah yelped in the hope that Tabor Jan would throw the apple.

"Best fruit in the Expanse."

Tabor Jan bit into the apple with such a sharp crunch that a watchman passing them on this west-facing wall looked back. "Is it one of the Coil-snake's?"

"That's it!" Tabor Jan half bowed to the watchman, a scrap of the apple's skin stuck between his teeth. "The island that looks like a snake all wound about. Master, you've seen it on the maps?"

"Stop by the shipyards tomorrow," the other watchman called as he walked away. "They're bringing in syrup from the Bracelet Isles."

Cal-raven reached down to scratch Hagah's head. "A new sensation every sunrise."

"You say that like it bothers you."

"How many days has it been since Cyndere gave me back to House Abascar? Twenty? And not a day has passed without the Bel Amicans chattering about something new that everyone must taste or see. These people are like Hagah as a pup—everything is their new favorite thing." He tugged on the hound's ear. "Isn't that right, friend?" The dog wagged both his tail and his tongue. He had been inseparable from Cal-raven since their reunion.

Tabor Jan wiped the loose sleeve of his gold watchman's jacket across his beard. "You don't like puppies anymore?"

"Abascar's gone blind with enchantment. We've played right into the Seers' hands. And now one of our own has gone missing."

"Look, I know I'm confused for lack of sleep," yawned Tabor Jan. "But let's remember—it's Warney that's gone missing. He was always a bit... unsteady."

Hagah's lips drew back, uncovering his fangs, and he growled. Cal-raven patted the dog's hard browbone. "That's just a statue, Hagah." He knocked on the forepaw of the howling wolf sculpted on the wall. Hagah barked again, a question this time. Then he slumped, clearly disappointed that he had not just rescued his master from danger.

Lingering fog teased Cal-raven with fleeting glimpses of the world below him as he leaned against the wolf. This was one of the most spectacular wall walks in Bel Amica, for it offered views of clustered palace structures, market platforms, stretches of train rail, gardens, factories, mills, paths, and multilayered residences below.

A girl wrapped in a white cape, a white scarf hooding her head, wound her way through a crowd of builders below. As the builders hunkered over sketches they had chalked on avenue stones, she looked up at Cal-raven. He turned away and put a hand to the claw scars on his cheek.

Keeper, what now? It can't end here.

Looking south to the inlet banks, he saw yellowed grass where the tents had been. Abascar was scattered now. Some lived in spare rooms of Bel Amicans; others stayed deep down in the rock or in bunkrooms left empty by island-bound sailors. They would repay their debts through their labor, or they'd be returned to tents, if not expelled to the wild.

Though the people bowed and still called Cal-raven king, the thought that they were incurring debt to Bel Amicans made him ashamed. The seduction of Abascar was well under way.

"When you have a plan, my king, you know I'll be ready to move on," said Tabor Jan.

"That's one. Will anyone join us?"

"Jes-hawk's ready."

"Jes-hawk's out riding with Ryllion."

"Jes-hawk's in the arrow yard, training." Tabor Jan tossed the apple core skyward. Hagah barked and leapt, but the fruit vanished in a flurry of netterbeak feathers before it could fall.

With his fingertip Cal-raven carved a circle in one of the rugged bricks. "The last time I walked here, I was a spy. It was frightening at first. Then I began to enjoy it. I stayed longer than I had to. Once I got back to the woods, I swore I'd never come back. It was all too dangerously appealing. I wanted something more."

A blanket of low, lavender clouds lay over the horizon as if offering the weary sun a soft place to land. A gem of light flickered like a lost earring. Cal-raven could almost believe it was an evening star. But no, it was the burn returning to his eye, that white scar flaring like one of the beacons that shone from the rock to ships in the fog.

That young woman was still staring, peering through a glass disc to see him more clearly.

He was distracted by a line of mule-rams straining to pull a parade of wagons with their cargo of broken boulders. Their hoofs knocking hard against the path, the animals dragged their burdens toward a broad avenue that led through an open marketplace.

"Seems like you've got a splinter in your boot today."

"How can I think clearly when wonders wait around every corner?"

"Forgive me, master, but not all Bel Amicans are villains. The food isn't poison. It's overwhelming, that's certain. And it's possible to lose your head in all of"—he waved his arms—"*this*. But there's nothing wrong with wanting to taste a Coilsnake apple. Don't you want New Abascar to enjoy abundance like this?"

Cal-raven ignored him, more interested in a rant than understanding. He pointed down at the avenue. "And what's worse, people keep staring!" But the white-draped girl was gone. "I'm the scarred king who lost his house, Bel Amica's biggest joke."

"Maybe this is a time to dream about what New Abascar will be. And what it won't be."

Cal-raven pounded his fist on the brick, and a flare of power went into the stone, fine-line fractures branching out. "How can I dream of New Abascar when the Old Abascar is melting into Bel Amica? These daily walks—I thought they would help me hold our people together. Instead, I'm witnessing a collapse. When they see me coming, their smiles weaken. They ask me not when we can leave but how much longer we can stay."

Tabor Jan yawned. "What are those mule-rams hauling, anyway?"

The animals had stopped at a crossing, tossing their spiral-horned heads as cars rattled past on iron rails, drawn by a wooden cylinder that vented blasts of steam. The passing train hauled the harvest—thinstalks for carpentry, bundles of feathergrass for weavers' looms, enormous shells tufted with moss and clusters of barnacles that spewed long lines of seawater like tiny fountains. As the freight disappeared into a tunnel, the mule-rams snorted as if insulted, then pulled on the settled weight of their load.

"They're not mining the foundation out from under themselves, are they?" asked the captain.

"No, those stones were hauled in from the sea. The Bel Amicans break them open to dig out lodes of crystal for glassmaking. Krystor told me all about it yesternight. He was exhausted but happy. Working in Bel Amica's glassworks is like waking to his favorite dream."

"Abascar never had windows like these." Tabor Jan gestured to the towers, where the afternoon light ignited hues of red, green, and gold. "Maybe New Abascar will."

Cal-raven could not restrain a sharp, bitter laugh.

"Am I wrong? Bel Amica's a wilderness like any other, full of dangers and ways to get lost. Lead us through it and on to the destination you've seen. Be our king."

"I'll make grudgers of our people."

"We could have died in Barnashum, master, but we didn't. Snyde hired killers to finish you, but you survived. We might have been ambushed getting here, but we weren't. We thought Ryllion would give us trouble, but he's been on patrol. We're more fit for travel now than before." Tabor Jan shrugged. "I'm not saying there aren't problems. I'm just saying it's been worse."

"I'm not so sure," said the king.

❧

Twenty days earlier, as Cal-raven lay broken and losing hope, the cell door had been flung aside like a curtain at a pageant. A man with a briar patch of a beard bowed as if to a stage audience.

"Time to crawl out of the crolca and into the glory," he announced, then leaned into the cell. "On the other hand, this really is a nice little chamber compared to that Cent Regus krammhole where I was imprisoned. My, my, a window. Luxury, if you're comparing."

"I wasn't," said Cal-raven.

The visitor gazed at the sunny spectacle, then clapped his hands sharply. "Get up, King of Abascar. Say good-bye to your favorite gulls. Come see what your patience has earned you."

"Who are you?"

The man grinned fiendishly and seized Cal-raven's hand. "I speak coarsely. A foul habit, I know. When I saw my mother again, she was more upset about my language than the horrors I described. Fall as deep as I fell, and you find out what's at the bottom. It changes you."

Cal-raven leaned in, looking for something familiar. Lines whorled about the eyes as if carved there by rivers. "Partayn?"

This hairy, muscled intruder was the sharp-nosed musician whose singing had enthralled him in a Bel Amican theater so many years ago. The one, once delicate and childlike, who had filled the stage with enough instruments for an orchestra and then proceeded to move about and play them all like a toddler with a room full of toys. After he had gone, the audience had remained seated as if trying to preserve some fragile spell.

"You could have knocked these walls down. But you followed Henryk's instructions. You trusted him and stayed. That gave us time to prepare everything for Abascar's protection before revealing your presence."

"Henryk got my message to Cyndere?"

"We've been working hard to persuade my mother ever since."

"Persuade her to what?"

Partayn seized Cal-raven's arm and drew him out of the cell, into the narrow, crooked corridor. "To welcome you officially and to give you charge over your people again. With supervision, of course." He led Cal-raven along a passage that seemed confused about its direction.

"We've something in common, you know," Partayn continued. "My people thought I was lost forever. And I returned. It blew their hair back. Your people are beginning to wonder if you're lost forever. Oh, Tabor Jan shovels so much crolca our way, telling us how you're out there shaping Abascar's future. I can't wait to see his face when he learns you've been here all along."

Still aching from his ordeal, Cal-raven struggled after Partayn up a steep stair. Partayn explained that this tunnel was part of a secret network laid out by the kings and queens of old to give them a way to slip through the palace unseen. "It's the only way we can move about our own house without being spied on."

The Seers, Cal-raven thought. *Partayn distrusts the Seers.*

"It's also the only way that Cyndere could steal away to question you. She asked me to give you her apology."

Cal-raven had already guessed, much to his chagrin, the identity of his visitor. "I appreciate your protection. We will not trouble you long."

"Of course you will," Partayn laughed. "Do you mean to take House Abascar back out to wander in the wilderness? As exhausted as they are?"

"We have a destination."

At the top of the stair, Partayn led him onto a wooden platform like a lift, but Cal-raven saw no ropes or pulleys. Nevertheless, it rose, lifted by a swift and silent mechanism. Now he could see that rods along the side of the flat were embedded in tracks along the walls.

"It must be magnificent, this destination." Partayn hesitated. "Did you know that the Seers have snatched your healer right back from the edge of death?"

Cal-raven followed Partayn into a dim chamber where heavy curtains veiled all but one window. He limped to a model of House Bel Amica, detailed down to its jeweled glass panes. "The Seers healed Say-ressa?"

"I'm willing to work toward some kind of a departure plan. But I'd advise you to let your people get their feet under them before you drag them back into the unknown. And even then, I recommend you give them a choice when you depart."

Warily, Cal-raven studied the intricate model—its marketplaces in miniature, its winding walls made of parchment scraps, its toothpick flags and towers carved from old wooden flutes—as if it were a sleeping wolf spider nest. "This is Bel Amica. They'll choose selfishly. I have a duty to the kings and queens who came before me to defend Abascar's people against enemies but also against themselves."

"An honorable conviction. But why not start here? We're establishing colonies on islands in the Mystery Sea, and there's room for new settlers. And you and I, we share some of the same enemies. I could use your help as I try to break the hold that the Seers have on our people. What is more, we think we may be able to break the Cent Regus curse. We need allies who share this vision." He drew back one of the curtains to reveal a sun-drenched balcony. "You don't inspire people by telling them they're wrong. You need to show them something extraordinary so they long to be part of it."

He walked out into that bowl of sunlight. Drawing a deep breath, he unleashed a banner of music, a song about an archer with a magical arrow named Mercy. The melody streamed into the sky and seemed to send the clouds roiling.

Cal-raven stayed in the shadows, listening. Then he inched closer to the edge and gazed down.

Caught in the wave of Partayn's bold voice, people put down what they were doing. Figures wandered out into the streets. People tilted back their heads and listened. They joined in. The windows resonated in harmonic tones.

After finishing his song, Partayn returned to the shadowy chamber.

"I've been deeper than darkness, and I can sing a stronger song for it," he said. "You know about finding a vision in the dark. You remind Cyndere of her Deuneroi. And I can already hear in your voice what she means."

Standing on the balcony, Cal-raven had suddenly understood the heir's kindness. He lifted a farglass that lay on the stone enclosure and scanned the inlet's edge where Abascar's tents were spread. He was looking at Lesyl, who stood at a fish-bone fence gazing fixedly at the tower.

She would not be staring in expectation of seeing him. Partayn's voice had drawn her as if he had called her by name. And while others drifted back to their work, she lingered.

"I think it's time that you took me to my people."

Partayn had smiled. "That is being arranged. Cyndere cannot wait to spring the surprise."

And then she had.

"A five-finned feast!" "Best with a bottle of bristleberry wine!" "Three... two...one...catch!"

The fish leapt up the line of fishermen, tossed from the boats to the docks to the great stone stairs, then up to the lowest platform tier, up rope ladders, and into a grand open-air market. These fish were massive, cold, and still flailing, for they had been towed along in nets behind the boats to keep them alive as long as possible. The fishermen tossed the fish to each other with mighty, practiced throws. A wriggling red creature twisted and turned in the air as if it might fling itself back to the water but then fell into the cradle of another fisherman's arms. With each catch the fishermen shouted in unison, carrying their struggling quarry up to the market.

There, some were dropped in great glass tanks for the customers to ogle and assess. Others were slit open to expose their meat and laid out in lines on tables that tilted down toward the onlookers.

Cal-raven and Tabor Jan cut through the fish line between tosses, past the sparkling bed of silver catches.

"A grundle!" "Look at this one. He was a fighter!" "Fifty-ale-bottles heavy!" "Called himself a king, he did!" "But he'll end up on a Bel Amican plate!"

Cal-raven kept walking, hoping he had not heard a veiled threat in those words. He scanned the crowds for any sign of Warney, while Tabor Jan lagged a few steps behind, staring at mountains of melons, heaps of crispleaf heads, and bundles of purple oceantendrils, which would cook up tender and sweet in their own wine-red juice.

Where would Warney go? What would attract him in this place?

Commanding Hagah to sit still, Cal-raven and Tabor Jan climbed an iron ladder to the top of the wall that divided the market yard from a vast stone flat. There, defenders practiced archery: running up from a trench, leaping over obstacles, then turning as one to fire their arrowcasters wherever a straw-stuffed target sprang up in surprise. When Cal-raven found Jes-hawk in their number, he winced to see his friend uniformed in the glossy armor made from hardened purple surfleaves.

The troop turned toward them in formation, then ran quickly back to the trench. But Jes-hawk broke from the line, approaching the wall. This provoked a reprimand from the exercise commander, who stood on the observation stage in a corner of the yard. Cal-raven waved to the commander to indicate that he was calling one of his own, a permission the queen had granted him. The commander surrendered his protest but not his glowering discontent.

When Jes-hawk climbed the ladder on his side of the wall, he knelt at once and removed his gleaming helmet of polished white seashell.

Cal-raven asked him to stand. But the archer was still wary.

"Jes-hawk, put this guilt behind you. It was your sister who betrayed Abascar, not you."

"Send me after her, master. I know where she is."

"I've a better idea." Cal-raven felt a flare of conviction. "Let's get about building a house that has learned from its mistakes." He glanced up at the fogbound rock behind them. "And the mistakes of others."

"That's what I like to hear," murmured Tabor Jan.

"This is weighing you down, Jes-hawk. Let Lynna go. I need you to be ready for departure."

Jes-hawk raised his eyes to the captain, then to the king. "When will that occur?"

The patrol commander was approaching from across the yard.

"Let's talk later." Cal-raven looked down at the soldiers in the arrow yard. "Be patient. You'll be among the first to know. Until then, watch for

Warney. He's been missing for three days. Keep your eyes wide open." He made a show of clapping Jes-hawk's shoulder in farewell. "We're off to check the infirmary."

As they climbed back down the wall, Tabor Jan said, "I doubt you'll find Warney there. But you'll find Brevolo."

"Is she ill?"

"Nightmares keep waking her. Dreams that walls are breaking open, and then she hears Bryndei screaming." He kicked at a loose stone in the path. "I could sure use some of that sleep she's not using."

Hedley, one of Cyndere's blue-robed sisterlies, scowled at Cal-raven's question. "I don't know anyone named Warney." She stood in the doorway, blocking his view, arms folded.

"Never mind then," he said. "Warney's not my only concern. I've come to visit others."

Begrudgingly, Hedley turned so he could enter.

In the faint light of blue glowstones, a man and a woman slept in coffin-shaped tanks, floating in a thick, milky solution. They remained as unresponsive as they had been since the Barnashum cave had collapsed on them.

"The Seers could probably wake them just as they did Say-ressa," Cal-raven muttered, kneeling. "They're taunting us."

The man's brow was cold to the touch, his skin so pale it was slightly translucent. Blue veins crisscrossed his body like elaborate tattoos. Glimmering crystals bobbed all around his head, clinking against each other quietly. The bath rippled as if troubled by something swimming beneath the surface. Even here, unconscious, with contusions on his head and legs, the man wore an expression of obstinate defiance, scowling beneath his overgrown mustache.

"Is it true," the sisterly continued, a reprimand in her voice, "that he was chained up to be punished when the cave walls crushed him?"

"Let us speak of him as if he still lives, shall we? Dane's a carpenter. Built houses in Abascar."

"Not very good ones." Tabor Jan yawned from the doorway.

Cal-raven cleared his throat and gave a loud, stern reply. "Brevolo would be thrilled to see you, Captain. Maybe you should pay her a visit."

Tabor Jan bowed in apology and departed down the corridor.

Cal-raven's nose burned as he breathed steam from the medicine bath. He eyed the scissors and spools of thread that hung from a rack to the side of the tub. "He's recovering, isn't he?"

"You'll have to ask Pretor Xa. He oversees the infirmary." The sisterly twisted the thick sponge she had just used to bathe the red-haired woman sleeping in the second tank.

"Yes, he was chained." Cal-raven sat on a nearby bench. "He'd been bitten by a feversnake. He suffered horrible visions and kept trying to run out into the wild. We had to restrain him to save his life. Darsey here, she was very ill, and we put her in the same cave so Say-ressa could attend to them both."

"Everywhere you go," Hedley mused, "the earth turns against you as if you belong somewhere else."

"It wasn't the earth that turned against us in Barnashum." Say-ressa, clad in the white gown of an infirmary attendant, stepped in. Her face was grim with memories. "It was something else."

A sickening dread burdened Cal-raven as he looked down at Darsey's ruined beauty. "There's something more than human wickedness at work here, something that takes pleasure in ensnaring and destroying anything good."

The sisterly took a staff and stirred the water. The crystals pulsed and cast strange lights across the bodies. "Why did you restrain him?"

"In his delusion he wanted to die."

"Why interfere?"

Say-ressa laughed, bewildered.

"His desire to throw his life away was inspired by confusion, a lie that the poison told him. We need him. And he needs us." Cal-raven stood up, and Say-ressa took hold of his arm.

The sisterly moved to a table and rinsed her hands in a bowl of steaming, sudsy water. "The world is full of trouble, and if someone wants to escape it, they should be helped on their way. I nearly gave birth last year, but my moon-spirit revealed to me that I was ill-equipped to raise anyone. I went to the Seers and made an offering to my moon-spirit. When I woke the next morning, my spirit had rescued the child and spared her so much pain."

Say-ressa's eyes filled with fire. "Rescued?" She let go of Cal-raven's arm.

"That's enough, Hedley." Cyndere's voice came from the doorway. The stranger holding her arm—a smiling, broad-shouldered man in a white robe whose wide eyes were staring into space—was clearly untroubled by the anger in the room. "Let Bauris and me have a moment with the king and the healer."

As the sisterly moved to the door, Cal-raven called after her, "In some cases with proper care, our weakest have become strong."

Hedley glanced back, and a shadow like a small dark bird alighted between her brows. "But you cannot trust them."

"Hedley!" Though she was smaller than the sisterly, Cyndere seized her and pushed her backward out the door.

When she turned, she took Bauris's arm again. The old man studied the ceiling, mouthing some kind of song to himself. "Forgive me. I appointed Hedley to serve here so she could apprise me of the Seers' activity. It seems that was a mistake. She was born with only one open ear. The Seers opened the other. Now she'll believe anything they say." She led Bauris to the foot of the tub where Dane floated.

Cal-raven gazed down at the floating woman. "Say-ressa, can you help them?"

Say-ressa knelt to touch the sleeping beauty's brow. "They're beyond my help. We were slipping away. All three of us. I don't like the Seers or their methods. I don't think they know much about life, but they negotiate cleverly with death."

Cyndere stepped close to him, her voice barely a whisper. "If you ask me to have them removed from the baths, I can do that. But it will be risky. If I fight the Seers on too many fronts, my mother stops listening to me. When I lost my husband, they came after me and wanted to put me in something like this. To numb the pain, they said. I ran to Tilianpurth to get as far away from them as possible."

The misty-eyed man inched to Cyndere's shoulder and murmured as if only she could hear him, "Is this the man they whisper about?"

Cal-raven gripped the edge of the tub. "Who's whispering about me? The Seers?"

Cyndere patted the old man's hand. "Bauris doesn't talk to the Seers. And the Seers think he's worthless, so they ignore him."

"He's going to find her again, Cyndere." Bauris pointed to a spot in the air where he seemed to be reading some invisible script. "It's one of my favorite parts. They talked about it on the boat."

"The boat?" Cyndere asked. "Bauris, you hate boats. When were you ever on a boat?"

"The rowboat." With his exasperated sigh, Bauris reminded Cal-raven of a small child trying to explain something to a grownup. "It's like I tried to show you. My drawings, Cyndere. My drawings."

"He's been like this since we found him in the forest. He talks as if he went away and lived somewhere else. Whatever it was, that dream kept him alive for a long time at the bottom of a well without any food or help."

Bauris turned and discovered Say-ressa observing him. As if recognizing an old friend, he ran to catch her up in an embrace and spun her around with such joy that she could only laugh. "I know who you are," he exclaimed, setting her down again. "One of the witnesses talks about you."

"What a...friendly man you are," the healer stammered.

Cyndere drew Bauris away, smiling in apology. "He was a fine soldier once. And he cared for me like an uncle. We keep him close by, or he gets into trouble."

"A witness watched you in the forest," Bauris said to Say-ressa as if they were the only two in the room. "From the trees. While you were sick."

"No one else sees what he sees." Cyndere shrugged.

"Curious," said Say-ressa. "We had a few like him in our care at Abascar. My husband called them the lucky ones. He meant it as a joke, but it was almost true—they lived as if nothing worried them." She turned to Cal-raven. "That reminds me, you need to speak to Luci and Margi. They miss their sister so much that they're convinced she's sending them messages from somewhere far away."

"Visitor," growled Bauris.

"Pretor Xa's coming," Cyndere told Cal-raven, as if translating. "It isn't safe here." She touched the king's arm, then led Bauris back to the doorway.

Cal-raven followed. He was surprised at his sudden and intense reluctance to part ways. Cyndere turned and looked expectantly, even eagerly, so he groped for something to say. "Thank you," he said, although he was not quite sure why.

"I'll do what I can for you," she replied. She could not entirely conceal the weariness behind those words. She looked back at the two sleepers. "I want to bring them out of here alive. I'll make some arrangement." She put her arm around Bauris, who was staring at Cal-raven the way a child gapes at a hero. "Come along, Bauris."

"My lady," Cal-raven called after her, "your care for us is a gift. I'll remember it."

She hesitated. But then she hastened her step and was gone.

Cal-raven turned to the tubs, and that feeling of helplessness crept over him again. "I've got to get us out of here."

"You will," said Say-ressa, and her faith was so convincing that it terrified him.

22

DESCENT INTO THE
BEL AMICAN NIGHT

Without any news of Warney's whereabouts, Cal-raven dragged him-self back to his chamber. The wounds from the attack at Mawr-nash were hot and furious. Sleep beckoned, offering escape.

A sweet, subtle scent on the air distracted him, as if someone had just slipped away with a bouquet of roses.

He crossed the room cautiously, almost expecting someone to leap out from behind a curtain. But he was alone, and the perfume was gone. There was only a bowl of oil with a floating wick on the windowsill—a moon-spirit prayer lamp. He blew it out.

It was not a spacious room—just a simple bed and one small, unglassed window. But it was a luxury compared to Barnashum. And it was midway up the Palace Tower, its window opening to a view across the avenue to the Heir's Tower, which was near enough that he could hear the sisterlies gossip-ing and laughing in their chambers beneath the rooms Partayn occupied.

He stared at himself in the mirror, examining the left side of his face—boyish, unscarred, familiar. Then he turned and felt sick at the sight. He seemed suddenly twenty years older, haunted, with three craters marking his cheek.

We didn't have mirrors in Barnashum. It was better that way.

The image changed as he watched. The mirror seemed to read his thoughts, for the scars faded to faint bruises until he could hardly see them anymore. He touched his face and felt them there, deep and severe.

He unwound the white fishercloth from his head and scratched hard until his matted braids splayed in all directions. Then he unfastened the belt of smooth seadisc shells with their delicate feathered texture and slipped out of the white robe. He sat on the edge of the bed and let the cool air from the window move over his aching body.

Images, conversations, and fears whirled about in his head with such frantic energy that he could not catch and hold any single line of thought. He fell back against the pillows and gazed out the window, looking beyond the silhouette of the Heir's Tower. He tried to imagine the shadow of the Keeper soaring through the darkling sapphire sky. But the memory of that sight had faded, and he saw only a few nightbirds and something that fluttered awkwardly about—a rockbat, perhaps.

The sea whispered, *Slumm-ber, slumm-ber, sleeeeep...*

But there was another sound too. A crowd was cheering somewhere down within the rock, somewhere in the busy caverns where people stayed up all night eating, drinking, laughing, pursuing their passions.

He lay there awhile, listening. The sound rekindled memories, years old but vivid as yesterday, and when he closed his eyes, he could walk down into the caverns of Bel Amica. During the day the world outside the foundation flourished, but at night that life withdrew into the rock like fire sinking into an ember. And when he was lonely and cold, it had been a warm and dazzling fire.

Joined by tunnels alive with light and color, the open spaces within Bel Amica's rock were altogether different from the labyrinths of Abascar's Underkeep or the bear caves and burrows in Barnashum's Blackstone Caves. These were vast stone sanctuaries, surrounded by walkways and crisscrossed with narrow bridges. Light fell in brilliant shafts, clouding with smoke from the incense ponds, giving him the sense that he was submerged in a deep pool while someone above poured in colorful streams of billowing dye. For every torch there were long rows of mirrors that caught and relayed the light— changing it in ways that slowed and entranced him.

There would be people everywhere down there tonight—moving in ravenous packs or pairing off in secretive strolls. At night, as if unsettled by the darkness and the sea's song, they filled the air with raucous music, with songs that competed from different caves and corners.

Was Lesyl singing somewhere?

He went to the window again and stared down at the avenue. The laughing people far below taunted him with their happiness.

"What good can I do here?" he muttered.

A flash of light from the tower across the avenue caught his eye. He scanned the windows and saw that the light was flickering from a piece of glass hanging in a window two levels above his own.

He stepped away and put his back to the wall. A diamond of light flitted across the floor, jittered on the far wall, across the bricks, tapestries, and the mirror.

He knew exactly what it meant.

"No," he said. "No. Not again. Not ever."

As if to escape a hunter, he dashed from the window to the door. He took up his white Bel Amican cloak, then put it back in favor of a black stormcloak with a hood.

Ignoring the complaints from his injuries, he limped back down the long stair.

He passed some of the queen's attendants and inquired about directions to the music hall. He had only one wish of his own tonight. He would not bother to raise it to any moon-spirit. He would either fulfill it or find a drink and retire to his bed.

"Lesyl's not here," said a tall, spindly man with thick discs of glass propped on a wire in front of his eyes. With a tray of precise tools before him, he was leaning beneath the open lid of what appeared to be a huge wooden desk, turning screws and straining a blanket of wires. The instrument hummed in answer.

"Did she say where she was going?" Cal-raven asked.

"Someone came to take her down to the Hall of the Red Walls," he said. "There's a storytelling contest tonight. Should be quite a crowd."

"Thank you," said Cal-raven. The thought of a storytelling contest encouraged him. Warney always loved a good story, always sat right among the children, leaning in, breathless with anticipation.

He would go look for Lesyl and Warney in the rock.

"Hoo!"

The girl blocking Cal-raven's path held glass discs up to her eyes, magnifying them.

"Why are you following me?" He wanted to be angry at her persistence but laughed the question at her owl-like appearance.

"Hoo, hoo, I've heard about you," she hooted, and she made her eyes grow and shrink by pushing the lenses farther from her face and pulling them back in. "I've never seen a real live king before."

He pulled up his hood, dismayed that he could be so easily recognized. He stepped out of the way of a crowd spilling from the corridor into this cavernous gathering hall and watched them hurry toward the stage at the other end where the storytelling contest was already under way. "Aren't you a little young to be out so late?" He leaned against the wall, and the stranger stayed in front of him as if this were just a step in a dance. "Who are you, anyway?"

"Hoo-hoo!" She handed him one of the discs, then held the other to her eye. "My name's Obrey."

Reluctantly he raised the glass to his eye in time to see her blush.

"I made this." She pushed and pulled the glass before her lips so he could see her crooked teeth up close. "I come from faraway north." She slapped her hand across her mouth to cover her gasp, as if she had just released some secret she'd sworn to keep. Embarrassed, she dashed off through the crowd in a flurry.

The gloves, he thought, watching her go. *Krystor was wearing the same white gloves when I saw him yesterday. This girl must serve at the glassworks.*

From a distance Obrey had been as annoying as an itch. Up close, she was more intriguing. And familiar.

Over the din of the crowd, a voice amplified by a horn announced that the final contestant in the storytelling contest was ready to take the stage.

Firecrackers sizzled and popped. The crowd cheered. Stars with streaming tails soared up to the ceiling of the auditorium and burst over the elevated stage. The storyteller, a brown-robed man with hair that frayed like a fan, led two elaborately painted, vawn-drawn carriages beneath the line of lanterns draped across the stage.

In the bowl-shaped cavern, the storyteller's voice bounced back from the walls so all could hear. As he spoke with great emotion, one carriage came apart, the walls swinging open and the roof unfolding, transforming it into a model of a colorless dome surrounded by a wall.

Cal-raven froze. *That's my father's palace,* he thought. He watched the curtain at the back of the stage, expecting the Seers to appear. Surely they had arranged this humiliation.

As he crept around the outer edge of the crowd, searching for Warney, the storyteller summarized Abascar's fall. Smoke and light burst from the dome, engulfing the stage. Actors behind the curtain screamed in convincing anguish. A dramatic silence followed while the smoke cleared. A small young man staggered out from that cloud, coughing and clutching his chest.

"A survivor!" announced the storyteller.

The crowd cheered, recognizing this as the central character.

Actors dressed as beastmen charged at the boy. Their costumes were impressive—wild manes and flashing eyes, teeth that stabbed from their mouths like knives. But the boy made a dash across the stage and dove into a water trough that had appeared while the audience was distracted.

The narrator described how the boy had floated on Deep Lake, certain he was dying. Staring at the rising moon, he called out. "I have heard that the moon watches over us," the boy sang in a faltering voice. "So, please, raise me up. My heart wants so much more."

A great angled mirror on the ceiling reflected this evening's moon. There was no fakery; Cal-raven had seen that very crescent on his approach.

From the ceiling's shadowy secrets, a rain of sparkling dust fell and settled over the floating boy. Wind chimes enhanced this silver shower with musical tones. The audience applauded, enthralled. "Moon-dust!" someone shouted. "His prayers are answered!"

The story unfolded in a way that Cal-raven could have predicted. The boy swam to shore and made his way to Bel Amica, where he became an apprentice to a tender-hearted Seer. The Seer explained that Abascar had fallen because its king had barred his people from following their desires. At the edge of the stage, another actor staggered into view, playing a drunken king, and then retreated backstage, his momentary appearance drawing laughter and applause.

The Seer was suddenly joined by Bel Amican soldiers, who were played by, yes, real Bel Amican soldiers. In their gleaming plate armor, they received an ovation fit for heroes. And the boy stood up, clearly amazed and worshipful.

Just then, a man in the audience rose, shoved others aside, and stormed out of the crowd, ranting. This, too, inspired laughter, but the distraction was quickly forgotten.

Cal-raven followed him.

"Krawg," he called, running to join the old Gatherer. "Krawg, where are you going?"

"Can't take any more of this krammed nonsense. They're just throwin' candy, givin' these folks what they want to hear. That isn't storytelling."

"Let it go, my friend. It's just one story."

"That's not what's stuck in my throat," he barked back. "It's what happened here before this story. Did you see it? Someone told the story of the tricksters. My story. My idea. Somebody stole it from Mawrnash, brought it over here, and pumped it full of noise and flash and dazzle. What good will it do me to tell stories if people just steal 'em and change 'em?"

"Jes-hawk told me your story. The Bel Amicans changed it?"

"They made that rebellious fool of a boy their hero. The one who broke the dollmaker's heart. He's no hero at all. He ruins everything."

"Let me get you a bottle of ale, and we'll talk this over."

The Gatherer paused and then blinked at him in surprise. "You? Buy me a bottle of drink, master?"

Cal-raven smiled.

He moved to the nearest ale wagon, and when the vendor saw who he was, he dutifully set out a bottle. Reaching into his pocket, Cal-raven asked if he might have another. "No coins," the vendor insisted. "You're our guest. But give me a few moments, as that's my last bottle."

Cal-raven thanked him, surprised, and gestured for Krawg to wait while the vendor shouted to an errand boy.

As he turned, he noticed two hooded drinkers at a nearby table. He found he could not move. Lesyl and Partayn were sipping ales and talking excitedly together, leaning close. To anyone passing, they would seem to have known each other for years.

Getting steadily louder, the storyteller was reaching the climax of his tale. The young survivor was now a Bel Amican hero, married to a beauty who had devoted her life to the moon-spirits. He had, through the blessing of the Seers' potions, become Ryllion's fastest battlefield runner. In the closing scene, an actor playing Ryllion commanded the boy to hunt down a beastman, and the crowd roared when he slashed a stuffed monster into pieces.

The pageant closed when the boy presented his sword to Ryllion, saying, "I am blessed by Bel Amica's greatest teacher. May the moon-spirits bless you as you lead this house to vanquish the curse."

"All hail Ryllion!" shouted a soldier from the crowd. This drew scattered applause from the crowd and shrieks of adoration from more than a few Bel Amican women.

Lesyl, recognizing Cal-raven, moved to get up, but Cal-raven urged her to stay. Partayn regarded Cal-raven with surprise, then waved for him to join them at the table. Glancing back at Krawg, Cal-raven repeated his gesture for patience, then slumped down onto a bench beside Lesyl rather than on the bench Partayn had offered him.

"Horrible," said Lesyl, nodding toward the stage. "Abascar's suffering exploited for Bel Amicans' pleasure." She looked pale as if the story had made her sick. "Is this really how Bel Amicans decide what is true—by what gets the loudest cheer?"

The heir took no offense. "The people got what they wanted—praise and affirmation. That's the Seers' way." Partayn scowled at his drink. "I'm tired of sitting on the sidelines and whining whenever the crowd applauds a bad story or a shoddy song."

"Truth doesn't win many cheers." Cal-raven scowled. As his gaze strayed from the spectacle, he noticed that Krawg was shuffling away without his ale.

"I'll sing something true," Partayn growled.

"They won't like that," said Lesyl.

"They will if I sing it," he said with a garish grin.

As Partayn walked to the platform, Lesyl watched him go. "What's troubling you, master?"

"It's smoky in here. Did you see? House Abascar collapsed." He uncorked his bottle and drank. He drank it all. Planting the bottle back on the table, he said, "Now those poor survivors will have to decide whether to stick together...or surrender to the appeal of Bel Amica."

They sat in a long and uncomfortable silence.

Then Lesyl said, "Krawg seems discouraged. You would think we'd be happier here than in Barnashum."

"Your second bottle!" the vendor called to Cal-raven.

"I'd better go after Krawg," Cal-raven sighed. "Lift his spirits. It's what Abascar's king should be doing, right?" He met her puzzled gaze for one more moment. "Try to keep from losing what we've fought so hard to preserve."

As he took the second bottle, the vendor again refused payment. "I worked with Deuneroi. Great fellow. Incredible what he did to try to help your people. Consider this a gift in honor of a courageous man."

Cal-raven thanked him again, wondering, *What exactly did Deuneroi do?* He followed after Krawg, but he could feel that somewhere along the way he had left something behind.

Meanwhile the crowd continued to cheer.

"Where are you going?"

Krawg halted, scowling and tugging at the loose flesh beneath his chin. "Down to the water. I like the waves."

"May I walk with you?" Cal-raven offered him the bottle.

Krawg took the bottle and embraced it tight against his chest. "Honored, my king."

Cal-raven limped away from the noise, out of the brightness, onto the dimly lit rubblestone paths that led toward the harbor. The Gatherer kept glancing back at him in disbelief.

"I'm sorry we haven't found Warney yet, Krawg. We will."

"Told him I was goin' out on a ship," Krawg groaned. "Thought I'd brave the waves with sailors. Warney got a rockbeetle in his belly over that. Tried to tie me down, bless his broken eye. Then them sailors wouldn't take me. Now I can't find Warney."

"You two have quite a history. Thieving. Hard years of harvesting. Then you rescued Auralia. And what a surprise she turned out to be."

Krawg paused on a broad stairway, his shoulders sinking. "We miss her so." His voice was hoarse and heavy.

Cal-raven put his hand on the old man's shoulder, and that spurred Krawg into descending again.

"Making stuff up," he rasped, "Auralia made it fun. She played harder than a yard full of kittens. Made things that surprised folks and got their eyes to go huge. But here, it's different. Everything's about gettin' cheered or bashed. Nobody plays." He paused, staring at something in the road. Cal-raven saw it was a seashell. Krawg put it to his ear. "Ballyworms," he whispered, amazed. "This one's magic too!"

"You're a good storyteller, Krawg. In New Abascar you'll tell Auralia's story."

"Have you heard what they've done to Auralia?" Krawg's lip curled in revulsion. "You haven't heard?" He threw the shell into the shadows. "Follow me."

They wound their way through marketplace pavilions, canvases rippling with the incoming breeze. The marketers' wares had all been cleared away, but a few figures lurked about, picking at the cobblestones under the tables like wild dogs or giant ruffled birds. Through the dusk blue air, Krawg led Cal-raven down a long aisle between the empty tables to a stair.

A stench wafted from below like a warning. "Where exactly are you taking me?"

"I was out lookin' for Warney. Thought I'd sniff about in places where the least of all Bel Amicans go—the worried, the tangled up, the sobbers and complainers. I found a nest of smelly critters..."

Covering his face, Cal-raven followed Krawg down to a platform that spread out just above the silverblue water. It was crowded with rickety, wheezy shacks, some dark and some alive with color and noise. Women's laughter cascaded from one. Men were shouting in fevered argument about numbers in another.

A formidable figure burst from the shadows and rushed toward Cal-raven. She wore little more than seashell necklaces above rustling skirts of dried seaweed. She was as large as the thugs that Captain Ark-robin had posted at Abascar's main gate, and her arms were thicker than most soldiers' legs. She walked in a cloud of perfumes that caused his eyes and throat to burn even before she came close enough to touch his arm. Through a flimsy veil that rippled with her breath, a mischievous smile shone.

"Please," she asked in a tremulous whisper, "Gelina's lost out here."

"You're lost?" Cal-raven fought the urge to run as her curling fingernails scratched faint lines up his arm.

"We're all lost down here," she moaned. "But Gelina's learned that being lost can be beautiful." A lascivious music had entered her voice. "And oh my. From a distance you strike quite a stature, but up close Gelina can sense that you're feeling lonesome and weary. Why don't we put our burdens down awhile. Maybe we can help each other."

"I'm busy."

"You don't even know what I'm offering you," she persisted, draping her arms around him and pressing her claws into the small of his back. "Gelina normally makes a man work hard to earn her privileges, but her moon-spirit has led her to you. It's her duty to fulfill..."

Krawg called after him from a distance, and Cal-raven dropped out of the woman's embrace. He ran, leaving her there, hearing her heave an expansive sigh.

Krawg waved the unopened bottle toward a crowd waiting outside a wedge-shaped structure near the platform's edge. Then he urged Cal-raven around a corner, out of sight of the crowd. Backing into a recess in the wall, he said, "You'll have to go in without me. They threw me out last time."

"Who?"

"They call themselves 'Auralia's Defenders.'"

23

AURALIA'S DEFENDERS

At first it seemed the darkest space in Bel Amica.

They have no mirrors, Cal-raven realized.

Then he noticed that the people crowding about the stage were all looking up. One enormous mirror hung suspended, tilted to reflect the people themselves, faces pale as blurred constellations on Deep Lake.

The stage itself was tiled with blue glowstones, cut so flat they seemed a frozen pond.

The purple curtain behind the stage still wavered where a small man had just emerged. In his simple brown robe, he might have been a stablehand, perhaps eight years old, still skin and bones.

In the mirror above, his image was cast in a blue shimmer. He performed his speech with his back to the crowd so that the mirror magnified his gaunt face to immense proportions. His eyes were fever wild, as if apprehending horrors no one else could see. The hair that framed his face was like silver feathers blown back by a gale-force wind. And his hands flashed about his face like angry birds.

"I know what we're all thinking!"

Cal-raven was reminded of a teacher he had suffered as a child, an imperious woman who had always said "we" when she really meant "you."

"I know," he continued, eyes like a predator bird above a fish-crowded lake. "We're thinking, *they* did this to her. *They* did it. And *they* should pay."

The tone was as seductive as it was punishing, but the voice did not match the face. Was the speaker just an actor mouthing words while the lecturer hid behind the curtain?

The crowd stared up into the sea of their own mournful faces. Many held bundles of black thread, squeezing them or winding and unwinding them. *A ritual,* he wondered, *or just a popular nervous habit?*

Their yarn twisting became fitful as a statue rose up through the stage floor. Cal-raven leaned to get a clearer view. It was a young woman hunched over and holding her head—a poor statue indeed, for the proportions of the child were wrong. The head was larger than it should have been, and the face twisted in exaggerated anguish. It was not the mirror's distortion. The eyes had been sculpted large so her pain could not be ignored.

The speaker lifted a whip from the base of the statue. "This," the speaker said, "is what *we* did to her. Again and again!" *Crack! Crack!*

Cal-raven recoiled.

"Do we understand? No, we do not. I tell you that it was you—*you*—who did this to poor Auralia. And I—Bahrage of Bel Amica—am guilty too. We never lived in House Abascar, but we denied what our dreams told us every night. The Keeper exists!"

"The Keeper exists," the assembly muttered in chorus.

"The Keeper exists," said Cal-raven, surprising himself.

"You say that now. But no one said it when Auralia was dragged before House Abascar's King Cal-marcus for claiming that very thing."

Cal-raven pushed his way closer to the stage.

"No one would believe her." The speaker's eyes burned red. Spittle flew from his lips as he groaned, "The shhhhhame!"

At the next whip crack, one woman sobbed and broke from the assembly to run for the door. A man stepped to block her escape.

"Where are you going?" the speaker laughed. "Do you think that just because you never set foot in Abascar, you're innocent? Her colors were meant to burn. Burn our guilty eyes."

Bahrage eyed them all like some disapproving schoolteacher. "We gave up on the guardian that visited us in our dreams. We forgot the Keeper and turned instead to the colors and sensations of the Expanse. We must withdraw and think only of the glory that waits beyond the Expanse—the glory that Auralia promised us. Then the Keeper may return to our dreams, bringing comfort and consolation. All else is frivolous. Folly."

Again the spitting.

"The Seers tell us to indulge our desires. But desire is the very root of all crime. We must surrender the paltry beauty of this world. Raise walls with me, brothers and sisters. Wait with me in dark rooms. The Keeper will see us. This life will not torment us much longer."

Cal-raven blinked.

"When we are asleep," Bahrage continued, pounding his fingertips against his forehead, "we are at our best, for then come the dreams. The Keeper draws near, and we cannot resist it. Our waking hours are fraught with dangers: food, drink, and distractions of the imagination."

He leapt down off the stage into the mob, and his voice became commanding. "Withdraw from the city and its corruptions. Withdraw from the sea and its seductions. Withdraw, my fellow maggots."

He walked to the woman who had tried to flee and put his arms around her. He was like a child embracing his mother, and she cradled his head under her chin and sobbed. He grinned out to the crowd. "Where can we hide from the Keeper? It hunts for us. We must withdraw from the world of pleasures and go where we belong: the darkness. When the Keeper finds us there, it will see that we are the awakened. Perhaps it will spare us the fire of its lash."

"The Keeper exists," they agreed.

"This miserable box—this is the only home for the awakened. We have something they do not have. What do we have?"

"Evidence," murmured the audience.

"Evidence," Bahrage hissed, ecstatic. He marched back to the stage, climbed the small rungs of the iron ladder, and stalked about the statue like a crane hunting in the shallows.

As he did, a strange tone began to shimmer from the mirror, and he hesitated, his face contorted in alarm. Cal-raven recognized the sound.

Partayn is singing.

Bahrage cast his arms wide, fingers pushing out as if he would break apart the sanctuary. "Do you hear that?" His robe swirled behind him, sweeping up clouds of white dust.

Every piece of glass or crystal in Bel Amica sang.

"They call this a gift. But this is corruption unless he sings the Keeper's name. What do you hear?" He cupped his massive hands to his ears. "It's a song of a man's love for a woman. Is this how we should waste our voices? Nothing is worth our attention but the Keeper."

"The Keeper exists," the mob chanted. Aggravated by the thought of Partayn singing a love song within reach of Lesyl, Cal-raven chanted with them.

"I hear laughter. Laughter up there in the halls of revelry. Laughter and filthy talk. But the only true laughter, my friends, is ours."

A bitter and condemning laughter rippled through the assembly.

"I hear appeals to moon-spirits." Bahrage lifted a small clay bowl like the kind used to light the prayer lamps. And then he cast it down, smashing it upon the glowstones. "The only prayers worth raising are appeals for mercy from our magnificent Keeper. We must beg our way back into its favor."

Suddenly aware that his hood had slipped, Cal-raven drew it over his head. The room was hot with the press of people. His hands felt heavy, and he brushed them together, only to find that they were grimy from the white grit clinging to the sweat on his flesh. *The Seers can see this. The dust is everywhere.* He glanced back toward the door.

"Some of us acknowledge how wretched we are. The rest are the Keeper's enemy and so our enemies as well. In its sacred name, we must assail them at every corner. Assail them with the truth."

He knelt down, took one of the sharp shards of the broken bowl, and then pressed its jagged edge into three of his fingertips, drawing dark drops of blood. "The Keeper's hands have three fingers and a thumb," he said.

Cal-raven almost laughed out loud.

"Let us bring forward that which Auralia left behind, those signs that our world is worthless and unworthy of our attention. Let us secure those things that they might not be lost, corrupted, mocked, or exploited by those who don't understand."

"Evidence," chanted the mob.

The speaker seemed impressed. "Provide the evidence."

The crowd was silent for a moment. Then a man raised his trembling hand. Bowing, he advanced like a guilty dog to a cruel master. He carried a glimmering glowstone, a gem split in two, revealing a core of shimmering crystal. Within that broken core, other gems had been placed, and in the center, the bloom of a thistle, which seemed as brilliantly alive now as it had been when it was planted.

As the man went forward, Cal-raven almost reached for his sleeve. For there was no question in his mind who had made this wonder.

"Tell us about this evidence you ask us to protect." The overseer seemed to swell with satisfaction.

At that, the man hesitated. "My name is Daryus. When my daughter fell ill in Abascar, she sank into a deep sleep. My wife and I carried her out to Deep Lake, and my wife found this stone on the shore beside an abandoned campfire. We believe it belonged to Auralia."

"It did, Daryus," sighed the overseer. "We will protect it." He reached out his hand.

"Evidence," came the chorus.

"We gave it to my daughter," Daryus continued. "We thought that if the Keeper had cared for Auralia, it might come and care for our daughter too. Even though she was asleep, she clutched this gemstone tightly with both hands. And in the morning, she was awake. When we came to work in Bel Amica, people laughed at our tale. So we are grateful to find others who revere Auralia and what she came to show us."

The overseer took the stone from Daryus—a little too eagerly, Cal-raven thought—and clutched it in his bleeding hand. "We mark the beauty," he sighed, "with the sign of the Keeper."

Meanwhile, Daryus walked bowed and burdened, reminding Cal-raven of the slow, laborious progress of a sunclinger across sharp stones.

"Evidence," murmured the overseer reverently. "Evidence has the power to persuade those who doubt. But doubters will have to come to us. For Auralia's work is fragile, just as we are fragile. We must protect her work as we protect ourselves. We do not dare go out from these walls and risk temptation. In our dark rooms with our strong walls, we can be clean and safe."

"Clean," chorused the faithful. "And safe."

Bahrage exhaled as if he were trying to pour something out upon them, some conviction rising from deep within. And they breathed it in.

"It is time for a testimony." Bahrage looked up to the mirror, searching for a volunteer.

In that reflection one man's face suddenly shone out, bobbing like grey driftwood on a dark sea. "I will testify!" Tears streamed from his eyes. His lips quivered beneath his mustache. He swiped his hand across the sweaty glaze of his bald head and came lurching through the crowd toward the front.

"Faithful Snyde," said Bahrage, "how long have you been with us? And yet you have been silent. You have kept your story bound up. It's time for the awakened to know. Your doubts are finished. You have stepped into the Keeper's favor."

And that's my signal. It's time to go. Cal-raven began to back slowly through the crowd.

"I was a man pumped up with pride," declared Snyde. "I sought to earn the favor of King Cal-marcus in Abascar. And that was my first mistake."

"Yes," agreed the chorus.

"A vain man, that Abascar king. He surrounded himself with the selfish. I was one of them." Snyde beat his chest with such violence that even Bahrage winced. "I despised the very idea of the Keeper, for I hated the thought that my selfish deeds were seen. I lied. I cheated. I stole. I took honors that were earned by others. The Keeper saw it all."

Cal-raven stood still, stunned.

Snyde turned to the mirror and raised his hands, wringing them so they were clearly visible to all. He seemed eager to appear miserable. "I was there when Auralia stood before the house. I approved of her imprisonment. I joined in her condemnation because she named the Keeper as her master."

"This world is full of worthless people," said Bahrage. "You had plenty of company."

"But after my most despicable deed, I was hunted down by—"

Bahrage lunged back into the center of the image. "Wait! We must know. What was that despicable deed?"

"I betrayed the king's son!" Snyde wailed as if casting off a burden. "I led killers to Cal-raven!"

Bahrage was silent, obviously surprised.

Cal-raven began again to inch toward the door.

"They took him away. But the Keeper must have spared him from my wickedness, for Cal-raven walks among us in Bel Amica."

"Ah," said the overseer, suddenly troubled. "Perhaps the Keeper has given Cal-raven another chance to become one of the awakened."

Snyde raised his voice as if competing with Bahrage for the crowd's attention. "But then the Keeper found me. I ran, but it caught me up in its claws. It could have crushed me. But it awakened me instead."

The overseer stepped forward, raising his hands as if he would catch the entire congregation. "The Keeper exists!"

"The Keeper exists!" the chorus shouted with conviction.

"It is great like a dragon," Snyde ranted. "It has hands with two clawed fingers and a thumb. It has the face of a ferocious hound, and the wrath of a fangbear burns in its tantrum. The Keeper has horns like a ram. And fire in its jaws."

"Snyde," said Bahrage, "you have seen the truth. You are transformed. All your curiosities, they are silenced. Your questions, they are answered."

He tried to lead Snyde out of the circle of light, but Snyde pulled free of his grasp and raised his hands. "I have more to say! I must apologize to the one I offended. And he is here tonight!"

At that joyous announcement, Cal-raven pressed himself against the back wall.

The mirror moved. It shifted so that Cal-raven's image filled the glass, as if this had been part of the pageant all along.

Snyde took a step off the platform, but Bahrage, his face racked with a mad delight, reached out and grabbed him by the collar. "No," he barked. "Make him come to you, just as we all must come to the truth. We all want to enjoy this moment when Cal-raven awakens."

The door was still blocked by that scowling brute.

Seeing that all eyes were upon him and the crowd was clearing a path, Cal-raven considered his options. Then he lurched forward, limping to the stage. Taking hold of the ladder, he climbed, each rung seeming strangely difficult.

When he arrived on the stage, Snyde came forward, clasped his hand in a tear-soaked grasp, and fell to his knees.

"Forgive me, master!" he whispered, and lines ran down from his nostrils. "I did not believe you."

"Let us celebrate," Bahrage instructed the crowd, "that the former king of Abascar has come to complete his journey tonight."

"I was a fool," Snyde spluttered. "You were right. Auralia was right."

"Auralia was right," Cal-raven repeated.

"Speak, former king of Abascar." Bahrage smiled. "There's no better place to proclaim your belief in the Keeper than here. In this, its true home."

Cal-raven looked out at the crowd. He tried to swallow. The faces of the observers seemed dim and faraway.

"Tell them," Snyde whispered. "Tell them about Auralia. And what our people did to her."

Cal-raven spoke, gently at first. "There has been a great deal of talk about what was done to Auralia. Perhaps we would do better to say a few words about what *Auralia* did."

Bahrage's smile began to seem forced. But Snyde squeezed Cal-raven's hand again. "Tell them, then," he pleaded. "Tell them about the colors."

"Since I first began dreaming of the Keeper, I wanted to find it," he heard himself saying. "I remember standing in my cradle and staring out a window. I saw a winged shape soaring in a great dance in the sky. I climbed out of my cradle to pursue it. I took my first steps that day."

The crowd sighed, delirious with pleasure.

"My mother thought I was running after a bird. So she named me Raven. Cal-raven, to honor one of the sons of Tammos Raak. But I remember what I was chasing. And I have sought the Keeper ever since."

Bahrage looked eager to interrupt, so Cal-raven faced the crowd—better that than the hovering glass of distortion—and continued.

"It became my life's obsession, to the delight of my teacher and to my parents' dismay. When Auralia came, revealing colors we'd never seen, she said the Keeper had sent her. The colors..." He glared at Bahrage. "Yes, they spoke of some great mystery—a better life, a better place. But Auralia did not bring them from far away. She found them in the Expanse. All things, she told me, are to be embraced. For everything in the Expanse speaks of the mystery we are to seek. And we are part of that mystery. Auralia even wove the hair of a beastman's mane into that glorious weave."

"Beastmen are abominations," Bahrage thundered. "The Keeper will trample them. They are abhorrent. Former king of Abascar, you are—"

"Former?" Cal-raven pointed at the statue. "I am going to lead my people out from here, and I will build a house that honors the Keeper. For I have seen Auralia. I held her hand. I beheld those colors with my own eyes. You've understood nothing."

He put his hands against that misshapen sculpture and began to soften it into clay.

"Auralia's colors should open our eyes, not narrow them. She loved the world and saw it more clearly than any of us. She does not want us to hoard what she revealed or lock it away. Those things were meant to inspire us. With each discovery I'm more determined to search until I find the place they point to, the place where we belong."

He clapped his hands together through the molten stone, and it exploded into a thousand pebbles that clattered across the stage and rolled off to the floor. The crowd backed up, amazed.

He faced them. "That is where I will build New Abascar."

"Snyde has seen the Keeper," rasped Bahrage. "Have you seen the Keeper? I think not. Or you would cower and be afraid."

"Snyde's never seen the Keeper," Cal-raven shouted.

Snyde gasped as if struck.

"Horns like a ram? Three fingers and a thumb? Nonsense. The Keeper looks nothing like that. I've seen it with my own eyes. It lifted me right off the ground at Barnashum."

Snyde came trembling to his feet, and his broken expression slowly began to piece itself together into a face that Cal-raven recognized—a face full of insolence and pride. Cal-raven felt more comfortable with this figure than with the broken, penitent Snyde.

"You attack me here?" Snyde shrieked. "You insult me yet again? I saw the Keeper." His head was purple as a beet. "The Keeper has horns like a ram."

"It is clear to me why Abascar's survivors have come to Bel Amica," Bahrage said, turning to the crowd, his chin high. "They're here for guidance, for they have misunderstood. We will show them the way. For we are the awakened."

Cal-raven opened his mouth to argue, but when he raised his hand high, he saw his hand enormously mirrored in the glass pane suspended above him, and he stopped. All three contenders on the stage stood in cold blue reflections. And it troubled him to see that he was one of them, pale as a corpse.

What am I doing?

"Enough of this!"

A woman's voice rang out. A figure slipped through the crowd, drawing back her hood, and the crowd gasped in recognition of the tousled golden hair, those piercing eyes.

"My lady?" Bahrage dropped to his knees.

Cal-raven stood still, watching Cyndere intently.

"I'm taking the king of Abascar out of here. I'm ordering the dissolution of this gathering. Bahrage, if I hear that you have spoken to an assembly like this again, I shall have you sent to shovel crolca in Wilus Caroon's stable at Tilianpurth."

"My lady, you would prevent these broken people from receiving the Keeper's comforts?"

"Comfort? I've seen threats, intimidation, and humiliation. I've seen you savoring shame and fear. You have insulted a guest of this house and drawn him into a most dishonorable debate."

Cal-raven winced at the look she gave him. He knew he deserved it. He stared out toward the corridor, and the white scar glimmered in the center of his vision.

I must get out of this house.

"My mother's going to hear about this. And the Seers will learn what you've said about them and their religion. And then how will you escape?"

Bahrage looked at her and smiled, seemingly delighted.

Cyndere faced the assembly. Those gathered seemed afraid and uncertain. "Are you feeling comforted? Is this joy and restoration?" She turned to

Cal-raven. "Come. You and I shall determine whether I should go further than boarding up this place."

He did not look at the crowd. He followed her as she moved up the mirrorless corridor. She did not look back or say a word until they were in the alley.

Outside, as she turned to him, Cal-raven bowed his head.

"My lady," he said, "I appreciate your care. But I assure you, I do not need protection."

"Don't be naive. Please." She held out her hand. He took it, surprised at how small and cold it was—or perhaps it only seemed cold, for he was hot with temper. "Of course you do."

"Why did you follow me?"

"I arrived before you did," she laughed. "I've been attending this gathering for a while, trying to find some flicker of the truth about Auralia."

"Why?" Cal-raven glanced anxiously back to the sanctuary. "This has almost nothing to do with Auralia."

"I was beginning to suspect as much. I have seen the influence of her work. It heals. But that...that was sickness." She shuddered. "Sometimes distortions can speak the truth. They confirm for me what is real by troubling me with something false."

She was still holding his hand. He withdrew his—too quickly, he realized, for she stepped away as if offended. "I'm sorry," he said. "My people might misunderstand."

"Of course," she said.

As she led him away, she folded her hands behind her back as if she were still offering them to him. They ascended the stair quickly, and Cal-raven gulped the cleaner air, feeling as if he were rising from a deep, polluted well.

"Sisterly Emeriene brought supper to your room tonight. She was hoping to meet with you."

Cal-raven bit his lip.

They emerged into the deserted marketplace, where the tents were swaying in a slow and eerie dance.

"You have avoided her since your arrival. You are never where she seeks you. Is it insulting to take orders from one of my helpers?"

"My lady, I have many people to attend to. Holding Abascar together is like trying to catch falling leaves and put them back on the tree. We'll take your leave soon." Even he was surprised at the force of his voice.

"Patience, Cal-raven ker Cal-marcus. I told you that I would send for you when I was ready to rescue your two friends from the infirmary. Surely you won't depart before we've restored them. Has your trust run out?" She seemed angry.

"Trust? I trusted you when I arrived here. Did you trust me? No. You hid behind a wall and questioned me."

She touched his lips to silence him. They stood among the wavering curtains and fluttering awnings in the empty marketplace. He realized that any of those ghostly canvases might conceal a spy.

Then she stepped very close to him and leaned in toward his shoulder. He could smell her perfume sweetening the salty breeze and see the details of the gems swinging gently from her ears.

"Let's not argue. I understand you, Cal-raven. Deeply, I do. The poisons and seductions spreading through our house make it difficult to live here day after day. Every morning when I walk along the water's edge, I long to keep walking or to sail away on a ship or to return to the deep forest and listen to birds instead of the constant bargaining and bickering. To stay is wearying and dangerous. But I must stay. I said I would complete what Deuneroi began. He risked his life trying to break the Cent Regus curse. And he died trying to save survivors from Abascar's ruins."

Cal-raven found himself holding Cyndere's shoulders, whether to support her or to hold himself up, he was unsure. "Deuneroi died in Abascar?" Then he found his arms around her. "I am sorry."

Cyndere did not resist his embrace. "To honor Deuneroi," she said, "I've set plans in motion that will bring strength to New Abascar. I cannot say more yet." She turned, and in the darkness her eyes were two pools flecked with stars. "You trusted me before. Trust me a little more."

He heard something more in her voice than a friend's confidence. It startled him. Even more startling was the surge of emotion that trapped his voice—a powerful pang of loneliness.

"Go back to your room, Cal-raven," she said. "The people have begun preparing for my mother's celebration. They'll be hanging banners on the towers tonight. Draw the curtains across your window so you can sleep. Tomorrow will be eventful."

He felt the urge to take her hand again.

But a clattering sound behind one of the nearby tables drew their attention. Then faint laughter.

"Who's there?" Cyndere demanded sharply. "Come out."

Two figures rose to their feet. Struggling to disentangle his arms from the seashell necklaces of his seductress, Krawg tried to apologize, but it sounded more like a man dying from some severe infection of the lungs. Gelina's enormous lips parted in the smug smile of a conqueror, and then she strutted off through the marketplace, a riot of clattering beads and swishing veils.

Wide-eyed, Cyndere laughed. "With that," she said, "I bid you good night." Wrapping her dark disguise more closely around her, she walked away determinedly, as if it required a great force of will.

Krawg hung his head like a dog who expects to be scolded. But Cal-raven only shook his head. "Come along."

Behind him the sea roared. He felt so fragile that the thought of going anywhere alone frightened him.

It may have been the incense or the reflections from a thousand murky mirrors. It may have been the endless parade—the haggard and haunted, the wide-eyed and the intoxicated. It may have been the shrouds of perfume they wore or the wave upon wave of music spilling from revelhouses, shacks, and gated gardens.

Whatever it was, Cal-raven forgot himself on the long ascent. Somewhere on the climb, Krawg left him. Stair after stair, avenue after avenue. The guards who laughed at him as he tripped crossing the wrong courtyard were unfamiliar. Was this the right tower? Was this the lift, and was this the right cord to pull to take him to his chamber?

He rose, passing window after window, catching glimpses of platforms, walls, walkways slung from the rock. Trains rolled along the rails, slithering in and out of passages like nocturnal serpents. He thought he saw children climbing ladders to string cords of tiny, sparkling glowstones.

When he stumbled back into his chamber, he patted a happy Hagah and snatched up the cold bottle of ale that waited on the table. The bottle was empty before he drew the towel off the food tray and found a loaf of fresh nectarbread, a small pitcher of cream, sliced ocean-vine apples, olives, crumbling wedges of fragrant blue-flecked cheese, and thick slices of spicy chump sausage. He devoured the sausage with the cheese, folded pieces of bread and dipped them in the cream, and then ate the apples, which proved to be a bit sour.

He was thirsty again but almost too tired to move. He lay back on the bed, wondering how soon the sun would rise. When he closed his eyes, there it was, the red moon's burn, flickering fiercely in his left eye.

He swung his feet back to the floor, stood up, and then stumbled to regain his balance.

The star he had seen in the chamber before, a diamond of light darting about his room, was back.

Cal-raven walked to the window. There again he saw the flash of the tiny glass in a curtained window of the Heir's Tower high above.

He knew what it was. Only a few years had passed since he had learned what it meant.

"You win," he said. "I give up."

Leaning out the window, he scanned the courtyard below. People were busy there with decorations. Already banners rippled beside his window, swaths of cloth bearing bright emblems of soaring eagles, fish curling in their talons. One of the tall ladders was propped against the wall just beyond his reach.

He climbed out the window.

Clinging to the tightly fitted blocks of the stone, his fingers burning with stonemastery, he spider-walked sideways until he reached the ladder. It extended a fair distance above his window, and he climbed up to the third rung from the top.

The ocean seemed nearer. Its voice was clearer, the waters roiling in the inlet and crashing on the shores. A bat hovered beside his head, squeaking after some frantic moth, and then was gone.

He waited for someone to shout at him, to tell him to get off the ladder. But the people far below were talking wearily amongst themselves.

The other window was right across the avenue from him now. The reflective glass was gone from the window. The curtains had been pulled shut.

This is going to be another mistake, he thought.

He climbed around the side of the ladder, and then he pushed off from the wall with a hand and a foot. The ladder swayed out from the wall, then brought him back to it. He waited. No one had noticed. He pushed off again.

The ladder moved easily upright, then tipped and fell fast toward the Heir's Tower. But the distance was far enough that it landed at a lesser incline, and he caught himself against the wall beside a window three levels below his target.

Sweat dripped down his forehead from the effort. He felt strangely exhilarated. Pushing his fingers into the stones, he climbed quickly without looking down. The voices below grew louder as he clambered onto the sill and leapt through the curtains.

He landed in a room surrounded by elegant white candles.

A woman in a white robe stood with her back to him, gazing into a mirror.

He brushed off his hands and said nothing.

"I was beginning to think you'd forgotten," said Emeriene in a quivering whisper. And then she took slow, uneven steps toward him. "That you'd never come back through my window."

24

AN OPEN WINDOW

Y ou should be scared of me right now." Emeriene set the small mirror behind one of the candles. It shot another golden ray to cross the others cast all around the chamber so that she moved in a web of light.

"Terrified," said Cal-raven, and he meant it. "You've been so generous to my people. But you should close the door against anyone who treats you with as much disrespect as I have."

"My door," she said, "is always closed these days. And barred."

"But your window was open."

"There is something worse than rejection," she snapped. "There's a long, slow starvation while I wait for someone to fulfill a vow."

"You deserve better than Cesylle." Cal-raven wondered if it was too late to turn back. "And you deserve so much better than me."

"Perhaps." She walked to him and without any hesitation reached up to cup her hand behind his head and drew him down to kiss her. Stepping back from him almost as quickly as she had approached, as if burned, she pressed her forearm to her lips and looked away. "But you see? I'm as weak now as you were cowardly then."

"I should never have run." He stepped forward, reaching out. "Does he hurt you?"

"Not in the way you mean." She walked around to the other side of the table. "I was once a beacon for Cesylle. But when he earned the Seers' favor, anything he could want became available to him. Now brighter things hold his attention. He's committed our sons to apprenticeships on the islands. He took them away from me, Cal-raven."

She went to the long, low wooden shelf and unwound her head scarf. Her dark hair spilled down past her shoulders, surprising him. Last he had touched her, that hair had been cut short and neat, just behind her ears.

"He's a blind man and an idiot," Cal-raven whispered. "I've been gone for six years. But you do not look a day older."

She paused, then finished unpinning the clusters of gems that hung at her temples. "I expect you to go on lying. If you don't, I'll throw you out." Then she held up a mirror with an oval the size of her small face, and he saw her eyes narrow. "You'll leave me again, won't you?"

"House Abascar's future is to the north."

He thought she might lash out at him or collapse into tears. Instead she bravely met his gaze. "Then stay for a while, King of Abascar. You never know what might happen. The queen might offer you an island."

"It would be a mistake."

"An island?"

"To stay."

"Trust me," she said. "In the Expanse every choice is some kind of mistake."

"I'm getting that feeling." He walked toward her then, and she sat down on the edge of her bed. He knelt and quietly reached beneath her robe, behind the calf of her right leg, and softly unbound the straps of the cast that protected it. "The Seers have not healed you yet?"

"They'll never lay a hand on me."

The cast parted like a shell, and he set it on the floor. Then he took her small foot in his hands. Her hand closed over his shoulder and tightened as if she were in pain.

"I've tried to forget you, Em," he said.

"I understand," she sighed. "I tried to forget Partayn when we thought he was dead. Then I met you. I asked you to tell me about your home. And you opened a door to places I'd never imagined. With you, I could forget what Partayn must have suffered when beastmen took his caravan. I could forget the dreams I had designed since childhood about what he and I might become. You...you were a whole new world. And then..."

"Then I abandoned you without a good-bye."

"It was worse with you. You were still alive out there somewhere, choosing other paths, choosing other company. You could have thrown yourself out this window and made it easier for me."

"I did not love anyone's company more than yours, Emeriene. But my father expected so much of me. I had to return to him. And now I've inherited his burdens, the calamity he prepared."

"You're still so principled," she said bitterly. "You and Partayn—both so much like Cyndere's Deuneroi. Always with an eye on some higher path than your own pleasure. Always giving up what you want for something more important. How could loving any of you be a mistake? I know that I am selfish. But the stars have gone out. I can't muster the courage for dreaming or hoping anymore. My boys are gone. Do I give up and drift aimlessly here? Or do I wait, and wait, and hope that the beacon that once shone for me comes around again?"

He closed his hands around her calf, bowed to press his forehead to her knee. "Are you really so alone?"

"I lean against Cyndere," she said, "my one true friend. And when she leaves me behind to attend to her own secrets, I feel as lost as a sailor clinging to wreckage on the sea."

"You're stronger than you think." He looked up into her face and almost lost his line of thought, for she was still, in all her sadness, so beautiful. Those dark brush strokes like storm clouds over her piercing gaze, that small red twitch of her lips. "You have not abandoned your husband though you have every right to throw him out a window. You do not condemn your children though they follow him."

"But how *could* I give them up? It's too costly." She combed her fingers through the braided lines of his hair. "Look what I've done. Here—a second chance for us. But I gave up too quickly. I made other promises, didn't I? It's too late. I cannot walk away with you."

He stood and, with one arm around the small of her back and another under her bending knees, he lifted her. "Let me carry you then." He smiled.

He took her through the balcony curtains and out into the air. They lay down on the cushioned bench. He cradled her head on his shoulder. She ran her fingers through the matted braids of his hair.

"Moonlight still loves you."

"And you," she said, smiling for the first time, "you look like you've been dragged across the floor of the Cragavar, facedown." She kissed her thumb, pressed it against the right side of his nose, and drew it across the scars. "Such wounds."

"Barnashum's been...challenging. It's made me careless when I shave."

Now she was laughing, closing his mouth with her palm. "I thought you'd died when Abascar fell. And then when the rumors about survivors came, I..." She pressed her hand against his chest. "You don't know how beautiful—"

He put his fingertips on her lips. "Look up."

The stars were so stark and cold against the night sky that it almost hurt to look at them.

He sighed and put a hand over his face. "You know why I climbed to your window. You know what I wanted. But I cannot make you any promise, Em. I would drag back the suns of so many days to return to that crossroads where we first met. If I ever find a way..."

"You're not the only one with a life and a calling, Raven. I made my promise. Empty as it now seems." She paused. "May I still call you Raven?"

"Of course," he said. "But only here, unless you want the world to know our secrets. Promise me, Em. Promise me you'll be safe."

"Cesylle spends most of his time beyond these walls, running errands for the Seers. He's jealous of Ryllion because he wants to be the Seers' favorite. I think he's forgotten all about me."

"And Partayn? Surely it is difficult seeing him all the time, knowing he'll be king."

"The heir came back with two thoughts in his head—he wants to sing, and he wants to save those suffering in the Cent Regus Core. And he's changed. He's become crass and impulsive. Braver, too. He devotes himself to planning the prisoners' rescue. He and Cyndere rarely sleep. They're two hands holding one sword, fighting their own house to save it."

Cal-raven stared out at the sea, and it seemed that she had spoken some word of incantation that turned loose troubling spirits. "What do you mean 'planning the prisoners' rescue'?"

Emeriene was silent for a while, then bowed her head. "Perhaps I'm not so good with promises after all. I said I wouldn't tell."

"I need to know this," he said.

"You'll find out soon," she said. "Cyndere has a scheme and a part for you to play in it. She knows you're a stonemaster, a strategist, a king with powers at his command."

"That's what she was hinting at. The plan!" He sat up straight. "Cyndere plans to rescue the Cent Regus captives. That beastman she sent to me. He's helping her, isn't he? He's going to help her save the prisoners!"

"Who do you think rescued Partayn?"

"Give me a moment." Cal-raven rose and paced back and forth on the balcony. "Oh, this world is too big. Too many slaves. Too many monsters. I am king of Abascar. That should mean something. I should be able to fix what is broken. But I cannot go to the Core to help the slaves. I have a clear vision, a path I must not stray from. Yet if I refuse to help Cyndere, what kind of man am I?"

When he closed his eyes, the white burn was waiting for him like a signal flare.

Somewhere down the avenues a woman had begun to sing. A familiar voice. Then another rose in harmony—and that voice, too, was known to him. Cal-raven looked out to sea.

Emeriene stood and limped to his side, threading her hands between his arms and sides, clasping them at his belt. "Forgive me for my jealousy."

"Jealousy?" He turned to her and drew swirling lines on her back with his fingertips. "You have no rival for my attention but a city, a destination."

"You love her, don't you? She's as beautiful as her singing voice."

He did not answer her.

She rested her cheek against his chest. "Go to New Abascar, Raven. Make a home with one whose heart is not already in pieces."

"The ax has already fallen. I'm alone, Emeriene."

"You can do something about that. Seers have persuasive potions you might slip into her drink."

In surprise he looked down into her sincere, suggestive gaze. And then the edge of her scowl quivered, and she broke into a laugh, pushing him against the railing. He pretended to push back, and she pretended to stagger, grabbing his tunic and leading them inside. She sat down on the edge of the bed again, then lay back. "I cannot send you away." Her eyes filled with tears. "It's so unfair. I never get what I want."

"Nor I."

"We could run away," she said, but her voice told him she knew they could not.

"And where would we live? Where would we have any kind of rest?" He set his elbows on the bed, pushed his arms beneath her shoulders, cupped the back of her head, and leaned in to kiss her. She turned her head.

"Let me give you what I can." She reached into a pocket of her robe and drew out a small glass vial. She opened it in the space between their eyes, and rich pungency, thick and soft as velvet, clouded the air.

"What…" He blinked as his view of her face began to blur. "Slumberseed oil. No, not…again…"

"A few hours of deep sleep." She touched the mouth of the vial, then dabbed his scars. The drops felt cool as tears.

He sank forward into her embrace, and they were both asleep, entangled like a puzzle. Painful needles stitched together their memories and their dreams.

Tabor Jan stared at the names carved into the bottom of the bunk above his own.

He tried memorizing them, closing his eyes and reciting them, hoping it would help him sleep. Here in the hollow of this watchman's wall, his mind was like a farglass in the hands of an anxious watchman, searching through the sights of the day, magnifying some, drawing back from others. So many new experiences had dazzled him, but there was so little time to make sense of anything or to ponder what to do about it.

In those moments when the memories began to shift into bizarre dreams, the soldier above him would turn and shake the rickety bunk.

Bunkrooms inside the walls—there would never have been any such thing in Abascar. Cal-marcus's walls had been meant to withstand trouble. Bel Amica did not seem designed to withstand any kind of siege, except insofar as every entrance was carefully watched and every visitor questioned.

At times he wondered if the watchmen were the engine that kept currency flowing in Bel Amica, for they spent their days gazing down at all the pleasures, delicacies, drinks, fashions, and opportunities being sold in the marketplace. He could see the boats sailing in from the mouth of Raak's Favor; he could see what they carried out to the islands of the Mystery Sea, where new communities would live, work, harvest, and play.

What kind of courage will it take for Cal-raven to blaze a new trail in view of all this?

He went to the window. A long path of stone branched out from the rock below and into the Rushtide's waters, a peninsula that formed one of the harbor's welcoming arms. The edges of those arms were pocked with caves where boats docked. He watched the boats come and go, watched the white burst of night-diving shallowbeaks flit from mast to mast so they could see fish rising and biting at bugs on the surface.

It's always feeding time in Bel Amica.

He looked to the horizon, where clouds were mustering.

Cal-raven is probably asking the Keeper for help.

The sailors and dock guards were, he noticed, all standing still, as if observing some ceremony. Taking a closer look, he could see that they were watching one particular figure—a tall, awkward character who strode solemnly along a boardwalk, examining the boats, examining the docks.

The Seers are watching the watchmen. Do they worry we might actually see something?

He made himself a promise to go to those docks and have a look.

"Keeper, if you can hear me, then you'll laugh, because I sound like a raving idiot. I don't believe anyone pays attention to people who toss questions into empty space. But for what it is worth, I'd like you to give us a plan. And while you're at it, show me what I'm supposed to do."

A tiny bell rang at the entrance.

The soldier on the upper bunk shifted and snorted like a prongbull facing a challenger. Tabor Jan went to pull back the curtain.

The bald, smiling, thickly mustached man facing him was dressed in an infirmary robe, and he held out an empty chair in front of him, leaning on it as if it were a crutch. Bauris. Tabor Jan remembered him from the infirmary. A strange character, clearly witless. But he had been a soldier once. That earned him some kind of respect.

"Abascar captain?" Bauris inquired.

"Yes, that's me."

"Message for you."

"From whom?"

"You'll need a disguise."

Tabor Jan waited for an explanation. When none came, impatience brought him close to shouting. "I must put on a disguise to hear the message?"

Behind him the slumbering watchman growled, smacked his lips together, and murmured, "I thought I saw one of them twitching."

Tabor Jan glanced backward. *I'm trapped between two ranting crazies. But the one standing in front of me is wide awake.*

"You're coming up to the challenge," Bauris continued. "You'll need a disguise. Take it, or you'll never get inside to learn the truth."

"Truth about what?"

"What the birds want to tell you. Here's the best part. You'll have witnesses."

"Witnesses? I'm afraid I don't understand."

Bauris shrugged sadly. "Certain fires will never be lit without kindling." He turned and, using the chair as if it would give him forelegs, he planted it out in front of him, then walked up to it and did this again, measuring his path step by step up the corridor.

"If you ever want your wits back," Tabor Jan muttered, "you'll find them at the bottom of the Tilianpurth well."

He went back to the window. A crestfisher, sitting on the flagpole that slanted from the wall outside, turned its massive fan-feathered head to stare at him.

"Got something to tell me?"

The bird dropped from the pole and soared a graceful line down around the opposite tower.

"We have to get a plan and get out of here," Tabor Jan sighed.

Trying to wake Cal-raven before dawn proved impossible. The slumberseed oil had drawn him down so deep that Emeriene could not inspire more than a moan.

"I'll kick myself for years." Shrugging off her robe, she quickly donned her modest blue gown and head scarf, then strapped the cast back on her leg. "I've imagined a night like tonight so many times, but it never played out like this. Dreams are kinder."

Cal-raven turned over so all she could see were his bare shoulders and his red braids hanging down to the pillow. His labored breathing would cease for long spells of silence, and then he would gasp or shout something, which made her worry that other sisterlies would hear a man's voice in her room.

"There it is!" the king of Abascar shouted. "Do you see it?"

"No," she laughed. "Why don't you tell me about it?" She seized him by the shoulders, sat him up, and drew his tunic over his head. "You'll never know I took this off you. And if you did know, you'd never believe that I did it to cool your fever."

He sat there with his head hung down, murmuring.

"This time," she said, "I'm not going to wait around for you to save me. It was a foolish dream. Cyndere gets up every day and pushes on, and she's lost so much more than I have."

She pulled his white jacket on, then drew that black stormcloak around his shoulders. "I'm taking you out of here as carefully as you came in."

She walked to one of the tiny recesses in the wall where a candlestick burned low. Blowing out the candle, she lifted the ribbon of cloth beneath and slid her fingers around the back edge of the slightly raised stone on which it rested.

On the other side of the room, the mirror came loose in its frame and turned slightly, opening a door just behind it. A salty breeze moved into the room, and a few bewildered moths stumbled into the air.

"Come on, then. Both our spirits need lifting, and I know just the thing." She brought a glass bottle from the table, uncorked it, and put it to Cal-raven's lips. He swallowed, choked, and leapt to his feet.

"Let's go for a stroll," she said.

Emeriene brought Cal-raven down through the old kings' secret passages with a blindfold over his eyes, which may have been necessary, but it was also fun. Cal-raven was still so muddled by the slumberseed oil he could not walk a straight line. She let him wander into more than a few pillars and gave him one long stairway to navigate by himself until his whispers were as angry as shouts.

"You deserve a lot more punishment than this," she said. "Wait until you see the tattoo I stained on your belly."

He paused, then drew a handful of stone from the wall, broke it to harmless pebbles, and cast them down after her. She was still laughing after the shower had gone silent.

Unmasking him, she led him onto the watchman's path over Queen Thesera's garden of rare foreign flowers and trees, and as they breathed in those strange perfumes, he began to relax.

They had walked here during the nights when he was a spy. She had come down to this walkway in the evening, retracing her steps in search of an earring that had gone missing. The earring did not turn up, but she did find a talkative, unfamiliar watchman who seemed quite uninterested in his work.

They had discussed what might live on those faraway stars, what treasures might be discovered along the bottom of the Mystery Sea. They imagined what they would do if given islands all their own. He made her laugh. But he also startled her with his willingness to invent things for his island— creatures, places, enchantments.

"Isn't it strange," she had said, "how most of us reach an age where we just fold up our imaginations and stuff them into our closets? I think I've learned more about you from these impossible dreams than from anything else you've said."

"Then let me tell you something impossible," he had said, turning and leaning her back against the wall.

Anticipating the nature of the pending announcement, she'd gasped, "Who are you?"

"I'm the prince of Abascar, commanded to break into Bel Amica and tear down the walls that conceal Queen Thesera's intent to destroy House Abascar."

She had laughed at that, waiting for him to surrender the joke.

"In truth," he said, "I've only come across one danger to report. There is a thief in Bel Amica who can, without giving any indication of her intentions, snatch something from my chest and leave me wondering what I must do to get it back."

Audacious. Ridiculous.

He had opened his hand to reveal a rose bloom exquisitely sculpted from stone, with the gem from her earring set in the middle.

For the next several nights, she had crept from her chamber to walk with him along the wall. He had been eager. She had been nervous. Their kisses were quiet promises that someday they would walk together beyond the circuit of their secret.

When the watchman assigned to that path returned, Emeriene directed Cal-raven to another stretch of Bel Amica's wall. She had taken to visiting Cyndere at night, and Cyndere, trusting her servant and asking no questions, let her climb out the window on a long rope to drop down and meet her mysterious friend.

"These memories are sweet," Cal-raven said now as they reached the pillar where he had first given her the rose. "And they're going to ruin my day."

"Oh, we have a destination," she assured him, bringing them at last around the eastern side of the rock. "Isn't that what you're concerned about these days? Destinations?"

Descending into a courtyard, they approached a great glass cone set into the rock. Panels of glass on its side blazed with reflected sunlight.

"When you last visited, the glassworks were impressive. Since then, they've been transformed. There's nothing like them in the sunrise."

"I don't have time for a tour."

"Cal-raven," she said firmly, "I'm saying good-bye to you today. You're leaving Bel Amica soon, but if I wait until then, I'm likely to change my mind. And that would be a disaster. You, Partayn, Cyndere—you are people of your word. And I would be the same. If I fail and decide to pursue you, you had better run."

He seemed frightened, even though he tried to laugh it off.

"While I stay true to my family, you had better fulfill your own vows. I want to see New Abascar someday, Raven." She paused. "*Cal*-raven. When I met you, you gave me something beautiful. It's my turn to give something back to you."

She raised her hand to knock, but the door opened before she could strike it.

"King of Abascar!" There, dressed in a white gown that sparkled with glassy dust, was that excitable girl who had called herself Obrey. "Don't just stand there! Come inside!"

25

THE GLASSWORKS

S ee? See?"

Obrey flicked the glass stars that hung from her ears, which stuck out from the white cloth that wrapped her head. Then she rustled the strands of her leafy skirts that were made from long strips of soft-edged glass. "I made these here."

The glassworks' reception room was a dizzying cocoon made of mirrored fragments. Alive with the light descending through openings in its shell, some pieces cast back truth, while others distorted it. Grey-feathered cooeys strutted around, puffing out purple chestfeathers, impressed with their reflections. Others flew at their images, flaring feathers and chirping challenges. Cal-raven would have laughed had he not observed how many of these head-bobbing fowl dragged broken wings.

Finding his balance, he stepped into an adjoining corridor and stopped in front of a full-length mirror. "Bloody gorreltraps." He pinched the space between his eyes. "I look like I've been attacked."

He turned and discovered that he was surrounded by versions of himself. In one, his eyes bulged hugely from his head. In another, he was narrow and bendy. He could regard himself as a muscular brute like Bowlder or as an ancient sage with withering flesh. Opening his mouth to speak, he stopped, for a particularly corpulent variation yawned a deep cave lined with massive, crooked teeth.

"Funny, huh?" said a hundred Obreys.

"And scary," he answered. He glimpsed another reflection from an adjoining passage, and he reached up to touch his face. "My scars. They're gone."

"Come outta there," Obrey murmured, and this time there was no pleasure in her voice. "Seers' mirrors. They're liars. Come with me. We've been making you something."

"Are you a glassmaker?"

"My grandfather was a gemstone miner up north. He made all kinds of glass there. But one day the Seers found him."

"The Seers brought you here?"

Obrey was running ahead of him now, and it seemed the girl walked right into—and *through*—the wall. He stopped. As her image grew smaller, he decided that it was a corridor, not a wall. He tried to follow her, holding out his hand in suspicion, and his fingertips pressed against a solid pane of glass.

"This way." Her voice came from the other side of the corridor, and he saw her running away. He started after her, realizing how quickly one could get lost in these illusions. He could hardly move. He wanted to just stand and stare at the shifting reflections, which offered him images from places all over House Bel Amica.

He was drawn to the sight of soldiers on horses. Abascar soldiers had depended on vawns, for most of their rides were in regions of forest. He had never seen so many horses nor such fine armor for those steeds, ready as if for war. Commanding their attention on a magnificent battlehorse was a man whose face was bandaged except for patches around his eyes. Framing that face, his mane was striped yellow and black. But the eyes that burned through all this—the eyes were red as if lit from within.

"Hello, Ryllion," Cal-raven murmured. "We meet at last."

"Good morning, Cal-raven."

He turned.

At first it seemed that five Cynderes approached him from different panels of glass, each wearing a revealing gown as if dressed for some courtship dance. She was younger. Those bruises of grief beneath her eyes had been erased. Her teeth gleamed with unnatural whiteness. Her lips were swollen and red. Her eyelashes were thick and dark. He glanced from one picture to the other, uncertain.

"Do you like our mirrors?" she asked.

It was someone else's voice.

It was the queen.

· The masks had come off. Standing in her courtroom, Cal-raven had not seen Thesera's face because of the ceremonial, painted shield she held in front of it. The queen seemed younger than her daughter, and her voice was like a melody accompanying some seductive dancer's steps.

"I walk here every morning to give attention to all that belongs to me," she said. "Let me show you a view of the islands. Our glass can bring them closer than any Abascar farglass. It's as good as being there." The sound of her gentle footsteps whispered to him from all around. When she lifted her hand as if to reach for him, he flinched and did not know which direction might give him an escape.

"A good place for a watchman," she said. "You can find almost anyone who concerns you. Even better, they do not know you're watching. I love to watch Ryllion." She spoke with lascivious enthusiasm. "There's a certain... ferocity in him."

"My lady." Cal-raven dropped to one knee and bowed. This relieved him of having to decide which image was really the queen. "I must address my people. I ask for an assembly tomorrow. The time has come for Abascar to move on. Autumn is coming."

She laughed. "What a shame to move on just when the fun is about to begin. Tonight's parade begins a week of revels in honor of my birthday. On the last day I'll sail away on our greatest ship, the *Escape*, to visit the islands my husband discovered. Our house is full of hope right now. We can cast off the problems of the past and be the house we were meant to be. Explorers from all around the Mystery Sea will present their newest discoveries as gifts. You'll see things you've never imagined. Let your people rest awhile longer, King of Abascar. Look there."

Five queens gestured, and he glanced about, bewildered, until she described the scene he should be seeking. "One of your own has joined our glassmakers. He has an eye for it." She laughed. "A sharp eye for fractures. He will help us perfect a new gallery of mirrors."

He could not find the person she described.

"Come. I'll show you something more. An unpleasant sight, to be sure. But you were a soldier once. You have seen this kind of thing before. See?

Those are the carcasses of beastmen. Cartloads of them. Ryllion is cleansing the forest of those who resist the Seers' endeavors."

"What endeavors?"

"You haven't heard? They aim to capture, tame, and train the beastmen to fight their own kind for us. Deuneroi dreamed of ending the curse. Ryllion is finding a way that will not cost us any soldiers' lives."

As she led him, her voice began to fade. Her reflections went out one by one as if someone were blowing out candles. Then she was gone altogether. And he was lost.

He stepped into a vast, open space and felt a great relief. For this was a space not of mirrors but windows.

He was in the high-ceilinged cone at the center of the glassworks. The brightening sunrise cast a gradation of pink, red, and purple against the failing night sky. This conflict played out on the curvature of the cone, and he walked forward staring up, transfixed. Pillars that supported the cone were also made of glass, and as he passed, small dark shapes within the pillars floated and darted about in swarms and schools.

Obrey was there, watching the drifting shadows. "Aha!" she said. "I thought you were playing Seek and Go Hiding."

"How do they feed the fish?" Cal-raven pressed his hand to the glass, trying to get a clear view of the creatures.

"There are no fish." Obrey knocked against a pane. "It's a trick. Look." She took him to a broad table where samples of glasswork were displayed. "Those glass bells will summon hoverbirds. Those will soften headaches. Those call dogs. These float-bubbles help our fishermen throw nets that will catch whole schools on the sea. Here's a glass teapot, made for Queen Glyndere, Thesera's mother. She'd take tea only from a glass teapot because she said that water tasted better boiled in glass. And here—this old stained-glass window opened and closed in the captain's quarters of King Helpryn's ship."

Cal-raven marveled at the intricate scene depicted on the small glass disc—a soaring eagle with a crown on its head, snatching a fish from a curling wave. "I thought King Helpryn's ship was lost."

"Sailors found some wreckage. Hard to believe that the window was not destroyed."

They walked across a crystal blue floor with the contours of rolling ocean waves. Cal-raven knelt to touch it. "It's like walking on the sea."

"The floor was sculpted by Lengle, one of the best glassmaking teachers."

As they moved through this high-ceilinged hall, he slowed to gaze up into a canopy of misty light where suspended inventions swayed slowly—flocks of glass geese flying in an arrowhead formation, their translucent bellies full of brilliant raindrops as if they had dined upon jewels.

Here the stained-glass walls were murals of ancient mountains. Or perhaps they were magnified views of faraway places—he was not sure. They were simple pictures, abstract, and yet clouds drifted, rivers glittered, trees swayed. As his eyes traced the jagged horizon, he thought, *I must not forget my vision. Fourteen bell towers of Inius Throan. They're waiting for me.*

"King Helpryn designed this hall for the queen. She comes every day."

"My mother had a garden," Cal-raven began but then stopped.

A man of deeply fissured, crimson skin stood among the floor's turbulent waves, studying Cal-raven thoughtfully as if considering him for a portrait. "Is this your special guest, Obrey?" He scratched his chin through a long, wispy beard that was swept back over his shoulder.

"He's ready," she laughed.

The old man winked. Then he turned, walked up over a wave, and descended out of sight.

"That's my grandfather," she said with deep affection. "Bel Amica's master mirrorcrafter."

"The miner. What's his name?"

"Fritsey, I call him. You can call him Frits. He makes glass trees that actually grow and flower. He makes walls speak about what the very best eyes have seen. He makes faces that tell stories."

They followed Frits's progress and came to a railing where the ocean floor fell away. On a level below them, lights flared—seven ferocious fires, a line of ovens set inside a soot-streaked wall.

"Furnaces," said Obrey.

They descended a stair of glass so white that it caught and purged the light, emanating an aura pure as snow under a blue sky. It led them halfway to the workshop floor, where they turned onto a crescent-shaped balcony. They sat to watch the forgers work.

Three glassworkers fitted pieces of glass to long steel poles, then thrust those instruments into the open mouths of three furnaces. Their arms were reddened from the years of blasting heat. Their faces were shielded by cloth masks with thick glass discs that covered their eyes. They looked as determined and yet as vulnerable as the dragonslayers Cal-raven had seen illustrated in his father's history scrolls. They withdrew molten shapes, blazing spheres that seemed to have been dipped into the cores of fiery stars.

The workers carried the rods to tables and set them down so their treasures hung suspended over the edge. Taking metal tweezers, they pinched the fiery pulp with one hand while rolling the pipes on the tabletop with the other. In this way they shaped and detailed the soft glass into spheres and cylinders, carving ridges and compressing slender lengths of stem beneath the bubbles that would become the bowls of chalices.

"They're making goblets. And one's for you." Obrey poked his hip with her elbow. "It was Emeriene's idea. She said you could choose an emblem for New Abascar."

He thought for a moment, then drew a stone from his pocket. He plied the clay into a shape he had crafted hundreds of times. "This," he said. "I want this figure upon it somewhere. The Keeper's true likeness."

"We can give you exactly that," said Obrey. She took the figure and danced down the stair and onto the workshop floor, where she handed the figure of the Keeper to one of the glassworkers. Then she ran away through the workshop, stooping occasionally to pick through the jagged and colorful throwaways.

If she were a few years older, I'd swear Auralia had returned from the ruins.

He turned to a glassworker who sat farther down the bench. "Don't you wish you saw the world the way she does?"

Even though her uniform cocooned her, the woman was clearly hypnotized by Obrey's play, watching the girl through thick eyeglasses and wringing her white-gloved hands. He decided that the winding white cloth of her shroud was muffling her hearing.

A line of glassworkers pushed a train of carts across the workshop floor, containers full of large green spheres linked by heavy ropes that framed a fishing net. Distracted by the crooked stride of the man at the end of the line, Cal-raven jumped up and ran along the rail, down the stairs, and across the workshop floor. "Warney!"

Catching up to the parade, he grabbed the old man's bony shoulder. But the face that turned and greeted him with a wide grin full of teeth gone wrong sent him stumbling backward. The man looking back at him had two eyes.

"I'm sorry. I thought you were... Warney?"

"Master!" Warney stepped out of the line and knelt down.

"Where have you been? Do you know that Krawg's been chewing his nails off, worried that you fell off a dock?"

Warney blinked his eyes. Both of them. "Krawg said he was headin' out to sea! So I went lookin' for somethin' to do." Then the gawky old Gatherer stood up—a rather unnerving endeavor, as it looked like his legs were performing separate dances. "Old Frits, he found me. Told me he'd like to fashion me a replacement eye, just to see how it looks. It doesn't work, but I'd rather wear this than that blasted old patch."

"And now you're a glassmaker?"

"Frits said that I've learned to use this one eye so good that it's better than it would be if I had two. Seems I can see flaws and fractures others can't. Today we're crafting a new chalice for Queen Thesera's birthday."

He leaned in and whispered, "King Cal-raven, what do you think?" He pointed across the floor to where Obrey had somehow linked a chain of glass from the broken pieces.

"She's a stonemaster," Cal-raven gasped.

"Does she remind you of anyone?"

Cal-raven met—or tried to meet—Warney's half-real gaze. Then he shook his head slowly. "It can't be her, Warney. Auralia came into Abascar so young that she'd be seventeen or eighteen years old now. Obrey...she seems younger."

Warney's real eye seemed to glow with hope. "A sister, maybe? Could Auralia..."

He quieted as Frits approached from across the workshop floor, a glass disc resting precariously on his left cheekbone so that it seemed to enlarge his left eye. With a knowing smile, he said, "You've noticed my granddaughter."

Cal-raven nodded. "She has a tremendous gift."

"Your king, Warney—he has good eyes." Frits winked at the Gatherer through his monocle.

"You're descendants of Tammos Raak, like me." Cal-raven shrugged. "I guess that makes us family."

Frits crossed his arms. "I have it on good authority that I can trust you, King Cal-raven. And I'm not a trusting sort. Not unless there's good pay involved."

"The Seers must be paying you well for you to pack up and leave your mine."

When Frits replied, his mirthful tone had faded. "Who said we chose to leave?"

Cal-raven cleared his throat and changed the subject. "Who's fooled you into trusting me?"

The glassmaker pointed at the departing line of wagons. "Warney, I'd appreciate it if you got back to your work."

Warney hobbled off sideways, glancing back at Cal-raven with a gleeful grin. "Tell Krawg," he said. "Tell him I've found what I'm for."

The glassmaker put his arm around Cal-raven and led him in the other direction, moving through the rivers of heat that poured from the ovens. "It's best you see this when Obrey's distracted. If she catches you in her playroom, you'll never escape it, for she'll feel compelled to show you her favorite things. And that includes everything. It's a very crowded room."

The glass burner who earlier had ignored or missed Cal-raven's question suddenly appeared at Frits's elbow, her message muffled through the scarf that wrapped all but the glass shields over her eyes. She raised one of her mittened hands to point to the entryway behind them.

Frits and Cal-raven turned to find Queen Thesera sweeping into the room, the train of her gown streaming along behind her. The sharp-eared whiskiro in her hand shuddered, eyes enormous at the sight of the roaring stoves.

"She's here to see our progress on her ceremonial chalice. I'll attend to her." Frits looked to the anxious glassworker. "Milora, my love, rescue King Cal-raven, would you? Take him to see...you know. But go quickly and quietly. Let no one follow you."

The woman, her eyes dark behind the murky glass lenses, would not meet Cal-raven's gaze.

"Another one from your mountain home?" he asked.

"The Seers dragged three of us from the mine in the mountains. Milora was sick. They promised to heal her with their potion work. It's how they managed to persuade me." He put his fist before his mouth to block his voice and muttered. "Funny thing. She wasn't sick before the Seers showed up."

Cal-raven watched the woman begrudgingly stride away to lead him.

"I almost forgot." Frits ungloved a hand and reached into his pocket. "You'll need this. I call it the lightkey."

He handed Cal-raven a piece of clear glass that seemed unremarkable— a teardrop cut down the middle. His hands, however, were remarkable indeed—brown and cracked as bread that's been baked too long, with such a web of scars upon scars it was difficult to find an unmarked spot.

Frits turned, drawing in a deep breath.

To avoid the queen's gaze, Cal-raven followed Milora, running to catch up as she rounded the far end of the ovens.

She led him out of the workshop and through a maze of passages lined with wonder after wonder that could only have been crafted by a child's imagination. Playful bursts of abstract shapes, like collisions of colored hoops pinned together in rising circles, bigger and more exuberant as they ascended. Some were outrageous animals, dangling from the wires of mobiles that spun in the wind of their passage—winged dragons chasing each other in circles.

"How old is Obrey?" Cal-raven asked.

Milora shrugged.

She led him up a stair into a room no larger than his own chamber back in the tower. Dark curtains encircled the high-ceilinged space. Resting on a workbench, she planted her heels beside a row of multicolored seaweed sandals. Cal-raven stood against the wall opposite her, awestruck. All about him on the floor were thin filaments of glass; spools of transparent, tinted threads; bottles of glue; sticks of waxy dye.

"This is where she plays?"

Milora gestured to a pile of blankets in the corner. He remembered the cushion where Hagah had slept in King Cal-marcus's library.

"Is this what you wanted to show me? Your daughter's window?"

Milora laughed behind her scarf, then leaned forward and gripped the bench tightly as if the question were a test of her patience.

"Frits told me that you've been sick. Is that why you cannot speak?"

"Oh, I can speak," she growled through the fabric, and at last she raised the lenses from her eyes to reveal a bruised and frightened expression. He felt an urge to unwind the strips of cloth that encased her, for she seemed so stifled. But she gestured to the long golden cord of the curtain hanging down the wall beside him. "Look. But don't linger."

The curtains drew back from the far end of the room, sliding around the curvature to unveil a tall, arched window. But the window's glass was not a solid pane—it was lace, filaments like a spider web of ice. Each line gleamed, each strand a different color. That it all held together was astonishing. Morning fog, moving out to sea from the mainland, teased the window, drifting into the chamber, so that the sunlight illuminating the glass infused the cloud with pulsing, shifting hues. It was as though the window were a sieve, straining colors from cloud.

He turned to her, amazed. "How did she—"

Milora was gone.

Obrey stood astonished in the doorway. The tiny "oh" of her mouth then burst into a glorious smile. "King Cal-raven! In my room!" She skipped across and took his hand, then danced about him in a circle. "Don't you love my window? It's my favorite thing in all of Bel Amica. It's like a map."

He looked at it again. "A map?"

Explanations exploded into the room as Obrey excitedly traced a river of blue lace down through green patches she found to be forests. She pointed out gleaming tips like mountains and golden patches of open plain. A dark swath near the top she believed to be the Forbidding Wall.

Cal-raven gestured to a spot just above that crescent of purple near the window's apex—an open space like an eye half closed. "And what, then, is that?" White hot with sunlight, whistling as cool air blew through, the space seemed strangely familiar.

"Didn't Grandfather give you the lightkey?"

Cal-raven drew the crystal shard from his pocket. "This?" He felt a prickly sensation across his skin.

Rummaging in a small closet, Obrey began to grunt and growl. "Here. You. Go!" she announced, dragging a heavy stepladder into the chamber. "You'll. Need. This!" It was heavy, for it was made of glass bricks. "I got in trouble...for using...the lightkey," she panted once the ladder stood in front of the window. "I couldn't reach. From the top step. So I had to stack things on top of it."

Cal-raven took a step up on the ladder, then reached out to touch the delicate lace with his fingertips. He was surprised by its warmth and strength. "Why does House Bel Amica hide this window? It's the most exquisite thing I've seen here."

"The people don't know about it." Obrey shrugged, spinning a glass top and watching it zigzag across the floor. "Frits and Milora decide who gets to see it. They know who they can trust."

"The colors remind me of something." He sat down on the stepladder, regarding the girl suspiciously. "But that was far away and long ago."

She blinked at him, tilting her head like a curious bird.

"Obrey, how old are you?"

"Not sure," she answered and started counting on her fingers. "Frits thinks I'm fourteen."

"Why did you end up here?"

"We didn't want to. But the Seers kept offering fortunes and fame. Milora got angry. She shouted at them. She was worried about what would happen to the stuff we were making."

"What happened?"

"Milora didn't wake up in the morning. Grandfather Frits got mad and yelled at the Seers. He said they'd poisoned her. It was bad. And noisy. Then the Seers promised they could wake her up if we brought her to Bel Amica.

They put her in the 'firmary." Obrey's face twitched and quivered with worry. "We work here 'til she's better."

"That's horrible," he said. "I'm sorry. What's wrong with her?"

"It's..." She knocked her knuckles against her head. "It's messy up here. That's what she says. Like somebody mixed up everything. Can't find what she needs. Makes it hurt to think." Obrey's play became more urgent. She mashed the pieces of glass together into a strange, alarming, jagged shape.

"I'm sorry," he said. "I shouldn't bring up painful things here in your playroom."

Absently, she pulled the scarf from her head and began to sweep broken glass into it. He was surprised to find that she was completely bald.

Was your hair ever silverbrown? he wondered. *Were you ever older?* The Seers had made Queen Thesera seem young again. Could they have drawn years out of Auralia?

She noticed his stare and patted her head. "It's the glassworks," she said. "They cut our hair so glass won't get caught in it. Folks get hurt when glass falls in their food or collects on their pillows."

He turned to ascend the stepladder, the lightkey in his hand. To reach the open space at the top of the window, he'd have to stand on the top step, with nothing to hold. A mistake could send him plunging through the intricate window. He spread both arms for balance, then reached up to the open space.

Ever so carefully, so as not to press it through to the other side, he fitted the lightkey into place.

"Get down!" Obrey laughed. "Quickly!"

As he descended, a force of heat and pressure struck him. But he saw nothing unusual, not until he looked back up at the lightkey.

That splinter of glass filled with sunlight. As it did, it became a whirling eye, a furnace of color. Reds, blues, and golds rushed through the strands of glassy lace as if they were veins. They spread and separated until the web was intricate with ever-changing hues. The mist enshrouding the window became infused with colors.

Cal-raven caught and trapped the name so he would not say it aloud. *Auralia.*

"This..." His robe glittering with slivers of glass, Frits had stepped into the room with Milora as close as his shadow. The glassmaker spread his arms as if to embrace the light streaming through the window. Colors trickled through his fingers. "This is our consolation until we can leave this place again."

"My friends." Cal-raven approached them, speaking in a surge of resolve. "Milora, I want you to visit Abascar's healer, Say-ressa. She may be able to help you. And I want to take all three of you with me when I lead House Abascar away. With this window you've already given Bel Amica more than it deserves. I'll take you back to your mine. And I will make sure the Seers do not bother you again."

He bowed, thanking all three of them—although Milora looked less than grateful—and then he excused himself, invigorated.

As he did, he overheard quiet laughter from the old glassmaker. "He wants to save everyone, doesn't he?"

26

A Sudden Change
of Plan

Three days?"
That was the first question Tabor Jan asked, but others followed so hard and fast that he stumbled on the path. His sleeplessness was beginning to scare him. He had begged for slumberseed oil, but Bel Amican watchmen were not allowed to use the stuff in case its lingering influence might interfere with their watchfulness.

He struggled to arrange words into coherent responses. How would they assemble the people? Would they get back the supplies that had been taken from them? Would the Bel Amicans offer them any protection? Were their vawns and horses in traveling condition?

As he pummeled Cal-raven with questions, the two men arrived at a railtrain platform deep inside Bel Amica. Here the train concluded its circuitous trip through the house. It would be rigged with a harness of hooks and chains and hauled up to a distant piece of sky through a shaft crowded with pulleys, gears, and ropes. At the top it would be set upon the rails again and begin its descent through courtyards and market squares.

"Tomorrow morning," Cal-raven was saying, "I'll address Abascar. I'll need your help to draw everyone together. They'll have three days to pack only what they can carry and to repair whatever needs patching. Partayn's convinced the queen to give us wagons, vawns, and packs for the journey, so long as we repay them, within three years' time, double what we take."

Others crowding the platform stared at them and gossiped. "So many people," Tabor Jan mumbled.

"They're assembling for the queen's parade. I'm to stand at the chamber window, like a puppet on a stage, and wave. Look at me, the humiliated king."

Tabor Jan snorted. "You're going along with it?"

The rail-train cars came rattling to a stop, sparks spitting from the wheels on the metal lines. He followed Cal-raven into the small crowd that formed to step aboard. As they settled in, the car jolted. The chains rattled. They were lifted. And he tried not to look out as the platform disappeared below.

"Partayn offered me a deal," said Cal-raven.

Tabor Jan waited, uncertain whether he wanted to hear what would come next.

"He has asked if I would give Lesyl to House Bel Amica. For her music. And she could teach them how to play the—"

"Give her up?" Tabor Jan grabbed Cal-raven by the collar. "You're turning us into currency?"

"You really do need to get some sleep, Captain." Cal-raven clenched his teeth.

Tabor Jan let go, suddenly afraid. "Forgive me. I don't know what—"

Cal-raven straightened his tunic. "The heir is moved by Lesyl's music."

"Begging your pardon, master, but I think he's moved by his—"

"Listen," Cal-raven snapped. "I told him I could not decide that for her."

"Good. For a moment you scared—"

"I told him the decision would be hers."

Tabor Jan's mouth slammed shut.

"He's going to invite her to stay."

At last the train arrived at the top of its lift, emerging into the daylight. The great wooden crane swung it around and set it down on the rails alongside another platform. They climbed out, and although Tabor Jan wanted to watch the train rumble off, Cal-raven headed to the palace-yard gate.

After the guards let them into the yard, they returned to Cal-raven's palace chamber, where Hagah's eyebrows twitched and his tail thumped once against the floor. The empty bowl beside him explained the dog's immobility.

"It'll be rough on Hagah, getting back out on the— Don't touch anything!"

Tabor Jan paused, his fingertips hovering over one of the overlapping maps.

"I'm charting the best possible routes. Here's our first campsite." Cal-raven tapped a corner of an open scroll.

Tabor Jan's eyes moved from one map to the other and back again. Either he was so tired that he was imagining things, or Cal-raven was taking them all the way to Fraughtenwood and beyond. "They'd better be giving us weapons as well."

"With Thesera gone to the islands, Partayn will have the power of the throne. He'll give us what we need."

"An armed escort?"

"Partayn's considering some whose loyalty to the throne is greater than their loyalty to Ryllion." The king tapped a few stones placed between the Cragavar and Fraughtenwood. "And I want to get a good distance from Bel Amica before the Seers have a chance to organize any interference."

"May I, master?" Tabor Jan sank onto the cushion beside the window. "I can already hear the parade. You're really going to stand at the window like a trained dog?"

"I'm not the only one." Cal-raven leaned on the sill and looked across the avenue. "Cyndere will be up there at her window, waving. Wait, there she is!"

Tabor Jan took the farglass Cal-raven offered him. He adjusted the eyepiece. "Don't trust my sight, but I don't think that's her."

Cal-raven took the farglass. "It's Emeriene, dressed as Cyndere." He put it down. "Why? Where is Cyndere?"

A sudden thump brought Hagah to his feet, woofing at the wall. Tabor Jan was already drawing his club from its belt loop. "Master..."

A section of the wall swung open as easily as a door on oiled hinges. A figure in the opening bowed to them. *Just Cal-raven's height, just Cal-raven's stature.* Tabor Jan was baffled as the king's equivalent stepped into the light. *That's Cal-raven's uniform. And it's a little darker, but that's Cal-raven's beard.* He turned to the king. "Is this a joke?"

"Yes," said Partayn, stretching out the word as he descended the stair behind the imposter. "Yes, to a few of us. This is Conyere. She's the closest Cyndere could find to your stature."

"She?" Cal-raven stepped closer.

"The beard's glued on," said the woman whose voice was soft but deep.

"Why do I need a twin?"

"Conyere will stand at the window for you." Partayn shrugged. "I know, it's kramming ridiculous, but she's going to play the part of Abascar's king. And Emeriene will play the part of Cyndere. In the meantime, good king, I suggest you come with me."

"Why the charade?" Tabor Jan rumbled.

Partayn laughed. "We're going to rescue two of your people from the Seers."

The king was already reaching for his hooded cloak. Casting it over his shoulders, he knelt and checked the dagger strapped to his calf. "We're taking back the injured from the Seers' suspension baths. They've had them long enough. Cyndere's found a way."

"I have one more piece for your costume," said Partayn, lifting a black strand of cloth. "You remember, don't you?"

Tabor Jan shifted uncomfortably as the Bel Amican heir blindfolded the scowling Cal-raven. "Take me with you. I don't like this."

"Stay here," said the king. "Study the maps. Think of everything that could possibly go wrong so we can be ready for it. And don't worry about me. I've made up my mind. We're leaving. It has already begun. I know our destination, and I won't make the Keeper wait anymore."

Smoldering, Tabor Jan watched Partayn lead the king away. When he saw Conyere's amusement, he had to restrain himself from smacking that smile off her face.

Before him, the map waited for his attention. He reached out for a stone Cal-raven had set down at Fraughtenwood's edge and then, with a chill, discovered another stone set beyond it somewhere among the mountains of the Forbidding Wall.

It was all Cal-raven could do to keep from stumbling as they descended a narrow, crooked stairway that would lead them out of the tower. He traced the wall with his fingertips, bracing for a misstep.

When they reached the bottom of the stair, hands smeared a cool putty across his cheeks and brow. His boots were removed, and his feet fumbled for the sandals set beside them.

"You cannot be recognized," Partayn said. "Not even by those infirmary workers."

Someone else entered the small room.

"Did it go well?"

"Ey there, my lord," said a gruff but familiar voice. "A little chancy. We'd almost given up. The empty boat never appeared. The Seers must be suspicious, because Ryllion's doubled the guard and put every perimeter station on alert. Either they know we're up to something, or they think there's some other danger to our house tonight."

Henryk, thought Cal-raven, *the guard who locked me up.*

"So," Partayn continued, "if the boat never appeared, how did you manage?"

"Our friend's a strong swimmer. Came in by the river and didn't draw a breath until he jumped up right in front of me. Ey, my! I nearly shouted out his name."

A firm hand gripped Cal-raven's arm. "Good to see you again, trespasser," said the guard.

"I'd say the same," said Cal-raven, "if only I could see."

"Good luck to you, Cal-raven," said Partayn. "I'm off to the parade. Officer Henryk will take you from here."

A slender figure wrapped in black waited in the ghostly light of the Seers' suspension baths.

Folding the blindfold, Henryk bowed. "I'll be at the end of the corridor. Remember...*haste*." He slipped away, past a huge guard wrapped in a stormcloak.

Cal-raven faced Cyndere. "What do we do?" he asked.

She held out a heavy flask, the sort carried for water on hunts. "This," she said, "is our best hope. If this does not revive your friends, we will have to put them back and hope the Seers will show them mercy. They're beyond any other kind of help."

He took the flask, sniffed at the opening. He recognized the scent even before Cyndere explained. "It's water from a deep well within the Cragavar. It's a secret that Partayn, Emeriene, and I have fiercely protected. Bauris may have learned a little too much about its power."

"I've tasted it," he said.

She was surprised. "At Tilianpurth?"

He began to describe Old Soro's well at Mawrnash, but the guard cleared his throat, impatient.

"Why keep it secret?" he asked. "Everyone should know."

"The Seers," said Cyndere. "They'd make people pay or seal it off for themselves. Imagine the riots. We might lose the best tool we've ever had for achieving our purpose."

"And what is that?"

She stepped close, eyes reflecting blue. "Breaking the Cent Regus curse."

He looked at the flask as if it were fragile. "Is it possible?"

"It's been done." She took his hand and pressed a small figurine into his palm. He looked down, and in the faint shimmer of the baths, he recognized the sculpture of the beastman he had given to Henryk.

A heavy hand came down on Cal-raven's shoulder, and a voice growled quietly, "rrrRemember?"

Cal-raven's throat constricted. He looked into a scarred and beastly visage, and he dropped the figurine. Without thinking, his hand reached for the knife on his leg. It was gone.

Cyndere seized him by the wrist. "This is Jordam. First of his kind—awakened from the curse. He risked his life to bring us this water, just as he takes it into the Cent Regus Core to awaken help."

Cal-raven leaned against Dane's bath tank, speechless.

"No one knows, Cal-raven, except you, me, my brother, and Emeriene. Oh, and Henryk. Henryk watches for Jordam down by the harbor. Jordam swims in by night beneath an empty rowboat. To anyone else, it looks like a bark broken free of its moorings."

"rrrNot this time," said Jordam. "rrRyllion's watching. Had to swim deep. Guards everywhere."

Cal-raven stared into those fiery eyes, those twitching black nostrils, that fanged muzzle, which seemed, against all reason, to be smiling with affection for Cyndere.

"He's here to save not only his own people but yours, Cal-raven."

"rrAgain," said Jordam.

Jordam knelt beside the tank. The body of the woman lay limp in his arms, her red hair spilling down to the floor and dripping the milky bath of the Seers' potion. Cyndere knelt, facing the beastman, her hand cupped behind the woman's head. Then she turned to Cal-raven.

"We're ready."

He opened the flask, then gently tilted it until the water dripped between the woman's parted lips.

"rrMore," said Jordam.

Cal-raven poured more, and her body jerked in sudden alarm. She choked, spraying water into Cyndere's face. Jordam held her steady, patient. He looked up, but Cal-raven could not meet his gaze.

The woman grasped Cyndere's shoulders, and Jordam turned to hide his face from the waking woman. "rrScarf!" he whispered anxiously to Cal-raven. "Scarf!"

Cal-raven put down the flask, then took the scarf draped over Jordam's shoulder and wrapped it around the beastman's face.

Blinking, the woman choked and tried to sit up. Jordam lifted her and placed her quickly in Cal-raven's arms, then turned his back and walked to the door. Cal-raven carried her to the bench across the room and wrapped her in one of the large, thick towels.

Jordam turned to the second tank, then bent low to lift the man from the bath. "rrHelp," he whispered.

Cal-raven quickly moved to the man's head and gave him a long draught of water from the flask. He swallowed as if already half awake and began to murmur.

Jordam carried him to the bench. Cal-raven spread a towel out so that the beastman could lay him there. He covered the man as Jordam returned to the doorway.

While Cyndere whispered to the waking survivors, Cal-raven walked to join the beastman.

"rrRemember?" Jordam quietly asked again.

Cal-raven nodded. He looked down at Jordam's right foot. "I wish I could forget. You did what you could to warn me about the siege. And you gave me Cyndere's message, even though I would not listen."

"rrMany Cent Regus still work for the white giant."

"I am not surprised." Cal-raven glanced anxiously to Cyndere. "What do the Seers want with Cent Regus?"

"Strength. Strength over every house."

"I could have done this without you, Cal-raven," said Cyndere quietly. "But I wanted you here. Some truths cannot be reduced to mere words. You have to see for yourself."

"You sound like my teacher." Cal-raven remembered how the mage had insisted he climb the tower of Tammos Raak and behold the view of Inius Throan with his own eyes.

"So you understand now," said Cyndere, "the power we have to help the beastmen. And even more importantly, we have an ally who is helping us prepare to rescue the prisoners of the Cent Regus. Prisoners, Cal-raven. Survivors. Many of whom are Bel Amicans. But many of them are your own. And if you could help us—"

Cal-raven walked to the doorway. "I cannot depart from my plan. There is too much broken that needs repair, and I must attend to the vision I've been given. The Expanse becomes more dangerous all the time. Should I delay and risk the safety of the people?"

"Of course you cannot repair all that has been broken. Before you speak to your people tomorrow, come to my father's assembly room. Partayn and I will show you our plan. You'll find we have a powerful alliance that gives us confidence of a rescue."

Cal-raven closed his eyes and clenched his teeth as the burn in his eye suddenly flared.

"rrRescue," grumbled Jordam. "O-raya's boy. Ale boy. He helps us."

"The ale boy? He's alive?" Cal-raven clapped his hand over his mouth as if to stifle a shout.

"That is not all," said Cyndere softly. "Jordam has other help in the Core. Some are beastmen. With your stonemastery and the boy's firebearing, we can close the tunnels, defend the prisoners, and carry them away."

"I don't speak Cent Regus. Neither do you. We only have this one." He gestured to Jordam. "How can we navigate through a labyrinth we've never seen?"

"We have someone who knows the Cent Regus Core." Cyndere took his hands in her own. "She's been a prisoner there for a long time."

Fear seized Cal-raven, and he felt a sudden urge to flee. "Auralia? Have you found Auralia?"

Jordam bowed his head. "No," he sighed.

"No," said Cyndere, and her voice had that familiar flutter. "It's your mother, Jaralaine. She's alive."

Cal-raven pulled his hands free.

He walked away from them, aimlessly at first. Then he thrust out his hands and struck the wall. It rippled. He pushed into it, immersing himself in disintegrating stone. Then, all at once, he surrendered the power. He stood paralyzed, encased in the wall.

He stood there a long time, emotions overpowering thought.

Then, deep within, he felt a cry beginning.

With a roar, he shattered the wall, stone crashing down in jagged shards all around him. He stood snarling like a cornered animal before Cyndere and the beastman.

"Help us, King of Abascar," Cyndere whispered while Jordam watched the corridor. "We'll show you the plan."

"You mistake me." Cal-raven felt his lips curl, and he gave a joyless laugh. "House Abascar is ruled by a queen. And she's hoping for rescue. I must go to her tonight."

27

HELPLESS IN THE GARDEN

When Cal-raven did not return to his chamber, Tabor Jan left the maps behind and descended to wander, troubled, through the rock.

Brevolo found him, leaned against his shoulder, and steered him down to the crowded corridors known as the Night Market. Amid the frantic energy and din inspired by the parade, they moved like watchful ghosts, murmuring in each other's ears ideas they'd like to carry with them to New Abascar.

Along an avenue where crafters sat, their legs folded beneath them on circles of elaborate carpet, Brevolo spoke with an old man whose skin was as dark as coal. When she praised the wooden pipes he had whittled into dragon shapes, his smile was shockingly bright. And even though Tabor Jan heard the coins fall in the craftsman's bowl, he did not know until later that Brevolo had slipped a piece from the collection into his pocket.

Steam burst from the kitchens that stayed busy all night long. Aromas spilled like rumors down the avenues: redfish on a grill; seaweed, braised and seasoned; peppered root-cakes fried in grease, then stacked and drenched in orange-cherry syrup. They wandered, sipping salty liquor served warm in small clay cups. From time to time, they joined crowds where musicians played loudly to be heard over the racket.

Every so often they would nod as they recognized someone else from Abascar. But these encounters troubled the captain. The people seemed dizzy with pleasure, inspired and relieved, as if Barnashum had been a bad dream and its stains could be washed away in this tide of sensual bedazzlement.

"Come along, Captain Scowlface." Brevolo punched him lightly in the jaw. "Have you become so accustomed to hardship that you're unable to relax anymore?"

"When our king is content, I'll rest," he said. "This is a stop on a journey. I fear we're forgetting."

"Then store up memories to keep you warm in the wild," she said.

"I had hoped," he mumbled, "that you'd keep me warm out there."

She smiled, but it seemed forced.

Light pealed from lanterns like music from bells, and the mirrors all around them gave wanderers a sense that the Night Market stretched on forever. Brevolo paused to admire an array of syrup-glazed, horn-shaped vegetables that seemed too brightly colored to be real. "You'll go back to the meager meals in the Cragavar after this?"

"We will," he insisted.

She did not respond to that.

They pushed their way at last to a viewpoint for some silent seagazing. Waves of incense wafted from shops on lower levels where craftsmen sold bowls and oils for moon-spirit lamps. Tabor Jan felt as if they had stepped out of an elaborate dance. And Brevolo seemed free of her grief for a while.

When he returned to his bunkroom, he almost slept.

Midmorning he found himself engulfed in sunlight, salt-stung and sleepy. Bel Amica's rock had cast its foggy blanket to the sea, and the marketplaces below were alive with activity.

"Three more days." The words tasted bittersweet, for he had let down his guard. He had enjoyed his adventure last night.

He pulled the pipe from his pocket. It was handsome, carved from marrowwood. Brevolo would have skipped an afternoon meal to save the coins for such a purchase.

He tucked some aromatic oceantree gum into the bowl and lit it with the flame of the moon-spirit lamp that sat glimmering on the wall. As he did, he saw Luci and Margi running along the avenue below. They saw him and waved. They shouted, but he could not hear them. He waved back, then stepped away from the low wall and leaned against the dark, porous stone, blinking woozily.

Pipe smoke shocked his lungs. When he exhaled, tension faded from his neck and shoulders.

The waves rolled. *Rest. Breathe. Rest. Breathe.* And then it seemed that their sighs said more: *Stay...Safety...*

Even as he clutched the pipe, he felt the distance between Brevolo and himself widen. She had made clear her affection for him. And here was this gift in his hand, smoke sweetly scenting the air. But they had spoken little of their future; she dreaded to imagine life beyond Bel Amica, but he could think of little else. Their past was washing away.

He thought of Brevolo riding on her first patrol with Captain Ryllion. She had told him so many stories from her days in the training yards, and most of them were accounts of Ryllion's strength and strategy—his hunts, his battles, the beastmen he had bullied into cooperation, the others he had slaughtered.

"Three days," he said, closing his eyes. "Three days, and I'm taking you back to a world that's true."

He heard a woman clear her throat.

He opened his eyes to a blue-robed figure standing in the morning's golden blur. At first he thought it was a child holding a lantern. Then he saw it was Emeriene. It was not a lantern she held but a cage housing five birds, each one no bigger than his thumb.

"I shouldn't be surprised to find you sleeping on the watch. The officers in your bunkhouse say you pace all night."

"I've a lot on my mind." He winced, hearing in his voice the boast of an obstinate child. He knocked the smoldering oceantree gum from the pipe. "You have a birdcage."

"Come with me."

She walked away, a blue cloud carrying a silver basket. A stone corridor breathed her in, swallowed her up. "You haven't been sleeping," she said as he followed, "and that's not good for a watchman. So it's time you met the Kneader."

They emerged from a mirror-lined tunnel onto a platform with tall, feathery trees and walls of woven vines. Emeriene led him through an ivy-bound archway into a maze of whispering leaves. The air was richly spiced, and men and women—most of them soldiers—wandered the paths as if sleepwalking.

"Our defenders enjoy this privilege after patrols."

Wary, he followed her into a small clearing and stopped abruptly. A strange chair leaned toward the cliff's edge as if someone were preparing to launch it off this stone jag and into the waters of the inlet far below. "I don't like heights."

"Take off your shields."

He grimaced.

"Your king has approved this."

As if stripping for a fistfight, he brusquely removed his shoulder guards, bracers, the cuirass, the chain-mail vest. Then he stood bowlegged in his trousers and loose-fitting shirt, arms out in the pose of a wrestler.

She showed him how to lean forward, not back, into the chair so that his face stared through a cushioned frame at the water. He studied their surroundings again as if something might pounce from behind. But then, with some coaxing, he found himself slumped against the leaning chair, arms hanging forward, knees bent and braced, his back and shoulders exposed as an enormous shadow appeared on the stone beside him. A formidable woman in a sisterly's gown leaned down to smile in welcome. She waved a hand mittened in a glove intricately beaded with small gems—some soft, some sharp.

"Cal-raven's supposed to assemble our people this morning. I don't understand how this is going to help—" His body felt a jolt like a blast of lightning, and then... "Oh."

A shock of heat rippled from the base of his neck through his shoulders and down his back, then spread through his whole body. The Kneader's hands suddenly felt like waves of an incoming tide, crashing and rolling, stripping away what burdened and pained him. He felt lighter. His hard, anxious thoughts softened and lost their shape. His view of the water blurred into a gauzy gold.

As he sank beneath the tide, Emeriene sat on a bench at the edge of his vision, set the birdcage on the ground by her feet, and spoke with sweet, flirtatious music.

"I've brought someone who wishes to speak with you."

He tried to lift his head but couldn't. A shapely figure in a green gown had joined Emeriene on the bench.

"I need you to be still, Captain." It was Cyndere's voice. "I've cleared the garden. The Kneader, you should know, lost her hearing in childhood. She listens through her fingers, and all she can hear right now is your body crying for rest. So we're alone. You can relax."

I am far too relaxed, he wanted to say. *I am disastrously relaxed.*

Cyndere explained that she had met Cal-raven at the infirmary and then revealed all that she had told him. Of Deuneroi. Of Jordam. Of the well at Tilianpurth and the hope for the Cent Regus.

Tabor Jan felt a knot tightening in his chest.

She spoke of learning from Jordam that beastmen were moving to besiege the survivors at Barnashum. She narrated Jordam's mission to find Cal-raven and described how Abascar's king had fought him and driven him away.

The Kneader shoved tiny pins into Tabor Jan's neck. Then she placed black seabugs on his arms, and they bit into his flesh with shiny fangs. Sweat poured down his brow.

"Jordam saved House Abascar," Cyndere continued. "He also went back to the Core and freed my brother, Partayn, from prison. He'll return to rescue others from the Cent Regus chieftain, many of whom are from—"

"No!" Tabor Jan shouted as if he had been kicked.

"Jordam was going to leave tomorrow," she continued softly. "But Cal-raven would not wait. He insisted they leave last night. He's determined to bring back as many as he can."

"Why?" Tabor Jan roared. He felt like a bull in a tantrum, but his hands hung useless before him. "Why not take me? What would compel—"

"Jaralaine," said Cyndere.

What Tabor Jan felt then was the queerest of sensations—a sense of losing all balance, of falling through space. "Why, for the glory of Harbaron's hindquarters, didn't he tell me?"

"You would have tried to stop him," said Cyndere. "I tried, believe me.

I asked him to wait and study maps of the labyrinth that his mother and the firebearer have provided for us."

He gasped. "The firebearer? Rescue's alive?"

Emeriene said, "As your tasker, I'm appointing you to protect Abascar's people and prepare them for departure upon Cal-raven's return. And your king approves."

"He's a fool." His voice was like a sob.

"He may be," Emeriene laughed. "But a better fool than most."

"I'm sworn to protect him. How can I keep my word when he leaves me behind? Charging off as if he has to do everything himself...when just a pinch of patience could...just asking for some help would..." His words diminished into a humiliating whimper, then a sigh of surrender.

Cyndere stood up. "And I thought my brother and Cal-raven were the last good men." Then she waved her hand to fan her reddening face. "I am feeling warm. I'm going to find water." The queen's daughter was gone.

Emeriene came up close to him. "Well, you've made an impression on one who is difficult to impress."

"You're not taking me seriously." He could not move a finger or a toe. "I'm not a man who stands and waits. What am I to do?"

"I'm taking you very seriously. Cal-raven's never needed you as much as he does now. Nobody knows him better, so no one can lead Abascar better than you."

"It's not enough."

"I know how you feel. I understand better than you might guess. You feel helpless. You feel disrespected. But you have to let him go, Tabor Jan. Even though you may be right. Cal-raven, with all the best intentions, may be taking the wrong path. Or he may surprise you, as Cyndere surprises me. Whatever the case, don't make things worse by missing the difference you can make right here. Cal-raven's off to face his own challenge. This, here, is yours."

"What can I do? I'm useless as a watchman. If I walk these walls any longer, I'll lose my mind." He stared down at the birdcage. "My challenge. The old man said my challenge was coming."

"Old man? What do you mean?"

"I had a visitor. The old man. Officer Droolface."

"Bauris? He came to visit you?"

"In the middle of the night."

"Bauris never visits anyone. He just wanders and talks to himself." Emeriene sat on the grass where she could look up into Tabor Jan's face, which only made him feel even more ridiculous. "What did he say?"

Tabor Jan pressed his lips together. Then he said, "It was nonsense. Something about the birds and what they would tell me."

"How remarkable. And he didn't even know."

"Know what?"

"Partayn has sent these tetherwings for you. My father trains tetherwings to chirp at any sign of danger. But these...these are special. He's trained them so they will respond only to beastmen. Otherwise, they are as silent as knuckle-nuts."

"That...would be useful. Are they for Ryllion?"

"In a manner of speaking. Partayn wants you to patrol the harbor caves with these birds. Tell no one about their...particular purpose."

"Why?"

"I'm not sure. But when Jordam the beastman came in last night, he told Officer Henryk that he smelled something. Something that doesn't belong."

"He smelled House Abascar," he snapped.

"No, no," she laughed. "Rest, Tabor Jan. You might as well since you won't be able to move for a while. Your body's sleeping. Let your mind follow. Just for a while." Emeriene motioned to the Kneader.

The Kneader seized him, lifted him from the chair, and set him in a wheelchair, where his arms hung limp at his sides. Emeriene planted the birdcage in his lap, then drew a circlet of feathers from a pocket in her robe and placed it on his head with great ceremony. "I crown you, Tabor Jan, king of tetherwings."

"Sleep? Bird-watching? I'm Abascar's captain of the guard."

"I wonder, did Cal-raven learn his insolence from you, or was it the other way around?" She smiled to the Kneader. "We'll let you find your own way out. When you're ready."

Emeriene and the Kneader walked away.

Tabor Jan tried to lift his head. He tried to lift an arm. But he could only sit and stare at the silent birds while the breeze teased the garden leaves.

28

NIGHT ON THE
BEASTMAN RIVER

A re you certain you won't rest?" Officer Henryk looked through the trees into the pond of fog that submerged the valley. "When this clears, you'll see it—the tower of Tilianpurth. We could get good rest there. Better meals. Would do you good, boyo."

Cal-raven tightened the clamp on the bow Cyndere had given him from her own collection, pulling the string taut again. "You keep calling me boyo, Officer."

"Do I?" Henryk gazed into the crumblewood campfire, turning the brascle over the flames. "Ey, now, forgive me. You just remind me so much of him."

"Who do I remind you of?"

"My son."

Cal-raven rose and walked a slow circle around the soldiers who were sharpening jags of heavy wood. They would sink a barrage of these bulky spears in the river near the Cent Regus Core to gut any boats that tried to follow them out.

"At what point do we come in after you?" Henryk asked. "And tell me twice."

"You don't. You don't come in after me."

Henryk puffed up his cheeks, then whistled long and low. "The courage of youth."

Cal-raven half turned, suspecting he was being insulted.

"Let us consider," Henryk continued, "the possibility that things could go wrong in the Core." He lifted the spit and shoved the dripping bird at

Cal-raven. "You end up slow-roasted over a fire, and with every turn you're thinking, 'Ey, now. I told them to stay. I told them I couldn't fail.'"

"Three days," said Cal-raven. "If I have not sent you some kind of sign in three days, then something is awry."

Henryk shook his head. "I wish my son had lived to see this. The king of Abascar taking a beastman as his guide."

A troubling rumble began beneath the fog, drawing their attention. Cal-raven stood up and put his hand on his hilt. "Maybe he does see it," he said. "If he does, he must be similarly surprised to see his father protecting an Abascar man."

"No," Henryk chuckled. "No, he would not be. He would know I'm doing this for him."

Cal-raven stared at him. "Of course," he said. "I've been a fool not to see it before." He smiled wryly at his protector. "You're Deuneroi's father."

A sour horn bleated, and the rumbling grew louder. Then as if emerging from the curtains of a stage, Jordam appeared astride a bellowing prongbull that thrashed the air with its powerful horns.

Henryk's men were on their feet with arrows to bows, but Cal-raven raised his hand. "Wait."

"Ey, now, would you look at that?" Henryk shook his head. "He's going to carry you on that?"

Jordam held the bull at bay for a moment, then urged him a few cautious steps toward the camp and turned him sideways. "You," Jordam grumbled to Cal-raven, "sit behind me."

Cal-raven could not take his attention off the animal's glowing red eyes.

"Ready?" Jordam laughed to the Bel Amicans. "rrKeep up."

Cal-raven clung to Jordam as the prongbull charged across rugged open ground.

As they passed through the northern stretches of Cent Regus territory, he searched every hillock for a familiar landmark. He came to suspect that the landscape here was as fluid as the nature of the beastmen—shapes changing as if the world had forgotten its design.

Jordam slowed at one point and gazed up a steep slope to an old, crumbling shelter—a disintegrating barn with a weather-battered shack leaning against it. The beastman sniffed the air like a hunting hound, then growled.

"Are we in danger?" Cal-raven almost asked, but the beastman spurred the bull forward again.

The animal's mercurial temper kept the whip in Jordam's hand. It became increasingly agitated the farther they moved toward the Cent Regus Core. It moved so quickly that Cal-raven could not imagine any creature capable of catching it—except the Keeper.

The thought caught him by surprise. He began to speak into the air as they rode, his words ripped from his lips by the rush of air. "Keeper, guide me. Keeper, protect me. Keeper, help me in the Core." But with every word he felt more foolish, for the Keeper had led him north to the vision. His way had been clear before him. He'd seen no tracks pointing him any other way. "I'll go north," he said. "Just help me bring my mother out of the dark."

As they came out of the hills and into the haze of the wasteland, the horizon faded in all directions. They moved through a stifling space beneath low clouds that looked like muddy rags. These clouds carried no rain—only dust that streamed down into his face like angry swarms of stingers.

Winding like a restless snake through reeds in the lowlands beneath them, a tributary of the Throanscall looked lost, resigned to a slow death among these hills. As Jordam brought the bull down to its bank, Cal-raven saw that the waters were foul with corruption and debris.

Jordam leapt off the bull, and not wanting to be stranded or launched into the sky, Cal-raven quickly followed. Jordam gave the bull's flank a sharp slap. The bull made a sound almost like a horse's whinny, then shook the ground with the force of its departure.

The reeds surrendered a long raft of oiltree bark, which Jordam had concealed for his return.

In Abascar, oiltree bark had made barn-stall walls strong against vawns and horses. In Bel Amica, it was valuable for ship's hulls. And for Jordam's purposes, it would serve to keep them dry on this reeking river.

"rrMore boats like this waiting," the beastman said. "Waiting for escape."

Jordam watched the dustclouds withdraw across the dry, cracked ground as if they'd grown too tired to pursue him down the river.

He pulled the cloth cover off the honeycomb candle, the only one he'd brought from the collection he had crafted to bless Auralia's caves with light.

He remembered finding a candle lying on its side in a corner of Auralia's chambers. He had studied it for a long time before realizing that he understood its basic construction. Auralia had pressed tiny beads into the wax—weaving intricate designs all around it. He could not begin to imagine how to achieve such pleasing patterns, but he could make the candle itself. And there would be nothing suspicious about a hunk of honeycomb among beastmen, so he could carry these candles into the Core to help the prisoners move through the dark, winding passages in their escape.

But the more candles he made, the more he made them for pleasure than for any practical purpose. He played with differing shapes and even tried threading grasses through their wax.

"I know what you need," said Cal-raven. Reaching into the water, he scooped up a heavy stone from the riverbed. His hands softened it like bread dough. Jordam watched him, amazed again and unsettled. It reminded him of falling through the collapsing floor of a cave as the king of Abascar sought to kill him.

Cal-raven elongated the claylike mass to the size of a bread loaf, then gouged a hollow within it. "There." He placed Jordam's invention inside, then carved a grip atop the stone so the beastman could carry it easily.

"Lantern," Jordam grunted. "rrGood."

When Jordam observed Cal-raven murmuring fitfully in a dream, he reached into the crude bag he had made from a sun-baked vawn bladder and pulled out a tiny blue vial. He let a drop of oil fall onto the edge of the muskgrazer skin Cal-raven had pulled over himself as a shield against biting riverbugs. Cal-raven quieted and soon was snoring softly.

Jordam smiled.

The day had passed without trouble, save for brascle sightings that caused Cal-raven to fitfully test his knife's sharpness. They had left Henryk's company far behind, trusting them to follow the river and set up a defense for their escape.

As dusk's blue darkened, Jordam scanned the land on both sides of the river relentlessly. Then he drew back the cover so Cal-raven could breathe the cooling air. Soon swarms of Cent Regus pests would gather over the river, and the cover would save him from poisons.

The beastman had become accustomed to strange sights like this—these almost-hairless people forgetting their fear of the Cent Regus. He had seen it in the Cent Regus Core while he helped the Treasure and the ale boy prepare the prisoners for escape. The slaves had not trusted him at first. But one by one their bravest began to risk it, following him to the underground caves where the river flowed. There, they had begun crafting rafts for the coming escape. With every raft constructed, their hope grew stronger. The first crowd would have to escape unobserved, or there would never be a second endeavor.

Jordam found hope in the determination of O-raya's boy.

That boy had been the first of the smooth-skinned people from beyond the Cent Regus world to travel with him, to ride upon his shoulders in a swift journey through winter's worst. The ale boy, he had called himself. But Cent Regus prisoners called him Rescue. A boy who could hold and play with fire. A boy who had learned, passage by passage, the network of tunnels in the Core, somehow evading the sight of his captors. He was tireless, but whenever anyone sought to show him gratitude, he told them to thank the Keeper who had brought him.

Jordam understood that. Without the Keeper, he never would have discovered Auralia's colors. He would have remained a savage, addicted to the Essence that corrupted his kind and filled them with violence.

"Jordam." Cal-raven was awake, but his eyelids were half closed. "You keep saying Auralia's name. Tell me what you know about her."

Jordam spoke of the young woman who lived in caves beside Deep Lake. He had crawled into those caves, injured from a terrible fall, and he had watched her spend mornings in the forest climbing trees, following animals, digging in the dirt, swimming in the lake. He described to Cal-raven the things she would bring back to the cave—stones, seeds, shells, bones and berries, tufts of fur and fangbear teeth, curtains of cobweb and ears of corn.

"rrWatched her," he said. "Watched her long, long time. Strange. Always I go away...better inside. Like having a belly full of good things."

"I must see these caves." Cal-raven stared into the blue light of Jordam's candle as they floated along. "You could show me the way someday."

"rrNo Auralia anymore."

"I know."

Jordam shrugged. "Someday."

"I'm a king, Jordam, and what have I ever done that could inspire anyone as Auralia did? I'd rather craft one meaningful thing, one beautiful work, than spend my days trying to hold a house together."

Jordam let go of an oar to scratch the scarring on his forehead. "Stone people."

"Oh. In the Hall of the Lost. How did you know I made them?" Before Jordam could answer, he saw Cal-raven's face contort. "You saw me changing stone. When I tried to..." The king looked down at the blue candle. "It surprised me. I didn't know I could be so hateful, so terrible as I was that day. I'm sorry."

"I scared you. I'm Cent Regus."

"Do you understand those words—'I'm sorry'? It's not fair of me to ask you to forget what I did to you. But I wish I had not been cruel. I wish I'd listened."

"Bel." Jordam looked off into the night. "Bel taught me. Me, sorry. Bel forgives." At Cal-raven's questioning expression, he added, "Sin-der. Bel." Then he scratched again at his forehead's scar, where the browbone had broken. "Want to forget many things. Essence. Killing. rrBrothers."

Cal-raven nodded. "Jordam, you don't scare me anymore."

As they sailed along, the ground rising on both sides, the breeze stiffened, and the light in the lantern leapt up in alarm and went out. Jordam sniffed the gale, then snarled, "Hide."

Cal-raven covered himself with the heavy skin.

The man's eyes would not be sharp enough, but Jordam could see that they were approaching a low bridge. A figure leaned over the edge, arms reaching down as if he might try to snatch him from the boat.

Jordam wrapped one hand around the grip of a shield, another around his spear. He had fought upon this bridge before. It had not gone well.

The stranger was a beastman not unlike himself—large, apelike, with a jutting jaw, a hound's nose, and powerful arms. And he could see now that the beastman would not attack them. It had collapsed on the bridge, sick and wounded as if it had barely escaped from a battle. It moaned and feebly groped at the air beside Jordam's head as they passed beneath the dark span.

"What did it say?" Cal-raven whispered beneath the blanket.

Jordam did not answer. He only stood and sniffed the air, his ears twitching as if searching for some kind of news in the hush.

A few hours later, the moonlight a sickly yellow through the ever-present haze, Cal-raven took cover again to escape the bombardment of heavy, droning insects.

"Jordam," he asked, "do you really think we can get the prisoners out?"

"Bel's plan—boats. rrFlat, hidden boats. Row them up the river at night. O-raya's boy can get prisoners to the boats. Underground. Not many Cent Regus there. But dangerous. rrMust work fast."

"Are you sure these other beastmen will help us?"

"Some," he said. "Weak beastmen. Bad legs from too many lashings. Can't run. But good arms. rrRow hard. Treasure promised them freedom. They like O-raya's colors. Makes them think the Treasure is more powerful than the chieftain."

"Auralia's colors—you have some of them there, in the Core?"

"You will see." Jordam scratched at his arm.

"What is happening to you?"

Jordam shrugged. "Change."

Deep in the Core, Jordam could move among the chieftain's servants without being questioned or suspected. None of them seemed to recognize him as one of those four brothers who had caused such trouble for the chieftain during the last winter. He still smelled like the Cent Regus, so long as he layered himself in their reeking, rotting skins and cloaks. He still spoke like them to his own kind, even if he whispered in careful, clumsy Common to the slaves.

But he was changing. His mane had thinned considerably, and patches of his head were bare. Similarly, the ragged fur of his legs and arms was shedding. His dark claws had grown brittle; three had crumbled from the tips of his fingers, and all the claws that once jutted out from his toes had come off in his running.

And then there was the matter of his skin. The bumps, white and sore, had spread across his body so that he had been forced to go without any woodscloak for a time. When the blisters burst, dried, and disintegrated, the skin all around those wounds had gone crisp and cracking, then fallen away. The new skin was smoother and softer—copper colored, even freckled. Sometimes when he scratched it, it seemed to shine.

The water from Auralia's well sharpened his thoughts, illuminated his memories. It was helping him to despise the very thought of the Essence that had once fueled his bloodthirst.

Partayn was the first one he had rescued. The endeavor had been easy, as the Cent Regus had no reason to suspect it. The trouble had come when they reached open ground. The feelers, sensing something uncorrupted by the Essence, had burst through and tried to seize Partayn. Jordam fought them back with a torch and a blade.

Later, as he hollowed out another boat from a tree in the Cragavar, west of Deep Lake, a whistle had sounded from Tilianpurth in the valley below.

He had learned to respond to this whistle—one carved from a tiny white stone into the shape of an oceandragon's skull. Just as he had learned what to do when he saw a white flag raised over Tilianpurth. He had known to go to Bel Amica. There he had found another white flag flying over a campsite near a bridge.

A soldier, Henryk, had met him there. Deuneroi's father. Deuneroi, who had died at Mordafey's hands in the ruins of Abascar. It had been difficult for Jordam to sit in Henryk's tent, for he was overcome with shame.

Henryk had explained that House Bel Amica was still too dangerous for

Jordam. The Seers would have him killed. Ryllion would destroy him. But the queen herself had faced him to thank him for bringing home her son.

It had been the most fleeting of meetings, the queen scratching and twitching and whimpering like a nervous pup. But Cyndere had embraced him and wept into his mane. And together they had plotted how to bring out more prisoners from the Core. Cyndere had shown him the whistle and told him to bring water to Bel Amica if he heard it.

And so in his shelter of woven shell-bark stalks high in the trees just southwest of Tilianpurth, he had listened. During the day, as he carved a fleet of light boats to match those Cyndere had shown him, he listened. And now he often ventured back into Cent Regus territory on the prongbull he had tamed, speaking only with the ale boy and the woman that Skell Wra called Treasure.

"Treasure," he muttered, shaking his head.

Cal-raven stirred.

Jordam said, "If others find us going in, must make you look like a slave. I captured you. rrBringing you to the chieftain."

"I have an idea," said Cal-raven, and for the first time Jordam heard him laugh—a strange sound in this wilderness. "I should do what I do best." He raised his hands as if they were weapons drawn for battle. "Stone people."

29

SUSPICION AT THE
HARBOR CAVES

No, I'm done with Abascar." Wynn put another damp, sweet-smelling barrel of Bel Amican syrup onto the cargo sled, then sat on its edge. To Tabor Jan, he looked like a wet rat in the warm rain. Dark circles under his eyes were a burglar's mask.

"That bad, huh?" Tabor Jan set the birdcage down and sat beside him on the sled so he could speak quietly with the boy, their conversation cloaked by the wavewash against the docks, the bumping of the boats, and the weary loaders' profanity.

The yearning for sleep had begun to confuse him. While he had to admit that the Kneader had drawn the pain out of his body, something inside him still strained for slumber. If only she could have worked on his aching eyeballs. *I think I've seen too much.*

"I coulda saved Cal-raven if he'd let me," Wynn was saying, bitterness in his bark. "He knows that, and yet he left me here doing meaningless work." He gestured to the barrels as if they were a pile of vawn dung.

Tabor Jan shrugged. "You have to earn his trust with simple things before you're given anything complicated. And so far you haven't convinced him."

He pulled his pipe from his pocket, stuffed some honeyweed into the bowl, then started searching the pockets of his watchman's jacket for a spark-stick. "And what do you mean—*meaningless work?* You're sharp enough to see what he's done. He's planted spies all over Bel Amica. You're Abascar's eyes and ears at the harbor caves. He could have thrown you to the wolves for your insolence, but he gave you an important position in the game. This is where you prove yourself, Wynn. Pay attention." He lit the pipe, and the honeyweed flared.

Wynn turned his nose away. "How do I prove myself here? I'm an invisible cargo boy."

"I know an ale boy who carried barrels around Abascar for years, Wynn. After all those seemingly insignificant errands, he played a heroic role during Abascar's calamity. That's because he'd been paying attention. Now they call him Rescue."

Wynn was silent. The story clearly impressed him, as he owed his own life to its hero.

"Looking back, it's like Rescue was training all along. He's down in the Cent Regus Core, trying to rescue prisoners. So pay attention, Wynn. Watch for your moment to serve." Tabor Jan suddenly heard his own message and began scanning the scene around him. "You see, Wynn, I don't like it any more than you do. But Cal-raven's risking the future of House Abascar on a vision he's been given by the Keeper. He can't afford surprises. He needs you to be vigilant, watching for any—"

"You don't drink what he's drinkin', do ya?" Wynn snapped. "The Keeper's just kids' play. I outgrowed that stuff ages ago. And besides, if something really was watchin' us, well. . ."

The captain knew that Wynn was thinking of his sister, Cortie. It had been a difficult moment when Wynn had asked him about Cortie. He hadn't said a word about the Deathweeds that had taken her. She was "missing"—that was all.

He drew sweet smoke into his mouth, tasted its burn in his nose and on the back of his tongue. "I suspect we're all wrong about a great deal in this world. I admit, it's harder to believe than not to."

"It's ridiculous. You ever seen the Keeper? Or a Northchild?"

Tabor Jan blew out a long stream of curling smoke and wished he could float away on it. "You ever seen the wind?" he asked. "No, I've never seen the Keeper outside of dreams. And I never saw those amazing colors that Auralia showed House Abascar. But kick me in the gut if I go calling Cal-raven a liar."

A voice from the boat slapped Wynn back to work. He tromped to the wavering raft and lifted another barrel to his chest. Tabor Jan took the birdcage and tried to look like a watchman on duty.

"What's in these tubs anyway?"

"Syrup, I think. From the islands. Syrup. Nuts. Grains. Cider. Seeds. Gemstones. I've moved it all." The way he said it, like someone who'd worked these docks a lifetime, made Tabor Jan shoot smoke through his nose.

A line of soldiers attending to a cargo flat at another dock began marching in a line to the mouth of a tunnel, burdened by heavy bags. A burly guard let them pass into a tunnel in Bel Amica's foundation. Tabor Jan eyed the guard and considered requesting passage. But the guard's answer was in his scowl and in the nasty, barbed club in his hand. Even his hair appeared threatening, braided in long thin ropes with metal barbs.

"That's Balax," said Wynn.

Tabor Jan walked back to the sled and sat down. "What does Balax guard?"

The boy did not look up, muttering out of the side of his mouth. "The loaders call it the Punchbowl. It's where King Helpryn used to build his ships in secret. He liked surprises. He'd sail them out when they were ready, and everybody'd be amazed. Now only Ryllion's best patrol soldiers go in there. And Seers sometimes."

"What're they building in there?" he mused. "And what's in those bags they're carrying?"

"The loaders say it's oil. Really smelly oil. Before I worked here, they dropped a bag, and it broke. Those who didn't jump in the water quick were knocked flat and slept for three days."

"Slumberseed oil." Tabor Jan smiled. "Think they'd sell me some?"

The guard suddenly looked troubled, and it was easy to see why. A painted woman draped in beads and veils had come dancing down the stairs from the marketplace, and now she tiptoed gleefully toward him. He crossed his arms to discourage her. But she placed her bejeweled hands on his shoulders.

"That's Gelina," Wynn grumbled. "Sometimes Balax goes inside with her and the others take his place."

Tabor Jan regarded two other guards who sat slumped against one another, sleeping.

"I hate her perfume," Wynn groaned. "Makes my skin turn red."

"She's approached you like this?"

"Not like that, no. But she's lonely. She asked if maybe she could go with us when the Abascar people move on to a new house. She's not thinking straight, you see."

As if he'd been bitten, Balax shouted and knocked Gelina down so that she curled like an injured bird. Tabor Jan fought the instinct to rush to her side. She climbed awkwardly to her feet, found her balance, and staggered toward the stairway, her chains of gems clattering like a beaded curtain.

Tabor Jan ambled toward the guard, holding the birdcage by its hook in his left hand, his right open and close to the knife hilt.

Balax regarded him with annoyance. "The Abascar captain." He glanced at the birdcage, and a pale scar that ran from his left eye to the corner of his mouth twitched. "I see you've found a task that suits your strengths." He spoke as if he were chewing a gob of root-gum.

"The tetherwings?" He fought the urge to boast that Partayn himself had assigned him to carry them. "Oh, they're sick. I'm supposed to take them to old Myrton for treatment. Otherwise, they might not do their job in the wild. And you? What's your assignment?"

The guard crossed his arms again and answered officiously. "Seers' business."

"I thought you answered to Ryllion."

Balax seemed suddenly afflicted by an itch on the back of his neck. "Think you understand how it all works, do you? You don't want to meddle in Ryllion's affairs, bird-man. I swept some teeth off the dock yesterday after Ryllion delivered a scolding."

"You'll do anything he says, then?"

"I'd scrub his vawn's hindquarters if it would please him. He's Bel Amica's future."

"Interesting. The name I'd heard was Partayn."

The guard's eyes flashed. "Here's a secret," he muttered. "Houses aren't ruled by half-crazy singers. They're ruled by strength. You'll see."

Tabor Jan felt an urge to distance himself, and right away. "Look," he said, "I need to get a message to an Abascar soldier who's gone into the Punchbowl. That's why I came down to—"

"No Abascars have passed me." Balax's teeth flashed nothing like a grin. "You're confused."

"Sorry. Must have misunderstood." He looked over Balax's shoulder into the tunnel's darkness.

Choo? hooted one of the tetherwings. Tabor Jan looked down in amazement.

Balax shifted closer to partially block his view. "Get those birds out of here. And keep your mouth shut about this place. Ryllion wouldn't want you spoiling his surprise for the queen. I'd rather not sweep up your teeth."

Choo? said another tetherwing.

Tabor Jan whisked the birdcage away and headed to the stairs.

Halfway up, he was startled by a pile of seashells and beads that suddenly approached. "And what can Gelina offer you tonight, good Abascar captain?" she sang suggestively.

The impulse to raise his sleeve to his nose was almost irresistible. "Funny you should ask. I need some help."

"You'll find," she said with a lascivious grin, "that I'm very, very helpful, so long as you offer me some help in return." She jingled a coin purse that was pinned to one of those seashell chains.

"Oh," he said, "I can offer you something better than coins. How about a home in New Abascar? How about a life under the king's protection, where no one will disrespect you again?"

All deviousness drained from her expression, replaced by a desperate hope. "What kind of help do you need, exactly?"

30

An Offering to
the Chieftain

"Vawn. Bull. Girl."

Cal-raven watched, grim with worry, as Jordam named the shapes he had sculpted from riverstones. "rrMusic?"

"Yes, this one's a bellerose drum," he said. "And this one, a hewson-pipe. Will the chieftain believe these are prizes from Abascar's ruins?"

Jordam knocked on the stone model, but it made nothing like a musical sound. He shrugged and lifted it into the boat alongside the largest sculpture—a detailed statue of a regal figure that stretched the length of the craft. Then he climbed across the statue to the gap in the front of the bark.

Cal-raven unwound the boat's tether from a tree root, climbed into the small space at the back, and surveyed their surroundings in the brown light of the Cent Regus dawn. Tomorrow by this time, Henryk would be settling in near this spot, armed and ready for the escapees.

I must not keep him waiting.

Jordam uprooted the oar from the soft bank, and Cal-raven pulled the muskgrazer blanket over himself.

We're ready, Mother. Will you know me?

In the waves of rising emotion, Cal-raven feared he would lose his reason. He felt he was sailing back through time toward a looming figure whose features were vague and shifting. He blinked back sudden tears, and he did not know if they came from weariness or anticipation, despair or hope. As they washed the air's dark grit from his eyes, the white scar remained, flashing its persistent warning, as if to say, *You're going the wrong way.*

The boat moved crookedly through the sludge, and Cal-raven saw Jordam straining to clear debris from their path.

He looked again at the statue covered by layers of shieldfern. He knew every inch of that figure; he'd crafted it quickly but carefully so nothing about it would arouse suspicion. And he had given it broad feet so it would stand firm.

At times his thoughts would drift into imagined scenes where he drew the sword that Henryk had given him and defended his mother from slavering beastmen.

The boat entered a haze of foul smoke.

"rrWrong," Jordam suddenly snarled. "Something wrong."

Silent, Cal-raven shuddered for fear of what he could not see.

But soon he found it difficult to breathe, even beneath the blanket. "Where's it coming from?" he whispered.

"Everywhere. Shh." Jordam crawled like a cat across the statue so he could speak softly to Cal-raven. "Trouble in the Core. Fire. Loud noise. rrBodies in the river."

"What kind of bodies?"

"rrCent Regus." Jordam stood up, sniffing the smoke, then turned and barked something in the rough, jagged Cent Regus tongue.

Something answered him with an ultimatum.

Cal-raven let his hands drift up and down his forearms, checking his sleeves for placement of the stabbing pins, thin spikes of stone with a textured grip.

"Trouble," Jordam wheezed again, fear in his voice. "rrGo now. Get in."

Cal-raven crawled forward beneath the covering to the feet of the statue. He touched the flat base, and a layer of stone dissolved, providing an opening to the statue's hollow core. He wriggled inside as if climbing into a suit of armor that had been fused into one piece from head to toe. He squirmed onto his back, then leaned forward so he could see through the statue's open eyes.

"Ready," he said.

Jordam lifted a stone plate with contours that matched the figure's feet and pounded it into place, sealing Cal-raven inside the statue.

The boat slowed. Cal-raven could hear more and more objects—or bodies, perhaps—bumping against the prow.

Jordam hissed and cursed. "rrMudgators."

The boat rocked, and Cal-raven heard a commotion. Jordam grunted once, twice, again. The statue shifted, rocked, rolled onto its side, and now through the array of smaller sculptures, he could see Jordam, teeth bared, thrusting the spear into the water. His hood had fallen back, and Cal-raven stared in bewilderment at that massive head with a fringe of hair around the base of the skull—what was left of the beastman's mane. Those eyes—narrow but white like any man's. Those teeth—bright, stained, bold, and wolfen. And those bare arms that had cast the cape back to work freely were bound in bandages at the wrists and elbows.

Jordam pulled the gory spear free, then slumped into the boat and let it coast. "All wrong," said Jordam. "All wrong. Trouble in the Core."

A short while later Cal-raven saw that they had come to a crooked stone arch caught in the coils of some strange disease, a colorless mold like the stem of a mushroom.

A creature clung to the arch with its talons. It was a bony, featherless bird-man with huge white eyes. From its curved beak streamed sentences of clicks and squawks. Somehow Jordam understood, and he gestured toward the statue with great appeals. The bird-guard blinked, then shrieked what sounded like a decision.

Jordam rowed again with greater fury, as if worried the guardian might change its mind. "rrBig problem," he murmured as if to himself. "New chieftain."

"What?"

"New chieftain. Skell Wra pulled down from his throne. Core full of fighting." He leaned in close to the statue. "rrBe ready. Strange camp ahead. Many Cent Regus."

The river twisted and turned restlessly as if looking for a path around what lay ahead.

Scowling, Jordam began fitting together pieces that Cal-raven had sculpted to disguise him. One long stone fang hung down from his lips. A dark tumor of stone fit over his left ear. He would not be recognized.

The boat sailed between slumping, shapeless hills, and in the distance, wavering like a mirage, the ruins of the city that was once House Cent Regus came into view. Between the river and the cracked walls, the world's seams were tearing, crevasses opening in crazed lines. But across one unbroken patch of ground, a shroud of white dust glittered. Cal-raven recognized the substance immediately—the chalky crystals of Mawrnash.

Seers.

Within that canopy of mineral mist, dark figures like a flock of black herons hunched, wings drawn protectively around them. But they were not birds at all.

Jordam cowered as if he might turn and throw himself into the river. "rrStrongbreed. Strongbreed, a new kind of Cent Regus."

"New? How?"

"Cent Regus born all kinds of ways, but not like men. These born as men. Men made to drink Essence. They change. rrBecome like Cent Regus, but thinking better. Thinking stronger. And some have powers."

Cal-raven drew a sharp breath. "Those are men? They're enormous. They're as big as..." The name stopped in his throat. *Ryllion.*

"Powers. Like yours."

"Stonemastery?" He flexed his hands. *The Cent Regus have begun to manifest the powers of Tammos Raak's descendants.*

"Melt stone. Run through fire. Stop us with screams like...like spears."

Cal-raven's stone shell seemed more stifling with every moment.

"There." Jordam pointed to the center of the camp. "New chieftain."

In the center of the army, a red curtain encircled the base of what looked like a broad-boughed, leafless tree. Its black and bristling branches thrashed as if caught in a storm. No, not branches. Tentacles. Limbs like the arms of some frantic ocean monster stranded on dry land.

Feelers. Deathweeds.

"The throne," Jordam rasped, clearly horrified by what he saw. "Skell Wra's throne. It's above ground. It walks. rrCarries a new chieftain." He turned and gripped the statue by the shoulders. His eyes were wide, and his cracked lips quivered. "rrQuiet. They've seen us."

White rat-beasts seized the stone sculptures from the boat and thrust them into a wagon. Cal-raven braced himself as the statue landed, propped up and facing backward. Through the eyes, he could see Jordam put his weight into pushing the wagon up the slope toward the camp.

Into the white dustcloud they moved. Long shadows lashing the ground like contentious serpents told Cal-raven that they were nearing the throne.

The Strongbreed stepped aside to give them passage, then turned to close in behind them—a barrier of rippling black cloaks. Giants indeed, the minions stared with red eyes, gripping spears with massive clawed fingers the color of old blood.

Jordam brought the wagon to a stop. Sweat rivered down the beastman's neck, and he pulled the hood of his stormcloak up. Then he fell forward, out of Cal-raven's sight, most likely to bow before these Cent Regus powers. Cold smoke reeked in the air.

Cal-raven pushed his hands up and began to close the openings in the statue's face. As he did, he leaned forward, trying to see clearly through the tiny slit he left open in the left eye.

"Skarggh!" One white-eyed rat advanced and lashed at Jordam with a whip. "Skenn-skenn," the rat repeated.

A familiar figure stepped into view, laughing at Jordam. Cal-raven held his breath.

One of the Seers.

A hissing like a nest of snakes filled the air. The Seer stepped aside as one of those black bristling branches wriggled into view, then coiled about Cal-raven's statue. Sharp teeth lined the tentacle, scraping against the surface as it tightened and dragged the statue through a break in the curtain toward the new chieftain.

Cal-raven fought for breath.

The towering, skeletal Seer—his everlasting grin still gleaming like the teeth of a polished skull—hissed with pleasure. "Gooood. A fine ornament. A resourceful servant has brought this for you, Chieftain."

The tentacle lifted the statue, turned it upside down, and Cal-raven winced as the top of his head struck the statue's stone cap. But the figure did not break.

Through the slit of the open eye, he could now behold the beastman. At first he could not tell the chieftain from the throne.

It seemed the throne's twitching tentacles had drawn in living prey as a spider clutches its meal. Sitting in the crux of trunk and branches, the beast-man looked likely to be torn apart, for some of the throne's branches penetrated the gaps between the ribs of his broad red chest.

The chieftain was a confusion of animals. Two powerful arms, plated with a skin of rough shields that scraped together when he moved, wielded hands backed with spines that he seemed eager to fling like daggers. He thrust out a jaw like a shovel, flaring red-stained teeth. The face rising from that fanged bowl resembled a man's. His head bore crisscrossing stitches; someone had opened it several ways, then sewn it up again. Behind his ears what remained of a thick black mane spilled down around his shoulders.

At times the creature seemed to direct the throne, to turn it like a rider turns a steed; yet, he was anchored to it like a puppet.

"You've seen the ruins of House Abascar, haven't you?" The Seer leaned in as if cooing to a nervous child. "A fitting prize for you."

From the chieftain's throat came a sound like a bone rattling in a wooden box. The eyes, which were small and sunken, unnerved Cal-raven, for they were such human eyes.

"It's a reminder of all that your kind have conquered. A prize to remind us of Cent Regus's sovereignty. He always was the greatest son of Tammos Raak."

Flattery, Cal-raven thought. *The Seer speaks to him just the way Pretor Xa speaks to Bel Amicans.*

"Show this prize to your predecessor, Master Cent Regus," sneered the Seer.

The statue rolled in the air, suspended suddenly before a small cage. Inside, a sniveling creature lay on its side, curled up like an infant. Its skin was blue with cold, and as it weakly lifted its head to stare at the statue, Cal-raven covered his mouth with both hands. The blue baby was not in any way healthy or human. Its hands were clawed, its face so swollen that its features were almost engulfed by the rolls of flesh. Like a newborn animal, it bleated from two separate mouths, one human and one strange and alien on a long throat lined with dark veins.

At the sound of the new chieftain's laughter—a hysterical cough and a sneer like a mocker-dog's—the caged child became enraged. He turned away, exposing a back that was deeply scarred. "Skell Wra," the chieftain was laughing. "Skell Wra."

The statue turned in the air again, several branches of the tyrant's living throne pawing at it and stroking it. Upright, Cal-raven was drawn closer to the chieftain's face.

Keeper, he silently spoke. *I would destroy this thing. Give me opportunity.*

The chieftain seemed curious about the statue's face. "Cal," he growled, "Marrrcusss." One of those dark, swaying branches over his head descended, carrying a trophy that the chieftain carefully regarded, grinning a wall of teeth so white and polished they might have been newly installed.

It was a skull, blackened and charred, staring back at Cal-raven through empty sockets.

When the chieftain spoke again, he spoke in the Common tongue. "Is thisss a good likeness?"

Cal-raven's breath caught in his throat.

"Hmmm?" The chieftain leaned forward. Cal-raven could hear him sniffing as if suspicious. "Cal." The voice slithered through the slit in the sculpture's eye. "Marcusssss."

Cal-raven brought his trembling hand down to his side to close over the hilt of his knife. *I will kill this abomination,* he silently vowed. *I will cut out his heart.*

"Your predecessor pillaged the ruins of Abascar," the Seer sang sweetly to the chieftain. "But you will do mightier things. Ryllion is ready. When Queen Thesera boards her ship tomorrow, she and her children will be within reach. They'll all be there, in full view of their people. Then those weak-minded Cent Regus fools you prepared will strike. They'll tear the royals to pieces. Ryllion will appear like the people's hero. He'll slay the fools you trained. And the grateful Bel Amicans will give him the throne."

The chieftain cackled, exuberant. "My servant."

"Though he knows not what he's become, the first of the Cent Regus Strongbreed will govern House Bel Amica. And when the time's right, I, Malefyk Xa, your creator, shall unleash you, the greatest of all Cent Regus. And you'll grip him just as you grip this statue of Abascar's King Cal-marcus."

Not in Barnashum, not in the slavers' pit, not even in the Bel Amican cell—Cal-raven had not felt so helpless since House Abascar burned and collapsed. Pictures of his people flowed past him. Tabor Jan walking the wall, blind to the danger. Lesyl, her voice raised, likely to be near Partayn at the time of the attack. Jes-hawk and Brevolo, working with Ryllion, unaware of the extent of his villainy.

We must go back.

Even as he thought this, he knew it was too late. He could never reach Bel Amica in time to save Cyndere or Partayn. And what would become of Emeriene? of Tabor Jan and Lesyl?

As he leaned back inside the statue, the stone began to soften, ready to release him. He shifted in alarm, and the chieftain turned his attention to the statue in surprise.

A rat-beast standing at the curtain squealed, distracting the chieftain. His purr resonated right through the arms of his throne, and Cal-raven felt the vibration through the stone. Then the chieftain dropped the statue to the ground, and Cal-raven heard a chip from the toe break away. Light gleamed through a crack that spread upward from the statue's heel to the knee. He worked his hand down to his left thigh, touched the stone encasement, and melted the crack shut before it could spread. Sweat trickled down his back.

The chieftain snarled a decision. The statue left the ground again, and the throne's tentacles carried it out through the curtain and planted it upright in the wagon. Cal-raven immediately parted the stone of the eyes and the mouth, drawing in deep breaths.

Jordam climbed wearily to his feet, and his eyes did not meet Cal-raven's. It was clear from the despair in his face that he had heard and understood every word.

One of the Strongbreed slammed its spear against a battered Jentan cymbal. Jordam, clearly terrified, lifted the wagon's shafts and pushed it on its grumbling wheels down the long aisle that opened through the assembly of unblinking half men.

"Ryllion," Cal-raven whispered, exhausted.

"rrStop," Jordam growled softly.

"He's going to kill—"

"Stop!" Jordam barked, as if forgetting that he was followed by rat-beasts.

"Cyndere, Jordam. Bel!"

Jordam roared and began to run down the hill. Cal-raven shut his mouth. Rat-beasts scampered up alongside, eying the statue suspiciously.

Jordam brought the wagon to a rest at the river's edge. Rat-beasts crowded around the wagon, glaring at the beastman. He lifted the statue to lay it in the boat. Cal-raven caught a glimpse of veins bulging from his forehead.

"rrThey're sending us in," Jordam mumbled to the statue's face. Then he let it tumble, facedown, into the boat, which rocked, jerked, spun, and was soon back in the current. It was swept along through the sludge and pulled violently down into the earth.

The river dropped steeply, and the boat was battered and tossed as it descended. The sculptures rolled, their sides grinding against one another. The breath was beat from Cal-raven's lungs. Sludge washed over the edges, filled the bottom of the boat, and began trickling into his confinement. He quickly sealed the eyes and opened a window on the back of the figure's head.

"Where are we going?" he called.

"Old dock for prisoners and prizes."

"What's waiting there?"

"rrNothing. Anymore."

Cal-raven felt the boat suddenly seize as if caught on some obstruction. Then it rocked, and he heard Jordam groaning with the weight of the bulky sculptures as he unloaded them.

"Are we alone?"

"Yes. rrStrange."

Cal-raven opened a larger cavity in the back of the statue's head so he could survey their predicament. They were at the jagged edge of a continent of stone, a plate that jutted out over the water, in a large underground cavern. Jordam stood on the edge of the shelf, lining up the sculptures.

Two half-starved vawns stood motionless and bony, as if they'd died on their feet. They were harnessed and hitched to wooden sleds on metal runners.

Jordam was about to jump back onto the boat for the statue, but he stopped when he saw Cal-raven's head protruding from the back of Cal-marcus's likeness. Cal-raven heard him laugh for the first time—a gruff guffaw.

"Is it safe enough yet?"

"No." He shoved Cal-raven's head back inside the statue.

"You said there were boats. Boats waiting to take us out of here."

Jordam stamped his foot. "Boats under the stone. rrReady."

Cal-raven lay down, took a deep breath, and decided to stop asking questions.

The sled's runners sang along, searing and scraping as Jordam drove one of the wretched animals around the corners of the rigorous corridor. Cal-raven felt it coast to a stop, heard Jordam speaking in the beastman tongue. Then the sled moved again, the feeble vawn groaning as its knees and spine crackled.

Cal-raven watched a female Cent Regus creature turning to study them as they passed, her face a monkey's mocking grin, teeth bared, while her long, hairless hands hugged a sagging, pregnant belly.

He had never seen such a thing before.

Jordam said his name. He opened the statue's eyes and looked forward. "rrVery close now."

The sled rested at a crossroads. "Wait. Stay." Jordam reached up and tugged the harness free from the vawn, then slapped its side. The signal would have sent any other vawn trotting away, but this one moaned, leaned against the wall, then sank to its knees and rested its snout on the ground.

Jordam gestured to a stairway that ascended from the crossing. "Abascar prisoners wait there. I bring them down." Then he spat out the jutting stone tusks, growling with relief.

"And when you bring them down..." Cal-raven's voice was trembling. *Who will be among them? Who lives?*

"If anyone comes." Jordam put his hands over Cal-raven's two small windows. "rrCover."

"Yes."

The beastman drew a long blade, its edges notched with scars. Then he dropped down on one knee so Cal-raven could hardly see him. "Thank you," said the beastman before he got up. "Thank you, King of Abascar."

My hopes are placed in a beastman.

He turned away from his father's eyes, looked out through the back of the head. Three passages led away—the long way back to the boat, a corridor so dark it may as well have been sealed, and another that led down a torchlit stair.

A shriek like the killing cry of a predatory bird cut the air. He twisted back to look through the statue's eyes but saw only a frantic clash of shadow and firelight on the walls.

Jordam's in trouble already.

A sharp hiss sounded behind him, and he pivoted once more to find two sniveling rat-beasts tugging at the back of the sled. He tried to bend his knees and duck out of sight, but the hollow within the statue was not large enough. He slipped his hands up into the statue's head and began pressing a thin layer of stone to cover the cavity.

The rats were now shouting at the slumped vawn and dragging it back to the sled. The ensuing screeches and roars told him the beast was not at all pleased. The sled suddenly jerked, then spun, and one of the wooden slats framing the wagon gave way. The statue fell backward out of the sled and thudded hard against the floor. Cal-raven's head rang as if his own skull had cracked. He called for Jordam in the dust-clouded space as the statue began to roll...

...and fall.

The statue of King Cal-marcus slid, feet first, down the stair.

It skidded to a stop in a dark, deserted space, then spun slowly on the pivot of Cal-marcus's hands, which were folded solemnly before him.

Cal-raven lay still. Warm blood ran from the back of his head down over his face, where it pooled inside his father's face.

"Go ahead, Tabor Jan," he muttered. "Keep on cursing my name. Biggest fool in the Cent Regus Core—that's what I am."

In the distance Jordam's fight continued. Whatever he fought was losing in a painful way.

Outside, the complaint of a metal hinge accompanied the snarl of a heavy door.

The statue moved. Someone was dragging it. He heard the voices of beastmen.

He groaned, turned his head sideways, and rested his cheek in blood that was draining out through the statue's eyes to the floor.

Moments later the statue was set upright. Back on his feet, Cal-raven blinked blood from his eyelashes. Through a dizzying haze, he saw a figure of radiant colors approaching.

31

REUNIONS

"C al-marcus?" The pregnant beastwoman staggered toward Cal-raven, clutching her belly. She spoke with the voice of a weary old woman. "Look. Look. The stone is weeping blood."

That's my blood, he thought. Then he remembered that he was still encased in the standing statue of his father.

His vision blurred, as if he were waking in a colorful garden. Those hues congealed, and the white scar burned in its center, bright as ever.

"You were such a fool, Cal-marcus," the voice from the dream continued. "Such a beautiful fool. What made us think we were ready?"

He blinked. There was no beastwoman. He was delirious. Someone was wiping blood and dirt from the statue's face with a rag.

"Fools, we were. Greater fools for bringing another into such darkness."

Carefully he looked out to see where he had been taken.

Figures were moving through a glow, in front of a shining curtain. Then the curtain moved too, and he saw that it was draped about someone's shoulders. The luminous stranger moved out of sight. The busy company that remained was outlined by spitting torches.

The figures were beastmen—five, burly and hushed. Like small fangbears they were, but with human faces. After unfolding and spreading out long strips of ragged fabric on the floor, they began to arrange feathered arrows in straight lines. This simple task seemed to require fierce concentration, as if straight lines were a new idea.

Bright colors flowered in his view again. The beastmen stopped and turned to watch the shining figure in fascination. Cal-raven's gaze followed, and he felt a thrill of certainty.

My eyes lie, or I have found Auralia.

Someone small—not a beastman, but a boy—hurried past in front of him. "Roll 'em up," said a youthful voice. "Wrap 'em. There's a fight in the corridor. I think Jordam's come back. If he has, then we should be ready to run. The time has come."

The woman's voice rang out again: "Raven!"

It struck him so sharply that he looked to the right, but the statue's head could not turn.

"Cal-raven," she said again, "we can't do this. It's too dangerous."

Cal-raven answered at once, without yet comprehending why the voice rang him like a bell. "Don't fear," he heard himself whisper.

The boy whirled. He drew back his hood and put a red, callous hand against his bald crown, which was crimson and cracked as if roasted in an oven. His eyes shone like white beacons.

The colors intensified, their source coming closer, and the boy darkened into a silhouette against the shining figure. As if asking a question, Cal-raven touched his finger where the Ring of Trust had rested.

But this was not Auralia—this woman embraced and illuminated by Auralia's colors, her hair short and silver and edged with the colors she wore, her eyes dark as caves, her face worn like stone after a hundred years of rain.

"The statue." The boy put his hand against Cal-raven's shell. "It spoke."

"I heard," she whispered. "Raven, I'm afraid. What if you're right? I heard you call out for the Keeper. I did not expect that anything would answer. But look... This is my husband's likeness."

"Don't be afraid, Mother," said Cal-raven, his heart knowing already what his mind did not understand. Tears stung his eyes even as he pressed his hands against the stone of his father's heart.

As Cal-raven staggered forward through the dissolving statue, the boy spread his arms and backed up, shielding the woman behind him. The beastmen came to their feet, growling.

"Don't be afraid," Cal-raven said again, rubble crumbling to the floor around his feet.

"Who are you?" the boy demanded.

"Raven," the woman whispered. "What's happening?"

"Forgive me." Cal-raven held up his bloodied hands as sand spilled from his sleeves. "I must look a fright."

The boy slowly brought his arms down to his sides. "She's...she's not talking to you."

"I was talking to my son," said the woman to Cal-raven, and she closed her hands fast over the boy's shoulders.

Cal-raven reached his left hand up to his right shoulder as if he could feel her grip. "What?" He took a shaky step forward and then sank to his knees. "No. I am Cal-raven. Don't you know me? I thought you were dead, or I would have come for you a long time ago."

The boy walked forward, raised a shaky hand, and brushed the blood-matted hair away from Cal-raven's eyes. "She doesn't know you, my king," he whispered. "It's been too many years for her. But me...I know you." Then he rested a hand on Cal-raven's shoulder. "I'm your ale boy."

"Rescue." Astonished, Cal-raven embraced the boy. "Jordam told me you were here."

The boy began to cry softly, and his small hand patted Cal-raven's back.

"I hardly recognize you, boy. And here you are, working to save Abascar all over again." He found it difficult to raise his eyes to that radiant figure who stood still in the center of the chamber.

"We're ready." The boy stepped away, wiping his hands on his filthy trousers. "Our plan's in place. We've got boats."

Cal-raven glanced to the beastmen, who were still looking from him to the statue's ruin in disbelief. "It's too dangerous. The river is difficult. And there are beastmen out there."

"Cal-raven, come away from him," said Jaralaine. Her voice, stern and fearful, was also familiar.

"She means me," the boy sighed. He turned to the woman. "Queen Jaralaine," he said. "I told you this would happen. You know it's true. I'm not your son. Here is Cal-raven." He took her hand and led her forward. Her hand-stitched leather slippers shuffled in small, reluctant steps.

Cal-raven's whole body began to quake.

"Some kind of..." The woman would not meet his gaze but stared beyond him. "Some kind of trick. He looks nothing like..." She stood stiffly, blinking as if sleepy.

Cal-raven stepped forward and drew his mother gently to him. She kept her arms at her sides for a while, then raised her hands awkwardly as if to test him in an embrace.

Crouched in a row across the chamber, the beastmen watched, uncomprehending. Then, one by one, they rose and returned to their work.

Through the shining cloth, Cal-raven could feel a brittle, bony figure, like a wooden frame the Abascar tailors had built to display new garments. "How can you be so small?" he murmured into her ears. He had not known what to expect. He had feared finding her senseless or maimed. But no, this was his mother—aged more by ordeal than by time. Through that mask of hardship, he glimpsed the face he remembered. Through her fear and confusion, he heard the voice that had comforted him after bad dreams and taught him the names of flowers and the lineage of his house.

For a moment he felt warm.

Then she hissed as if stung and broke free of the embrace. "No." She turned away. "No, this is not my son." She flattened her hand at about the height of the ale boy's head. "He is not grown yet. I still..." Her voice became faint. She looked around. "I cannot let..." She pressed her hands against her head. "What's happening? Time. Time. Did you tell me, my son?" She reached out for the ale boy. "Forgive me, but I've forgotten. I need to walk in my garden. But the garden is dead. Cal-marcus. He's so worried about me. He sent me this, you know." She bundled the colors tightly around her as if the chamber had gone cold.

"My lady, you should put something on your feet," the boy said. "We will go now to the boats."

Cal-raven's mother hesitated. He thought she might turn back to him and change her mind. But she did not. She walked slowly to the other side of the chamber and knelt in a corner to sort through a pile of rags.

The boy took Cal-raven's hand. "Give her time, master. She's broken. But she's alive."

Cal-raven pressed his hand against his chest. "Isn't that...the cloak..."

"Auralia's colors, yes. Don't ask me how it got here." The ale boy squeezed the king's hand. "Forgive me, master, but perhaps it would help if we cleaned you up a bit."

Cal-raven felt the knots within him tightening as his mother approached the beastmen and surveyed their work. "Good," she said. "The arrows are ready. Now the shields. Where are the shields?"

"Those beastmen, they're gonna help. Weak in the legs, but strong arms. They'll row us upriver."

"They won't hurt her?"

"None of the beastmen will hurt her. The chieftain made them swear to protect her. She's his greatest prize."

"Yes, but Skell Wra's been overthrown."

The sound of someone rapidly descending the stairs drew their attention to the dark beyond the barred gate. A beastman lunged into view. His breath was ragged, and a wound on his left shoulder bled down his arm.

"rrMust...hurry."

"Jordam!" The ale boy ran to the bars.

"They know," Jordam groaned. "rrCouldn't catch them all. They'll tell." He looked down at the boy. "It hurts. Hurts to kill."

Cal-raven ran to the bars. "What do we do?"

Jordam shrugged. "Prisoners...not all where they should be. rrMust find the rest. Up there, somewhere."

Cal-raven shook his head. "Let's take who we have and go. I have to get her...get them out of here."

"I'll go get the others," said the ale boy.

"No," shouted Jaralaine. She walked to the bars and clasped Jordam's hand as assuredly as if he were family. "I'll go. I promised Abascar's people I would get them out of here. All of them. Nothing will stand in my way. This is how I pay my debt."

Cal-raven reached for Jaralaine's arm, but the room began to spin. He opened his mouth to object, but the words he spoke were slurred.

"He's bleeding," said the ale boy. "His head."

"The statue," Jordam growled. He held out a vawnskin flask to the ale boy. Cal-raven blinked at it, then realized how thirsty he was.

The voices faded. All he could see were Auralia's colors, and then nothing.

He awoke to the sound of Abascar's Early Morning Verse and to the sight of red lines rippling across the ceiling of a vast cavern.

He recognized another sound—the echo of the river. He was lying on the stone plate, his head on a warm pillow wet with water. Its scent was familiar.

The well water.

Someone caressed his brow, saying, "Shhhhhh."

He turned his head slightly to see her, but she touched his cheek and said, "Don't move. Rest, King of Abascar."

He tried to rise, and his head came up dripping from the pillow. "Where's my mother?"

"The queen has gone to get the rest of us. Lie down, master. Your head's a bruised apple. I'm Nella Bye. I was a Gatherer. I am here with your people."

My people. Turning his head, Cal-raven could see more than a hundred sitting on the stone plate, clustered together in groups as if for warmth. Their clothes were mere rags, their faces dark, and all of them looked at him, even as they sang softly.

The river here broadened into a vast lake under a high ceiling. The recesses above were alive with chattering cave bats. On the far side, Cal-raven could see a rocky bank and a deep passage that continued under a low ceiling. Behind him, the wall of rock was solid save for the tunnel where he and Jordam had ventured into the labyrinth.

"The boats are ready."

"But we can't go out there."

"The new chieftain is on the move," said a voice. Cal-raven turned his head and saw an old man braiding a long, grey, filthy beard and rocking back and forth, his naked shoulders jutting forward. "Jordam said the conquerors are scouring the Core, destroying Skell Wra's faithful. But they won't find many. Beastmen are fickle."

"Irimus Rain!" Cal-raven had never before been happy to see the old Abascar strategist.

"Lie down," said Nella Bye sternly. "Listen to the song. Soon we'll rise and sing it together in the sunlight. Sunlight, master. We haven't seen it in so long."

Pushing her arm away, Cal-raven got shakily to his feet and gazed into the faces of the crowd. *It's like I'm surrounded by ghosts.*

They sang on, but as they did, they came to their feet one by one. Some stood quickly, hands placed over their hearts. Others needed help. They moved to encircle him. He began to recognize faces he had carved in the Hall of the Lost, people he had not seen since they passed him on the avenue in House Abascar.

"Tell me, my lord—have you seen my sister, Chalis?"

"And me, my lord—my grandfather Jak!"

Like a spark that catches a runnel of oil, the questions began and spread, and Cal-raven had to raise his hands as the people pressed in. It was old, cranky Irimus Rain who shouted down the clamor.

"The time for stories will come," Cal-raven said when the people quieted. "Have patience."

One child Cal-raven recognized as Owen-mark—a tough upstart of a Gatherer who had ventured beyond the bounds set for harvesters. Cal-raven's patrol had rescued him from the coils of a ravenous squeezer-tooth. "Rescue asked us all to call out for the Keeper," the boy said.

"Rescue was right. The Keeper's been leading me." But even as Cal-raven said this, he felt a pang of doubt.

"I've been here the whole time," Owen boasted. "Some of us only been here a while." The boy described the filthy, exhausting work of clearing the stone and soil so that feelers could push their way faster and farther. He told of how the slaves collected in carts what had been dragged down by the monstrosity's wide-reaching arms—bodies, broken people, animals, trees.

"Why do the feelers drag the living into the Core? Animals can't be slaves."

"Some can," said Irimus. "But those that can't are carried down deeper.

No one knows what happens. We suspect it has something to do with the Essence."

As he spoke, the crowd parted, and Nella Bye came forward. And this time Cal-raven choked in disbelief. For in the woman's arms lay a child asleep—a girl with golden hair.

"Cortie."

"You know her?" asked Owen in surprise. "The feelers dragged her in."

Cal-raven looked up as the five bear-beasts marched in a sullen line into the cavern. Each carried rolled bundles of arrows under one arm and a pile of shields under the other.

"Perhaps it's time we show them," he said, "that there are powers greater than claw and curse." Behind his eyes, the cliffs of Barnashum were coming alive with light, and the very stones that the beastmen climbed were turning against them. "We've surprised them once. We'll surprise them again."

"We'll ask the Keeper to fight for us," said Owen.

Cal-raven reached down and mussed the boy's hair.

The five beastmen knelt along the edge of the stone plate. Paw over paw, the bear-beasts drew on ropes that disappeared under the edge of the platform. As they did, Cal-raven felt a faint vibration beneath his feet.

Broad, misshapen boats of oiltree bark scraped under the stone until they were out and rocking on the slow, filthy water like dry, curling leaves.

"Here they come," said Nella Bye, and Cal-raven beheld a small crowd emerging from the corridor, led by the ale boy and his mother. Jordam brought up the rear, walking backward, a spear in each hand.

"This is it," said the ale boy. "We've gathered all the Abascar prisoners. But there are more."

∾

Plosh, said something ahead in the murky waters.

Jordam leaned forward from his perch at the front of the foremost boat. It might have been a gator.

These boats are like turtles, he thought as the three chains of rafts lurched, stroke by stroke, against the current.

Each boat was packed with survivors. Passengers around the edges held up dark, reflective shields facing outward, giving each raft the look of a domed shell. He thought of Goreth; his twin brother had been strangely fond of turtles.

Jordam had watched these survivors, fascinated by how much they risked in order to stay together. He was beginning to understand. His thoughts, like his body, were shedding the curse as well. He felt as if he were moving into new territory—sunlit, open, colorful.

It was all so different from what went on in the Core among beastmen.

There had been a frenzied battle in the throne room as the new chieftain took control. The Strongbreed had torn the paltry resistance to shreds. Jordam had slaughtered many of his own kind in the past, just as the Old Dog had taught him. But now he felt an ache every time one beastman turned upon another.

Laying his shield across his lap, he brushed bogflies from it and stared at his reflection. His mane was falling away. His forehead, where a browbone had once protruded, was now grown over with rugged flesh. He looked the way he felt—like a lonely creature stranded between two worlds.

But these people cared about him. Especially the ale boy.

Jordam stood up and looked back across the line of boats. The ale boy sat next to Owen at the back of the boat just behind this one. Seeing Jordam's attention, his countenance brightened. As if he knew what the beastman was thinking, the boy spoke quietly, for he knew that Jordam would hear him even if others with their weaker ears could not. "You've grown so much."

Jordam laughed, a strange gruff cough. And there it was again, that tickle of water in his eyes.

He turned to look up the tunnel, reminding himself of the need for vigilance, and he raised his shield. "rrNot free yet."

Cal-raven, sitting beside him, glanced back down the dark tunnel. Jordam could hear the man's heart pounding as rapidly as prey in flight from a predator. "I should seal the passage behind us," Cal-raven said. "It would prevent them from following."

"But the tunnel, my lord," said Irimus. "The river's flowing in. It would fill the tunnel."

Cal-raven grimaced. "Perhaps I should just raise a reef beneath the water then, something boats can't cross."

"rrDon't get into the water," Jordam growled.

"Don't block the river," said Jaralaine, who sat enshrouded in a plain grey cape on the opposite side of the boat, clutching a bundle of cloth against her breast. Jordam had noticed how the Abascar king jumped whenever she spoke. "We're coming back. There are more prisoners. Bel Amicans, merchants, and others."

Cal-raven looked around. "Why did they keep Abascar separate?"

Irimus shrugged. "They supposed that Abascar people knew how to dig."

"When the Cent Regus learn that my mother and the Abascar slaves have escaped, they'll watch this passage. We'll have to find another way."

Jaralaine narrowed her eyes. "Don't talk like you know this place."

Jordam saw Cal-raven smile and wondered why such a stern order would please him.

He turned his attention back to the slow roll of the ugly waves. One of the bear-beasts glanced at him nervously, and Jordam spoke to him in the Cent Regus tongue. "No more beatings. No more chieftain. You can drink more water from O-raya's well. Soon. rrRow harder. Watch the tunnels. We can't let any others find us here."

The people were silent, peering out from between the shields.

There—Jordam could smell open air. They would need every arrow. They would need Cal-raven's stonemastery. The ale boy claimed to have called for the Keeper. Jordam remembered his encounter with the Keeper. He had no desire to see that creature again.

Plup.

Something had gone into the water.

He looked back, glanced to the banks on either side, listened. No one said anything.

"What did you hear?" asked Cal-raven.

He shrugged and turned forward again. "rrWatch close," he warned the rowers.

"Jordam," said Irimus, "the feelers have not come for us."

"Feelers," he said, "don't hunt here. Unless Skell Wra tells them to. But Skell Wra is not the chieftain. Maybe the feelers are confused."

"And the observers," said Irimus. "What of them?"

"The white giants protect the new chieftain," Jordam growled.

"I am proud of my father," said Cal-raven suddenly. "He made our house the only one that utterly refused to do business with the Seers."

Abascar's queen looked up. The words seemed to amaze her.

"But what game are they playing?" asked Irimus.

The river's reflections swirled above them the color of blue flame. Then Owen quietly asked, "Is it time to sing yet?"

Jaralaine looked back at him. "Not until the Morning Verse. Soon. But we may have to whisper this time. Follow my son's example."

Cal-raven looked up at her, but the queen was looking back across the rafts. "My son," she said softly. "Where is my son?"

"Mother?" Cal-raven answered softly.

"No!" she shouted, rising to her feet. "Not you. Where is my son?"

"rrQuiet!" Jordam whined.

"He was right there!" she shrieked, and then she tried to step through those around her as if she would jump to the boat behind them.

Cal-raven stood up.

Everyone turned.

Owen bowed his head.

"Where's the ale boy?" Cal-raven asked. "Where's Rescue?"

Jordam responded at once. He leapt off the boat into the water. The river was just shallow enough that he could stride. Step by step, he searched the waters behind the boats, the cold, slimy current coursing all about him. "O-raya's boy!" he roared.

Cal-raven stepped to the next boat and knelt beside Owen. "Did you see anything?"

"Master," said Owen, "I promised I wouldn't say."

"You promised what?"

Owen sighed. "He said he'd done his part. The Keeper's coming to help him find the others who need rescuing."

"That boy wants to save the whole world," Irimus wheezed.

"rrMust keep going," Jordam growled. "Can't stop now."

A tremendous splash sounded, and everyone turned.

Jaralaine had gone into the water.

They did not see her come up until she staggered onto the rocky river-bank, soaked in sludge, her arms wrapped tight around the bundle she had brought to the boat. "Son!" she was crying.

Jordam held up his hands to Cal-raven. "rrStay! No stopping the boats!"

Cal-raven followed his mother into the water.

Jordam turned, terrified. *They will awaken things. The Cent Regus will come after us.* He pushed against the current but saw Cal-raven's head bob as he was carried past. Struggling to surface, the man grabbed hold of a rolling tree branch. Jordam surged after him. Out of the corner of his eye, he saw Jaralaine disappear into a crevasse in the wall.

Jordam reached out and seized the tree branch, then drew it close until he could grasp Cal-raven's sleeve. Soon he had the man in his arms.

"We've. Got to. Catch her." Cal-raven coughed out sludge.

Jordam carried Cal-raven to the shore, and the man stumbled into a run.

Jordam turned to the boats. "Go on," he said. "Arrows ready. We will find you." He stared intensely at the oarsman who steered the last boat. "rrDon't fail me."

Charging into the tunnels, he could hear both of them—Jaralaine's frantic breath, her light footsteps, Cal-raven's calls for her to stop, his swift heartbeat.

Jordam bounded up seven stairs at a time.

Behind him he heard the Abascar slaves whispering. The bear-beasts grunted with quiet, urgent complaints. The rafts bumped against one another.

If I can hear all this, then others will too.

He smelled rat-beasts. He heard their scuttling.

And then, boots. The altered guard. Strongbreed. They were coming.

By the time he reached the crossing, the passage behind him was silent. The passengers had managed to quiet themselves.

I do not know this corridor.

He smelled blood. Something deep inside him opened up, begging for

Essence that would give him strength. He growled, fighting against that itch. He had not given in for so long, and he did not dare give in now. Essence would make him faster, yes, and stronger. But it would also weaken his mind and heart.

Where did they go? He stopped and listened.

He felt a dark and open space to his left. Someone was there. He unsheathed his blade and turned.

A mighty hand struck his, the shield on the back of the glove jarring the knife from his grip. Another hand struck him in the jaw, lifting him from the ground and throwing him back against the wall. The impact stole the breath from his lungs, and before he could get his feet under him, one of the altered guard seized him by the throat, lifted him, and cast him into the adjoining corridor, where three more guards were waiting.

Jordam fought them, brandishing his remaining claws like knives. He smelled their blood—a mingling scent of human and animal—heard their excitement, smelled Essence on their breath. Two guards held his feet, two more held his hands, and one, his armor painted red, drew a long gleaming pin from a sheath and drove it into his back, paralyzing him so fast that he froze in a contorted twist.

The guards turned and carried him down the dark corridor, laughing. "What are you?" one of them asked him. "Running around with slaves? Trying to steal a few for yourself?"

They don't know about the boats, he thought.

"rrNo," he barked. "Abascar slave tried to switch camps. rrRan from the diggers to the scavengers. The Treasure is chasing him. No trouble."

"Don't explain to us," they said. "Explain to the chieftain."

They broke into a run, carrying Jordam between them.

When they stepped through the gates into the throne room, they flung him forward as if casting wood on a fire. He skidded on his chest through puddles and piles of carnage and came to a stop facedown at the foot of the dais.

It was quiet, but he knew there were Cent Regus all around, watching, uncertain, wondering how this new chieftain would behave. He heard the labored breathing of the creature at the top of the dais stair.

"rrMy massster," Jordam wheezed, wishing he could get his disguise back. "I welcome...and honor you."

At that, he heard the sound of snakes uncoiling—great, slithering sounds of the throne's arms. He felt one of those tentacles coil about his ankles, and suddenly he was lifted through the air, his head a pendulum. He was carried up the stairs, his forehead slamming against the edge of each step until his head was full of light, and he sneezed blood. The arm turned him around and raised him up, and he saw the chieftain lean forward in eager anticipation.

Through flashes of pain, he saw the face of this chieftain and was thoroughly bewildered. For he was not like any Cent Regus he had seen before.

"You," said the chieftain, "smell wrong."

This beastman had been cut open and sewn shut. This was something new, and Jordam knew at once that the white giants had been hard at work, giving the Cent Regus curse a new shape.

"Only one Cent Regus was ever such a fool as to refuse Essence," said the chieftain.

Something smelled familiar.

"Mordafey told you once," said the chieftain's voice in soft delight. "He told you that if you ever betrayed him, he would meet you again in some dark place. And you would not recognize him."

Everything within Jordam strained to writhe in shock and sudden, overwhelming fear.

Mordafey.

The creature went on, emboldened. In his rising enthusiasm, his voice had become many—a predator bird, a slavering wolf, a serpent—the tones of a cluster of creatures twisted together within his body. "Four brothers," said Mordafey. "You all could have been here. Beside Mordafey. Do you even think about the brothers, Jordam?"

"rrBetter things. To think about," Jordam spluttered. "You'll never know what I know."

Mordafey drew Jordam in closer, hanging him like a piece of meat on a rack, and as he spoke, he spat in Jordam's face. "Jorn, sssshot by an old Bel Amican man. Goreth, ripped into pieces. And Mordafey—you spit poison into Mordafey's face. Mordafey could hardly run fast enough to escape the arrows. And then...then the white giant punished Mordafey."

"rrLooks like the white giant gave you everything you wanted," Jordam answered. "You don't need brothers anymore. You never wanted them anyway."

Mordafey laughed long, loud, triumphant. "Mordafey holds the whole Expanse in his new arms. You can't escape him. Not even on a prongbull. Nor can you refuse his gifts. So take this, Jordam, as your second chance. Mordafey wants to see you kill again."

Jordam was driven hard and fast down through a steaming vent that had opened in the floor. Headfirst he was carried down, down, down.

He saw the cauldron of boiling Essence for only a moment, dark as a bottomless pit, before he was submerged in it.

32

SUBTERFUGE

Much to Wynn's dismay, Gelina wore even more perfume when she returned to the harbor dock the following night. Even among stacks of damp cargo crates and the scent of hot torch oil, he could smell her before he saw her, and so the scratching began.

Slinking down the marketplace stair, she pranced past the ogling harbor workers, a cork in her crooked white teeth and a beveled green glass bottle in her hand.

Balax the guard stood up from his guard post like a dog smelling dinner. Whether he rose for the cider or the seductress, Wynn did not know or care. "Like a bull-gully fish to a big fat worm," he muttered.

Gelina's beads clicked and snapped together, strategically strung over her gown, every visible region of her buxom body dancing as she frolicked up to Balax. Balax's eyes were on the bottle. She set the cider on the step in front of the forbidden corridor. "Don't touch," she laughed. "You're on duty."

Balax glanced about.

Alert as cats in a fishyard, Balax's brothers, Biggas and Broot, were on their feet, all but drooling for a taste of the cider.

Balax snatched the bottle, lumbered out to the edge of the dock, and made as if to cast it into the harbor.

Wynn held his breath. Gelina cried out, "Stop!"

Then Balax laughed. "Had you worried, didn't I?" He took one quick swig. "Just to clear my throat, mind you." Returning to his post, he handed the bottle to his brothers. "No more than a drop," he admonished them.

"And afterward, we'll have orange-chew. Can't have Captain Ryllion sniffing your beards for drink."

He sat down on the step of the tunnel's entrance. Gelina sat beside him, drew the guard's head down to her bosom, and rested her chin on his ear.

Wynn waited, scratching his elbows, hoping the perfume and cider would work their magic.

Slowly Balax raised one of his hands and spread his fingers as if he had never seen them before in his life. He voiced an unintelligible question, confused. Gelina began to laugh that rolling, resonant music. Balax giggled. They rose together, and Gelina drew him back into the tunnel. Just before the darkness erased them both, she cast an urgent glance at Wynn.

Biggas and Broot replaced Balax on the step and set the bottle between them, eying it as if it might attack them.

Drink the cider. Sleep.

Biggas picked up the bottle, sniffed it, then took a deep gulp.

Broot leapt to his feet and cursed. "Has your head come off? Ryllion will open you up and pour that swallow out on the rocks! We're gonna get the lash!" He marched past the pallet of barrels, muttering, "If I'm gonna be the last one standing, I'd better clear my head." He knelt to scoop cold water onto his face. "Gotta wake up."

Biggas was already failing, his hands hanging down to his ankles, his head swaying low. He fell forward so that his forehead hit the boards, held that awkward pose, and then collapsed onto his side, asleep.

Wynn climbed onto one of the barrels and peered into an empty space among them. "Now."

Tabor Jan stood up, then ducked back down. "One of them's still awake!"

"Broot's not gonna drink it," Wynn whispered back. "Go now, while he's talking to himself!"

"Too risky." Tabor Jan remained in the shadows.

Shouts broke the quiet. Wynn looked across the harbor. One of the boats listed, and a violent clamor came from its hull. Red torches converged on the dock beside the boat, and men were calling for arrows and axes.

"The scourge," Wynn whispered.

"What's that?"

"Something's been sinking boats. Haven't you heard? Something in the water."

Broot, his face dripping, had noticed the disturbance. Turning back to his brother, he shouted, "Biggas! It's striking again!"

Wynn held still, his hand frozen in a firm command to Tabor Jan to stay down.

"Biggas?" Broot came to his feet, gaping at the sight of his sprawled, sleeping brother. "Biggas, are you awake?"

Wynn had a clear view of the baffled guard as something like the tail of a giant eel rose up from the water behind him, coiled around his legs, and pulled him sharply from the dock. Broot disappeared into the waves without even time to cry out.

"Sacred backside of Tammos Raak!" Wynn gasped. "What was that?"

In the confusion Tabor Jan sprang from hiding and made his move, carrying the birdcage before him in both hands.

❧

A column of smoke billowed black against the dusk. A cargo ship was in flames.

Something had breached the hull, flooding the cargo hold. Now the whole craft would go down.

It wasn't the first time. Ryllion had heard the horrific accounts, but he had always been out on patrol. He knew what skulked below the surface. He had seen the feelers in the wild. In Cent Regus territory he had seen them burst up, coil about a lurkdasher, and drag it squealing down into the ground. His own patrols had reported tentacles descending from the canopy of branches in the Cragavar forest. Abascar survivors had spoken of something rising up through the stone of Barnashum. All these frightful descriptions fit what the shipyard workers had glimpsed—bristling, serpentine limbs attacking the hulls of ships as if hungry for the living things inside.

The Seers had, for once, lacked answers.

As he stormed through the closing marketplace, Ryllion heard the vendors' heartbeats quicken, heard their excited whispers. "There goes Ryllion. He's off to fight that monster in the harbor. He's going to pull it up like a weed."

But he was not on his way to save the ship. With all of Bel Amica distracted by this horror, he'd seize the opportunity to get some work done in secret.

"Spirit," he murmured, "you've given me this desire for the throne. You've given me these gifts—these claws, these senses, this strength. You've prepared me. Give me success today, and I will turn the attention of everyone to the moon-spirits."

He dashed down a staircase onto the dock. Across the waters of the inlet, flame bloomed along the collapsing hull of that historic vessel, *Helpryn's Vision.* The firelight illuminated the queen's own ship alongside—the *Escape.*

But as he reached the tunnel to the Punchbowl, he stopped, snarling. Biggas was crumpled in a heap. Balax and Broot were nowhere to be seen.

His clawed hands opened.

"Captain?" squeaked a voice.

It was that meddlesome Abascar boy. The fool was standing by the door of the tunnel, holding Balax's club.

"Get away from that door, rodent!" Ryllion barked.

"I'm guarding it," he yelped. "Can't you see? These useless guards got all drunk. But I'm dependable." He brandished the club with pride.

Amusing, Ryllion thought. *Might make a good soldier someday.* "Where are the others?"

"Balax? I don't know. But Broot… I saw something pull him into the water."

"Did anyone go inside?"

The boy hesitated a moment. His pause was worrying. Ryllion pushed him aside and lunged into the tunnel.

There it was again, that low rumble in his chest. The noise had become an involuntary response to his anger. He had grown strong under the Seer's care, but his improvement carried a heavy price. Certain manifestations of his body were now beyond his control—his pungent scent, the rapid growth of bristling hair on his limbs, the dark lines of veins that pulsed across his face and chest. The Seers had tried to help him with makeup, just as they had treated his burns after a venomous beastman spat in his face. He was weary of seeing people flinch as he passed by.

But here he did not mind the growl. He wanted to frighten anyone who might have gone inside.

His keen nose caught a whiff of perfume. "Gelina," he scoffed. "That smelly seductress again? Balax, your head's no better than what most people sit on."

At a fork in the path, he listened for a moment. All was quiet.

The urge to surprise and torment Balax was difficult to resist. Both he and Gelina were fools. But fools could be useful pawns. He would spare them this time, so long as Gelina had not gone as far as the Punchbowl.

A stairway to his left lead to an observation corridor lined with windows from which the king had watched the construction of his ships down in the Punchbowl. Ryllion heard nothing, smelled nothing there.

To his right, another stair led down to the floor of the Punchbowl itself.

He took neither path. He marched straight ahead, onto the stone arm that reached out over the Punchbowl. The Seer would be there, watching over their secret.

He could hear Pretor Xa's voice, like a searing alarm, echoing in the vast cavern. He smelled the Punchbowl's salty brine, heard something like the panting of a pack of wild pigs.

Ryllion walked onto that long ray of stone. It broadened to form a platform where Pretor Xa stood between a large wooden barrel and a massive, chalk-white crystal that burned with ghostly light. He was leaning against a tall wooden lever that protruded from the stone like a flagpole while his left hand twirled a staff like a baton. His lidless eyes were large and his skullish grin triumphant.

"They're ready," seethed the Seer.

Reaching the end of the promontory, Ryllion gazed down to the shallow pool of seawater. The snarl in his chest slowed, became a flutter of pleasure as he found that all was as it should be.

A boat lay on its side, as if waiting to be released through the stone gate into the inlet. The water was almost still, but on one side of the cave it was troubled by the activity in a large cage.

Beastmen—thirty, perhaps forty of them. Wolf-men skulking and spitting. Reptiles hissing and slamming their tails in the shallow water. Monsters like bears shaking the bars and howling at their captors.

"They're loud," Ryllion worried. He tapped his claws on the lid of the wooden cistern at the platform's edge. "Too loud."

"We're deep down. Out of sight," said the Seer. "And look at them. Eager. Hungry." He then struck the sheer stone of the promontory with his staff. The silver ferrule at the end released a blast of light and a low sound that shook the cavern walls.

The beastmen quieted, attentive. The ripples around the cage slowed and stilled.

"Many of you were at Barnashum," Ryllion called down to the creatures. "Many of you heard my instructions to destroy the remnant of House Abascar. You failed me there. You made not a scratch on that host of weak, half-starved survivors. You could not even get through the door."

Pretor Xa translated his words into the crude Cent Regus tongue. But Ryllion knew that some of the beastmen understood already, for even before the translation began, he discerned a spiteful murmur among them.

"Tomorrow morning," said Ryllion, "you will have a second chance. We have kept you sedated." He patted the side of the cistern. This barrel had released a steady drip of slumberseed oil into the pool, the haze of its aroma rendering the beastmen dormant for days. "Tomorrow morning you will awake, sharpen your claws, and claim great treasure."

He gestured to the heavy door strung from chains and ropes. "Beyond that gate is the Rushtide Inlet. And with this"—he put his hand atop the wooden lever—"I can open that gate and let the water pour in. But I will not. No, tomorrow morning the Seer will release you. You will climb into the boat. And then he will open the gate, let the tide rush in, and raise the boat for sailing. You will stay hidden inside the boat. And silent. The Seer will steer the boat out through the harbor. He will bring it alongside a great ship. On that ship the queen and her children will be waiting."

This provoked a change among the beastmen. Their thirst for blood was greater than their impatience.

Ryllion held up his hand. "The Seer will release you. Kill everyone on that ship as fast as you can. And I shall reward you for your work. You will have prizes unlike any in the Cent Regus world."

Hysteria broke out in the cage. The beastmen were ravenous now, ready to do this simple task, ready for the reward.

Except one.

"What?" The Seer translated the voice that hushed the other predators. "We kill your queen. You kill us after."

Ryllion growled. "No." He hammered his fist against the cistern. "If you do right, I will use you again. After we have taken House Bel Amica, we will go back and take House Cent Regus. I will bring down the chieftain, and we will reign over the Expanse together."

The Seer knelt and reached around the barrel to the spout. A few drops of the slumberseed oil splashed into the shallow water.

Ryllion covered his face to avoid catching any whiff of the oil and turned to leave. The beastmen groaned as the aroma spread below.

As Ryllion and the Seer retreated through the corridor, Ryllion's misgivings began to scratch at him. "How can it fail?" he muttered. "As soon as the beastmen leap into view…as soon as the first scream sounds…the queen, Cyndere, and Partayn will hurry below deck."

"If they make it that far, you'll be waiting there to finish them in secret," said the Seer. "And then you'll appear on the deck of the ship in full view of the people. Everyone will see you cut down those beastmen. We've prepared you for this. Your soldiers won't even have time to put arrows to their bows. The people will mourn their loss, but they'll know that you saved the rest of them from a Cent Regus invasion."

"They'll find the boat—"

"I'll sink our boat. Put aside your worries, boy. The beastmen aren't the weakness in our plan."

"The weakness?" Ryllion sought to suppress that rising growl. "You see a problem?"

The Seer was silent, waiting, as he walked alongside.

"You think I won't kill the queen."

"We know you can kill Thesera. And we know you'll enjoy cutting up Partayn. But Cyndere..." The Seer dragged his staff along the floor and said no more.

"After tomorrow," he said, "you won't doubt me anymore. Cyndere humiliated me at Tilianpurth. She ran away with a beastman. Who knows what corruption she carries now. She's a blight on House Bel Amica."

"When you take Bel Amica's throne, you'll be the ruler of three houses. My kindred and I will give you a gift beyond measure. A steed upon which you will conquer the last great house."

"A steed."

"House Jenta has always sought a way to master the air. Wait until they see their conqueror coming for them astride a winged beast."

"A winged horse?"

"Better. Malefyk Xa is tending to a little collection. Wait until you see them. You'll rule the Expanse, both land and sea, from the air. You'll fly." The Seer rapped him on his maned head, then turned and stalked back toward the Punchbowl.

Ryllion walked in a daze, his future coming into view...until he saw two figures crowding the passage ahead.

"Get out!" he barked. One turned back, startled.

It was Gelina. Her wide, frightened eyes quickly narrowed. "Dreams come true," she gushed. "It's Captain Ryllion. Surely he'll be my companion for the rest of this evening."

"If I ever touch you," Ryllion scoffed, "it'll be with a bludgeon."

Clad in similarly frail scraps of veil and strings of gaudy beads, another broad-shouldered figure cowered against the wall. This one moved in a cloud of the same dizzymaking perfume but leaned shyly toward the wall as if eager to let Ryllion pass.

Ryllion seized both of the costumed seductresses and pushed them toward the smoky air at the end of the tunnel. "This corridor is forbidden for anyone but my troops. You hear? Get out. If I find you near these caves again, I'll send you to Mawrnash. You know how they treat your kind there, don't you?"

He looked down at the other woman's alarmingly thick and hairy arms, her large hands. Then he saw that those hands were holding the ring atop a birdcage. With one curling nail, he lifted the soft blue cloth that covered the cage. Inside, seven tetherwings chirped at him madly. "What," he murmured, "is this?"

"A gift," laughed Gelina. "A gift from one of our customers."

Ryllion stared at the birds. Something about this bothered him.

Fierce light and explosive noise from the harbor pulled his attention away. He watched as *Helpryn's Vision* was reduced to floating, fiery scraps. But the proud *Escape* was safe, waiting for the queen's morning voyage.

He turned to the Abascar boy, who still stood dutifully beside the tunnel's open mouth. "You keep watch," he said to the boy. "I'm sending down more guards. And if I hear that you let anyone past, I'm going to feed you to the thing that took poor Broot. You understand?"

Leaving the dock, the water, and the flames behind, Tabor Jan urged Gelina to hurry ahead of him. He could not get back to her chambers fast enough to shed these veils, these beads, and this long, braided wig. He wanted to throw himself into the inlet and scrub himself with sand until every last hint of the rose-honey was gone from his skin.

Gelina guided him through an alley and then up a rickety wooden stair in the back of the gamblerhouse where she lived.

His throat burned from wearing Gelina's perfume. But entering her rooms was like swallowing a torch. He could barely see through the incense haze to find his way among pillows, trays of perfume and lotion bottles, the dangling racks of silken costumes. Gamblers were shouting in the room below the feeble floorboards.

"Did you find what you were looking for?" she asked, stepping behind a screen and tossing away strings of beads and layers of veil.

He stepped behind another screen and nearly wept for joy at the sight of his watchman's uniform. He heard fabric tear as he frantically broke free of his disguise.

Before he could answer—and what would he have answered, considering all that he had seen and heard?—Gelina was regaling him with stories of her life. She spoke about the child she had brought into the world right here, in this closet she called a home. She had almost died, with the infant struggling beside her on the hard floor. But a stranger had heard her cries and come up the stairs.

"It may be the only time a man came into this room out of pity rather than lust," she sighed. "And such a strange man too. Smelled of earth and leaves and grass. He knew how to hold a newborn. Next thing I knew, it was morning. I was in bed. I felt no pain. My child was sleeping beside me. The stranger was gone."

As he fastened his trousers and buttoned his jacket, Tabor Jan asked, "What became of your child?"

"Oh, I didn't have any way to raise her. What a miserable life she would have had. I gave her to the Seers. They promised they'd find a home for her. Somewhere she'd be useful. They promised she'd become part of a grand endeavor and someday I would be surprised." She looked at him searchingly. "Do you think I did wrong?"

33

WHAT CAME
BY INVITATION

B oots coated in the river's sludge, Cal-raven stumbled in the damp of
the low-ceilinged tunnel, landed hard on his hands and knees, and
then was up and running again. As he rounded the corner, just a few anxious
breaths behind his mother, his eagerness nearly carried him over a precipice.
His heels slipped, shot out from under him, and he sat on the edge of an abyss.

Glowstones in the steeply slanted walls pulsed faintly, green and yellow—
just enough light to reveal the narrow stone bridge over the drop. He saw the
queen pause between two flaring torches, halfway across, and look back. At
first he thought she might wait for him. But she lifted a torch from its stand
and ran on in search of the ale boy.

You're afraid of me, but you won't leave me in the dark.

Her strength bewildered him, for he was already out of breath. Had she
spent years like this, running from one distress after another?

He started across the bridge, but a sound stopped him. He dared a look
over the edge.

The menacing darkness swirled, a deep pool. Something down there was
groaning, a sound that spoke of hopelessness. There seemed to be movement
along the walls. Then he saw them—thick, living cords intertwining like
roots, rising up from that bottomless shaft and then disappearing into the
walls. From there he knew they were reaching out through the Expanse, a
patternless web, twitching with something like life.

He knew this sensation. He had felt it deep beneath House Abascar in
the Underkeep. The terror that the miners abhorred.

"Go back!" came a shrill cry. His mother had reached the other side of the bridge. "They need you."

He got to his feet and moved forward. "It's you they need," he called after her. "You're their queen."

"Not anymore." Her voice was a sad echo. "Abascar's yours now."

"Mine?" He paused. "Do you know me, Mother?"

She looked away. Sparks from her torch sprang free and drifted down into the shaft like shooting stars. "He's getting away," she whispered. "I cannot leave him."

"Don't leave us again," he pleaded. He immediately regretted it, for she hunched over as if a burden had suddenly become too heavy.

"I can hold back the beastmen," she said. "It will give you time. But if you follow me—"

"I won't leave without you."

His call fell like a fading spark. She was gone into the wall.

Jaralaine arrived at a crossroads and found a Strongbreed host there, standing still like a forest of ragged trees. As two of them grasped her arms with their clawed hands, the other half-human creatures stared coldly through slats in their pointed helms, then looked down at their other prisoner with quiet contempt.

Shivering in his tattered rags and embracing Jordam's water flask against his chest, the ale boy looked at her and said, "Don't be afraid. The Keeper is coming."

"My boy," she said to him. "Still so full of dreams." Just as she had on the first night she had found him, telling Auralia's story to the prisoners, Jaralaine felt a thrill at the boy's fearlessness. But she also marveled at his calm, for he did not thrust his courage in the faces of his captors. He spoke quietly as if offering them insight. "The Keeper brought me here," he continued. "And I don't believe I've finished my work." His countenance was humble, his hairless head like a single red scar.

"Do you have the colors?" he asked, a note of hope in his voice. "We need them now."

She was surprised, for she had forgotten the contents of that bundle she clutched so tightly. She did not draw them out, for her arms were held fast by the guards.

One of the Strongbreed approached her. He did not say a thing, just stared at her in expectation. She gestured to the boy. "Bel Amican slave," she announced with authority. "He got lost during the uprising. I'm taking him back to the slaves so he can serve the new chieftain. As I do."

The blank, blue stare from that helmet slit gave her no indication that the Strongbreed understood. After years of learning to understand and predict the beastmen, their enslavement to the Essence, their shows of power, she worried about these new invaders. They gave her no clues to their thinking. Where the beastmen could be swayed by appetite, the Strongbreed seemed immovable unless ordered by the new chieftain or the Seer. Even when the Seer was gone, they looked up as if listening to the crystal stones implanted between their eyes.

"Let me take him to serve with the Bel Amican prisoners," she insisted. No one moved.

Three more Strongbreed stomped into the crossroads. They gripped the arms of her pursuer—the young man with the scars on his face, his red braids muddied with sludge from the river. He reminded her of Cal-marcus.

One creature pointed a scale-gloved hand back to the tunnel from which they had come. "No," she said, perhaps a little too quickly. "Not that way. These two belong with the Bel Amican slaves."

Ignoring her, twelve of the Strongbreed departed in single file, dutiful as drones, pushing the ale boy and the Abascar man before them. They left ten more with her.

The boy looked back before he disappeared. "Thank you," he called to her.

"My boy!" Her knees buckled. "Let him go!"

That man from Abascar—he, too, looked back. His hands were out, his fingers spread, and he fought as if striving to seize hold of the edge of the tunnel. Baring his teeth, he shouted, "Mother!"

She turned away. "You're killing me," she said. She wanted to fall to the floor, but the guards dragged her, kicking, to her feet and pulled her backward into the larger corridor. And as they did, her breath caught in her throat.

What were those figures who followed, who filled the corridor and pursued without making a sound?

"Northchildren," she whispered.

The Strongbreed did not turn to look. They were not listening as they marched toward the new chieftain's chambers.

In the tumult of the marching Strongbreed, Cal-raven could hear the ale boy whispering just ahead of him. At first he thought the boy was trying to speak to him. He caught a murmured plea for help. And then he heard him say, "Keeper."

Even as Cal-raven strained against his captors' grip, grasping for the wall, the edges of the doors, the floor, anything made of stone, he wondered why he was not crying out for the creature who had lifted him from the brambles at the base of Barnashum's cliffs. That all seemed so far away now, so long ago.

"Keeper," he said. "Keeper, come. If you don't hear the boy, then hear me." Already he was surrendering the fight to grab the stone. "You sent Auralia's colors to Abascar, to remind us of all we'd forgotten. To summon us home to Inius Throan. Come for us now. Save us and we'll follow you."

The Strongbreed emerged in single file onto a path that was little more than a ledge above the abyss. The altered guard were taking them back down to the bridge, back to the river.

A flare burned in the vast open space—the one remaining torch on the bridge. The bridge came into view. But the space was brighter now. He looked up and saw a faint shower of golden daylight from an opening far, far above.

Shoved by the guard behind him, the ale boy stumbled onto the bridge. Cal-raven could see him tensing, trying to slow the march. He, too, knew that this was it—the place where things would have to change. The boy walked toward the middle of the span. There were seven, then eight, then ten guards on the bridge.

Cal-raven hesitated, four steps from the span. He dug in his heels, pressing backward. The guards' claws pierced his shoulders, forced him forward.

Arriving at the middle of the bridge, beside the lonely, flickering torch, the boy turned suddenly, raising Jordam's flask of water. "Before we go any farther, I think you should drink from this. It will help you see more clearly."

The Strongbreed paused as if trying to translate the boy's speech.

"It may save your life," he added.

The falling, golden light wavered, dimmed.

The ale boy, inspiring no response from the Strongbreed, took a drink from the flask and then closed it tight. "I'm sorry," he said. "It's the only help I had to offer you. But now it's too late."

Cal-raven looked up toward that distant window.

Something was there. A shadow like the pupil of a bright eye.

In the next few moments, much happened very quickly.

The ale boy leapt to grab the heavy torch. He brandished it like a sword before a ceremonial duel, then held it high and poured the hissing oil over his head and shoulders. Fire engulfed him. He cast the torch away, raised his blazing arms, and ran back at the line of guards.

The guards stumbled, roaring with voices that shook the bridge. They cast their spears aside and unsheathed long, curved swords.

"Keeper!" the boy shouted. "Keeper!"

"Keeper," Cal-raven whispered.

The shadow descended, fire lacing its fanged jaws, layers of wings unfolding to soften its descent. A long, reptilian tail whipped the air beneath it, and its talons were poised like those of a predator bird in a dive. The torchlight seemed brighter in the reflection of those scales on its belly, and its eyes were spheres full of whirling colors.

In that moment of distraction, Cal-raven pulled his arms free of his captors' grasp, dropped to his knees, and planted his palms against the span of the bridge. Immediately before him, three guards sank into softening stone, submerged up to their knees. Cal-raven lifted his hands and let the stone go solid again, leaving the guards trapped and helpless. As he stood, he dug a handful of stone free of the bridge, turned, and struck the helm of the guard behind him. The guard hurtled into the open space, flailing through the dark.

Cal-raven heard the wingbeats, felt a powerful thrust of wind. The creature hung suspended over the bridge. It lunged, jaws open, toward the guards imprisoned in the stone. Flames rushed like a river from its tongue.

Cal-raven dove off the bridge. He twisted as he fell, reaching out to sink his fingers into the wall of the abyss, digging himself a grip to break his fall. His feet swung over darkness, and he kicked himself a foothold. A wave of heat flushed through the wall. Strongbreed were screaming in voices that cracked stone. The smell of burnt hair and flesh flared in Cal-raven's nostrils. One fell past him, fire spewing from the eye slit of its helmet.

Then the creature turned and smashed the bridge with its tail, snapping its span like a twig. Cal-raven choked, astonished. The two halves, the guards—all of it fell in a blazing rain of ruin.

And the ale boy was gone.

Everything became still, the sound and trouble swallowed by the pit.

The creature clung to the wall, upside down, like a massive bat.

Cal-raven held to the wall, paralyzed.

This? This was what had haunted his dreams? This was the power that had answered the ale boy's call?

From somewhere far below, that unearthly groan rose again. Anguish. Despair.

The creature raised its head and took up a similar cry in answer, a word of such fathomless sadness that Cal-raven fought the urge to crawl into the wall and seal himself inside.

But then, as quickly as it had struck, the creature set its eyes fixedly upon the corridor through which the guards had pushed the prisoners, a passage far too narrow for anything of such girth. And it leapt into that tunnel, slipping through as easily as a snake into its hole. A flick of its golden tail, and it was gone.

Cal-raven clung to the rock and stared down into the dark.

Gulping in deep breaths, he tightened his hold, driving energy out to his fingertips. The stone responded. Sculpting ridges, he pulled himself up, rung by rung, back to the ledge. He collapsed there and stared across the chasm. A jag of stone was all that remained of the bridge. It was the only path he knew that could take him back to the boats.

Jordam opened his burning eyes.

He was upside down again, suspended by a foot, his arms dangling. He could hear the Essence spilling from his head, shoulders, and hands, splashing into a widening pool on the floor of the chieftain's throne room. Rat-beasts licked their lips, ready to clean up the mess. He was cloaked, toe to head in a cast of the very stew he had refused himself for so long. Essence stung his nostrils, scorched his throat, smoldered in his lungs. The measure he had swallowed burned through his veins.

"Jordam, Mordafey's last brother." Mordafey somehow flexed the muscle within that powerful branch that bound Jordam's foot, drawing him close again. "Jordam tried to poison Mordafey," he continued, narrating for the Strongbreed that guarded him. "Jordam spit a smelly poison into Mordafey's face. Mordafey could not run. Mordafey fell again and again. Bel Amican hunter got close with his arrows. Too close."

Mordafey lay back against the rise of wavering arms that fanned up from the living throne, and he slapped at his bloated belly with his hands. "But Mordafey lives. Eats what he pleases. Maybe today, he eats his brother."

Jordam held his breath as Mordafey's jaws opened. He closed his eyes, felt Mordafey lick Essence from his side. His thoughts were like pieces of hot, broken glass, and he struggled to fit them together.

What was I doing? Why was I here?

He knew this feeling—the heightening waves of strength, the desire to destroy. Soon thought would be extinguished. He would surrender to the call of action and the ecstasy of power. At this moment he was the most dangerous beastman in the Expanse.

Mordafey laughed. "Good," he said. "Jordam is a proper Cent Regus fighter again. Jordam is ready to rediscover what it is like to be powerful. Shall I pull the pin from your back, brother? Free your arms to move?"

Pin?

"Let's test the last brother. Send you on a hunt. Go and fetch Skell Wra's Treasure for the new chieftain. Bring her back here on a spear. Wait, no... She might be tough meat to chew. Maybe something softer. Yes. Like that boy." Mordafey leaned forward, excited. "Jordam, fetch your chieftain that meddling boy. You let him get away from me. Twice. Show us you have learned your lesson, and Mordafey will make you a Cent Regus captain." He shook Jordam like a toy for a hound. "Yesss. That would be a tasty finish."

Boy? Ale boy. O-raya's boy.

Jordam stared into his brother's eyes. They were the only piece of this frightful puzzle he recognized. "A tasty finish?" he asked. He noted the large curved blade that lay across Mordafey's lap. "Jordam will give Mordafey a tasty finish."

The pin that had pierced his back and paralyzed him—Mordafey thought it was still there. But as the tentacles had retrieved Jordam from the cauldron of Essence, the lip of the bowl had caught the edge of the pin, pulling it free.

So as Mordafey laughed, Jordam let that burgeoning strength fill his arms. Then, with swift and precise claws, he reached out to the thick threads that crisscrossed Mordafey's chest, slashed the stitches loose so that the newly sewn seam burst open. Mordafey sucked in a gasp of surprise, and Jordam plunged his hands inside. Before Mordafey could close his jaws, his mouth was dripping with all that Jordam had drawn from his open chest.

The tentacle holding Jordam by the feet recoiled and thrashed. But Jordam had caught Mordafey's blade, and he swung it around to cleave the end of that powerful limb. He flew across the throne room in a fountain of the limb's hot blood. After landing on his back, he rolled and leapt up, snarling and quaking with strength.

Mordafey's eyes bulged. His hands clawed uselessly at the throne, and then he lurched forward, straining those thick black cords connected to his back. His jaw clacked open and shut. "Essence," Mordafey choked. "Sssstrength." Then the throne swallowed what was left of Mordafey, whipping at the air with its arms and beating upon the stone dais until it cracked.

Jordam turned to face the two altered guards who came after him. Their

Strongbreed screams would paralyze a weaker creature. But Jordam left them staring at the ceiling with no arms to raise.

Fleeing the throne room, he howled in the rush of bloodthirst and strength. He was free. Free from the threat of Mordafey forever.

Stop, cried a voice inside him. *Stop, Jordam. You are forgetting things.*

He charged on.

Ahead in the corridor, a mass of Strongbreed advanced, spears at the ready. He welcomed them, a whirlwind with a silver sword. He sent the blade through the eye slit of a helmet, caught the broach of the falling guard's cape, drew it around himself, and dove at the others.

Stop. That voice was pleading with him now. *You said never again.*

This was done to me, he answered back. *Maybe I can use the strength to set us all free.*

Standing proud as a conqueror, he surveyed the bloody scene. No Strongbreed remained able to pursue him. Only one lived, and he crawled along the ground as if he were swimming. Jordam stalked him, raised Mordafey's blade, and finished him.

His laughter stopped when he saw an arm emerge from beneath a fallen guard. Jordam raised his blade again, then stopped. This hand was small and hairless, slender and fair.

He dropped his knife. He reached down and drew two of the bodies aside.

Jaralaine lay contorted beneath them, one of the Strongbreed's spears jutting up from where it had pierced her in the fall. Her eyes were wide in surprise, and her hand pinched at the air. Jordam took her hand and crashed down to his knees, shaking.

"Help me, Jordam," she whispered. "I'm freezing."

"rrWater," Jordam whimpered. "Good water. Where?"

I gave my flask to the ale boy.

"Bring me my son."

He put his arms beneath her, lifted her, and walked swiftly up the corridor to the crossroads. He paused there, releasing a howl of anguish and confusion.

Strongbreed came in answer—bold figures of black and red—from one corridor, then another, then another.

Jordam held the queen close to him, baring his teeth. He had left the blade in the corridor.

But then, from another passage, came an altogether different noise.

Jordam had time to see the creature's head burst through the corridor and into the crossroads. He had time to see the dark glass spheres of its eyes wild with lights, to feel its hot breath. His memory sent him a fierce, irresistible warning.

Run.

Strongbreed soldiers turned and fired their arrows into the creature's open maw.

Those jaws smashed shut, arrows sticking out between its teeth like toothpicks. It cocked its head, eying the Strongbreed thoughtfully, and Jordam sensed a deep, bewildered sadness in that expression. Then the jaws came open, and the creature inhaled. Somewhere in that narrow passage, as its body expanded with breath to fill the space, dark cracks slashed through the earth.

Jordam turned and ran up the only open corridor, toward daylight.

The creature laughed out a flood of flames that rushed up the corridor, crashing over Jordam like a wave and sending him scorched and seared onto the open ground of the Cent Regus wasteland. Kneeling, he held the broken queen before him, his roar drowned out by the sound of the creature's conflagration.

Jordam would never forget the ruin of Cal-raven's soot-smeared face or the desolation in his cries as the Abascar king emerged through the gate. Along the way the king had slung one of the Strongbreed bows over his shoulder and lifted one of their heavy blades. But he cast these things aside when he saw his mother in the open, as the silver sun sank into grey, dusty morning.

Jordam would hear those cries in his sleep for a long time to come. He would never forget how small and feeble both the woman and her son seemed as Cal-raven lifted her and carried her into the empty prongbull stable beside the main gate.

"rrShe needs the water," Jordam told the Abascar king. "O-raya's boy has it."

"The ale boy is dead!" Cal-raven had shouted.

That brought Jordam to his feet. He looked through the open door of the stable to that dark, smoking, open throat, the entrance to the Longhouse.

Cal-raven's talk had then devolved into curses until his mother's hand came up from the dry, dead weeds of the floor to touch his face.

"Can you see?" Cal-raven weakly asked. "Do you hear my voice?"

Jaralaine nodded, staring blankly past her son's shoulder into a shaft of yellow morning light that drifted down through the broken beams of the stable roof.

"The one who did this to her," Cal-raven growled to Jordam. "Tell me you killed him."

Jordam paused, cringing. "rrTore out chieftain's heart." The lie gave him no relief from the truth's punishing burn.

"What will we do?" Cal-raven leaned forward, pressing his forehead against his mother's breast.

"Your people," Jordam reminded him. "Go back and try to save them. Come, Abascar king."

"You go," Cal-raven shouted. "If the Keeper cares at all, it will do as I asked and save my people. But it let the ale boy fall, Jordam. And my mother..."

As shame for his lie pierced him, Jordam took backward steps through the door of the stable. But as he did, his ears twitched and turned to gather news from the sky to the south. "Brascles."

At any moment the birds would be here. Following, beastmen on the ground would converge from all directions, knowing that the source of the Essence was unguarded, that they could drink from the chieftain's reservoir. In the fight that would ensue, one would triumph. One would find himself seized by the throne's strong arms, embraced and empowered by a direct channel to the Essence. A new chieftain. The Core would fill with beastmen.

And Jordam was certain they would soon find the boats moving north across the wasteland, if they hadn't already.

"rrGet her out of here," he muttered. "Cent Regus come. Too many. Get back to the boats."

"We can't go back," Cal-raven barked bitterly. "The Keeper has broken the bridge."

Jordam grunted in surprise, then turned toward the gate, seething with distress.

Jaralaine reached up suddenly and clasped Cal-raven's face. "Cal-marcus?"

"No," Cal-raven wept. "I'm not Cal-marcus. But he loved you, Mother. He loved you so fiercely, like stars that shine in the summer night."

Jordam looked up into the morning sky. *Like stars.*

"He never gave up searching for you," he said. "Had he known you were here, he would have torn apart the Cent Regus Core in his fury. Don't leave me now. Please."

Jordam had never felt so powerless. He had caused this broken scene, and he could not repair it. He clenched his teeth and looked off into the distance. "I go to the boats," he announced. "Come after me. Find the river. Follow." He pointed north and then west. Then he came and took Cal-raven's shoulder in a powerful grip—so strong that Cal-raven cried out. "rrGet away fast. The Cent Regus come."

Jordam dragged the heavy wooden door of the prongbull stable closed behind him, sealing them inside in hope of hiding them from the approaching beastmen. Then he turned and walked down into the throat of the Longhouse, summoning all that he knew of the labyrinth in his mind, seeking a way down to the boats, wondering what he would find there, wondering if anything was left for him to save.

❧

"Cal-marcus," said Jaralaine again, staring over Cal-raven's shoulder into the light.

"Mother." Cal-raven stroked her face. "Don't you know me yet?"

"Not you," she said firmly. "Him."

The hair on the back of his neck rose, and he felt a chill. Terrified, he could not bring himself to turn, for in her eyes he saw a figure outlined in the cloud of light.

"Marcus"—she smiled, and tears filled her eyes—"Marcus, you've come. Look at you. Such strange dress. So who is this?" She put her hand again on Cal-raven's face, reading him eagerly with her fingertips.

"Raven," he whispered. "Raven."

"Your father tells me you'll remember," she whispered back.

"Remember?" He listened but heard no voice behind him. "Remember what?"

"The light's too bright," she said. "Your eyes aren't strong enough to see. You must look instead at the wonders it shines on. The wonders it shines on and through." She patted his face with affection. "You'll remember."

"Remember what?"

But she did not hear him. "I made so many mistakes," she gasped. "Chasing wonders. Trying to throw my arms around them. But they weren't meant to be caught. They were to lead. But now I cannot follow them any farther. The ground stops, my little Raven. And then there's only cloud. Who can climb a cloud?"

"Sleep, mother," he whispered. "I'll carry you down to the boats. We have to find someone who can help you." But he knew that he could not move her, and who on those boats could treat so wicked a wound?

"More?" she suddenly asked. And she turned to look over his shoulder again. "I see all of it and more, Raven! Shining through! Such colors."

Cal-raven turned to shout at the figure, to frighten it away. But his voice caught in his throat, for there was not one figure. There was a great and silent host of phantoms in translucent, shimmering veils. Their eyes sparkled, and lines of diamonds rained from their faces. The one standing closest to him gazed down at Jaralaine. Slowly its hand rose, enshrouded in that strange, diaphanous lace.

A slow change came over Jaralaine's eyes as she released a sigh of deep relief. Her hand fell from Cal-raven's cheek.

He heard breath as fierce as the roar of a furnace, and he knew even before he turned that the Keeper was there. He stood up, lifting his mother, walked to the door, and kicked it open.

The creature's long-fingered hands clawed at the ground, pulling its enormous body halfway out of the Longhouse and into the open. Flames and sparks still flickered about the creature's jaws. When it turned its attention toward them, those eyes holding a cosmos of color, it seemed unconcerned, as if they were only part of the scenery.

"Help us," Cal-raven said. "Please."

The creature's upper lip curled to reveal its teeth, as if anyone needed reminding.

Cal-raven waited. "You don't even understand what you've done, do you?" he asked.

The creature groaned, coughed a burst of flame, then looked away northward and sniffed the air.

"You've come too late," he said.

The creature's nostrils flared, and it looked toward Cal-raven, a disgruntled scowl on its muzzle, almost as if it was about to make some sharp retort.

Cal-raven laid his mother on the dry grass, keeping his body between her and the shimmering crowd. But as he knelt beside her, the creature suddenly reached forward and, with one of those massive, clawed hands, gathered up Jaralaine's body. That hand carried her back into the tunnel while the Keeper's gaze remained fixed on Cal-raven as if this were some sort of challenge.

A wind rose.

Cal-raven looked down at the stain of his mother's blood on the ground. "I've sought you my whole life," he said to the creature. "I've sought you, thinking you were immortal. Thinking you were kind. And this is my reward? To see you fail? To see you destroy those I came to save? What are you?"

The ground began to quake.

"If you're my hope," he whispered, his voice a dry scratch, "it's not enough. The dream of you was better." He began to back away from that gaze, those scrabbling claws. "In the dream you were stronger than the world."

He turned and walked away.

The ground shuddered more violently. He was certain the creature was crawling after him. He kept walking.

But nothing caught up to him. And when he heard the creature cry out in alarm, he turned.

The ground was breaking open. The creature was turning, shrieking, as something serpentine and black coiled around its body. Twisting onto its back, the creature thrashed, trying to break free of the tunnel. A violent tug pulled it back so that only its head and neck remained in view. Cal-raven breathed a sharp, familiar stench—the same putrescence he had encountered on the bridge over the chasm.

Feelers.

He found he could not move as the magnificent creature fought, coughing out smoke and sparks. Cracks spread across the dry ground. More fanged tentacles—tough as roots, wild as snakes—broke through, whipping the creature's head and raking bloody wounds. It reared up in one mighty lunge for freedom, trying to spread its wings into the air. Then it crashed down, and a gust of hot smoke burst through its nostrils.

The creature's eyes turned once to Cal-raven as if to ask for help. Then it trembled, and colors drained like tears from those dark, glassy spheres and soaked into the ground. As its color faded, so did the witnesses gathered outside the stable, and Cal-raven thought he heard a chorus of anguished cries.

He was certain the feelers would come after him now. But the branches released their victim silently as if their work was finished. Then they retracted as swiftly as they had appeared.

Cal-raven watched the last tendrils of smoke drift slowly from its nostrils.

He had stood there and done nothing. Now he was alone.

He turned to see a tide of beastmen sweeping across the open ground. Like night arriving early, they rushed through the ruins of the old House Cent Regus village toward the gate.

Cal-raven ran into the prongbull stable, pulled its wooden door closed, and pressed himself into a far corner, shivering, ankle deep in dung, dragging piles of weeds to bury himself. Outside, the passing beastman horde howled like a storm. He could hear them climbing over each other in an eager madness, desperate to push their way past the enormous carcass and rush into the throne room, where the Essence waited unguarded.

When the cacophony diminished, sinking down into the Core, Cal-raven emerged. Too terrified to set eyes on what remained of the magnificent creature, he ran like a wild animal fleeing a forest fire.

34

QUEEN THESERA'S
BIRTHDAY SURPRISE

O ceanhawk eggs." Lifting the copper cover from the plate, Queen
Thesera inhaled a cloud of spicy fragrance. "This is my favorite."

The blinking puffball on her shoulder wiggled its pink nose and sighed
with pleasure.

While the ruler of Bel Amica smiled down on the fried eggs, each having been neatly rolled like a napkin, Tabor Jan reminded himself that staring
would not improve his chances of winning her favor.

But how could he not stare at a woman who looked, for all the world,
like her daughter's daughter? The seams that stretched from her ears to her
jaw line made him wonder what her true face might have been.

As sisterlies placed more plates on the crescent table, Tabor Jan tried
to ignore the aromas of tempting but insubstantial fare that had become all
too familiar for him in the markets. Nectarblooms. Salty sand-digger cakes.
Slices of mushy, syrupy meyerfruit. Handfuls of crunchy pulmynuts, appealing but hard and hollow.

He stood at the foot of the dining dais like a man waiting to be
sentenced.

Cyndere and Partayn sat on the near side of the curved table, half-
turned in their cushioned chairs. They offered him apologetic smiles as they,
too, waited for Thesera to grant him permission to speak.

"If you're here out of concern for your king," said Thesera at last, "I'm
told he's in good hands."

The rail train rumbled below, its vibration upsetting the levels of hot
seaweed tea in the glass goblets.

"Henryk and his troop are waiting at the edge of the Core," said Partayn. "Our mission has a greater chance of success if Cal-raven and Jordam stay inconspicuous."

"I notice you stayed here," Tabor Jan said curtly.

"You're enough of a strategist to know I need to stay at the planning table." Partayn's glare was a clear reprimand. "But believe me, Captain, I understand your frustration. I wanted Cal-raven to stay. I needed him here. He wouldn't listen. He demanded we let him go."

"Is this breakfast conversation?" The queen sounded exasperated. Tabor Jan had to stifle a laugh when he saw the bright red grin that the fruit had painted across her face.

"It's my birthday," Thesera continued. "We can talk of the world's troubles anytime. Today, my mind is on escape." She glanced to the window. "Or rather, *the Escape*. I saw the most magnificent oceanhawk sweep past the tower this morning. Your father would have taken it as a sign. Perhaps we should perform Helpryn's eagle ceremony to bring blessings on our voyage."

"I thought the Seers discouraged the old signs and ceremonies." Cyndere smiled sideways at Emeriene.

"I have not forgotten the moon-spirits," came the queen's sour retort. "My moon-spirit will grant me my wish. I'll have a safe voyage, far from trouble, where I can rest and recover from my...improvements."

Seated on a couch beneath an arching, stained-glass window, Emeriene gazed into the sunlight that blazed through that morning rush of fog. But Tabor Jan could hear the tension in her voice. "It's not any concern for his king that brings Tabor Jan to this table. I do hope we will hear his appeal before you set sail for the islands."

Cyndere put down her glass, choking on her drink. Clearing her throat, she said, "Forgive us, Tabor Jan. There's urgency in your visit."

"There is duty in my visit," he replied. "I carry out my king's pledge to serve House Bel Amica during our short"—he paused, then repeated the word—"*short* stay here. Last night down at the docks..." He stumbled to a stop. "Queen Thesera, you are in danger."

"You speak of the ship that burned," the queen replied. "There is danger, yes. Ryllion has dealt with it."

"My discovery has nothing to do with the trouble in the harbor waters."

"Summon Ryllion," the queen interrupted, waving a hand at Partayn. "If there is a threat, he'll take care of it."

Tabor Jan glanced about at the large mirrors that surrounded the room. He felt exposed, as if the Seers might sweep in and upset his errand.

"Ryllion is busy, Mother," said Partayn. "He is on the *Escape*, examining every inch to ensure it will carry you safely."

"So, what kind of threat—"

"Beastmen, my lady," Tabor Jan blurted.

The queen paused, lips parted, a forkful of eggs halfway to her mouth. She closed her mouth, rested her wrist on the edge of the table. Then she laughed. "We have some frightening old fellows down by the docks. Only dead beastmen are allowed in House Bel Amica. And believe me, I sought to prevent it."

"It would be so much better if I could take you to see for yourself what troubles me."

"You're offering to show me something upsetting on the morning of my birthday voyage? How charming!"

"How," chirped the whiskiro.

"Queen Thesera," said Emeriene, "Tabor Jan has been to Helpryn's Punchbowl."

The forkful of eggs had almost reached the queen's mouth again. It hovered there, and then she lowered it back to the plate. "The Punchbowl's been sealed for years."

"How would he describe it to me if he hadn't been there?"

"I saw forty beastmen. In the Punchbowl." Tabor Jan hesitated, then took a step that felt like a dive. "Ryllion and a Seer were speaking to them."

The queen sat still. There was no longer any steam rising from the shred of egg on her fork.

"It's heavily guarded."

"Then how did you get in?"

"I had..." He cleared his throat. "I had a disguise."

Thesera rapped the fork on the tabletop, fragments of egg flying into the air. "Am I being mocked?" And then she laughed like a young girl being tickled. She aimed a sharp kick at her son's shin under the table. "It's been so many years since anyone's attempted a good birthday prank. I cry mercy."

"This isn't a ruse, Mother," Cyndere said.

The queen's mirth dissolved. "Listen," she said. "I'll not miss my ceremony. I am departing this house as planned. My boat awaits. The crowd's assembled. Like Tammos Raak, I set out to discover a new land, one that the moon-spirits have promised me."

"Me," chirped the whiskiro.

She stood, took hold of her cup with its howling wolf emblem. Then she lifted her fork as if to strike its glassy bowl in a pronouncement. "I'll have Ryllion search the Punchbowl for beastmen, and the matter will be settled."

"Ryllion *is* a beastman," Tabor Jan muttered.

"I will go with him!" Cyndere announced, leaping to her feet.

"The Seers have corrupted Ryllion with the Cent Regus curse," Tabor Jan persisted.

"Be silent," the queen growled. "Ryllion *slays* beastmen. He's shown me their bodies. It's a mercy, I say, to wipe them from the Expanse. All of them. Yes, Cyndere, even your ugly friend. Imagine the fear that creature must feel, the confusion. How can a life like that be worth living?"

"They were not carcasses that you saw," said Tabor Jan. "They were sleeping. Now they're awake."

"Mother, I'll investigate," said Partayn.

"I'm going too," said Cyndere. "We'll take father's secret stair. I'm sorry, though, Captain. You'll have to wear a blindfold." She lifted the breakfast napkin from the table, then descended from the dais, walked around behind him, and tied it over his eyes.

Ryllion stood on the prow of the *Escape* and watched for glimpses of Bel Amica as the morning sun began to break through the heavy cloud bank. He clawed neat lines into the polished wooden railing, rehearsing the simple steps of the plan. He had not slept, but he was not tired. Zeal ran as hot as the blood in his veins.

Zeal and fear. Fear that he would disappoint his moon-spirit. Fear that the Seers would determine he was not fit for this venture.

The tide has begun to recede.

He had imagined it all so many times. Before sunset, Bel Amica would hail him a hero. He would fulfill the promise he had made to himself—that he would break free from his family's lowly and humiliating history. His father had been weak, his mother ashamed. But he had escaped a life of service in the shipyards, grown stronger than any who stood in his way, and seized what could be taken.

His first plan had failed. He had slain Deuneroi in secret, plotting to catch the widowed heiress in her grief. But Cyndere had resisted him, and Partayn had returned as Bel Amica's heir. No matter. Pleading with his moon-spirit for greater strength, Ryllion had been satisfied. While he did not like the troubling changes in his body, he told himself it was only a temporary blessing to help him gain the throne. He would reign as a king, the first ruler of the full Expanse since Tammos Raak himself.

Rain fell in wind-swept curtains to the south, concealing the descending moon. The Seers would not like it. It was more difficult, they said, for the moon-spirits to hear calls for help or to observe the virtue of faithful and obedient servants when clouds got in the way.

"Captain?"

He turned to find Cesylle, Emeriene's miserable, cowering husband standing behind him on the deck. Behind Cesylle, he saw Cesylle in miniature—a small, neatly jacketed toddler with the same haunted, bitter expression, his chubby fingers gripping a toy harpoon.

"The tide is high. Pretor Xa is on his way to let the beastmen into the boat."

Ryllion started. "They told you this?"

"They tell me everything," Cesylle boasted. He had a bad habit of trying to smile when all he could do was sneer.

"Get out of here," Ryllion woofed. "I must be single-minded."

Cesylle chuckled. "They told me to wait here. In case you need help. When you take the throne, I'll be promoted to the court's high judge."

"That will be for me to decide," Ryllion growled, although, in truth, he could not remember the proper procedure for installing his officials and council.

Cesylle shuffled up closer. His young son scowled, glancing about as if in serious anticipation of some threat. "Have you heard?" he asked. "We're going to have a skydragon, Ryllion. We will soar on the back of a winged steed."

"Pretor Xa told me. They'd best hope it isn't the Keeper." He paused long enough to enjoy Cesylle's look of concern, and then he laughed and shoved the little man's shoulder. A little too hard, perhaps. The silence that followed, as they watched the gate, was strained.

The Seers have sent Cesylle to this ship. Ryllion gripped the railing so tightly the hardened wood splintered. *They mean for me to let the beastmen kill him. That will bring Emeriene back within my reach. They know my desires better than I thought.*

Suddenly impatient, he pounded on the rail, and it broke. Cesylle winced, alarmed.

Ryllion growled, "Where is the queen? And where are Partayn and Cyndere? They should be approaching by now. The tide is high."

"They should be here by now," Cesylle agreed, lifting his son onto his shoulders.

"I'll enjoy cutting those monsters to pieces. Beastmen are abominations. They live for violence. Nothing will please me more than to prove myself stronger than they are."

Where is the queen? Spirit, I have followed your voice. I am ready. Raise me up.

Wynn sat on top of the stack of logs, trunks with bark smooth as marble and just as fluid in swirling color. He was of no use to the loaders, and so another day was passing uneventfully.

Elbows on his knees, his chin on his knuckles, he pounded out an uneven rhythm with his heels against the logs.

The air still carried the tang of old smoke. Wynn gazed across to the inlet's far shore. A grand ship, the *Escape.* Cyndere's sisterlies and Partayn's brotherhood hurried up and down the dock, taking turns in the lifts to festoon its riggings with banners and ribbons, set the Bel Amican flags to flying, and light moon-spirit lamps all along its railings.

The docks were crowded with grim-faced guards carrying torches, spears, and powerful bows.

I could stow away on that ship, he thought. *Cortie's gone, so I might as well.*

"Wynn?"

Luci and Margi stood smiling and holding hands behind him. Luci still looked at him as if he were some great hero, and Margi still regarded him with suspicion and disgust.

"Go away," he said. "I've got work to do."

"But don't you want to see it happen?" Luci asked. "It's happening soon. In there." She pointed to the new guard, the one who had replaced Balax and his brothers. "Madi's going to be there to see it."

"I don't know what you're talking about," he snapped. "Madi's gone, just like Cortie. Wipe those smiles off your faces, or I'll smack 'em off."

"You're wrong," grumped Margi. "Madi's told us that Cortie's with Cal-raven."

Wynn stood up, crossing his arms and scowling down at them. "Don't."

"We're going in," said Luci.

"You can't get past that guard."

"Who?" Margi glared at the guard, who raised his eyes to them as if they were filthy mice. "That big lunk? He usually guards a bakery. And when nobody's lookin', he steals the bread himself."

"Watch that talk, rodent!" the guard bellowed. "I'll pull out your tongue and feed it to the fishes."

"Just try and catch us." Margi turned up her nose and pointed at him, defiant. "We'll be past you before you can take a step."

The guard glanced left, right, then slowly stood and rolled up his sleeves. "It's not my usual kind of fun to punish little girls," he growled.

"Come on, Wynn," said Luci. "Let's go before Margi gets us all in trouble." Then she laughed at the guard. "Clearly this one's too smart for us."

Margi let go of Luci's hand and skipped away, her nose in the air. Luci waited for Wynn. He wouldn't take her hand, so she sighed and rolled her eyes and skipped off after Margi. Wynn ambled behind them, curious to know where they were leading him as they took the next cargo tunnel, the unguarded one, and disappeared into the dark.

"What," he asked quietly as he ventured into its shadow, "are we doing?" He paused. The corridor was quiet. In the faintest trace of light from the dock, he could see Luci smiling. Margi, meanwhile, was pressing her hands against the tunnel wall. "Oh," he said.

And so they stepped through the wall and into the tunnel behind the guard. He was holding a seashell to his ear and had forgotten all about them.

Margi looked at him triumphantly. But Luci grabbed her by the back of her shirt and pulled her away. "No," she whispered. "He'll chase us."

"Will he?" Margi asked loudly, and the guard spun and dropped the shell, which shattered on the boards at his feet.

"You!" the guard roared.

"Before you even take a step," Margi laughed.

The guard charged into the corridor, picking up his spear. As he ran toward her, Margi knelt down and touched the stone floor. The guard stumbled, his spear flying forward and skidding along the ground past Margi, finally stopping at Wynn's feet. The floor of the tunnel had melted beneath him, and as soon as he fell, Margi stood up, turned, and walked away. The stone solidified, leaving the guard stuck there on his knees, breathless with astonishment.

"Come on," said Wynn, picking up the spear. "He'll bring trouble."

"But trouble will be too late." Margi stood up, brushing her hands clean. "Madi told us. She's with the Northchildren now, and she says—"

Shush! came the thought into her head, sharp and clear as a shard of glass.

"Shush!" said Luci aloud.

I've told you more than I meant to.

"What?" asked Wynn, confounded. "What are you talking about?"

"Never mind," said Margi. "Let's go."

They hurried up the corridor, until they came to the torchlit cross-roads. Luci was giddy with excitement, and Margi had to admit that she, too, felt a thrill at being directed by a voice from somewhere beyond sight and sound.

"Which way now?" asked Wynn. "And where are we going? How do you know what to do?"

"I don't," said Margi. "I just...I just know that something's happening. Witnesses are gathering." She turned to Luci. "Up, forward, or down?"

"Witnesses to what?"

Boys, thought Margi. *Why do they always need to have the answers?*

"I think Madi wants us to go down," said Luci. "I feel something about it."

The sisters hurried, close together, down the steep, damp tunnel. Wynn lagged behind. "Scared?" Luci asked him.

"Course not," he snorted. "Remember, I led you on our last adventure. And it was more dangerous than this."

"No," said Luci. "No, it wasn't."

As they came to a deep cave of cold, milky light, they slowed to creep along the wall. They could hear wild animal-like voices and a shrill, harsh response.

"Look," said Wynn.

The cave was blocked off from a larger, echoing space by a wall of scattered driftwood and seaweed-strewn stones. Chilly light filtered through, and shadows moved past in the grand cavern beyond.

Wynn climbed into the clutter, cautious of slippery branches. The girls climbed up beside him, peering through the jungle of pale grey boughs.

"What's that smell?"

"Slumberseed oil," Wynn whispered. "Try not to breathe too much."

Now they could see that the driftwood formed a ring almost all the way around the high-ceilinged cavern. Below the driftwood ring, water pooled, shallow and strewn with debris.

In the water, a long vessel with a bulky hull and a flat deck leaned on its side as if waiting for water to rise and right it. Slots for oars lined the sides, but there were no windows.

Whoever rides in there, Margi thought, *is being punished.*

Margi scanned the circle again as voices drew her attention. She saw a Seer striding through the shallow water around the boat, examining it. The Seer looked sharply to their left, and Margi discovered there was something else in the ring not far from the vessel. A cage—a wide cage with a low ceiling, penning in a large pack of beastmen.

"My moment," said Wynn. "This is it."

Luci began to whimper, and Margi grabbed her arm. *Shhhh. If they hear us, the Seer will turn the beastmen loose.*

They're here, came Madi's excited thoughts from somewhere else. *They're gathering to watch. Can you see them? Wynn's going to do something brave.*

"What's Wynn going to do?" Luci whispered, and Margi turned to silence her. But then they both noticed that Wynn was gone.

Where'd he go?

I don't know. Maybe he got scared. We should go.

No, Madi wants us to stay.

The ring of driftwood was broken in one place where a great stone gate, hanging on slack chains, rested shut. Water trickled down its edges.

It's keeping out the tidewater.

I want to get out of here.

Wait. I want to see what Madi sees.

Margi looked up at the high, dark walls of the cavern. A stone promontory jutted out like the prow of a ship. At the platform on the promontory's point, a tall white crystal sparkled like a monument. Beside it stood a barrel with a spout.

"What," wheezed one of the beastmen, surprising Margi with his Common speech. He was bearlike in the breadth of his shoulders, with a face like one of the brutal apes from Fraughtenwood. "What if Cent Regus get hurt? *Gurr.* What if Cent Regus—*gurr*—run away?"

Pretor Xa stalked about the leaning vessel as if inspecting it, his long white robes dragging in the shallows. Then he pointed up at the crystal and addressed the beastmen. "You see that?" he hissed. "That is why you won't run away. It's a piece of the moon itself. A sliver from the eye that watches the world."

The beastmen collectively raised their wild eyes to view the source of the cavern's snow-white luminescence.

"What these stones see, we see. We're spreading them across the Expanse so we can see it all, everything that we shall eventually possess. If you run away, we'll watch you wherever you go." Pretor Xa clapped his long-fingered hands together, and white dust clouded into the air.

Where's Wynn?

I don't see him. Where's Madi?

I'm here.

Where?

You can't see me? Strange. I can see you. I can see everything now.

Make yourself seen, Madi!

It's not for me to do. Your eyes need repairing. You'll see. Someday.

The Seer stalked right up to the cage, and now the girls could see that he was even taller than the beastmen—a giant, gripping the bars and staring down at them with a cold, skullish grin and wide, wild eyes. "So follow my instructions. Take the queen's pathetic ship. Remove her from her throne, destroy her bothersome offspring. And then we shall see a beastman wear Bel Amica's crown. And you will be exalted as his faithful followers, free to run and hunt and have what you wish."

One of the beastmen turned and translated these words to the horde. The grumbling mob bristled, gathering closer to the bars. Margi suddenly understood.

"He's going to turn them loose?" Luci whimpered. "We should go back." Margi punched her in the arm.

"Many, many times our moon has risen and fallen," the Seer intoned, and he climbed onto the tilting deck of the ship, unlatched a hatch, and opened it. "But the time has come."

Luci's mouth popped open again, and Margi slapped her hand across it.

"No more, then." The beastman rattled the bars again. "No more sleep. No more poison."

The Seer pointed up to the wooden cask and smiled. "The time has come to wake."

He walked to the cage. "You remember what it felt like, don't you?" He grinned. "You remember that glorious night when you gathered in the depths of Abascar's ruins? When you watched as Ryllion ran a sword through Deuneroi's back?" He raised his hand to the lock that bound the cage door shut. "You delivered Bel Amica from its future king. You spilled his blood in the dark. And today, in full view of the people of Bel Amica, you will slaughter the rest of—"

He stopped. The key fell from his hand. He staggered a bit to the side, then lurched away from the beastmen.

Luci shrieked, but the Seer did not respond. He stood there, teetering, his trembling hands rising—one to grasp the feathered shaft of the enormous arrow that had penetrated his right temple, the other to grasp the sharp barb that had come out the other side.

Margi lifted her eyes to see Tabor Jan standing in one of those high windows. But Tabor Jan was not holding the bow.

Cyndere stood beside him, the bow raised. She was far away, but Margi could see her shaking, and then her voice rang out.

"Deuneroi!"

The Seer crashed down on all fours, his dark cape enveloping him like the wings of an injured bat. He crawled forward through the water, raised himself onto his knees, reached for the ends of the arrow again, and with a vicious hiss snapped the barb off one end and then pulled the arrow out of the other side of his skull.

Much to Margi's disgust and amazement, not a drop of blood spilled out.

"You're finished, Pretor Xa!" roared Tabor Jan. "The queen has not gone to her ship. And she will reckon with you and Ryllion for everything—everything—you have done!"

The Seer had his back to Tabor Jan and Cyndere. He must have looked like a dying dog crawling away from them. But Margi was in front of him, staring at him through the driftwood. And she could hear him laughing.

"Fools," he hissed, "you have no idea." Then he turned and shrieked, "Your arrows cannot stop us. And you don't have enough for all the beastmen." He reached the cage, snatched the key, and unlocked it.

The beastmen burst out, howling with bloodthirst. They splashed through the water and climbed onto the boat's canted deck. They roared at Tabor Jan and Cyndere and lashed at the air with their claws.

But then the cask on the platform began to rock. It moved closer to the edge of the stone.

Wynn!

Yes, now you see, came Madi's gleeful thought. *Isn't he brave? His moment has come.*

"It's my moment too." Margi, moving on an impulse she could not understand, shoved a piece of driftwood aside and clambered through it, then fell down onto the pool's sandy shore. The Seer did not hear her, did not turn, for his attention was focused on his assailants. She waded into the water, then reached down through the shallows and pressed her hands against the rocky floor of the cave.

A resonant pulse rippled through the cavern.

The Seer staggered and fell forward again as the ground moved beneath him.

Margi stood up and scrambled backward. *He won't get away now.*

Look out, Margi!

She turned and saw the great barrel of oil topple from its perch. It hurtled down through the air and struck the edge of the ship and exploded.

As its contents spilled across the boat, a powerful wave of perfume struck the girls as hard as any rush of water. Margi looked up to see Wynn standing where the barrel had been. And then she ran for the driftwood barrier and clambered over it as her consciousness collapsed.

"Cover your face!" Tabor Jan shouted, throwing himself backward from the balcony and casting his arms across his face. Cyndere dove with him.

They heard the sound of the barrel of slumberseed oil strike the boat. There was a cacophony of splashing for a few short moments. Then, silence.

The pungent aroma seeped through their sleeves as they fought to stay awake. But the power of the oil was too much. Cyndere, leaning against Tabor Jan, looked anxiously into his eyes, and then she was asleep.

He settled her against the wall. Then he crawled to the edge and looked down to see Wynn lying on the edge of the promontory beside the crystal, fast asleep, just inches from a fall that would have killed him. He saw the Seer in the water, tugging as if his hands and feet were stuck to the floor beneath the shallows. Sprawled and scattered all around him were the motionless bodies of the slumbering beastmen.

Everything began to blur.

And then there were others with him on the balcony. Was that Partayn?

He looked down again to see a figure walking onto the promontory—a woman in an extravagant gown with a gleaming circle on her head. She was pressing her sleeve to her face and striding forward as if moving up a steep incline. She shouted a shrill question to Pretor Xa. The Seer screamed back up at her in a fury.

Then the woman put her hand upon the wheel and began to turn it.

The heavy stone gate that held back the waters of the Rushtide Inlet began to rise.

The tide burst in.

A wall of water came sweeping into the Punchbowl, filling it up almost to the edge of the promontory. The boat rose, righting itself, swaying, spinning, and smashing itself against that jutting arm of stone.

Water crashed against the sides of the cave. It fractured driftwood. It churned and roiled in such a way that Tabor Jan finally understood why it was called a Punchbowl.

But all this was quickly forgotten, for he was asleep. Asleep at last.

35

CAL-RAVEN, LOST

*I*f *Jordam doesn't come back, then my people got away.*

Cal-raven paused, holding his arms across his face as a stinging gust of dustcloud struck him. *I must not rest until I find the river. They may be waiting for me.*

The only features in this blasted landscape were the sinking, collapsing Cent Regus structures, less than empty, devoid of symmetry, besieged by some strange and colorless mold.

Cal-raven stumbled among them feeling as if he had died beside his mother in the prongbull's stable. The midday sun was hot, but the light was drained of health or hue. Each step he took scared ghosts of ash from some slow, invisible burning into anxious southward flight. How could he be sure of a direction north and west? The world around him was disintegrating; he saw nothing he might have recognized.

If I hadn't insisted on hastening the rescue... If I hadn't left Bel Amica...

He walked down a deserted avenue, finding momentary relief in the shelter of the decrepit walls. As he skirted the edge of a deep break in the ground, he looked down to where dust swirled over scattered bones that did not resemble anything human or animal. Looking up, he saw a weather-beaten rope swinging between two long, sagging structures. Strung from that rope were half skeletons of creatures ruined and displayed for all to see.

If there never was a Keeper, there will never be any kind of reckoning. And all my belief that my father might be waiting for me, all the hope in my mother's dying gaze, is folly.

He coughed, and the sound echoed. He needed water, and he had no sense of where to find it.

A gorrel crept out from under an abandoned wagon. It blinked at him, and then bolted off, leaving a grey stripe of cloud to mark its path.

If there is no Keeper, those tracks I sought and found were not leading me anywhere. My discoveries were mere luck and nothing more. I was not being led. I was not meant to find anything. It was just an animal.

He put his hands into his pockets and found that the wind had filled them with dust that could not be molded.

If there is no Keeper, even Scharr ben Fray is deceived.

What would he say if he saw his people again? How could he tell them that he had watched the creature he had claimed was leading them die?

The ale boy was caught up in the same madness, thinking that it led him to save so many lives. But did I not see the creature snapping the bridge like a twig and the boy falling, on fire, into the abyss?

He stopped and regarded a block of stone that upheld great, sculpted feet. Once a statue had stood there, perhaps a monument to Cent Regus himself, that famous son of Tammos Raak who had rebelled against his father and chased him to his death. But the creatures that his descendants had become had broken it off at the ankles, and who knows what had become of it?

He ducked behind the block at the sound of an approaching steed. A wheezing vawn came charging down the avenue bearing a figure wrapped in white rags.

The Seer. Malefyk Xa.

The reptile did not even pause, its rider leaning forward on some urgent mission.

If there is no Keeper, then what power in this world can stop the Seers? Cal-raven closed his eyes, remembering his proud claims in that dark Bel Amican sanctuary where the name Auralia had been twisted into something troubling and wrong. *What a fool.*

It came to him suddenly—Auralia's colors. They had gone with his mother, to wherever that creature had left her body.

If there is no Keeper, Auralia was either a liar or greatly deceived. And yet. . .

He stood up and staggered back onto the avenue. "Could I have killed the Keeper?" he asked. "By failing to help it escape, did I destroy the creature in everyone's dreams?"

He moved on, but the desire to go back was taking hold. He wanted confirmation that the creature had, indeed, died there in the Longhouse gate. And he wanted to find Auralia's colors again.

He walked through a dense wave of haze to discover that he had moved in a circle, and there indeed was the Longhouse, its maw still open wide. He began to run, his question compelling his aching body just a bit farther.

He found the creature's body there, contorted and still. It was a horrible sight, for it had been crushed and scarred by the beastmen that had clawed their way past it and burrowed down into the labyrinth.

No. Something isn't right.

The creature's body was caving in on itself. It was empty.

Cal-raven approached and found that the body had no head. All that remained was the thick husk of the creature's breast—a thick shell of silvery scales, beaded with gold. Other scraps of scaly skin had been cast aside like a discarded garment.

He saw tracks—fresh tracks—marking the dust.

The creature has sloughed off its skin. It has crawled free of its own dying shell.

The tracks led away from the tunnel.

"Alive," he said aloud.

He walked in dim bewilderment. But as he followed the disturbance through the dust, his steps quickened. He scanned the landscape, in hope that the creature's shape might rise up, wild and beautiful, triumphant over even his rash doubts.

For hours he followed. Past the carcasses of monstrous cattle, the bones of ruined beastmen, the shelters and storehouses of Cent Regus history engulfed in the spreading disease. His throat was parched, his skin blasted by the stinging dust. "Please," he said, his tongue swollen and cracked. "If you are the creature Auralia spoke of, if you have sought to watch over and protect my people, forgive me."

At the effort of his words, the white scar flared, insistent, like a signal waiting to be understood.

The tracks were steady, but they were increasingly difficult to discern. Then, at the crest of an ashen rise, they stopped.

Beyond the rise, the ground fell away into a canyon, a rift that ran in a jagged line. He began to wander along the top of the ridge, pushing through patches of shoulder-high weeds that grew without any hint of green or blossom—rough, brown branches with dark black stripes.

Then he felt the creature's voice, a vibration in the ground. It was a menacing music, a warning. He crouched down in the weeds, but as he did, he knew it was too late. He had surely been seen, and there was nowhere to hide.

But the creature did not come for him. It was walking slowly along a trail at the base of the canyon not far ahead. The trail was lined with rubble that had fallen from the walls. Its wings were spread out as if to intimidate anything it might encounter, but its nose was low to the ground, and Cal-raven could hear it breathing deeply as if hunting.

It was as vast as a fleet of ships, armored in new emerald scales, and its wings were like sails, layer upon layer of feathered canvas filled with wind and singing. He wondered why it bothered with the ground. Streaks of light rippled down its tail, and there sparks burned like red jewels in its dusty wake. Beholding it again, he asked himself how he could have refused to help this creature. It had taken him up in its claws and treated him gently. It had comforted him in dreams and given him courage in the wilderness.

Did I really see all that I thought I saw? Did I really understand? This must be the Keeper.

Now it swayed from side to side, and then it reared up on its mighty hind legs and cupped its wings around its head. It howled a sound like a question, and the bell of its wings magnified its voice so that it resounded through the canyon and shook showers of stone from the walls.

When the sounds diminished into silence, Cal-raven felt a strange foreboding, for the creature was still, its wings cast out as if it might catch something in return.

An answer did come, a high shriek like a bird's.

The creature retracted those wings—a sound like sheets being shaken out—and began to march eagerly forward. Cal-raven knew he could not move fast enough to follow.

Nevertheless, he studied the precipice and then let himself down over the edge, his hands working only feeble enchantment on the cliff face, for he was exhausted. His fingers found faint holds, and he cautiously worked his way toward a place where the sheer drop became a faint incline, a place where he could turn and slide down.

But then a sharp twang of wire stung the air, and he turned.

The creature lurched, hissing with the force of a river breaking through a dam. Golden wires had sprung up from the ground, coiling about its legs. The creature roared, shattering plates of stone from the walls and shaking Cal-raven free. He fell upon that slant of stone and slid head first down its rugged incline until he tumbled into a thicket of lifeless weeds.

When he got back to his feet, he watched the creature breathe streams of fire across the ground as if trying to fight some unseen assailant. But the wires had a life of their own, tightening their grasp. He had heard of Bel Amica's cruel beastman trap-wires, but this seemed a frightful new invention. And it brought the creature crashing down. He breathed the scent of hot blood, and he choked. The creature fought on, thrashing with such ferocity that Cal-raven could hardly see it for the dust.

From a ledge above, a great black tarpaulin weighted with large green spheres was cast out like a net, and it pinned the distraught behemoth to the ground. Dark figures ran from their hiding places in the rocks to seize the cover and tighten the cords along its edge.

Strongbreed.

There were sharp shouts from a tall figure on the overlook. Cal-raven recognized the white-wound Seer at once.

There was nothing he could do but watch in silent, aching horror as the Strongbreed tightened the black, oily trap around their prey. The creature fell hard on its side, groaning, unable to fight.

More of the altered guard emerged from the base of the canyon wall, leading harnessed prongbulls. They were dwarfed by this creature, and yet they formed an obedient line as the Strongbreed bound their harnesses to their struggling captive.

The Seer disappeared from the promontory, and Cal-raven began to climb, concentrating on each handhold. At times deep pangs of grief would leave him breathless, clinging to the wall while tempted to surrender and fall away.

Evening deepened into night as Cal-raven crept westward along the canyon's edge toward the setting sun, following this nightmare parade. There was just enough light for him to see that the trail turned a corner. He woke from something near sleepwalking when he heard a cacophony of beastly voices. He heard the Seer giving orders, and he dropped to his belly, hoping no one had seen him silhouetted against the sky. He crawled to the rim and peered over.

Set into the canyon face was a line of fourteen caves—great, dark caverns carved into the opposite wall. Bars of dark metal—thick as tree trunks—closed off those caves.

Behind the bars of twelve caves, similarly tremendous creatures paced, groaning and spewing fire—each one magnificent and terrible, each one different. The creature that had found Cal-raven in the brambles outside Barnashum was being hauled into the space of the thirteenth cavern, dragged beneath the bars that had been raised by a mechanism in the wall.

Malefyk Xa walked along the avenue, keeping a fair distance from the bars, a whip in his hand. He shouted in the Cent Regus tongue, but Cal-raven understood the sound of mockery in that voice. The Seer was reveling in his dominion, taunting his captures.

Thirteen of them.

When the latest catch was through the arch of its prison, the bars crashed back down into their deep holes, trapping the animal.

The black canvas fell away, and the creature hurled itself against the bars in a fiery tirade. The canyon wall shuddered with the impact.

In the cell alongside, a creature slammed against its gate with its heavy, curled horns, clutching the bars of its cage with massive, reptilian claws.

Ram's horns, Cal-raven realized. *And those claws—two fingers and a thumb. Just as Snyde said.*

Cal-raven crawled away from the view. Then he got to his feet, his thoughts in shambles, and staggered off into the night.

The hard wind took what was left of his understanding. Detail faded from the landscape. The white scar, still pulsing the memory of a distant beacon, was all that Cal-raven could see, even as he sensed someone cautiously approaching.

"Jordam," Cal-raven whispered, "I'm lost."

Strong arms caught him, lifted him, and carried him away.

Three days after Queen Thesera's orders that the Seers be imprisoned and Ryllion slain, the soldier was still missing, and the Seers remained locked inside their invulnerable laboratories.

The riots that had broken out shocked Bel Amica's defenders. They withdrew to enforce the walls around the palace towers, restraining the tide of people who believed they could not live without the solace of the Seers' potions.

And yet, on this third morning of unrest, some things went on as if these were ordinary days. The fog bank moved out to sea, as it always did, crashing over Bel Amica's rock like a mighty wave. The marketplaces were busy. The seabirds fussed and sang their complaints.

Tabor Jan woke from a deep sleep to find an invitation on his pillow. He rose and followed its instructions. He went down to the glassworks, where he was met by Krawg and—much to his surprise—Warney.

"You're lookin' better, there, Captain!" Warney exclaimed.

"I slept. I've slept two long nights now." Tabor Jan stared, bewildered, trying to figure out what about Warney had changed. "Did you shave your beard or something?"

"How'd it be…" Krawg interrupted, fidgeting with the fringe of his yellow scarf. "What if I walked with you on the wall this evening?"

"Why's that?"

"Seein' how you're a sort of hero now, folks will want to hear tell of Tabor Jan's courage and the nest of beastman invaders. I reckon there'd be no better source for details than the man who made it happen. And I'd like to tell that story before anybody has a chance to get it wrong."

"I'll give it some thought." The captain was happy to see the old men together again. "You'll have to include Wynn and how his humble service on the docks gave him the opportunity for a brave act. And don't forget

Cyndere's perfect arrow. Or the girls, Margi and Luci, who almost drowned when the water came in."

Krawg was tying the scarf in knots now. "Yes, we've got to do this story right."

"Oh, and Krawg...make it short." Tabor Jan forced a straight face. "Too many characters, too much description—an audience won't have patience for that."

Krawg looked crestfallen. "I would."

Leaving the old Gatherers to ponder the future of Krawg's art, Tabor Jan walked through the open door of the glassworks.

Inside, he meandered through the bewildering reflections until he found Cyndere and Emeriene waiting in the glassmakers' workshop. Cyndere seemed fidgety, lifting herself up on tiptoe several times and smiling a little more than seemed necessary. Then she took his arm and led him deeper into the glassworks, straight into a small room littered with paints, bottles of glue, and pieces of glass.

Obrey sat on the floor playing a game with Bauris and two very young boys. Emeriene, who sat between the boys with her arms spread like wings around them, introduced them as her sons, Tenno and Terryn. Her hands were locked on their shoulders as if she worried someone might snatch the boys away at any moment. Cyndere explained that they'd been found hiding on the queen's ship, unattended and afraid, when soldiers stormed it in search of Ryllion. Emeriene's husband, Cesylle, was missing—most likely hiding or fleeing into the Cragavar with Ryllion. Cesylle, like Ryllion, was a fugitive student of the Seers.

Tabor Jan expected Bauris to greet him, but the old man was absorbed in his play. Beside him sprawled an enormous viscorcat. Tabor Jan watched the animal carefully, hoping it was, indeed, tame.

"After seeing the worst our house has to offer," said Emeriene, "Cyndere thought you deserved to see some of what's best."

When Cyndere pulled back a heavy curtain, Tabor Jan stood mesmerized as crescendos of light pulsed through the intricate glass lace of Obrey's window. "Must you keep this hidden?"

"You saw how people have lost respect for true beauty in this house," sighed Cyndere. "Best to leave this where it will be preserved."

"Strange," said Tabor Jan. "Strange that they riot because you've punished those who sought to kill their queen." He sighed and turned back to the light. "Forgive me, but I'm ready to leave for New Abascar."

They were quiet for a time while Obrey, Bauris, Emeriene, and the sisterly's sons rolled marbles back and forth across the colorful floor.

"Bauris," said Tabor Jan quietly, "Thank you. I don't understand how you knew, but you were right. The tetherwings...they did have something to tell me."

Bauris rose to sit in the large, cushioned bear-chair like a king on a throne, smiling as if he knew a world of secrets.

"May I?" Tabor Jan knelt to stroke the viscorcat who lay purring drowsily in a sunbeam. "Never touched a viscorcat before." As he ran his strong hands down the cat's silky black fur, he wished that he could purr as well. He dug his fingernails in behind the cat's left ear, which so thrilled the animal that he stretched out his hind legs and let out a *rrrrowwlll* of pleasure.

"That's Dukas," said Bauris. "He's happy today. He's so happy to have her around again."

The cat sighed contentedly as if to agree.

"Who?"

"My favorite." Bauris beamed at his visitors. "She's come back." He looked from one visitor to the other, then shrugged. "Nobody's paying attention."

When Frits stepped into the room, holding a bundle of golden cloth, he furrowed his brow. "Such a gloomy crowd. And I'd been told this was a playroom."

"It is a playroom!" shouted Obrey. "Will you join the game?"

He laughed. "Perhaps later, Granddaughter. You should chase out all these serious adults before Milora finds them. You know how she feels about people disrupting your play."

Cyndere was sitting on Obrey's workbench, and Frits approached her, unwrapping the treasure. "Here it is. Your mother's new chalice."

They gathered around and stared at its exquisite complexity, at the way it caught and cut the light, opening it up and refracting rays of radiant color. "It's for her voyage. See how the eagle's feathers ripple when you turn it in the light? I took this down to the *Escape* for her departure ceremony, but things did not go as planned, did they?"

"No. Partayn's with Mother now," said Cyndere. "She's having difficulty adjusting to life without her puppeteers."

"When she's ready, she can drink from it on the shore of some new world."

Cyndere smiled sadly. "Our own world needs a bit more attention before that happens. She won't sail until we sort some things out."

Incredulous, Tabor Jan turned to Cyndere. "Your mother's still going to make the voyage?"

"It will be best," said Cyndere, "if she's away for a while. We're encouraging her to go. She's so distraught. I caught her trying to unstitch her new face last night. She needs to get away from here. And Bel Amica will be better off with Partayn on the throne."

"If I can be of any help while I wait for Cal-raven, well...you'll have to interrogate your defenders, I assume."

Cyndere raised a hand to assure him. "You're generous. And, yes, some of our defenders will have to be questioned and even imprisoned. Most are reaffirming loyalty to the queen. Many served my father, so they're ready to tear Ryllion to pieces." Cyndere took the goblet from Frits. "I'd like to have a house worth defending again. A house full of beauty like this."

"You'll observe," said Frits in hushed enthusiasm, "that we included no moon-spirit symbols in the chalice's engravings. No wolves howling. We went back to early Bel Amican rituals. This blackstone symbol is a gem from a necklace that Queen Bel Amica herself wore when her throne was first established."

He pointed to the outline of a small silver bell, the kind that might hang in a tower.

"Mother once told me a story about Queen Bel Amica and her obsession with bells." Cyndere ran her finger over the smoothly sculpted symbol. "There was a certain tone she heard when she awoke in the morning. She had no memory of where she might have heard such a thing. No bellmaster ever found its equal. Many tried. Bel Amica used to be full of bells instead of mirrors."

"We should have a contest," said Obrey, "to make the most beautiful bell."

"Frits could craft us a bell made of glass," said Cyndere, turning the chalice upside down and tapping it lightly with her nail. "Please take no offense if my mother barely notices the chalice, Frits. The best things dazzle us so slowly."

And that, thought Tabor Jan, *is why House Abascar cannot stay.*

"What was that?" Emeriene looked at the captain.

Realizing he had spoken aloud, Tabor Jan said, "I only meant that we learned to be patient and attentive during our hardships in Barnashum. While we're grateful for your help, we mustn't delay. We've become distracted from our own story."

"You cannot rush such a huge endeavor as rebuilding a house." Emeriene took her youngest son's hands in her own and showed him how to snip the marble toward a bracket that Obrey held in place.

"No." Tabor Jan smiled sadly, looking into Obrey's window. "Careful as we've been, we've lost so many important pieces along the way. New Abascar will be a cold and blustery place for a while."

"Look," whispered Cyndere, "the sun's coming through."

It was true—sunlight was streaming into the room in bold rays, captured and focused by breaks in the glass.

Tabor Jan watched Cyndere's face, which was canted into the effusion of light, and he thought to himself that, broken as she was, the queen's daughter was as extravagant as Obrey's window.

"Frits," said Cyndere, "I've asked Abascar's healer to spend time with Milora. We must restore her health so the three of you can go home."

"You are gracious," said Frits.

"I suspect," said Cyndere, "as you do, that the Seers made her sick just to force you to come to Bel Amica and work here. We want to make this right. You should be working in freedom, following your own vision rather than flattering my mother."

"They can go north under Abascar's protection," Tabor Jan said quickly. "Cal-raven has a particular care for those who catch light and color in this world." He looked up to Obrey's window. "He once gave his strongest pledge of protection for a girl called Auralia who—"

"Auralia. Yes, her name is known in Bel Amica," said Cyndere.

"She was young," said Tabor Jan. "No family to speak of, her history a secret. Cal-raven spoke with her for only a few moments. But she won his heart by her way with colors."

Bauris stood and elbowed the captain. "This is my favorite part," he whispered. Tabor Jan patted his arm, uncomprehending.

Obrey snipped a red marble to Emeriene, and it ricocheted off the side of the bracket, careening across the room. It bounced off Frits's boot and rolled to the doorway. Emeriene's older boy rose to chase it, but Milora, just arriving on the scene, stopped it with her bare toes.

Seeing Milora scowl in disapproval at the solemn crowd, Cyndere clapped her hands together. "We should leave Obrey to her play."

"My work!" said Obrey solemnly. "It's my work!"

Milora rolled the marble under the ball of her foot, clearly impatient.

Stifling a laugh, Cyndere turned to Tabor Jan. "I know you have much to do to prepare your people, Captain. But Cal-raven and Henryk will not be back for several days. I hope you can take the time to join us for a quiet meal tonight—Emeriene, her boys, Frits, my brother, and myself."

The captain's expression revealed his surprise. "You honor me too much."

"I'd like to light a ceremonial lamp and place it in the center of the table. And around it, we'll speak of wishes and dreams. The future."

"After all that has happened," he said, "you want to call to the moon-spirits?"

"To call whatever power we believe is listening. The Keeper. Ghosts of our loved ones. Whoever might be out there weaving our threads together."

"Will there be wine?" Tabor Jan asked.

"You saved my life and the lives of my family. For that, I'll personally fill your glass."

He smiled. "Just a glass?"

"Come now," she laughed. "Let's not get greedy."

"Let's go, boys." Emeriene drew her sons away from the game and toward the door.

Cyndere followed, threading her arm through Tabor Jan's and leaning into him a little. He lost the rhythm of his step for a moment but quickly found it again, letting events unfold without a plan.

❧

Bauris returned his attention to Auralia's cat.

"She loves you, Dukas," he whispered. "She told me so while I was away. She told me how you used to carry her through the forest. But now that she's come back over the wall, she has to remember everything again. Give her some time. She'll play with you."

Obrey stared up at him, her face full of unresolved questions. Bauris knew that his words were making her uncomfortable. But then, his words made most people uncomfortable. What could he do?

He had come back through the well on certain conditions. He was forbidden to speak directly of those gentle, shimmering strangers who had found him at the bottom of the well and carried him upstream to revelation. He was forbidden to speak of all they had shown him.

He could not make his friends see what he could see—the witnesses passing through the chambers, through the corridors, through the walls. Nor could he explain for these poor, half-blind people why all his fears had dissolved, why his joy endured through every trouble.

The pact had to hold. The people of the Expanse would never really know the truth unless they found it for themselves, made that climb, beheld that view. They had to discover—or better, remember—the golden thread within them and follow it home. Telling them would never do.

Milora took a broom in her white glassworking mitts, and proceeding cautiously on her bare feet, she swept marbles and fragments of colored glass aside.

"Everybody marvels at my window," grumbled Obrey, "but they never thank you for it."

"That's because they all think *you* made the window," Milora sighed. "They assume so many things. Since I live with you and your grandfather, well...I *must* be your mother, right? Since I know glasswork, I *must've* grown up in Frits's clan, right? If they asked more questions, they'd learn how wrong they are. But oh well. Scissors and scraps. It's not important. So long as they don't disrupt your play, what harm can that do?"

"Why do they think I made the window?"

"Because since the day I made it for your playroom, everyone has called it Obrey's window. And it *is* your window, my dear. It's there to inspire you because I love to watch you play. I'm sure I used to mess around like you do. But life's got a way of beating the play right out of you." She knelt, set the broom down, and put her arms around Obrey. "I'll never, ever let life beat the play out of you, my dear."

Bauris bit his tongue until it hurt.

Milora narrowed her eyes. "Why do you look at me like that?"

"This is my favorite part," he said.

Milora sat down on the workbench and studied the window, unbinding her head scarf. "I'll have to ask Frits to cut my hair again." As the scarf slipped to the ground, the viscorcat got to his feet. Purring so rapturously it was almost a snarl, he rubbed a furry cheek against her shoulder, then threw himself down to playfully wrestle the loose scarf.

She rubbed the cat under the chin. He pressed his eyes shut, smiling, and groaned. "You want me to take off my mitts don't you?" She began to slowly unwind the strips of her mitts. "Cal-raven," she said absently. "He's a strange, impulsive man."

"He has a funny name," Obrey announced.

Milora cocked her head. "He does, doesn't he? Well, he's lucky to have a name that means something, I guess."

"What's wrong with 'Milora'?"

"Nuthin's wrong with it." She spread her unwrapped fingers, and the white strips fluttered to the floor. "I like it because Frits gave it to me. But I want my real name."

"Must've been weird for Grandfather. Findin' a grown woman lyin' bare by the river like that. I remember him carryin' you in. Even though you were asleep, you wouldn't let go of those milora flowers in your hand."

"No clothes. No memories." Milora pushed her hand through the air toward Bauris. "Erased. *Whoooosh*."

The emerjade ring on her finger caught his attention. She fingered it with curiosity, tracing the shape of the figure that she saw so vividly in dreams. Then she shrugged and reached down to scratch the cat behind his ear. "Dukas," she murmured.

"I hope Cal-raven's back soon," said Obrey. "I like him. I want him to live with us."

Milora smiled, amused, then whispered his name again as if it were strangely familiar, and she watched Obrey get lost in her play.

A Guide to the Characters

House Abascar (AB-uh-skar)

ale boy—A former errand-runner in Abascar; friend of Auralia; gifted as a firewalker who can pass through fire without burning; now a survivor responsible for leading hundreds from the rubble of Abascar and south to the gathering in the Cliffs of Barnashum. Some call him "Rescue."

Auralia (o-RAY-lee-uh)—A young, artistic girl discovered by Krawg in the wilderness when she was an infant. Her artistry was an extraordinary revelation of color that inspired many and stirred up dissension in House Abascar. She disappeared in the calamity of House Abascar's fall, and only the ale boy witnessed what happened to her.

Bowlder (BOL-der)—An Abascar defender, distinct in his size and strength.

Brevolo (BREV-o-lo)—A swordswoman; daughter of Galarand, sister of Bryndei.

Bryndei (BRIN-day)—An archer; daughter of Galarand, sister of Brevolo.

Cal-raven (cal-RAY-ven)—A stonemaster; king of House Abascar; son of Cal-marcus.

Cortie (KOR-tee)—The young daughter of the merchants Joss and Juney.

Jaralaine (JAYR-uh-layn)—Former queen of House Abascar and wife of King Cal-Marcus; ran away from the house and disappeared when Cal-raven was young.

Jes-hawk (JES-hawk)—The finest archer among Abascar's defenders.

Krawg (KROG)—Formerly a thief in House Abascar, known as "the Midnight Swindler"; arrested and cast out to be a Gatherer; now a harvester, famous for discovering Auralia.

Krystor (KRIS-tor)—A glass crafter of the remnant of Abascar.

Lesyl (LES-el)—A musician who was restricted to singing songs of praise for the king during the reign of Cal-marcus.

Say-ressa (say-RESS-uh)—A healer; wife of the former captain of the guard, Ark-robin, who was killed in the Abascar calamity.

Snyde—(SNIDE)—Formerly King Cal-marcus's director of arts; now a
  leader of the resistance (the "grudgers") against Cal-raven.

Tabor Jan (TAY-bor JAN)—Formerly man-at-arms to Prince Cal-raven
  during the reign of Cal-Marcus; now captain of the Abascar guard.

triplets—Luci, Madi, and Margi (LOO-see, MAD-ee, MAR-gee)—
  Three young Abascar survivors gifted with the extraordinary powers
  of stonemastery and thoughtspeaking.

Warney (WOR-nee)—Formerly a thief known as the "One-Eyed Bandit"; then a Gatherer; now a harvester in the remnant of Abascar.

Wynn (WIN)—The young son of the merchants Joss and Juney.

House Bel Amica (bel AM-i-kuh)

Cesylle (SES-il)—Emeriene's husband; a court representative in Bel Amica.

Cyndere (SIN-der)—The daughter of Queen Thesera and King Helpryn; widow of Deuneroi; sister of Partayn.

Deuneroi (DOON-er-oy)—A court representative; husband to Cyndere;
  murdered while striving to rescue the people of House Abascar after
  the collapse of that house.

Emeriene (EM-er-een)—Cyndere's closest friend since childhood and
  highest-ranking of her attendants, the sisterlies.

Gelina (jel-EE-na)—A prostitute.

Hedley (HED-lee)—One of the sisterlies, assistants to Cyndere.

Helpryn (HEL-prin)—King of House Bel Amica; husband to Thesera;
  father of Cyndere and Partayn; died in a shipwreck while exploring
  the islands of the Mystery Sea.

Henryk (HEN-rik)—A Bel Amican soldier serving as a guard at the
  harbor caves.

Malefyk Xa (MAL-uh-fik kZAH)—One of the Seers; master hunter
  and trapper; devotee of the faith of the moon-spirits who advise
  Queen Thesera.

Panner Xa (PAN-er kZAH)—One of the Seers; overseer of the Mawrnash mine; devotee of the faith of the moon-spirits.

Partayn (par-TAYN)—Cyndere's older brother; heir to the throne of Bel
  Amica; a gifted musician.

Pretor Xa (PRE-ter kZAH)—One of the Seers, devotees of the faith of
  the moon-spirits who advise Queen Thesera.

Ryllion (RIL-ee-un)—Captain of the guard at House Bel Amica; apprentice to the Seers.

Thesera (TES-er-uh)—Queen of House Bel Amica; widow of King
    Helpryn; mother of Cyndere and Partayn.

Tyriban Xa (TEER-i-ban kZAH)—One of the Seers; master of surgery
    and alteration; devotee of the faith of the moon-spirits who advise
    Queen Thesera.

Wilus Caroon (WIL-us ka-ROON)—A guard at the Bel Amican out-
    post of Tilianpurth.

House Cent Regus (KENT REJ-us)

Jordam (JOR-dum)—One of four beastman brothers, twin to Goreth;
    the first beastman to overcome the Cent Regus curse through the
    influence of Auralia's colors.

Mordafey (MOR-duh-fay)—Jordam's oldest brother.

Skell Wra (SKEL RA)—The chieftain of the Cent Regus beastmen; con-
    troller of the Essence.

Between the houses

Dukas (DOOK-us)—A viscorcat; once a faithful companion of Auralia
    in the forest. Injured by an arrow, he was eventually captured in the
    wild and adopted by Deuneroi.

the Keeper—A massive, mysterious creature who appears in the dreams of
    all children, and some say the adults as well. It is perceived by chil-
    dren as a benevolent guardian, but most determine that it is only a
    figment of dreams, probably imagined out of a need for comfort.
    Some believe it is real and moving about in the wild with vast powers
    of perception and influence.

Rumpa (RUMP-uh)—A vawn tamed by Scharr ben Fray; carried the ale
    boy through adventures in *Cyndere's Midnight*.

Scharr ben Fray (SHAR ben FRAY)—A renowned mage, a wandering
    stonemaster, and a wildspeaker; formerly an advisor to Abascar's
    King Cal-marcus, and a mentor to Cal-raven.

Tammos Raak (TAM-os RAK)—Legendary ancestor of the four houses'
    royal families. Stories say he led the peoples of the Expanse in a
    daring escape from an oppressor, bringing them over the Forbid-
    ding Wall, a line of mountains in the north, to settle in the
    Expanse. Accounts disagree regarding the manner and cause of
    his disappearance.

ACKNOWLEDGMENTS

First, thanks to all who have encouraged me at LookingCloser.org, Facebook (facebook.com/jeffreyoverstreet), and Twitter (twitter.com/Jeff_Overstreet) this year. When I need a break from writing, you provide immediate, inspiring company.

To write *Raven's Ladder* in less than a year while working a full-time job and fulfilling other commitments, I needed patience, grace, and encouragement from a whole community. I'm grateful to friends and family who were understanding and respectful when Anne and I regretfully declined invitations to coffee, breakfasts, lunches, dinners, birthday parties, movies, concerts, readings, recitals, sporting events, getaways, housewarmings, going-away parties, book-release parties, etc. To climb *Raven's Ladder*, we needed every evening and every weekend. I hope you like the story that was born while the sign read Do Not Disturb.

WaterBrook Press—especially editor Shannon Marchese, who understands my vision for The Auralia Thread—has been patient with me, giving me time to tell the whole story. Mick Silva has given me encouragement and counsel. Kristopher Orr and Mike Heath have created another breathtaking cover illustration. I'm so grateful.

In some future novel I should name a hero after editor Steve Parolini (www.noveldoctor.com), who asked thoughtful questions about every single page and answered the phone when I needed help with a storytelling crisis. I have a lot to learn from Steve.

I'm blessed to have an agent who is also a great friend. Lee Hough at Alive Communications is generous with his time and expertise and is passionate for my work and well-being.

Thanks to you, Carol Bartley, and your crackerjack team of copyeditors. If this book earns any praise, you deserve so much credit for your meticulous attention to details. You helped me see what needed repair and revision.

Thanks to those who provided other substantial help: Tommy Fong and Vivian Bennett gave Anne and me a fabulous place to live and work. Dave Von Bieker gave me a better Web site. Adrienne Lema offered good, blunt criticism. She, Anastasia Solano, and Claire Wilson all brought extraordinary meals on days when Anne and I were hunched over hot laptops. Claire and her husband Tom, Rachel and Steve Beatty, and Danny Walter were always there when we needed them. Kristin Wilhite at The Grinder served me countless cups of coffee with a smile, even when I was grouchy. I found more hospitality and caffeine at the Laughing Ladies cafe and Richmond Beach Coffee Company during long Saturdays of rewrites.

Jennifer Gilnett and my co-workers at Seattle Pacific University, Gregory Wolfe at *Image* journal, Mark Moring at *Christianity Today*, and the team at Filmwell.org were all patient when I was exhausted and late with assignments. It's great when your editors and supervisors are also your friends.

Thanks to Bob and Laurie Denst; Bryan and Tara Owens; Rick Paul and Wendi Poole; Robert Clark; Bart Cusveller and his family; Peter van Dijk; Julie Mullins, Mary Kenagy Mitchell, and Anna Johnson at *Image*; Wayne Proctor and the Thomas Parker Society; Mike Capps and Kimberly Alexander at the Trinity Arts Conference; Steven Purcell and Marcus Goodyear at Laity Lodge; John Wilson, Luci Shaw, John Hoyte, Walter Wangerin Jr., Eugene Peterson, Gina Oschner, Matthew Dickerson, and others in the Chrysostom Society.

Raven's Ladder is about preserving a vision of hope through doubt, disappointment, distraction, and disaster. I found inspiration in the music of Over the Rhine (Linford Detweiler and Karin Bergquist) and Sam Phillips. Thank you, my inspirations and my friends, for such a feast of beauty. "I hear music up above…"

If I've found a family among writers, then I've found a sister in Sara Zarr. Her telephone pep talks have been a blessing.

And finally, thanks to my parents, whose prayers make such a difference.

ABOUT THE AUTHOR

JEFFREY OVERSTREET grew up in Portland, Oregon. He is writing the fourth and final volume of The Auralia Thread. The first two volumes, *Auralia's Colors* and *Cyndere's Midnight*, were published in 2007 and 2008 by WaterBrook Press. Since 1996, Overstreet's award-winning writing about art—especially cinema—has been posted at his Web site, LookingCloser.org. His work has also appeared in *Image: A Journal of the Arts and Religion*, *Paste*, and *Christianity Today*. His "travelogue of dangerous moviegoing," *Through a Screen Darkly*, was published by Regal Books in February 2007.

Jeffrey and his wife, a poet and freelance editor named Anne, spend time writing in the coffee shops of Shoreline, Washington, every week. He works in Seattle as the contributing editor for Seattle Pacific University's *Response* magazine.